Acts of Violet

Also by Margarita Montimore

Oona Out of Order

Acts of Violet

Margarita Montimore

FLATIRON
BOOKS
NEW YORK

ACTS OF VIOLET. Copyright © 2022 by Margarita Montimore. All rights reserved. Printed in the United States of America. For information, address Flatiron Books, 120 Broadway, New York, NY 10271.

www.flatironbooks.com

Designed by Donna Sinisgalli Noetzel

Library of Congress Cataloging-in-Publication Data

Names: Montimore, Margarita, author.
Title: Acts of violet / Margarita Montimore.
Description: First edition. | New York : Flatiron Books, 2022.
Identifiers: LCCN 2021060877 | ISBN 9781250815064 (hardcover) |
    ISBN 9781250862211 (international, sold outside the U.S., subject to
    rights availability) | ISBN 9781250815071 (ebook)
Subjects: LCGFT: Novels.
Classification: LCC PS3613.O54898 A64 2022 | DDC 813/.6—dc23
    /eng/20211216
LC record available at https://lccn.loc.gov/2021060877

Our books may be purchased in bulk for promotional, educational, or business use. Please contact your local bookseller or the Macmillan Corporate and Premium Sales Department at 1-800-221-7945, extension 5442, or by email at MacmillanSpecialMarkets@macmillan.com.

First U.S. Edition: 2022
First International Edition: 2022

10 9 8 7 6 5 4 3 2 1

For Terry Montimore, who fills my life with magic

(stop rolling your eyes, it's true)

With love and fhqwhgads

I didn't disappear, I was present for all of it.

—BRIT MARLING AND ZAL BATMANGLIJ, *THE OA*

Don't be the real you.

Be the better you.

Be the astonishing you.

Be the you no one can ignore.

—VIOLET VOLK, *YOU ARE MAGIC*

Acts of Violet

Strange Exits Podcast

Season 1: "Vanishing Violet"
Extended Trailer

[MALE VOICE 1]: Anyone who tells you they knew Violet Volk is a liar. I was married to her, and I still couldn't tell you who the "real" VV was. Because nothing was real with her. Her life, her career, it was all a series of illusions.

[FEMALE VOICE 1]: Violet was a strange one. Part gutter punk, part diva. She was unpredictable, whip-smart, charismatic as hell. Not conventionally beautiful but alluring, in the way that self-assurance gives people a special magnetism.

[MALE VOICE 1]: There was this . . . malleable quality to her. Sometimes Violet could be the most gorgeous woman you've ever seen and other times she was utterly hideous. Either way, it was impossible to take your eyes off of her.

[FEMALE VOICE 2]: I worshipped her. I think a lot of girls in the nineties did.

[MALE VOICE 2]: She was a phony, and she made millions off people buying her lies.

CAMERON FRANK: Violet Volk was the greatest magician of our generation, arguably of all time. Her act was jaw-dropping, with illusions that defied explanation—some even believed she was gifted with special abilities that extended beyond those of a skilled magician.

[MALE VOICE 3]: Nobody could do what she did. I don't know what you'd even call it . . . it was more than magic. There are tricks she performed that nobody's figured out to this day. All that stuff with fire and blood and levitation—it was mind-blowing. Deep down, you knew these things had a logical explanation, but sometimes you still felt like you were watching something . . . miraculous. Violet Volk didn't perform magic—she *was* magic.

[MALE VOICE 2]: You know how many guys can do what she did? *Pfft.* If Violet wasn't a sexy chick, we wouldn't even be talking about her.

[FEMALE VOICE 1]: Stage magic has always been a boys' club—even today, over ninety percent of professional magicians are male. History has forgotten greats like Adelaide Herrmann, Dell O'Dell, Celeste Evans, and Dorothy Dietrich, and relegated women to serving as little more than pretty props. Violet made a name for herself in this boys' club and showed us we can be more than pretty props, onstage and off. History will not forget Violet Volk.

[FEMALE VOICE 3]: A feminist icon? Gimme a break. Less performance artist, more con artist, if you ask me.

CAMERON FRANK: Whether you loved or hated her, whether she inspired you or pushed your buttons, you have to give her credit for how provocative she was. Being neutral about Volk was not an option—you were bound to have a strong opinion.

[FEMALE VOICE 4]: Violet's biggest talent was knowing how to provoke attention. Some find that admirable. I think it's cheap and disgusting. She's not worth the spotlight . . . Sorry if I sound bitter, but that bitch broke my heart.

[MALE VOICE 3]: She was a visionary. And like all visionaries, she faced her share of being misunderstood, judged, and criticized. That doesn't make her any less brilliant.

CAMERON FRANK: From her meteoric rise in stage magic and pivot to self-help guru, to her salacious romantic entanglements, to a muddy personal history filled with contradictions and obfuscations, VV was perennially complex and enigmatic. If there was one thing you could rely on her to deliver, it was the unexpected.

[FEMALE VOICE 2]: How could this have happened? There were so many witnesses . . . hundreds, thousands of us. And nobody saw a thing?

[FEMALE VOICE 3]: We all thought it was a giant publicity stunt at first . . . but as weeks passed, then months . . . Now it's been almost ten years. You gotta start to wonder if . . . maybe we'll never see her again. Maybe she's not with us anymore.

[MALE VOICE 4]: I heard she was hiding out somewhere in the Amazon.

CAMERON FRANK: In the years since her mysterious disappearance, she continues to capture public curiosity and spark speculation. There have been various unconfirmed sightings of Volk and countless theories persist around her vanishing.

[FEMALE VOICE 3]: I don't think she's dead. There were some . . . unpleasant realities VV was about to face . . . and she was getting tired of her fame and notoriety. She had plenty of reasons to want to start a new life. Staging her disappearance would be the perfect way to do it.

[MALE VOICE 1]: Violet once told me, "When you're rich and famous, you can get away with anything. You have no idea what I've gotten away with." The thing is, she looked scared when she said that.

[DISGUISED VOICE]: There were people who had grown tired of her antics and felt threatened by her. I don't know how much more I can say. I wouldn't want those people coming after me . . .

[MALE VOICE 2]: We're never gonna know what really happened. Someone as clever as Violet? If she doesn't want to be found, she won't be.

[FEMALE VOICE 2]: I miss her every day. And I'll never stop looking for her.

[FEMALE VOICE 3]: She *loves* being a puzzle—she *prides* herself on it. Violet reveals different pieces of herself to different people, and nobody ever gets to see the full picture.

CAMERON FRANK: Join us on *Strange Exits* as we put together the pieces and try to solve the puzzle of Violet Volk.

Vanishing Volk Causes Riot

By Cameron Frank

FEBRUARY 24, 2008

Friday night, two thousand people packed the Witkin Theater in Willow Glen to see legendary magician Violet Volk perform her first stage show in years. People came from around the world to see Volk's act, with some paying over a thousand dollars per seat from resellers. They were expecting an extraordinary night. Little did they know, they'd be witnesses to the last confirmed sighting of this mercurial performer.

Violet Volk was one of the most popular stage magicians of the 1990s, her numerous tours and television appearances, along with a residency in Las Vegas, making her a household name. In the early 2000s, she reinvented herself as a self-help author and toured the world as a motivational speaker. While she incorporated some effects into her seminars, questions persisted, from fans and press alike, as to whether she'd ever return to the stage as a full-fledged magician. It wasn't until early 2008 that they received a satisfying answer, when Volk announced a special performance in her hometown of Willow Glen, New Jersey. One night only, but many believed a proper tour would follow.

After Friday's show, nobody is sure what to believe.

The performance was stripped down compared to her TV specials or Las Vegas show—*Violet Volk Unplugged*, relatively speaking. There were no acrobats or dancers providing colorful misdirection, no screen projections, and, apart from the final illusion, few pyrotechnics or elaborate set pieces. The restrained approach made Volk all the more astonishing to watch, and the audience was enraptured for a full hour until the Flaming Angel, one of her trademark disappearing acts. The effect proceeded smoothly until it was time for Volk to reappear. She never did. The confusion that ensued caused a stampede, with twenty-nine people hospitalized for minor injuries.

The Flaming Angel involved four hoops suspended six feet above the stage floor and lit on fire, followed by the magician, clad in a white bodysuit and matching angel wings, levitating and passing through them. While navigating the fourth hoop, her wings would burst into flame and she'd vanish in a puff of smoke and an explosion of feathers. Moments later, she'd reappear in a different part of the theater. Last night's iteration was entirely unprecedented. When the spotlight trained its beam on the upper balcony, where it was supposed to find the performer, now wearing a (supposedly charred) black bodysuit and wings, it remained fixed on an empty space.

A theater crew member who wished to remain anonymous said, "We rehearsed it dozens of times. When she didn't reappear, we were scared there was a tech malfunction. We checked the rigs and equipment but saw nothing wrong. So we went all over the theater, hoping we'd find her quickly enough that the audience would think it was part of the act."

At first, they did. "Everybody was looking around, trying to figure out where she'd reappear," said Nancy Martin, a fan who traveled from Vancouver for a front-row seat to the spectacle. "But I knew something was off. I saw Violet perform dozens of times back in the day, and the way the stagehands were rushing around felt sloppy and panicked, not rehearsed at all. I could tell right away it wasn't part of the show."

When Volk failed to reappear after a few minutes, the music was cut, and the house lights came on. "You could hear a worried murmur go through the crowd," Martin said. "Then there was this announcement apologizing for technical difficulties and asking us to please remain in our seats. I got scared when I saw security guards walking down the aisle, and when the police showed up a few minutes later, I got *really* scared. Then somebody asked if there was an active shooter and all hell broke loose."

"The manager of the theater called to report the disappearance," said Willow Glen Chief of Police Howard Donegan. "It happened during the show, so we were concerned about foul play and wanted everyone to stay put. If that theater was a crime scene, we needed to preserve it and keep track of everyone present. You're looking at hundreds of potential witnesses and there's no telling if any might've been accomplices. But you also have to bear in mind the whole thing could be a big stunt."

Law enforcement couldn't confirm who initiated the panic that caused people to flee the theater.

"I don't know what would've given someone the mistaken idea that we had an active shooter in our midst. One minute, everyone was sitting calmly in their seats, the next, it was a mob scene," said Chief Donegan. "We're lucky nobody was grievously injured."

After the theater manager confirmed Volk's disappearance was not part of her show, officers and theater security officials searched the area. They have yet to find any trace of her.

Volk's sister, Sasha Dwyer, was in the audience Friday night, appearing composed and only mildly concerned, stating, "Violet's been known to fall off the radar now and again. I have no idea what happened tonight, but I'm confident she'll turn up soon." Could she know more than she's letting on?

Some audience members took a more cynical approach. "The whole thing was a setup to grab more headlines," said one man, who preferred to remain anonymous. "No one generates publicity better than Violet Volk."

A representative for the performer disputes the notion that her disappearance was staged. "Violet has deviated from the script before, which is what makes her such a compelling entertainer. But her vanishing is not a publicity stunt and is of serious concern to us. We urge the public to reach out if they have any information on her whereabouts."

While police are unsure whether to treat this as a legitimate missing person case, they are erring on the side of caution. "She's a grown woman and has the right to go missing," said Chief Donegan. "That said, the circumstances surrounding this disappearance are unusual, and, given Volk's high profile, we need to rule out foul play. If she went missing voluntarily, we ask that she notify law enforcement to let us know she's in no danger, so we can focus our resources elsewhere. Otherwise, for the meantime, we'll keep looking."

Violet Mania in Full Bloom

By Reggie Moser

JANUARY 10, 2018

It's hard to believe nearly a decade has passed since Violet Volk disappeared, considering how her legend endures. Video clips of her magic routines and motivational talks continue to get millions of views online, her signature alterna-glam-goth style still echoes in today's fashion trends, and her books periodically reappear on best-seller lists, her brand of inspirational tough love still resonant today.

February 22 will mark ten years since Volk's final performance and her mysterious vanishing. As this somber anniversary draws near, VV's absence will be felt more acutely than ever, and thousands are expected to flock to the annual candlelight vigil in Willow Glen, New Jersey. If you can't make it there, you'll have plenty of other opportunities to celebrate the magical performer. Here are some noteworthy Violet-centric projects to have on your radar:

- #violetisback—This trending hashtag is accompanying posts of current photos that supposedly feature Violet Volk. Most are amusing impersonations, but some are striving for verisimilitude. This social media fad has seemingly come out of nowhere. Is it a marketing ploy? A sign of an imminent comeback? An organic outpouring of fan appreciation? Nobody can say for sure, but if we can't have the real thing, we'll take these wannabe Violets any day.
- *Strange Exits* (Podcast, Sidecar Studios, January 23)—Journalist Cameron Frank delves into the life, the controversies, and the disappearance of our favorite magician. This podcast promises to be a revelatory examination of Volk, and after listening to a preview of the first few episodes, we believe the hype. Rumor has it Frank will be airing interviews with some of the most press-shy members of Volk's inner circle—including her sister, Sasha Dwyer.
- *Violet Volk: Behind the Magic* (Saltworks Press, March 13)— This expanded reissue of Noriko Tomlin's 2012 unauthorized

biography contains a new foreword by illusionist Jenn Junk, whose current Vegas residency includes an homage to Volk. While the veracity of Tomlin's chronicle has been called into question by sources close to the performer, it still makes for compulsive reading. We're already saving a place for this one in our beach tote.

- *Light & Magic* (Limited Series, Vumi, Streaming May 11)—Focusing more on Volk's early years, this eight-episode series traces her path from Jersey to Vegas, from obscurity to stardom. If the trailer is any indication, *Light & Magic* promises to be a feast for the senses, with a killer trip hop/dream pop soundtrack, stunning production design, and eye-popping special effects.

- *In the Picture: A Retrospective of Violet Volk* (Touring Exhibit, Fall)—Celebrity photographer Mayuree Sakda (who was romantically linked to Volk in the early 2000s) shares her most iconic images of the performer both onstage and off, along with never-before-seen private moments. An accompanying coffee table book is also forthcoming, so go ahead and add that one to your wish list now.

COMMENTS (582):

RUNNINGWITHWOLFPACK: Did I read that right?? Sasha Dwyer is gonna spill the tea about her sister on a podcast?? Won't that, like, short-circuit her robot programming?

PLANTSOVERPEOPLE: Can you blame Sasha for avoiding the media when she gets bullied by the Wolf Pack every time she doesn't worship at her sister's altar?

WOLFPACKJACK: Yes, I can blame her, cuz keeping media attention on a missing person case is EVERYTHING if you don't want it to go cold. Sasha's done nothing to help.

DAGLITTERBOMB: Dude, you're talking about a missing chick who's rich + famous + white. You don't need Sasha putting up billboards and shit when the FBI is already on it. And you don't know her sister's life. Everyone grieves differently.

RUNNINGWITHWOLFPACK: Or not at all, if you're VV's sis.

PLANTSOVERPEOPLE: Would exploiting VV's memory be better? Sasha could've made bank doing interviews, writing books about her sister—she even turned down an offer to do a reality show. I'm curious what she'll say when she finally does talk.

DAGLITTERBOMB: Same. Maybe the WP will finally see her as a decent, loving sister and get off her ass.

RUNNINGWITHWOLFPACK: *side-eye* Yeah, and maybe Sasha will confess she's kept Violet in her attic all this time.

PLANTSOVERPEOPLE: Like you wouldn't already know with all the stalking and trespassing.

RUNNINGWITHWOLFPACK: I didn't do any of that shit and don't condone it. All respect to my fellow Wolfies, but some of y'all are giving the fandom a bad name. Drag Sasha all you want online, but don't fuck w/ her IRL.

Sasha

January 9, 2018

When I get home from work, the first thing I see is that stack of flyers, hot pink papers glowing from the top of the credenza like they're radioactive. I drop my keys into a candy dish beside the stack. These damn things are plastered all over town, and now they're in my home.

I grab the flyers without looking at them and follow the sound of lighthearted bickering coming from the kitchen.

"Do you know how many sudoku apps there are out there? You can do, like, *millions* of puzzles for free, without killing trees." Quinn's earnest voice trails down the hall. I reach the doorway and find her at the stove with Gabriel, both facing away from me.

"But I get so much more pleasure from sudoku when tree murder is involved," Gabriel says, stirring a pot of chili, which infuses the room with an aromatic combo of garlic and cumin. "And you won't bring the trees back to life by taking that away from me."

Quinn holds up a paperback with *222 Sudoku* printed across the glossy cover in blue letters. "It's just such a waste. I hope you'll at least recycle it." With a scoff, she tosses it onto the dining table.

"Careful, kiddo, you're starting to sound like that preachy vegan you brought to Thanksgiving last year." He spots me before Quinn does and winks, tilting his head at our daughter as if to say, Can you believe this one?

"I'm nowhere near as annoying as Nancy Travino. How dare you?" Her head whips over to see what Gabriel is looking at. "Tell him, Mom."

"I don't know, I think you're one earnest lecture away from Travino territory. You need to cut us old people some slack when it comes to printed media. Besides, I have something better for the recycling bin." A satisfying thud as I drop the stack of flyers on the counter. "Why do we have these? And since when do I not get a proper hello?"

"Hi, Mom." Quinn shuffles over to me. "Should we hug now or after we argue?" She uses her palms as imaginary scales, weighing the decision.

Opening my arms, I say, "I'll take a hug now. And we don't need to argue at all."

Embracing my daughter feels like hugging a rack of clothing with all the layers she's wearing, a nesting doll of baggy T-shirts, sweaters, and hoodies. "I see you decided it would be easier to wear all your clothes instead of packing a bag." Over Quinn's shoulder, Gabriel looks up from stirring and breaks into a grin. *Good one*, he mouths at me. I air-kiss him and then real-kiss Quinn's cheek, catching a whiff of the cinnamon gum she's always chomping on. "Aren't you supposed to be on your way to Baltimore for some job fair?" It'll be months before Quinn graduates from college and moves out, though I'm already bracing myself for a wicked and prolonged bout of empty-nest syndrome.

"It's a renewable energy conference *and* career fair. I decided to have dinner with my parents and drive down early tomorrow instead. Because I'm a good daughter like that."

"You're *okay*, I suppose." I ruffle her short mop of dark wavy hair, which she inherited from Gabriel, and she squirms away, casting a nervous look at the sheaf of pink flyers. "All right, enough with the niceties. What's the deal with those?"

Uncertainty flutters across her face and settles into the tight corners of her mouth. "Funny story. Maybe not funny, but . . . So I was at Lowe's the other week—the smoke tree needs to be repotted, and if I don't do it no one will—and I ran into Mrs. Toback. We checked out the gardening area, and she did her nosy thing, asking how my last year at SJU was going and did I know what I was gonna do after graduating. I told her I dropped out months ago to fulfill my beekeeping dreams and start my own line of artisanal honey."

"Quinn . . ."

"Okay, so maybe I told her I could go different ways with an environmental science degree, and I was still figuring that out, and maybe the topic of bees didn't come up. But we got to talking about Aunt Violet because Mrs. T always finds some way to mention her—and of course the vigil came up, and her being one of the organizers. She asked was I sure I didn't want to say a few words or read a poem or something because it would mean so much for a family member to speak, and we all know it's not gonna be you."

My nostrils flare. "She did *not* say that last part."

"Stop trying to freak out your mother, kiddo." Gabriel gives me a don't-mind-her shake of his head.

"Of course she didn't say that . . . but it was kinda implied." Her shoulder twitches up in a partial shrug.

"I swear, that woman is such a pest. She gets judgy because I don't feel comfortable addressing a horde of thousands, and now she's hounding you to do it." I open the fridge and rummage around for salad ingredients, feeling a sudden urge to chop things up with a big knife. "So how'd you get out of being roped into her vigil shenanigans?" I ask her.

A pause and her dark doe eyes glint. "I told her to fuck off."

My gasp is involuntary. "You did not."

"Mom, can you stop acting like we've never met before? I was super polite to Mrs. Toback. Like always. I even insisted on carrying a twenty-pound bag of fertilizer to her car for her, which is when I told her I'm not so great with the public speaking . . ." She grabs my wrist before I can reach for the knife block. "Actually, could we have the rest of this conversation away from the sharp objects?"

I back away from the counter slowly until my hip grazes the kitchen table. "What's going on? What did you do that I'm gonna hate?" A downward glance at the stack of flyers, and I see now these are different from the ones wallpapering Willow Glen. There's a new name in the list of featured speakers. "Quinn, what the fuck?"

"Mrs. T thinks this would be good for me." Raising her chin to a stubborn angle, her voice is firm as she says, "I think so, too."

"Good for you how?" Oh, how I want to sweep those flyers to the floor or, better yet, shred each one by hand. She doesn't remember the fallout from the last time she had that many eyeballs on her. She believes her anxiety and phobias are innate, like the mole above her lip or her strawberry allergy. "You throw up anytime you have to give a speech to more than two people. You won't even do karaoke."

"All the more reason I should speak at the vigil. Face my fears and all that." She grabs the stack of flyers and holds them to her chest like a shield.

"Face your fears . . . in front of thousands of strangers. Like an extreme form of immersion therapy." Nodding, I pretend this is a sound plan. "So when you were a kid and went through your phase of being deathly afraid of water, should I have taken you on a cruise and thrown you overboard? Because that's kinda what Mrs. Toback is doing to you here."

Quinn goes pale at the suggestion and mutters, "I thought parents were supposed to be supportive and shit."

Before I can respond, Gabriel steps in, putting a hand on each of our shoulders. "Okay, let's take it down a notch." He turns to me. "I know you're just looking out for our daughter, but we gotta trust her to make her own decisions and take risks once in a while." He turns to Quinn. "And you know your parents are supportive 'and shit,' but I think you might be forgetting how hard it is on your mother dealing with all the extra ten-year anniversary hysteria."

Still sullen, Quinn shoots me a doubtful look. "Is it hard on you, though? You seem more annoyed than anything."

Of course I'm annoyed. I've been immersed in the purgatory of my sister's disappearance for the past decade. I think about her every fucking day. But since I prefer to avoid big emotional displays, I get criticized for not caring enough about her absence (mostly by people I don't know, sometimes by the one I gave birth to). It's bad enough every anniversary brings up extra Violet worship, but something about round numbers makes people lose their minds. Why is ten years more noteworthy than nine or eleven? It's all so arbitrary. Yet I'm being inundated with reminders of my sister—online and off—when avoiding the tidal pull of her memory is already impossible. So yeah, I'm annoyed, along with other things I can't verbalize, not even to my husband or daughter.

Something about my weary silence chastens Quinn. "Sorry, Mom," she relents. "Is that #violetisback stuff messing with you, too? I know I shouldn't, but I can't stop checking the posts . . ."

Oh god, all I need is for her to get her hopes up again. "You know none of the photos are really her, right? It's all a fad or some bullshit marketing gimmick . . ." Gabriel squeezes my shoulder, silently urging me to take it easy. "But yeah. It is kind of messing with me, to be honest." My hands need something to do, so I rinse off the head of lettuce and tear it by hand into a salad bowl. "There's just *so much* happening all at once. Books, podcasts, TV shows. It's easier to handle when it's more sporadic, you know?"

"Yeah. It's a lot."

"If I can be extra honest," I say, "I didn't even want to go to the vigil this year."

"You never want to go," Gabriel and Quinn say in unison. "Jinx," they add and share a chuckle. Must be nice to be so in sync.

I return to the knife block, grab a blade, and take my frustration out on the tomatoes.

"At least this year we can skip the I'm-not-going-to-the-vigil tug-of-war," Quinn says.

"Right." I don't turn around as I chop away. "Because being the grieving sister and supportive mother takes top priority. And how lucky am I? This year, not only do I get to be judged by more people than ever, but I also get to worry about my daughter having a panic attack in front of all those extra people. Can't wait." Damn. We were so close to having a pleasant dinner.

A glance over my shoulder and I catch the reassuring smile Gabriel gives Quinn, the let-me-handle-this nod. But I won't be handled, not this time.

"Sweetheart. Don't get upset," Gabriel murmurs in my ear and massages the back of my neck. "I know how much it sucks for you to go."

No, he doesn't. Nobody does.

Just recalling last year's vigil makes my skin crawl—the pain and tedium of the whole thing. How many times would I have to endure the same compliments heaped on my sister by people who didn't actually know her, the same questions and speculations? Every year, by the time we get to the moment of silence, I have to clench my jaw shut to keep from uttering the screams that have been boiling inside me for hours.

"How could you all let her fool you for so long?" I want to shout. *"She didn't care about entertaining or enlightening anyone, she only wanted to get paid."*

I'll be standing there, fake-smiling as someone blathers on about how Violet changed their life and wasn't her work so important and wasn't she a gift taken from us too soon, and it'll be all I can do not to shatter that reverence and howl, *"She wasn't a hero, she was a liar and a cheat. None of us meant anything to her, not even me. We were all just her marks."*

Every year, I have to listen and stay silent.

This year, I'll also have to listen to my daughter heap accolades on a woman who almost killed her. And stay silent.

I don't know if I can show that much restraint.

"I'm not gonna have a panic attack, Mom." Quinn's exasperation brings me back to the present. "I've been taking my meds, I'll make sure I eat right and sleep enough, and I'm gonna practice my speech like a thousand times beforehand."

"Do you even know what you're going to say?" I ask.

"Not really. I can't remember much since I was what, in second grade the last time I talked to her? Weird how none of us had contact with her for years before she went missing." Her words are sharp and launched with target precision. "And maybe I'd have more to say if you actually told me more about her. Unless you prefer to share your thoughts with the internet?"

I shove the cutting board away from me and whip around. "What is *that* supposed to mean?"

"Nothing."

"Quinn, is this about that takedown? You can't possibly think I was behind it."

"If you say so." Her eyes remain narrowed.

A month before Violet vanished, a website called violetisafraud.com went viral. Its sole content was a scathing anonymous essay ripping my sister to shreds. Naturally, the immediate consensus was that only someone close to Violet could author something so intimate and furious. Naturally, I was the prime suspect. I thought I'd managed to convince at least my own daughter that it wasn't me. Apparently not. Ironically, I *did* manage to convince Quinn the majority of that takedown was baseless drivel, so she wouldn't believe the worst things about her aunt. Maybe that was a mistake.

"I don't get it," Quinn continues. "Why is it such a big deal for you to come out once a year to honor Aunt Violet? I mean, it makes me miss her like crazy, but I like people celebrating and remembering her—those strangers tell me more about her than you ever do." Her skepticism of me mutates into something worse: disappointment. "You won't even say why you wanna skip it—I mean the real reason instead of bullshit excuses about it being too emotional for you. What's the real story? Jealousy? I mean, you obviously hate her being one of my role models."

"No, I don't." That's a lie. It eats at me that my daughter looks up to someone unworthy of her adoration, and I've been sorely tempted to tell her the harsh truth. But I won't. Life will find endless ways to carve cynical edges into her. Is it so wrong to want to keep her bubble-wrapped and protected a little longer? "It's not jealousy. Violet and I weren't on the best terms when she disappeared, but I think I was starting to understand her a little better. I actually felt kind of sorry for her." That used to be a lie, but over the years, my vitriol has evolved into pity. I saw what fame and money had done to her. "I just feel like I'm reliving the immediate aftermath—all the worst parts—of her going missing every time I go to the vigils. It . . . resurfaces things."

"Yeah, for me, too." Quinn's eyes go big and shiny. "But you had decades with her. I have only some childhood memories. Remembering her, thinking about losing her, it all hurts. But not honoring her at all . . . I don't know, I feel like that would hurt me more."

"Are you sure?" I don't know if she's right about that. "Listen, sweetheart." Placing my hands on her shoulders, I measure my words like a chemist with beakers of volatile compounds. "I know this takes a toll on you, too. I don't want you to be let down again."

Every vigil, Quinn paces the crowd. The first time, I thought it was her way of shedding nervous energy and expressing her grief. It would be a lot for any twelve-year-old to handle. The following year, just after we entered the park, she sprinted away from me, over to a bench where a slender, dark-haired woman in a trench coat sat reading a magazine. By the time I caught up, I heard Quinn say, "Oh. Never mind," which earned her a sympathetic smile from the woman.

My heart found a new way to break that day.

Ever since, my discomfort at the vigils is compounded by Quinn's scrutiny of the attendees and her yearning to discover her aunt among them. Seeing that hopeful glint in her eyes get extinguished year after year is brutal.

Back in the kitchen, Quinn stares up at me, her jaw set. "I want to speak at the vigil, and I need you to have my back on this, Mom."

That's it, then. "Of course."

Gabriel links an arm around my waist and offers Quinn a soft smile. "Having your back is pretty much our mission statement, kiddo."

Bolstered by her advantage, Quinn adopts a gentler tone. "I understand why you want to skip this thing. But people in Willow Glen talk. I don't want them to become suspicious again that you're hiding something or that there's bad blood between you two."

Me neither. Because I am. And there is.

It's not about hiding it from the residents of Willow Glen, though. I don't care what this town thinks, or Violet's fans, or anyone except for the freckled girl standing before me who's no longer a girl, who inherited my husband's soulful eyes, and my dimpled chin.

Somehow, she also managed to inherit my sister's fiery convictions.

Gesturing to the pot of chili, Gabriel says, "Now can we eat dinner like a family who likes each other?"

At the table, he and Quinn are too busy talking true crime shows to notice I'm not saying or eating much. They chatter on about which dramatizations they're most excited about: Versace, Tupac and Biggie Smalls, or Waco. I wonder how many similar conversations are going on elsewhere and how many are including the Violet miniseries. Does her case count as true crime if we don't know what happened?

Over the years, I've had family members of other missing people reach out to me. It's a club nobody wants to be part of, and you don't get a choice whether you join. Sometimes it was comforting to hear from other people forced to live in this limbo; most of the time it made me feel like I wasn't sad or desperate enough to find Violet. That's the accusation I've gotten more than any other, from the press, from the Wolf Pack, from this town, even from my own daughter. How much am I supposed to put on hold for this search, and how do I stop feeling like an asshole for trying to get on with my life? Not to mention, how long and hard should I look for someone who might not want to be found? Nearly ten years later, the questions still linger.

They call themselves survivors, the loved ones of those who went missing. But that's not what I am, not really. I wish there was a special word for those of us living with ambiguous loss. There isn't a language that feels right, a sensical way to parse out and assign definitions to the thoughts and emotions. Usually, I don't think of myself as surviving anything. Usually, I see myself as someone who was left behind.

All this criticism over the last decade about how I wasn't doing enough to find Violet, how I wasn't grieving her loss correctly, and not once has anyone ever pointed out that I'm still here. Ten years I've remained in the same house, kept the same phone number. Ten years I've held my tongue.

Tonight, it's easy being quiet.

Tomorrow, it might not be so easy.

There's only so long I'll be able to remain silent.

Violet thrived on secrecy; it was the fuel that made her engine run. Her entire sense of self was built on making others believe she possessed hidden knowledge and abilities.

I'm not built the same way. Keeping Violet's secrets has been like living with a bomb planted inside me.

Tick-tock, tick-tock.

One of these days, it's going to detonate, and it won't be pretty.

Date: January 10, 2018, at 7:42 AM
To: cfrank@sidecarstudios.com
From: twoods@sidecarstudios.com
Subject: Sasha

Cameron,

Okay numbers on the *Strange Exits* teaser so far but it would've been nice
to include a sound bite from the sister.

Where are we with the Dwyer interview?

—TW
Tobin Woods
Editorial Director & Cofounder
Sidecar Studios

Date: January 10, 2018, at 10:01 AM
To: twoods@sidecarstudios.com
From: cfrank@sidecarstudios.com
Subject: Re: Sasha

I'd say the teaser is doing better than okay. We've gotten 20K new *Exits*
subs in the last forty-eight hours, without the Sasha sound bite. Look at
all the chatter around that *EnWhen* piece. Could be better to have people
wondering will she/won't she instead of announcing her participation out-
right. We can hook listeners with the big mystery of Violet but tease them
with the smaller mystery of her sister to keep them on the line.

The Sasha interview is coming. I've been in regular contact with her, and
she's interested but has a lot going on right now. She's swamped with vigil
prep—Willow Glen is expecting more visitors than ever for the ten-year, and
she does a lot behind the scenes. We may be looking at a postvigil interview.

Guaranteed, *Strange Exits* will be one of the biggest shows you've ever had,
with or without Sasha.

—CF

Date: January 10, 2018, at 10:04 AM
To: cfrank@sidecarstudios.com
From: twoods@sidecarstudios.com
Subject: Re: Re: Sasha

The reason you were hired over more experienced podcasters was because you claimed being local to the area gave you deeper insight into the case and better access to Violet's associates and family, particularly her sister. Yes, the show is guaranteed to be a success with or without Sasha, but your future with Sidecar is not guaranteed if you don't deliver on what you promised.

—TW

Date: January 10, 2018, at 11:02 AM
To: info@volksalon.com
From: cfrank@sidecarstudios.com
Subject: Attn: Sasha Dwyer-PLEASE READ

Dear Sasha,

I don't know if you've received any of my prior emails. If you did, but chose to ignore them, fair enough. I hope you won't ignore this one.

I'm a podcast producer and host, currently working with Sidecar Studios, an up-and-coming audio media network in the United States. The podcast I'm developing, *Strange Exits*, focuses on mysterious deaths and disappearances, as its title suggests. The first season, "Vanishing Violet," is about . . . well, by now, you can probably guess.

I can't imagine what you've been through since your sister went missing, how difficult it must be to find meaningful closure . . . I don't know about you, but I've always been frustrated that law enforcement didn't do more. Last year, I decided to start researching your sister's case myself. I hope getting it more exposure with this podcast will generate some new leads.

This isn't merely an intriguing story I'm chasing. I grew up (and still reside) in Finchley. Being ten miles from Willow Glen, our town thought of Violet as an adjacent local hero. On a personal note, I'm a great admirer of your sister's work. A friend gave me a copy of *You Are Magic* when I was in a dark place in my life, and the book inspired me to make positive changes. When that friend became terminally ill, the only thing that comforted her was watching Violet's TV specials with me, and after she died, those shows were the only thing that comforted me.

Look, I'll level with you. Sidecar has a respectable listenership, but we're not NPR or anything. If you decided to speak on the record, you could surely have your pick of any media outlet. But I'm still asking you to say yes to me.

On *Strange Exits*, I intend to approach your sister's disappearance with utmost respect and an open mind, examining all possibilities and various aspects of her life. There are likely many sides of your sister still hidden from the public. While I've secured interviews with some of her friends and associates, I believe you'd illuminate other aspects of Violet better than anyone. My hope is that these accounts will not only pay tribute to her, but may even help us find her. It can also be an opportunity for you to share your story. If VV was such a compelling character, I have no doubt her sister is, too.

I'm sure you're a busy woman, and I will gladly accommodate your schedule if you're willing to speak with me. Since I'm local, I could meet you in person, at your salon or anywhere else that might be convenient.

I hope you'll give my offer serious consideration.

Best regards,
Cameron Frank

Date: January 13, 2018, at 3:05 PM
To: cfrank@sidecarstudios.com
From: info@volksalon.com
Subject: Re: Attn: Sasha Dwyer-PLEASE READ

Cameron,

I don't recall any prior emails from you—could be a smart spam folder kept them out of my inbox. Normally, I'd reply a simple "thanks but no thanks" to your request, like I typically do when I get these (if I reply at all). Normally, I also wouldn't take time to research the sender. But in your case, I made an exception on both counts. Something about your pseudo-earnestness got me curious. And now that I know more, I can't dismiss you with a polite form letter.

A quick online search revealed there are already rumors flying that I'm gonna be on your podcast. You wouldn't have anything to do with that, would you?

I also found your numerous contributions to blogs as well as the podcast you cohosted before this one. What a goodie bag of paranoia and paranormal *Theory X* was. But nowhere near as popular as I expect *Strange Exits* will be, so I understand the branding pivot. I may just be a small-town hairdresser with an infamous sister, but I'm also a business owner married to a marketing smarty-pants, and I've learned a lot from him over the years.

Let me guess: aliens and Bigfoot don't bring in sponsors like the dead and the missing. Hitching your wagon to the true crime train is a much more lucrative bet, isn't it? Now you've got a chance to get the mattress companies and fancy toothbrushes and meal-kit delivery services on board. Do you personally get a cut of the ad revenue? Even if you don't, you'll surely make something off your merchandise sales. While Stand Out/Don't Disappear is hardly the catchiest slogan, I'm guessing you'll still sell quite a few tees, totes, and mugs. And how industrious for you to set up an online shop before the first episode has even aired!

At first glance, it would be easy to assume you're using other people's tragedy for your personal profit. But you donate *10 whole percent* of those merch sales to the National Center for Missing and Exploited Children! How ever does NCMEC function without your generous support? Then there's your insistence on bringing attention to unsolved cases in the hopes that new info will provide answers to heartsick families. Wow. How goddamn touching. Tell me, Cameron, are you officially eligible for sainthood? If not, you must be *so* close.

Oh, but that's not all. If you're lucky and *Strange Exits* really takes off, you can take the show on the road, have hundreds—thousands?—of people pay to sit and listen to you speculate about my sister in real time. Though the ultimate goal is, of course, a TV deal. Right? I bet you get a little hard just thinking about the day some cable network or streaming service comes knocking. A book deal wouldn't be bad, either, but TV is more lucrative. Meanwhile, more listeners means selling more merch, perhaps expanding the line—you gotta think big here: branded body bags, coffins . . .

I wonder how many new listeners I could help bring in. What a coup it would be, convincing Violet's sister to say yes to you when she said no to everybody else. According to *EntertainmentWhenever*, I've pretty much already said yes! And you wouldn't be exploiting my sister to make all this money, oh no. You'd be super respectful. After all, it's not like you have any interest in conspiracy theories or sensational speculations, right?

I'm glad my sister's work had a positive impact on your life, but let's not pretend you've got noble intentions here. You really think *Strange Exits* will lead to a break in Violet's case? Let's get real. While I appreciate your generous offer to stalk me—ahem, sorry, I mean "meet me in person," I'd rather clean slimy hairballs out of the drain with my bare hands than take you up on it. My sister told me never to trust a man with two first names, and while a lot of what she said was nonsense, I'll take her at her word on that one.

Regards,
Sasha

Strange Exits

◦

Episode 0.5: "Bloody Gorgeous"

CAMERON FRANK: One thing there's no shortage of when you start re-searching Violet Volk: stories. Rumors, anecdotes, legends, all of which have a way of blurring together. Before we dive into the VV rabbit hole and explore some of these stories, I'd like to share my own.

I first saw Violet Volk on *Later Tonight with Jackson Cleo* in 1995. I'll link to the YouTube clip in the show notes—if you haven't seen it, you *need* to.

This was when I was a junior in high school, a humbling year for me, because I came down with a bad case of mono. I didn't even get it the fun way: my best friend got it from making out with the cute girl who worked at Hot Topic while I caught it from sharing his soda. I was out of school for a month, which quickly lost its novelty, since I was mostly bedridden and incapable of doing more than watching TV all day. It was fun to stay up late, though, and the best part of that was getting to watch *Later Tonight* every night. Jackson Cleo was famous for going off script, ad-libbing his opening monologues, having im-promptu conversations with audience members, and steering celebrity interviews into uncharted and uncomfortable territory. For those brave enough to run his gauntlet, it elevated their fame and made for mem-orable water cooler moments.

At this point, Violet was still unknown, working at Marabou, a burlesque club on the Lower East Side of Manhattan. Jackson Cleo had been to the club for a bachelor party and was blown away by Violet, the only burlesque performer to incorporate magic into her routine. He went back to see her act a few times, and raved about it on the show every time, joking that she wasn't a magician, she had to be a witch—it was the only way to explain some of her impossible tricks. His producers hadn't been able to get her on the show, so he extended a personal invitation right on TV for her to drop by *Later Tonight*. A few days later, Jackson got a life-size skeleton made of candy along with a note from Violet saying she couldn't make it because she had a meetup with her coven in Salem. Jackson showed off the skeleton on the show and had a good laugh over it. But, of course, this also got him even more worked up. It turned into a regular bit between them. He'd implore her on the air to be his guest, promising he wouldn't drown her or stick needles in her because he had a progressive attitude toward witches. She kept turning him down: her broom was broken so she had no transportation, she was busy scrubbing her cauldron, you get the idea.

When she finally did appear, a few months after their back-and-forth, she came out in a prim white dress that covered every inch of her body from the neck down; imagine a Victorian nightgown. Quite a departure from the sexy, flashy ensembles Jackson had mentioned when describing her performances.

As soon as she sat down, Jackson teased her about her modest look, asking if she had a date with Ebenezer Scrooge later, saying he would've brought ingredients to make s'mores if he'd known they were having a slumber party, that sort of thing.

Violet laughed along, ever the good sport, and said she wanted to look sweet and virginal for him, which made Jackson go tongue-tied. It was rare for him to appear nervous in front of a guest—this guy kept his cool when interviewing supermodels, presidents, some of the most famous people in the world.

Did he have a crush on her? That was the real reason he'd been chasing her for months to be on his show, right? Violet stated this hypothesis playfully, but Jackson stuttered and squirmed in his chair, waving away the audience's hoots at his flummoxed state.

Then things got more interesting.

When asked about doing burlesque, Violet said it was all about being tantalizing, hinting at what you *might* reveal—the best burlesque dancers could drive a man crazy just by taking off their gloves. She asked if he'd like a demonstration and Jackson just about fell out of his chair. The band started up classic old-timey stripper music and Violet stood.

What followed was arguably the world's most erotic below-the-elbow undressing. First, she teased Jackson (and the audience) by tugging up her sleeves, revealing long white gloves with tiny satin buttons. The removal itself felt both agonizingly slow and over much too quickly, each unfastened button a delicious torment. We gradually glimpsed the bare skin of her arms, then wrists, then palms, then fingers, and there was a collective gasp when her nails were revealed. Claws might be the better term here. They were metallic and pointed, like some kind of strange, sexy love child of Wolverine and Edward Scissorhands.

When Jackson asked if her nails were as razor-sharp as they looked, Violet grinned and said, "You tell me." Then she tossed her gloves in the air, waved her hands at warp speed, and slashed the fabric into ribbons, then the ribbons into smaller pieces, which became handfuls of confetti. Violet blew the confetti at Jackson, who now looked like he was covered in fake snow.

The good-natured host laughed while brushing the confetti off his suit jacket, then stopped abruptly.

"Violet, you're bleeding." He pointed at his temple.

Still standing, Violet wiped at the trickle of blood running down the side of her face with her sleeve, saying she must've accidentally nicked herself. In the process of trying to clean up, she cut herself several additional times with those metal talons, until blood was pouring out of her head cartoonishly, staining the top of her dress red.

"Should we call you an ambulance?" Jackson lobbed the question as a joke, but there was genuine horror creeping into his face. "I'm starting to feel like we're remaking *Carrie* here."

At this point, the audience was shrieking. Every time Violet tried to wipe up the bleeding, she only did more damage until the blood was gushing out of her, soaking the rest of her dress, which was now entirely red.

Unsure of how to react, Jackson asked what he could do to help.

Violet smiled sweetly, tilted her head, and batted her eyelashes like a southern belle. "Do you have a handkerchief I could borrow? I think I have a little something . . ." She pointed at her face, which was covered in red smears.

Jackson slid over a box of tissues, but Violet waved them away, said, "Never mind. I just need to do something about these wet clothes." She slashed at the lower part of her dress and exclaimed with delight when she found a box of matches at her feet, saying this would help speed things along.

The camera zoomed in close on her face for a moment, and she flashed the scariest and sexiest smile before setting her dress on fire.

"Oh no!" she screamed and spun around, trying to put herself out.

Somebody from offstage ran in with a fire extinguisher and aimed the nozzle at Violet. A cloud of white smoke enveloped the entire area around Jackson's desk. A few seconds later, it began to clear. Violet was now perched on the desk wearing a skimpy red dress covered in sequins and fringe, not a drop of blood on her.

From my sickbed at home, I felt like I was watching a delirious dream. Within a year, everybody would know who Violet Volk was. And yet, to this day, I wonder if anyone can truthfully say they really knew her.

July 31, 1989

Dear Violet,

How are you? How is magic camp?

You're not missing much in Brigantine. A bunch of crappy stuff happened. Our car was stolen right after we got here, Dad got food poisoning, and Mom yelled at me when she saw I wasn't wearing my red string bracelet (five seconds after I tore it off behind her back). She kept going on about protecting me from the evil eye and tied more red string around my wrist with like a thousand knots. I said I didn't know how a piece of string would protect me from car thieves or bad calamari, but she gave me that Scary Crazy Russian look so I shut up.

She still thinks this place is totally cursed! Then again . . . first Brigantine Castle closed, then the pier burned down, then you left me (sob) . . .

So what else is new? Uncle Slava's girlfriend Julie moved in with her daughter Lisa, right before we got here and there are still boxes everywhere. I have to sleep in Lisa's new room, which is covered with teeny-bopper posters and reeks of Electric Youth perfume. She's ten and keeps asking me which of the New Kids on the Block is my favorite until I want to scream. She's never even heard of the Beastie Boys or seen a Barbra Streisand movie! I practically had to twist her arm to watch *The Lost Boys* with me, and she cried because she found it too scary.

That's not all. Lisa and I have to share a bed, and it takes forever to fall asleep because she won't shut up about how she's going to grow up to be a famous dancer and marry Joey McIntyre and be best friends with Debbie Gibson. It's torture. She must snore or something, too, because I sometimes wake up on the living room sofa or patio lounger. When she gets up before me, she gets all pouty and says I don't like her. What a baby!

Speaking of the Beastie Boys, did you get my care package with *Paul's Boutique*? I was gonna wait until you got back from camp so we could get it together, but Dad kept calling me *kislaya* and got tired of my moping, so he took me to Tune City for new tapes. Do you hate the new Beasties as much as me? It's weird and not nearly as good as *License to Ill*. I've been listening to Madonna more than anything. I wish you liked her more, I think she's my favorite now.

Gotta go, Lisa is bugging me to take her to the beach. Have you learned how to cut people in half yet?

222,
Sasha

August 8, 1989

Violet,

What's up? I got a favor to ask you: knock it off. It's my own fault I got kicked out of magic camp. I was the one crying over those rabbits living in cages and it was my idea to free them, remember?? I unlocked the hatches and let them loose. You had no part in it. Stop feeling bad. My sleights sucked, anyway. Yours are a million times better. "The future of magic is in good hands," as Moses Deprince told us every single day, but it's better in your hands than mine.

I'd rather spend more time practicing rhymes, anyway. I came up with this one for you:

She's crafty, she gets around/Her card manip is the best in town.

(Fine, I borrowed the first part of that from the Beastie Boys.)

Are you still driving your bunkmates crazy listening to *Paul's Boutique* over and over? Mom is so sick of me blasting it, we get into fights about it every day. She says the Beasties sound like "loud boys with very bad manners," which cracks me up. Dad promised to get me a Walkman for my birthday if I stay on her good side. When it's him and me in the car, he cranks the music like he's Mr. Cool Guy. It's not the same thing when it's the Eagles, but I'd be a dick if I told him that.

In case your brain is too crammed with card techniques and patter, these are the horror movies you need to watch as soon as you get home: *Phantasm, Halloween, Sleepaway Camp, April Fool's Day*, and since you like *The Lost Boys* so much, another great vampire movie to check out is *Fright Night*. If you like any of these, I'll give you more.

All my friends are away, and I'm bored as hell, so you better write back!

—Gabe

Date: January 13, 2018, at 5:21 PM
To: info@volksalon.com
From: cfrank@sidecarstudios.com
Subject: Re: Re: Attn: Sasha Dwyer-PLEASE READ

Sasha,

You're absolutely right: I need you more than you need me. And I *am* jumping on the true crime bandwagon, hoping it'll be lucrative. If that's not honest enough, I'll lay it all out for you.

Prior to blogging and podcasting, I worked as a reporter for the *Finchley Free Press*. Two years ago, the paper was shuttered, and despite my best efforts, I wasn't able to find another full-time job in journalism. I freelanced when I could, but not enough to earn a livable income. That was the first domino that set off a Rube Goldberg machine of my life going to shit. It was followed by my wife also getting laid off, which led to our house being foreclosed on, which led to our divorce (that was right around the time my friend died, too).

Up until a couple of months ago, I was working as a cashier at Target for the health insurance and to cover basic living expenses. Considering how much time I spend in a job that brings me zero joy and fulfillment, the last thing I want to do is fill my free time with more things I don't enjoy. Podcasting has always been a labor of love for me.

As I was developing a new show based on your sister's life and disappearance, I got a lucky break when Sidecar hired me to do the same thing full-time, under the umbrella of their podcast network.

Is *Strange Exits* a cash grab? Maybe for my bosses, but for me, it's a chance to rebuild my life. Pay off my crippling credit card debt, move out of my grandma's condo and get my own place, that sort of thing. It's a chance to prove myself, and a chance to learn the truth about what happened to your sister.

The fact is, I don't know if I can do this without you.

I'm not looking to exploit Violet or to stalk you at your salon. Please know I have zero ill will toward you or your family.

Best,
Cameron

Date: January 15, 2018, at 1:27 AM
To: cfrank@sidecarstudios.com
From: info@volksalon.com
Subject: Re: Re: Re: Attn: Sasha Dwyer-PLEASE READ

Cameron,

Look, I'm sorry life has been kicking you in the nuts. And I appreciate your persistence . . .

Who am I kidding? I find your persistence annoying as hell, I'm just trying to be polite. Yeah, I know you worked as a reporter for the *FFP*. Remember that sentence you wrote?

"Could she know more than she's letting on?"

I'm not saying that one little sentence in your article made the town and the precious Wolf Pack suspicious of me, or that it put my business in jeopardy, but it didn't help. Shortly after that piece came out, somebody thought it would be cute to throw a Molotov cocktail through my salon's front window and spray paint "U R NOT MAGIC, U R A CUNT" on the awning above it.

Whatever you're looking to prove, you'll be doing it without me.

I will say this much: when it comes to Violet, "truth" is a word that should be used in quotes.

Sasha

Date: January 26, 2018, at 1:05 AM
To: cfrank@sidecarstudios.com
From: info@volksalon.com
Subject: Re: Re: Re: Attn: Sasha Dwyer-PLEASE READ

Cameron,

Seriously? You're gonna give up that easily? No wonder you couldn't hack it as a journalist. Unless that sob story was a ploy to get my sympathy . . .

Either way, I'm a little disappointed in your lack of tenacity.

What happened to needing me? Not being able to do this without me?

Tell you what, I'll give you another chance. Come by the salon on Sunday at 4:00 PM. I can't promise I'll share every personal detail I know about Violet, but I'm sure you'll be able to coax some good info out of me.

Don't bother responding, just show up on Sunday. You may be in for the scoop of the decade.

Sasha

Sasha

January 28, 2018

"We're getting extra security, and the township is closing off the streets bordering Cordova Park as a precaution. Nobody knows for sure, but some are estimating there could be as many as *a hundred thousand* attendees this year. Can you imagine? And how marvelous to get Quinn as a speaker! You must be so proud of her."

It's Sunday, Eleanor Toback is here for her monthly haircut, and she hasn't stopped chattering about the candlelight vigil since she sat down.

"I'm proud of Quinn for many reasons." This one being pretty low on the list.

"She's a delightful young woman, I'm sure she'll dazzle the crowd."

Before I can formulate a snarky reply I won't say out loud, Mrs. Toback emits a surprised coo. "I don't think I've seen this one before. May I?" She leans away from the trajectory of my spray bottle to get a closer look at a framed photo beside the mirror. In it, my sister and I are posed on a beach with a pier behind us.

The salon is filled with photos of Violet—not something I was in favor of, but Gabriel insists it helps draw in clientele and keeps her fans happy. It was also his idea to name the place Volk Salon instead of Dwyer like I wanted to—I took his name, so why shouldn't our business? But Gabriel's marketing acumen prevailed, so my sister's name and image are all over this place. I've gotten used to operating within a Violet shrine, but some days are more insufferable than others. Particularly the ones when Mrs. Toback comes in for her monthly appointment, and a land mine–filled stroll down memory lane ensues.

"How old are the two of you here, seven, eight?" She examines the picture intently.

"She's eight, I'm seven."

"That's Brigantine Castle, right?"

"Yeah. We used to spend summers in Brigantine when we were little. My uncle had a house down there." My voice softens at the memory. "We loved that pier. I think this was taken the last year it was open. Not long after that, it burned to the ground right before they were set to demolish it. Violet and I cried when we saw what was left."

Brigantine was part of the secret code we used to sign our notes, emails, texts . . . when we were on speaking terms. At first it was "BBB" for Brigantine (our favorite place), Bottle Caps (our favorite candy), and Barbra Streisand (our favorite actress by osmosis—Mom watched her movies nonstop). After several failed attempts by our parents to teach us Russian (we were lazy, and the alphabet, which looked like jumbled spiders, scared us), we experimented with creating our own secret language by swapping the letters of the alphabet for numbers. "BBB" became "222"—not exactly something it would've taken Alan Turing to crack. It wasn't long before we grew tired of how tedious it was to encrypt and decrypt simple messages like "Bugs and birds live in Mrs. Toback's hair," so we opted for phonetic Pig Latin when we wanted to be stealthy, keeping our "222" sign-off.

In early 2008, when I heard Violet was playing the Witkin Theater on February 22, I wondered if she was sending me a coded message, taking a step toward reconciliation. A couple of days later, when I received three front-row tickets to the show with a note saying she hoped we'd be able to make it—its humble wording a far cry from the hubris and entitlement I'd come to expect from Violet—I was able to briefly set aside the years of resentment. It was like I'd been wearing a backpack filled with bricks, and suddenly the bottom gave way, releasing a burden I didn't realize I'd been carrying around.

Maybe I'll get my sister back.

But then, of course, February 22 came, she went, and I was left to make sense of it all. Though I never could. Still can't.

"How darling. Violet looked like she was ready for the stage even back then." Mrs. Toback's face is somber as she hands me back the photo. "Oh, Sasha, you poor dear. The time around her vigil must be terribly arduous for you. Especially with this being the decennial." Only Mrs. Toback could casually drop words like "arduous" and "decennial" into a conversation. I bet her favorite gift to give anyone is a dictionary. "What do you make of this recent spate of sightings?"

"It is what it is." I cringe at my monosyllabic nonresponse. It's been thirty years since she was my teacher, yet I still feel like she's silently grading our interactions. "I don't think there's any legitimacy to them. It's just the latest social media fad. People got tired of dumping buckets of ice water on themselves and pretending to be mannequins so now they're pretending to be my sister. Some don't recognize the artifice for what it is." There, that should score me extra vocab points with her.

"I think you're right." Her thoughtful tone makes me stand taller (I am too old to be seeking validation from this woman). "I also believe, while the intentions behind this copycat behavior aren't malicious . . . it's grossly inconsiderate toward you and your family."

The sting in my eyes is sudden, and I purposefully drop a comb so I can wipe away my tears in private as I bend down to retrieve it. Gabriel, Quinn, and I made a pact not to search the hashtag, but every night we break it, furtively scrolling on our individual screens as we pretend to watch TV. For weeks now, I've been asking myself what's worse, having no hope or false hope? It has to be the second one . . . right?

"How old would she have been now, forty-one?" Mrs. Toback asks.

"Forty-three. Not would've been, *is*. Legalities aside, last I checked, they haven't found a body." I swallow the lump in my throat and hold up a lock of her hair between two fingers. "How short are we going today, Mrs. Toback?"

"Just a trim. And please, it's Eleanor."

But there's something unnerving about calling a teacher by their first name, even as an adult. It's too intimate, like I'd be seeing Mrs. Toback in her underwear.

"How are Sophocles and Euripides?" Asking about her cats is usually an effective way to change the subject.

"Oh, they're fine, fine. Still a little lackluster since we lost Aeschylus, but they're recovering. We all are." Uh-oh. There's that sentimental gleam in her eyes. I know what's coming next. "I can't imagine what it must have been like for you, all these years, wondering what happened to your sister."

There it is. I should've known we weren't done with Violet talk.

Every month it's the same thing, getting verbally prodded under the guise of sympathy. It's like conversational *Groundhog Day* with this woman, being asked over and over how I've been getting along since my sister vanished (fine) and what I think happened to her (no idea).

"That surely can't be the correct time?" Mrs. Toback looks at the wall clock, perplexed, then bends over to root around in her handbag. Go right ahead, sudden movements are my favorite when I'm wielding sharp scissors next to someone's head. "I must've left my phone in the car." She sits back up and I zip my shears away from her ear a second before it's impaled.

I check the digital clock above the washing stations. 2:22 PM. Mrs. Toback's appointment was at 2:30, so unless time has moved so painfully slowly it's gone backward (which I wouldn't entirely discount), that can't be right. Let's check the iPhone.

"It's 3:05," I say. "Guess I need to get a new battery." One of Violet's many superstitions was making a wish whenever the clock showed repeating numbers (11:11, 2:22, 3:33, and so on). It was silly even to my childish brain, but eventually she persuaded me to make a wish whenever the time read 2:22. I shoot a disdainful look at the stopped wall clock. *That doesn't count.*

The minutes drag on as I trim Mrs. Toback's hair, which is so thick, it takes the better part of an hour to cut. An hour filled with mediocre chitchat and dodging intrusive questions, inspiring gruesome fantasies about using the pointed ends of my shears (or better yet, my styling razor) to put one or both of us out of our misery. Not that I'd ever go Sweeney Todd on her, but good grief is that woman taxing. Luckily, she prefers her hair to air dry, so that's an extra half hour I don't need to maintain my politeness.

After Mrs. Toback pays her bill (tipping me exactly 10 percent, not a penny more or less), she stops outside the salon to accost a thirty-something blond guy I've never seen before. I busy myself with organizing a box of receipts and invoices. Moments later, the bell above the front door trills, and that same blond guy approaches the counter.

"Sasha, right?" He flashes a nervous grimace-slash-smile.

"That's me. How can I help you?"

"I'm Cameron." He extends a hand. When I look down at it with-out moving or responding, he adds, "Cameron Frank. From the *Strange Exits* podcast. We've been emailing each other."

"Right . . . and you promised you wouldn't stalk me at my sa-lon . . . yet here you are." I take a step back and bump into a shelf of olive oil hair treatments. One of the amber glass vials topples to the floor and shatters, permeating the air with rosemary and lavender, two calming scents that are not doing their job.

There's nothing threatening in Cameron's outward demeanor. Broad-shouldered and tall, he stands hunched over and tucks his hands into his pockets, as if trying to come across as less imposing. His ex-pression is meek. Nevertheless, he turned up after I specifically told him to stay away. Unnerving much?

Cameron cranes his neck like he's misheard something. "I don't understand. You asked me to come by."

The doorbell trills behind him.

"Shit, I meant to get here sooner." Gabriel rushes in, combing har-ried fingers through his mess of dark hair, which is in a perpetual state of bedhead. He casts an uneasy look between Cameron and me. "A call with a distributor ran late."

"I thought we were doing inventory later . . ." The three of us stand there, staring at each other, unmoving.

"Is anyone else thinking of that scene from *Reservoir Dogs*?" Cam-eron's snicker is halfhearted.

"No, but my scissors *are* sharp enough to take off an ear," I snap at him and turn to my husband. "Did you have something to do with this?"

Instead of answering me, Gabriel introduces himself to Cameron. "Let me have a quick chat with my wife in the back, clear up a few things." He heads toward the supply closet, motioning for me to fol-low, but I don't budge.

"I think I can figure it out without a quick chat," I say, crossing my arms, digging my nails into my biceps. Mustn't look too long at Gabriel in case laser beams shoot out of my eyes and maim him. "You found Cameron's email and replied from the salon account, inviting him here. Even though I already made it clear I had no interest in being interviewed for the podcast." Gritting my teeth, I manage a tight smile at Cameron and tell him, "I'm sorry you came out here for nothing. False pretenses and all that."

"Oh, I was meeting a friend for dinner nearby, anyway," Cameron assures me, like I give even a single fuck about his schedule.

"How about we all take a minute—" Gabriel interrupts himself to sniff the air and squint at me. "Did you spill something back there?"

"I sure did." Sidestepping the oily puddle, I come out from behind the counter and march toward the front door. "Feel free to clean that up—feel free to clean *all* of this up." My hand sweeps an exaggerated circle in Cameron's direction. "I'll be at Better Beans."

The front door doesn't slam, and the trill of bells echoing in my wake undercuts my angry exit. I stomp to the coffee shop two doors down, admonishing myself for doing only half of my usual run this morning. Those extra endorphins would be nice right about now.

"Medium unsweetened iced tea, please," I order and dig into my jeans pockets for money.

"That'll be two dollars and twenty-two cents."

I fish out a five-dollar bill and hand it over.

Gabriel comes in as I'm poking a straw through the plastic lid of my beverage. "You have every right to be pissed off."

He didn't leave that guy alone in the salon, did he? A rush to the front window reveals Cameron in the same spot by the counter, shuffling his weight from one foot to the other, glancing around. When he catches sight of me, relief flashes on his face only to be replaced with uncertainty.

"Sasha, please."

I turn and face my husband, take a long sip of tea. It's strong, bitter.

"I'm sorry I emailed him under your name. Let me explain." An elderly couple approaches, and we go quiet as they take what feels like a full hour to saunter by. "Can we please go back in? Just give me five minutes." Whenever Gabriel gives me that beseeching look, his eyebrows triangular in distress, he looks like a little boy suffering. It's too much.

"Yeah, fine."

Back in the salon, I grab a windup timer from one of the stations. "Gabriel and I are gonna have that quick chat you've been hearing so much about," I tell Cameron. "I can trust you not to steal anything, right?"

"God, of course." Horrified at the thought, as if he wouldn't love a souvenir of my sister, as if he's any better than the other people who nab framed photos of her when my back is turned (it took less than a year before I switched to color copies and picture frames from Goodwill). "I can even wait outside if you want," he adds.

"Not necessary, you can just take a seat somewhere."

I gesture to the chairs by the front door and follow my husband to the supply room.

Once Gabriel closes the door behind us, I take the timer—which I usually use for bleaching and dye processes—and twist it several notches. "You have five minutes. Go."

A faint ticking echoes between us.

"Didn't think you'd be quite so literal about it, but okay," he begins. "First off, I'm sorry for going behind your back like that."

"Were you snooping on me?"

"No, I was looking for a purchase order and came across Cameron's emails. The guy's been through a lot. I thought it would be nice to give him a break."

"We've all been through a lot. And you wouldn't be the one giving him a break, *I* would. For years now, what's the only thing I've been asking for? To have nothing to do with my sister. Every time I try to draw a line in the sand, you push me over it. Bad enough I caved on the salon."

"Which was a smart business decision. Let's not make me out to be some kind of bully here. When you didn't want to sell T-shirts or other Violet memorabilia, I gave in on that one—though it might've helped us repay that second mortgage. And I've always supported your decision to avoid the media." His jaw twitches, belying the effort it takes to offer this support.

"After how many hours of going back and forth on it?" How he tried to coax me to talk to the press. It would be therapeutic for me, it might get new leads on Violet, it could end up being lucrative for our family—he tackled it from every angle, but I remained firm. There was no way I'd get through an interview without letting a negative sound bite slip, and the last time I did that (I had the nerve to admit I didn't think my sister possessed any superpowers), our house got egged and the salon was boycotted for a month. "And what about all the stupid vigils I let you drag me to?"

"That's to protect you. To stop people from gossiping about you."

"How exactly would participating in this podcast protect me?"

"Maybe it wouldn't. But you'd get to control the story. Maybe that's what you need more than protection." He takes my hands in his and looks into my eyes like he's searching for something long lost. "If not this, you need *something*. I get that therapy isn't your thing. But you're not eating enough and you're starting to exercise too much again. And your sleep issues—"

"I've been restless. Sometimes it helps me to sleep in other parts of the house."

"Like the kitchen floor? Whatever it is, I don't think you've ever fully dealt with the Violet situation, and this could be an opportunity. Maybe sharing it with me or your friends is tough because it's too close, and sharing with a counselor would make you feel self-conscious or scrutinized—"

"But sharing with lord-knows-how-many podcast listeners is gonna be easier?" Even as my eyebrows shoot up, something loosens inside me, like a pebble at the bottom of a rock pile.

"In a weird way, yeah, maybe it will be easier."

"You're just saying all this so you can find a way for us to get in on the profits."

"If money were the only thing I cared about, I would've bugged you to do the reality show. Or pursue that book deal."

I don't even feel my jaw dropping open, only Gabriel's fingertip under my chin pushing it closed again.

"Yeah, I know about all of it." His tone is gentle, resigned. "And I get why you had to hide it from me. It makes me feel shitty that you reached that point. Rather, that I got you to that point. I'm sorry for that."

"It's okay." My eyes feel gritty and I blink away threatening tears. "It just bothers me when you look for ways to use my sister's name so we can make a quick buck."

"After everything Violet put us through, I think we have the right to use her name to give us any advantage we can. Just my opinion and not what's important here." Gabriel holds a hand up to my cheek. "People have underestimated you for a long time. They thought because Violet was the loud one, you were the quiet one. That's never been true. Violet just drowned you out." The timer goes off, a tinny ring that echoes through the small room. "Maybe she even made you lose your voice a little."

Maybe. But years of putting up with her drama have left me too worn-out to speak.

His face says the power is mine, the power of truth, the power to expose, to be vulnerable.

But it doesn't feel like power, it feels like baring my neck to the guillotine.

"I have to protect Quinn," I say.

"She already knows the tooth fairy and Santa Claus aren't real." His tone is tender, coaxing. "But she still has Violet up on that pedestal. Might be time for you to knock it over. Maybe it's what Quinn needs to fully grow up."

"Or maybe she'll shoot the messenger. Or not believe the messenger. Or find a way to make me the villain of the whole thing." When you really don't want to believe something, you'll create a new logic to circumvent the truth; sometimes necessity isn't the mother of invention so much as denial. Alternately, Quinn could resent me for keeping secrets from her all these years. She already kinda does, she just doesn't know the specifics. "Besides, can you imagine what the Wolf Pack would do if I gave an honest interview? They'd burn this place to the ground. Again."

"We have better insurance now. If it would help you, it would be worth it," he urges, giving my arm a squeeze.

Would it help, though? And at what cost? Never mind the salon. If there's even a minute chance I could lose Quinn, it's not worth the risk.

"I'm sorry, I can't," I tell Gabriel, casting my eyes down so I don't have to see his disappointment. "Nothing matters more than Quinn."

"I think she'd understand."

"There's no way to know for sure. And if I can't talk to her, I'm not ready for a podcast audience." My eyes drift over to a box of latex gloves on the shelf beside me. A blue sticker on the side reads *Inspected by #222*. What's the deal with all these twos? Doesn't matter. There are more important things to focus on. "Please tell Cameron I'm out."

When he leaves, I peel off the sticker, tear it up, and throw away the sticky pieces.

Date: January 28, 2018, at 6:00 PM
To: quinndwyer@sju.edu
From: gabrieldwyer@gmail.com
Subject: like I said . . .

. . . good intentions, bad idea. At least you had enough sense to give me a heads-up. We'll come up with a way you can repay me for taking the blame. In the meantime, you're welcome.

Love you, kiddo.

Strange Exits

Episode 1: "Violet's Early Years"

CAMERON FRANK [STUDIO]: Whether you regard Violet Volk as a hero or villain, one thing both have in common is an origin story. This week, we're going to examine the magician's early years with the help of someone who knew her back in the day. I recently had the pleasure of speaking with Eleanor Toback, who taught Violet Volk at Willow Glen Elementary School.

Before we hear from Eleanor, I want to start with a bit of background on Violet herself.

She was born Varushka Volkov on January 25, 1975, in Newark, New Jersey, to Russian immigrants. Early the following January, sister Sasha was born. Their father, Anatoly, was a tailor and mother, Regina, was a hairdresser. Rising crime rates in the late 1970s and early 1980s drove the family to move downstate, to Willow Glen, a quiet middle-class suburb in South Jersey.

Willow Glen Township is the type of place where you could have an uneventful childhood. It's also the type of place that any young person with lofty ambitions would want to escape.

Trust me, I know what I'm talking about. I've spent most of my life in a nearby town similar to Willow Glen, wishing I'd left.

But enough about me. Let's meet our first guest, Eleanor Toback. After teaching at Willow Glen Elementary for twenty-four years, she transitioned to a position at the local library, where she still works today, and where we recorded our conversation. Eleanor is a petite woman in her late sixties with thick curly gray hair she wears down to her shoulders. Her blue eyes are sharp, her posture and vocabulary are better than yours, and she will verbally eviscerate you if you bring up the subject of retirement. Something else you should know about Eleanor: her memory is impeccable. She knows the Dewey Decimal System by heart and can name and describe every student she's ever taught. Lucky for me, that includes Violet. Here's our chat:

CAMERON FRANK: Thanks for speaking with me, Eleanor. And for letting us use the library after hours.

ELEANOR TOBACK: Well, you requested a quiet place, and this seemed fitting.

CAMERON FRANK: What years did you teach Violet?

ELEANOR TOBACK: Let's see now . . .'85 to '88. Fourth through sixth grade. Willow Glen Elementary was experimenting with looping, a system wherein teachers remained with a single class over the course of consecutive years. Its proponents believe fostering consistent student-teacher relationships offers an enhanced learning experience and improved academic performance. While Sasha was initially in the year below Violet, she was terribly bright and skipped the fourth grade, joining my fifth-grade class. Thus I had the chance to teach both Volkov sisters.

CAMERON FRANK: And was Varushka already known as Violet when she entered your class?

ELEANOR TOBACK: Not quite. The metamorphosis occurred a few weeks into fourth grade. She loathed the way her classmates pronounced her name and constantly corrected them. You see, you're supposed to roll the *r* and hit the first syllable—VA-roosh-ka—but most of the kids called her va-ROOSH-ka and didn't know how to roll their *r*s.

One morning, I gave the class an assignment to write and illustrate a short poem. In the afternoon, we hung up everyone's work on the back wall, and the kids took turns reading their poems aloud. I still remember what Violet wrote, word for word:

Roses are red
Varushka is dead
Violet is me
And now I am free

Such boldness in that child! Such a declaration of autonomy!

From then on, she was Violet. She changed her name in all her schoolbooks and refused to answer to any other. I'm not sure when she changed it legally . . .

CAMERON FRANK: It was 1993, when she moved to New York City. That's also when she shortened her last name to Volk.

ELEANOR TOBACK: Ah yes. Her sister, Sasha—who I'm very friendly with—once mentioned that their father went gray at a very young age and was nicknamed "Sery Volk," which translates to "Gray Wolf."

CAMERON FRANK [STUDIO]: For those of you wondering, yes, that is why Volk's most ardent fans call themselves the Wolf Pack.

ELEANOR TOBACK: Perhaps the adopted moniker was a tribute to him. Nevertheless, from that day in class, Varushka ceased to exist.

CAMERON FRANK: It sounds like Violet had a flair for the dramatic even back then.

ELEANOR TOBACK: To an extent . . . I'd call it a sense of restlessness more than anything.

CAMERON FRANK: Restless in what way?

ELEANOR TOBACK: Well, you could tell there was something about her that was unsatisfied, unresolved, searching. Her moods didn't oscillate, per se, but this inexplicable cloud of frustration surrounded her.

Perhaps that's why Violet had trouble sitting still. Whenever I looked at her, she'd be drumming her fingers on the desk or tapping her foot or braiding and unbraiding her hair. She wasn't disruptive the way some of my other pupils were, and she was hardly the only child who fidgeted in class . . . but there was something excessive about her movements. I wondered if that might be an indicator of something more serious. Back then, you didn't get a lot of children diagnosed with attention deficit disorder, so I presumed it was a nervous condition of sorts. I brought it up at the first parent-teacher conference her mother and father attended.

CAMERON FRANK: How did they react?

ELEANOR TOBACK: Her father did something most unexpected. He produced a quarter from his pocket, handed it to me, and promised Violet would settle down in class if I gave her the coin and let her fiddle with it.

At my bewilderment, he explained that her previous teacher didn't allow her to have the coin in class, claiming it was a distraction to the other children. You see, she wasn't merely playing with the coin, she was manipulating it, practicing sleight of hand techniques, and her teacher punished her anytime she was caught.

CAMERON FRANK: Punished her how?

ELEANOR TOBACK: I'm uncomfortable revealing this, but . . . Anatoly said it was a while before he noticed the marks on his daughter. Mind you, it wasn't uncommon for certain teachers to employ corporal punishment back then, but apparently the evidence of violence he saw was brutal. That poor girl. She never said a word about it for months. This was the catalyst for the Volkovs to leave Newark.

CAMERON FRANK: How awful. Did he say whether the teacher faced any consequences?

ELEANOR TOBACK: I asked if they had filed a report with the principal or the police, and he said his brother took care of it . . .

CAMERON FRANK [STUDIO]: Slava Volkov, Violet's uncle, worked in construction and was also a known card shark. He was rumored to have been involved with the Allegro crime family, which operated along the Jersey Shore since the days of Prohibition, helping them rig high-stakes poker games. And if you're wondering if he introduced Violet to magic, your assumptions are correct. We'll get into that later on.

ELEANOR TOBACK: After the parent-teacher conference, I had a private conversation with Violet, and we made a deal. I couldn't have her distracting the class with coin tricks, but if a quarter would serve as her safety blanket, I'd let her fidget with it so long as she did so in a way that the other children couldn't see. Her initial reaction was unease, until I swore I'd never hurt her—at worst, I'd take the quarter away if it proved disruptive. She accepted the deal. Perked up quite a bit, too. I think giving it a covert angle made it that much more appealing.

CAMERON FRANK: Makes sense, considering magicians need to be adept at hiding things. What happened after that?

ELEANOR TOBACK: She became a different person. More focused and attentive. No more squirming, no more tapping—I couldn't believe a coin could cause such a transformation. And she was so skillful at keeping the quarter out of sight. It was only at recess that she showed off her tricks.

CAMERON FRANK: Could you see her emerging talent as a magician back then?

ELEANOR TOBACK: Oh, yes. She could make a quarter dance around her fingers as if it had a life of its own, make it vanish and reappear in myriad ways, have it jump up into her hand as if defying gravity . . . It was quite remarkable.

CAMERON FRANK: How did Violet's classmates react to her talents?

ELEANOR TOBACK: It's a funny thing. They were a tougher audience than we teachers were. They appreciated Violet's tricks but were suspicious and rigorous in their attempts to figure out her routines or catch her in a mistake. She learned to show off only her most polished material and not to perform it too many times.

CAMERON FRANK: Because otherwise they'd catch on to how she did the trick?

ELEANOR TOBACK: Once in a rare while—if a palmed coin slipped out of her hand, for example. Usually, the children would lose interest once they were fully stumped and Violet made it clear she wouldn't reveal how a trick was done. The novelty wore off surprisingly quickly for them, though it never did for her. There was an obsessiveness in the way she practiced. Often she asked to spend recess in my classroom so that she could rehearse a trick without the other kids seeing her.

CAMERON FRANK: Did you let her?

ELEANOR TOBACK: About fifty percent of the time. I felt it was important for her to socialize with her classmates, but I also knew she had a gift. Not only that, she possessed the compulsive drive that someone gifted needs in order to elevate themselves. It was remarkable, how Violet never seemed to tire of practicing. She could spend a half hour repeating the same series of finger movements without expressing a hint of boredom or frustration.

CAMERON FRANK: How did things change the following year, when Sasha skipped a grade and entered your class?

ELEANOR TOBACK: Honestly, the biggest change I noticed was that Violet incorporated playing cards into her lunchtime practices.

In terms of how she was with her sister . . . There was something . . . inscrutable about them. They were cordial enough to each other, and I did catch them passing notes from time to time, but there was also . . . Sometimes I picked up a sense of apprehension, particularly from Violet. Perhaps it was envy?

CAMERON FRANK: Envy toward Sasha?

ELEANOR TOBACK: Yes. Sasha was a beautiful child. Don't get me wrong, they were both lovely girls, but Violet . . . she was not as outwardly striking as her sister. Both had dark hair and blue eyes, but Sasha's hair fell in perfect waves, her eyes were large and vivid like cobalt glass, and her skin had a rosy glow—she's still luminous today, and without a stitch of makeup. Violet's hair was more unkempt and had less luster, her eyes smaller and cloudier, her skin pale and waxy. One of the downsides of spending so much time indoors practicing magic tricks, I suppose. She was also small for her age, whereas Sasha had an early growth spurt, which made many think she was the older sister—goodness, did Violet find that irksome.

There was something about Sasha that was sweet, effortless, and drew people to her. She was quick to loan her school supplies, share her snacks, help a classmate struggling with an assignment. If it was easy to be kind to Sasha because she was pretty, it became easier once she mirrored that kindness. Perhaps that created a positive feedback loop. Whereas Violet, who did not possess the same genetic advantage and had endured physical abuse from a trusted figure early in life, was more guarded, prickly.

CAMERON FRANK: Did Violet have a tougher time making friends?

ELEANOR TOBACK: Yes, though it was clear Violet wanted to make friends. And Sasha, who collected friends effortlessly, tried to include her sister but was met with resistance. Violet wanted to earn the attention and admiration from her classmates on her own terms. That didn't happen until Cyndi Yanoff's eleventh birthday party.

CAMERON FRANK: Why don't you take us through that party?

ELEANOR TOBACK: It took place the weekend after Halloween. Cyndi's father owned a number of successful car dealerships, and while he could've easily afforded to move the family to a tonier area like Haddonfield or Mullica Hill, they decided to stay local. I guess he liked being a big fish in a little pond. The Yanoffs lived in a custom mansion and threw lavish parties. Half the town must've been invited to Cyndi's birthday celebration. It was unlike anything I've ever seen. There was a petting zoo, an inflatable ball pit, a cotton candy machine, face painting . . . the works. The Yanoffs also had a stage area set up in the backyard and hired a magician to perform just before the cake was served. A fellow named Ace Morgan, who embodied the typical look of a magician: top hat, vest, cape, all of it. You should've heard the gasp that came out of Violet when she saw him.

CAMERON FRANK: Was he any good?

ELEANOR TOBACK: I'm no expert, but he struck me as proficient. He did the standard fare with playing cards, silk scarves, coins, metal rings. It was entertaining, but it got more interesting when he asked for a volunteer and Violet joined him onstage.

He had her pick a card, which she showed to all of us while he turned around. Now, my memory is good, but not that good, so let's say it was the five of clubs. Once we all saw the card, Ace had her put it back in the deck, which he shuffled and had her cut. He flourished the top card and she shook her head. Another shuffle and cut, another card brandished, and once again, it was not the five of clubs. Then Ace contorted his face and said he had something in his teeth. He rooted around in his mouth and took out a folded playing card. At this point, we were all certain this would be the five of clubs.

It wasn't.

When Ace unfolded the card and Violet shook her head again, he accused her of lying. He tried to be playful about it, but you could tell he was frustrated. Violet calmly named her card, and we all backed her up, since we'd all seen it. Then she gave him this wicked little smile and said she hid the card, and he would never guess where.

At this point, Ace was having trouble hiding his impatience, but he remained even-tempered, asking where she'd hidden the card.

Violet pointed to a table near the stage holding a sheet cake covered in pink icing roses. She told Cyndi to cut herself the corner piece with the biggest rose. Before anyone could stop her, Cyndi ran over to the cake and, in her excitement, didn't bother with any utensils. She grabbed at the corner of the cake with her bare hand and shrieked as she pulled out a playing card. It was smeared with vanilla icing, but it was unmistakably the five of clubs.

CAMERON FRANK: Wow. So, was Violet part of the act?

ELEANOR TOBACK: That's what I thought at first, but Ace's confusion seemed genuine. He jumped offstage and ran over to examine the card himself. It wasn't until he uttered an expletive that I began to suspect Violet had somehow hijacked his trick. He just kept staring back and forth between the five of clubs that had come out of the cake and the ten-year-old girl with the tangled hair and crooked smile who'd somehow upstaged him.

Finally, he raised his hands in surrender and led us in a round of applause for Violet, who was still onstage, watching us like this was what she'd been waiting for. She bowed, held up a finger, and took a few slow backward steps. She outstretched her arms and . . .

Now, this was broad daylight and I saw no wires, no harnesses, no way she could've—but she *did*—the girl *levitated off the stage*, a good ten inches, and just *hovered in place* for what felt like a full minute before lowering herself back down.

We were all stunned, Ace Morgan included, but at that point I was sure Violet had to be part of the show. What other explanation was there?

[MALE VOICE]: She wasn't part of the show. I still can't figure that one out.

CAMERON FRANK [STUDIO]: That's Ace Morgan. We'll hear more from him in a later episode.

August 30, 1990

Dear Violet,

Congrats on nailing the diagonal palm shift! I don't know why you're surprised. You practice so much, you probably do card manip in your sleep. Do you even need magic camp anymore? Haven't you learned everything by now?

My summer has been a snooze fest, except for a trip to Hershey Park (the Flying Falcon was awesome!).

Big news. You better sit down for this.

What's the craziest and coolest thing that could happen?

No, Mike D, Ad Rock, and MCA haven't asked me to be the fourth Beastie.

We're moving!

I think it has something to do with the "vacation" Mom's been on (she's still in Florida taking care of her "sick friend"). Dad stopped shaving and smelled like beer all the time until Aunt Carol came to stay with us. She's kinda bossy but her grilled cheese was the best thing I ever ate after weeks of nothing but cereal. Aunt Carol kept telling Dad "get ahold of yourself!" and "forget that floozy!" Finally, he decided he was sick of Pennsylvania and sick of the college he writes grants for (grants are like fancy letters asking for money, except when I wrote him a fancy letter asking him to raise my allowance, it didn't work, so I guess he's better at it than I am). He was probably sick of his sister bossing him, too. Long story short: he got a new job. Only this one isn't at a college. It's at the Witkin Theater. You know what that means?

We're moving to Willow Glen!

I know, I know, you think Willow Glen is the most boring place on earth, but there's no way it's more boring than Carlisle. And duh, you won't be bored with me around.

No! Sleep! 'Til Jersey!

—Gabe

P.S. For the record, *Evil Dead 2* is not better than *The Evil Dead*. *ED2* is funny and has the big effects, but you gotta give props to the original, which is a horror classic.

February 20, 1991

V—

This is stupid. You've been giving us the silent treatment for weeks. If you don't want to be friends with me because I like your sister, that's on you. But you can't keep ignoring Sasha. She didn't do anything wrong. Neither of us did. I thought you were cooler than that.

If you want to stop being lame, come hang out with us at lunch tomorrow. Sasha and I will be in the locker hall outside the computer lab. I brought in the latest *Fangoria*, but it was too big to fit in your locker. It's a special 100th issue—very awesome, you need to see it. If you're nice, you can borrow it.

If you're extra nice, I'll get my dad to sneak us into the Witkin again next week so you can practice your magic onstage . . .

—G.

YOU ARE MAGIC

By Violet Volk

For QD
May your wings and fins never fail you

AUTHOR'S NOTE

Let's get one thing out of the way right now: I fucking hate self-help books.

Anybody who claims to be an expert at living a better life is an asshole and should be avoided at all costs. We're all blindly running around our existential rat mazes, hoping to find a piece of cheese. I'm not here to feed you so-called wisdom cloaked in platitudes, encouraging you to take baby steps to nowhere.

In other words, I'm not an expert, and I'm not here to help you. I'm here to grab you by the shoulders and wake you up.

Actually, I need *you* to help *me*.

You read that right. I need your help. Because our world is in a precarious state. There is an ever-widening sinkhole of mediocrity trying to consume us all and we need to find higher ground.

If you love your life, every last crumb of it, put down this book right now and go back to living it—you don't need me. (P.S. You're probably lying to yourself; I'll be here when you've figured that out.)

But if your life could use more inspiration, more spice, more (and I roll my eyes as I write this, but my editor insists) *magic*, I'll tell you what's worked for me. And for the record, despite what the gossip rags might say, I fucking love my life.

Magicians are not supposed to reveal their secrets, but I'm seeing so many people drowning in misery or denial, feeling untethered and incapable of being their best selves, it's time for me to step in and divulge a few things. Dedicating my life to magic has given me a unique existential perspective. Performing an effective illusion involves mastery: over yourself, the audience, and the elements involved in creating a sense of wonder.

So, am I here to teach you how to be more deceptive?

Yes and no.

Like I said, I'm not claiming to be an expert. I'm just here to show you how to discover your personal flavor of magic. What you do with it is up to you. What I *hope* you do is use it to astonish others.

And if you're not interested in being astonishing, if you're content with a "happy" or "good" or "simple" life, I have three words for you:

Fuck. That. Noise.

We're on this planet for a millisecond, a blink of an eye. Don't accept your innate insignificance. Don't settle for being content. Aim higher than good or simple. Make that blink count. Your best self will emerge from the strife that accompanies chasing glory, from the climb to greatness, the quest for astonishment.

Dream bigger, aspire harder, pursue the impossible, and find that fucking magic.

Don't worry, I'll show you how.

—Violet Volk, August 28, 2002

Sasha

It's cold and dark, and this mattress is so uncomfortable, like sleeping on tiny rocks. I turn my head and squint against the glare of a street-light.

What.

The.

Fuck.

I swear, what seemed like a minute ago, I was in bed, fighting to keep my eyes open to finish one more chapter of the sci-fi novel I was reading. Now I'm lying on some gravel path, still in my pajamas, coat-less and shoeless.

I shake off the fog of sleep and scramble to my feet. How the hell did I get here? Where, exactly, is *here* anyway?

Frenzied, I look every which way. Behind me is a parking lot and before me is an ashy brick building. It has arched windows and so many cornices it looks like it was attacked by an overzealous cake decorator with a piping bag and too much gray icing. The Witkin Theater. The last place I saw my sister, almost ten years ago. Wow, my subconscious mind has all the subtlety of an avalanche.

There are no cars in the lot, which means I walked here. It's only a few blocks from home, but I have no recollection of this little jaunt.

It's one thing for me to wake up in different parts of the house, but another to wake up outside it. I thought my sleepwalking was harmless, insignificant, cute, even.

This is not cute. I need to get back home. Now. Before my husband or daughter wakes up and starts worrying. Before an opportunistic criminal cruising the Jersey burbs sees me as a way to get his own *Dateline* special.

I hurry to my house, hoping nobody spots me, hoping this sleepwalking-with-expanded-radius is a one-off. I don't want to be one of those people who has to be strapped into bed every night so I don't go wandering off.

Thankfully, I make it back without incident. I reach for the front door and—it's locked. Damn it. If I'd gotten that Hide-A-Key, I could let myself back in no problem, but Gabriel and Quinn, their minds saturated with true crime paranoia, were vehemently against it.

"Mom?" Quinn peeks at me through the window beside the front door. "What are you doing out there?" She unlocks the door and lets me in. "Is something wrong?"

Something is very wrong. "No, nothing is wrong. I was in the backyard getting some air and accidentally locked myself out. Thought I'd see if maybe we left the front door unlocked."

"Like it's the 1950s or something? Yeah, I don't think so." Her voice is hushed as she trails me down the hall.

"Dad still sleeping?" I ask.

"As far as I know. It's weird I never heard you come downstairs." Quinn's eyes sweep me head to toe.

"I guess I'm just stealthy like that. You studying?" I point to the open laptop on the kitchen table.

"Working on my thesis. Are you sure you're okay?"

Not at all, but I force a smile and kiss her forehead. "Of course. I'm gonna head back to bed. Don't be up too late."

"Mom." The sharpness of her tone sends a whisper of dread through me.

"What's up, honey?"

"You do realize I'm pretty much an adult at this point, and I'm not gonna blindly believe everything you tell me, right?"

That knocks the wind out of me. "Quinn, where is all this suspicion coming from?"

"You weren't out for some air in the middle of the night. If you don't want to tell me where you really were, fine, but enough with the lame excuses. After a while, it gets insulting."

Bowing my head, I say, "You're right. I didn't want you to worry, but . . . I was sleepwalking again. I woke up in the backyard and found myself locked out."

"That's better." How grateful she seems, even to get the half-truth. "You usually don't wander outside."

"The vigil stress must be getting to me."

"You keep saying that. Maybe you should talk to someone about it."

"Maybe. But for now, could we keep this between us? Your father doesn't need to know."

"Because you don't want him to worry, either."

"Right."

"'Kay." She motions to her laptop. "I should get back to it. Night, Mom." Her nod releases me.

As I leave the kitchen, my eyes wander to the digital clock above the stove. The blue numbers glow 2:22.

Tiptoeing upstairs, I tell myself it doesn't mean anything.

It must be like when you learn a new word and see it everywhere. The anniversary of Violet's disappearance is coming up, and 222 was our special sign-off, so that's why I'm noticing it more. What's it called when the brain tries to make meaning out of something random? Pareidolia? But instead of seeing faces in clouds or hearing hidden messages in songs, I'm haunted by triple twos.

It's human nature to notice patterns. That's all this is, a pattern. A series of coincidences; nothing worth ascribing meaning to. I don't understand why people feel the need to do that, assign fake significance to happenstance. Guess it's more comforting to believe the universe sends signs and omens, that there's a method to its madness, instead of accepting the true chaos of our reality.

Violet was quick to find a deeper meaning in such things, eager to ascribe a universal subtext. Three words I never need to hear again in my life: "It's a *sign*." Insert liberal exclamation marks from her, eye-rolling from me.

And yet, as I scrub the grit off my bare feet and sneak back into bed, I can't help but wonder about number patterns and my sleepwalking and whether there's something here I'm missing.

More likely, it's my brain's way of reminding me there's someone *not* here I'm missing.

The bigger concern is how far afield my brain might lead my sleeping body. Tonight, I avoided what could've been a dangerous situation.

It might be time for some outside help.

Strange Exits

Episode 2: "Violet's Legacy"

CAMERON FRANK [STUDIO]: It's a Thursday night and I'm in an industrial-chic duplex hotel suite in Lower Manhattan. I've never seen accommodations like these, not outside of movies and magazines. We're talking exposed brick walls, floor-to-ceiling factory windows, polished concrete floors, furniture that resembles Tetris pieces, and copper accents. You could throw a party for fifty in here and it wouldn't feel crowded, but there's only five of us, drinking wine and getting to know each other. Our lux surroundings, while excellent for social engagement, are terrible for taping a podcast. Luckily, the bedroom is sound treated, so that's where we gather, wineglasses in tow.

It isn't long before the conversation gets lively.

[FEMALE VOICE 1]: I worshipped her. I think a lot of girls in the nineties did. Watching Violet Volk do what she did gave me this sense of . . . possibility. It made me feel like my life had no limits. She was a consummate performer and the feminist icon us Gen Xers didn't know we needed.

CAMERON FRANK [STUDIO]: That's Noriko Tomlin, author of the unauthorized biography *Violet Volk: Behind the Magic*, which is getting rereleased next month with bonus content. Noriko is also a self-professed "VV scholar," and many consider her to be the unofficial leader of the Wolf Pack.

[FEMALE VOICE 2]: While I see merit in Volk's contribution to stage magic, I have problems with the blind idolatry associated with her, given how self-serving and potentially damaging she was as a public figure. There's no question celebrity culture has been on a downhill slide for a number of years, and while many like to attribute this to reality television and the famous-for-being-famous set, I'd go back earlier and say the descent began with Violet Volk.

CAMERON FRANK [STUDIO]: That's Janet Lurie, documentary filmmaker, essayist, and social historian and commentator. Her latest film, *Where Things Are Hollow*, an examination of fame and beauty standards in the age of social media, is making the rounds at film festivals and already receiving critical acclaim.

[MALE VOICE 1]: There are tricks she performed that nobody's figured out to this day. All that stuff with fire and blood and levitation—it was mind-blowing. Even knowing deep down these things had to have a logical explanation, sometimes you still felt like you were watching something . . . miraculous. Violet Volk didn't perform magic—she *was* magic.

CAMERON FRANK [STUDIO]: That's Viva Vox, television personality, magician, and drag performer, best known for his work as a Violet Volk impersonator. He's currently performing on Broadway, and this is his hotel suite. Also, in case anyone's wondering, Viva has no preferred pronouns but is typically referred to as he/him when out of drag, and he's not dolled up tonight.

[MALE VOICE 2]: I call bullshit. You know how many guys can do what she did? *Pfft.* If Violet wasn't a sexy chick, we wouldn't even be talking about her. And if we're gonna be honest, she was no great beauty, either.

CAMERON FRANK [STUDIO]: And that is Ron Vest, former chairman of the board for the Alcazar, an exclusive members-only club for magicians and magic aficionados. He's retired now but worked there for over thirty years in various capacities, including talent booker and head of operations before joining the board of directors. Numerous stage magicians have crossed his path at various points in their careers, and those who've crossed him have been lucky to have any career at all.

Before we delve deeper into Violet's personal history, I thought it was important to discuss her legacy. For better or worse, she left an indelible impression on the entertainment industry, on popular culture, and on countless people who encountered her work.

In selecting this specific group of participants, I wanted to ensure a balanced roundtable discussion, including detractors alongside devotees. I found it necessary to show varied opinions and interpretations of Volk and her legacy, from the perspective of a superfan, cultural critic, current performer, and magic industry insider.

Let's get back to it.

NORIKO TOMLIN: Way to contradict yourself, Ron. Which is it, that she used her sex appeal to get ahead or that she wasn't sexy? You can't have it both ways. And both opinions are disgusting.

RON VEST: Violet did the best she could with what she had. She never rang my bell, but those tight pants did it for plenty of other guys . . . and girls.

JANET LURIE: I find it interesting how quickly we pounce on personal appearance as soon as we're discussing a woman's accomplishments.

It brings to mind Minerva, one of Houdini's contemporaries whose ability was comparable to his but who was sexualized in a way that he never was. She did a water barrel escape, and despite being more heavily bound than Houdini, people fixated on how her clothes clung to her when she came out of the barrel soaking wet. You could perhaps understand that line of thinking in the early 1900s, when women still lacked the right to vote—incidentally, the leader of the women's suffrage movement was paid to get sawed in half at magic shows. But for women today to still be assessed on their looks in conjunction with their societal and cultural contributions . . . it's disappointing, to say the least.

VIVA VOX: I can see both sides here. Do women get judged more harshly for their looks than men? No question. But it's naive to ignore how much appearances matter, especially in the entertainment industry. I'd argue VV deserves more credit for achieving what she did without relying on her looks. And she came up in the decade when we were worshipping supermodels. It's interesting how she was a fan of Barbra Streisand because, like Babs—and I mean this with no disrespect to either diva—Violet was not what you would call beautiful in the traditional sense. Both women had to hone their talents to get noticed.

RON VEST: Funny how Jackson Cleo noticed Violet's "talents" in a strip club.

VIVA VOX: I don't have the energy to explain the difference between burlesque and stripping to you.

RON VEST: Both involve shaking tits and ass, so I don't see much difference.

NORIKO TOMLIN: Funny how much you're sounding like the douchelord who wrote the Violet takedown. Of course, you couldn't have written it—

RON VEST: Why, 'cause it has too many big words?

NORIKO TOMLIN: Way to step on my punch line.

RON VEST: Serves you right for using stale material.

CAMERON FRANK: Let's all play nice.

VIVA VOX: Ron, interesting you mention tits and ass. Let's say Jackson Cleo did go to Marabou for those two reasons. Violet Volk didn't have much of either. I'd bet all my wigs there were women at that club who were better eye candy than Violet. Obviously it was her magic act that set her apart and captivated him.

NORIKO TOMLIN: And when you watch her on *Later Tonight*, you'd be an idiot to suggest she was there for any reason other than her talent. Come on, Ron, even you have to admit that was an impressive piece of magic.

RON VEST: It was fine. A little showy for my taste.

VIVA VOX: Being showy in showbiz, *quelle horreur!*

[SOUNDS OF ESCALATING VOICES TALKING OVER EACH OTHER]

CAMERON FRANK [STUDIO]: This continued on until I flashed the bedroom lights and they quieted down.

CAMERON FRANK: I love the passion you're all bringing to this discussion, but let's give everyone a chance to speak. Janet, you look like you want to say something.

JANET LURIE: I do, but I don't want to get dragged by Noriko and Viva.

VIVA VOX: Dragged? I see what you did there.

CAMERON FRANK: Healthy debate is encouraged, Janet. You can speak freely.

JANET LURIE: All right then. It's not the showiness that bothers me, it's her overall lack of sincerity. This is a woman whose entire brand is based on artifice. She *loves* being a puzzle—she *prides* herself on it. Violet reveals different pieces of herself to different people, and nobody ever gets to see the full picture. I wonder if any of the pieces she revealed were genuine. In some ways, she was a precursor to the influencer culture we see today wherein people curate their lives for reality television, social media, et cetera.

VIVA VOX: Violet would've killed it on social media. She'd have so many followers, she'd be more popular today than ever.

JANET LURIE: You say that like it's a good thing.

VIVA VOX: Do you know how much you can get for a single sponsored post? Thousands if you're midlist. Hundreds of thousands if you're A-list. And if you're doing video content? Hell, there are ten-year-olds making millions on YouTube.

JANET LURIE: I would argue all this vying for empty accolades and exorbitant wealth is not healthy for society. I'm not saying Violet invented the cult-of-celebrity concept, but it does feel like she turned it up several notches during the height of her popularity. Don't get me wrong, I'm not bothered by the accolades she received for her stage work—magic isn't my preferred avenue of entertainment, but I won't deny she was talented and dynamic. What does bother me is how she never stopped performing. How her entire being, from her public behavior to her written work, seemed to promote the cultivation of artifice. Particularly her second book, *Life's Great Illusion*, where she essentially offered a blueprint for how to live a lie. It's challenging enough to discover your authentic self without having a bold voice encouraging you to wear a mask instead.

NORIKO TOMLIN: That's a warped way to look at it. Violet wasn't telling us to live a lie, she told us to bravely pursue the life we wanted, with no limits and no apologies. Did you ever attend one of her motivational seminars?

JANET LURIE: I've seen some of the bootlegged video footage: the light show, dramatic music, her over-the-top costumes . . . literal smoke and mirrors. Seemed like the usual pomp and circumstance but with more talking and fewer actual magic tricks.

NORIKO TOMLIN: Yeah, none of those crappy recordings come close to what it was like to be there in person. I spent a summer following her *You Are Magic* tour. The audio sensory experience she created night after night was . . . transcendent. It was a spectacle, sure, but only Violet could've pulled off something so inspiring and moving. This wasn't your typical motivational speaker, walking around an empty stage being too earnest or high-octane or smug. Violet was a badass high priestess reaching her hand into your soul and switching on your inner light.

RON VEST: If she "switched on your inner light," as you put it, why'd you need to go back again and again? Did she turn that light off at the end of the night to get more money from all you suckers?

NORIKO TOMLIN: Have you heard your favorite song or eaten your favorite food only one time? Had only one orgasm your entire life? No. We like to re-create our best experiences, chase that exhilaration. That's what Violet's shows were for me. Pure exhilaration. And each one was a little different. You never knew what to expect. You could be crying cathartic tears as she led a funeral service for the death of your former self. You could be dancing in a conga line made up of hundreds of people. You could be covered in glitter, feathers, Silly String, fake blood, flower petals. Night after night, here was this tiny woman commanding the stage, being nothing short of astonishing.

VIVA VOX: Honey, she was that way from day one. It was her brand of charisma. Violet didn't try to look like anyone else or follow fashion trends—she'd wear combat boots with ball gowns and look *amazing*—and she said things no one else had the guts to say, like calling out TV presenters when they were being sexist or homophobic. She didn't play the fame game; she created a new game of her own. It felt like her very sense of being was revolutionary.

JANET LURIE: Why, because she was outspoken, wore outrageous garb, and challenged gender and sexuality norms? Plenty of celebrities who came before her did that, from Marlene Dietrich and Katharine Hepburn, to Cher and Bette Midler, to Madonna and Courtney Love. The 1990s in particular were rife with feminist assertions—between the riot grrrls, vampire slayers, warrior princesses, and endless calls for "girl power," I'd say Volk was part of the bandwagon, not leading it.

VIVA VOX: All the people you just referred to were musicians or actors. Violet started out as a magician, dominating in a male-dominated field, which made her stand out that much more. I wouldn't have the career

I have today without her, though of course I'm not the magician she ever was.

RON VEST: You got that right. I must've been on vacation when you got booked at the Alcazar, because when I saw your parlor act, I was underwhelmed, to say the least. You have that in common with Violet.

NORIKO TOMLIN: Ron's just bad-mouthing Violet because she turned down his advances.

RON VEST: I don't appreciate your little accusation there. I may be old-school about some things, but I've never been inappropriate with women. There were some jackoffs at the Alcazar back in my day—probably still are—but I was quick to ban anyone who was disrespectful, men *and* women.

CAMERON FRANK: Why was Violet banned? Was she disrespectful?

RON VEST: There was an incident the first night she performed. A security guard caught her threatening a magician who will remain nameless. I can say this much: he was one of the old-timers, well known and beloved, and there was Violet cornering him in a supply closet, one hand around his throat and the other pointing a dagger—one of the antique ones she used in her act—at his dick. I threw her out then and there and banned her for life.

VIVA VOX: Did you ever wonder what the circumstances surrounding that might've been? Like maybe Violet was defending herself?

RON VEST: This guy was ancient—no way was he putting her in danger. And if he was getting frisky, she should've reported it instead of going all *Thelma & Louise* on him.

NORIKO TOMLIN: Because you would've *totally* believed her over a "well-known and beloved" old-timer, right? And let me guess, *he* wasn't banned from the Alcazar, right?

RON VEST: Actually, he was, Miss Know-it-all. Not that night, and not while I worked there. It was a decision made by new management. Just like it was their decision to unban Violet and name her Magician of the Year in 2003. She declined the award and never set foot in the Alcazar again. Such nerve. To this day, that's some of the highest recognition you can receive as a magician. Nobody ever turned down that award before—or since.

NORIKO TOMLIN: Which is a shame, considering Violet was only one of—what, four women who were named Magician of the Year by your little boys' club? Two of whom were part of a husband/wife duo. Versus dozens of male performers recognized over the years.

JANET LURIE: This is actually something I looked into. Up until recent years, women have made up approximately eight percent of the magic population. Between 1964 and 2014, four women and forty-eight men were given the Alcazar's Magician of the Year Award, factoring in the husband/wife teams you mentioned. That breaks down to eight percent of the recipients being female, which is in line with the portion of the magic community they represent.

NORIKO TOMLIN: You're kinda downplaying the tragedy of this eight percent statistic. There's no other creative industry where women are outnumbered by men to such an appalling degree. And it's easy to see why: the lack of mentorship and resources for girls and women, the history of ingrained misogyny . . .

JANET LURIE: If we're going to take the historical route, it's also worth mentioning witchcraft hysteria. We're going back hundreds of years, to be sure, but considering all the women accused, persecuted, and even executed for being witches, I could see, even in more contemporary times, a woman performing stage magic getting muddled with her per-forming actual sorcery.

RON VEST: Or it could be that men are just better at magic than women.

[SOUNDS OF ANGRY VOICES FOLLOWED BY SHATTERING GLASS]

CAMERON FRANK [STUDIO]: This seemed like a good time to take a break and let tempers cool. Once the mess was tidied up, we resumed the final part of our discussion.

CAMERON FRANK: I appreciate everyone bringing their knowledge, experience, and impassioned opinions to this roundtable. I'd like to close out with a lightning round of sorts. I'll throw out a question for each of you to answer briefly.

First question: Who do you think wrote the *Violet Is a Fraud* take-down? Janet, let's start with you.

JANET LURIE: It's mere conjecture, but the amount of intimate information conveyed leads to Sasha Dwyer being the most likely author.

NORIKO TOMLIN: Yep, I think it was Sasha, too. Or maybe Violet's ex-husband, Benjamin.

VIVA VOX: See, I get a professional bitterness vibe outta the whole thing. My money's on Ace Morgan.

RON VEST: Don't know, don't care. Next question.

CAMERON FRANK: Do you think Violet possessed any otherworldly powers? Telekinesis, levitation, any of it? Noriko, this time let's begin with you.

NORIKO TOMLIN: I flip-flop on this one. I want to believe Violet really *was* magic. But in the literal special-powers kind of way? I don't know. Can I be a maybe?

VIVA VOX: There's no way I could prove it, but I've been trying to replicate parts of her act religiously for seven years—I've worked with all kinds of experts and consultants and there are some effects that seem *impossible* to pull off without some . . . extra ability. So my answer is yes.

RON VEST: Get the fuck out of here.

JANET LURIE: I find the notion far-fetched, so no from me, too.

CAMERON FRANK: In one or two sentences, what do you see as Violet Volk's ultimate legacy? Viva, you're up.

VIVA VOX: Thanks to Violet, stage magic will continue to undergo an edgy and female-led revolution, while also gaining more credibility as a legitimate art form.

RON VEST: And less talented chicks will get picked over men in the name of feminism. Good times.

JANET LURIE: I believe Violet will continue to inspire people—particularly women and girls—to create delusional and unattainable ideas of what their lives should look like. Eventually most will be disappointed by the harsh reality that being a rich, glamorous, eternally adored celebrity is out of their reach.

NORIKO TOMLIN: Violet showed the world you can start out as a no-body with nothing, and become somebody special, by working hard, dreaming hard, and believing in a world with no boundaries. She challenged us to find and create our own magic, and those of us who rise to that challenge will always be better for it.

CAMERON FRANK: Last question: What do you think happened to Violet and will we see her again?

RON VEST: If I had to guess? I don't know what happened, but I think she pissed off the wrong people and ended up dead.

JANET LURIE: I don't think she's dead. There were some . . . unpleasant realities VV was about to face . . . and she was getting tired of her fame and notoriety. She had plenty of reasons to want to start a new life. Staging her disappearance would be the perfect way to do it. I don't think we'll see her again.

VIVA VOX: I agree with Janet on first part, but I do think we'll see her again. Or, I don't know, I want to believe we will.

NORIKO TOMLIN: I think the whole thing—all of it, even the five of us having this conversation—is part of her greatest illusion yet. She's just not finished performing it.

We'll see her again. There's no question.

July 16, 1993

VV,

How's NYC treating you? You sound good on your answering machine. And for the two seconds we get to hear your voice before you hang up on us. Maybe we could have a real conversation one of these days? It's been a month. We're not in high school anymore, so how about we act like grown-ups?

I get it, you're angry. At your mom for getting sick. At your uncle for roping your dad into a bad business deal. At your dad for getting roped in. At Sasha and me for not moving to New York with you.

New York was the plan. But plans change.

You have no idea how much is on Sasha's shoulders. I saw how you were around your mother, treating her like she has a bad cold instead of MS. You think some soup and positive thinking is going to make it all go away. This is serious. Regina can barely walk, barely work. Even with your dad's help at home and my support, between the salon and everything else, Sasha is fucking overwhelmed.

The last thing she needs right now is your petty bullshit.

Here's what's gonna happen. You're gonna get over yourself and call your sister (Monday mornings are less busy, and she's back from her run by 9:00). You're gonna apologize to her for being such a child, tell her how much you miss her, and invite her to visit you. You'll show her a great time around the city, being the cool and fun Violet we know and love. I'll send you a check so you can take her to a Broadway show, a nice restaurant, etc. You can pay me back when you book your first big magic gig.

You know we're rooting for you, right? Sasha might not be the magic nerd I am, but we always talk about how you're gonna be big-time. We're so sure of it. The point is, you might wanna be a little nicer to the people who believe in you the most.

Oh, and Sasha would kick my ass if she knew about this letter, so it stays between you and me.

—Gabriel

Notecard from Sofia's House of Flowers

August 9, 1993

Dear Violet,
Best. Weekend. Ever.
Best. Sister. Ever.
You rock!!!
222,
Sasha

Legendary Performer Declared Legally Dead

By Jennifer Lansing

APRIL 28, 2013

Five years after her disappearance, in accordance with New Jersey presumption of death requirements, stage magician and self-help guru Violet Volk has been declared legally dead.

An extensive investigation was launched when Volk vanished from the Witkin Theater during a performance on February 22, 2008. After a week with no leads, the Willow Glen police department turned over the case to the FBI. While an indication of kidnapping or other illegal activity involving crossing state lines is normally required to bring in federal assistance, Volk's high profile and the peculiar circumstance surrounding her disappearance added urgency to the case.

In the ensuing years, authorities have remained tight-lipped about Volk, offering no insight into her absence. None of the reported sightings have been verified, and if any clues to her whereabouts have been discovered, they have not been shared with the public.

"As my sister's only next of kin, I had a very difficult decision to make, and I gave it proper consideration," said Volk's sister, Sasha Dwyer, to reporters gathered outside the Atlantic County Courthouse. She read from a prepared statement. "I am grateful to law enforcement and everyone else who supported our search for Violet these last five years. As much as we want to believe she's out there somewhere, alive and well, unfortunately there has been no evidence to support that, and practical matters must be taken into account. I would like to assure everyone that my family had no personal stake with regards to the financial aspects of this matter. The majority of my sister's estate will be used to pay off outstanding debt and the remainder will be donated to the wildlife conservation charities specified in her will.

"This is a sad day for me and my family, and I hope you will respect our privacy. No matter what court documents say, Violet will live on in our hearts."

Despite today's court ruling, which has issued Violet Volk's death certificate, her case remains open. If you have any information concerning her disappearance, please contact your local FBI office.

Sasha

February 12, 2018

Renatta Nelson's office is on the outskirts of Finchley, on a street with Victorian houses converted for commercial use, mostly law and medical services. Less of a chance I'll run into someone I know out here, apart from a certain podcast host.

I park in a small lot behind a powder-blue house with white trim. When I ring the bell and announce myself, a low buttery voice says she'll be with me in a few minutes and I can wait inside.

Her voice was one of the reasons I chose her, in addition to her credentials, and a last-minute cancellation that enabled me to see her so soon. I figure if I'm going to subject myself to a therapist, at least I could talk to one whose voice provides a modicum of comfort.

There's nobody in the waiting area, so I'm spared awkward chitchat with a receptionist or other patients. On the coffee table is a stack of magazines. I pick up a copy of *Psychology Today* and start thumbing through it.

A door opens at the far end of the room. "Sasha Dwyer?" A heavyset forty-ish Black woman in a maroon shift dress steps out. Her eyebrows are perfectly sculpted and her mouth is set in a smile, but there's a scrutiny in her stare, like she's trying to figure me out before our session even begins.

I greet her and hold out the magazine. "You're not worried the patients might learn your trade secrets and decide to fend for themselves?"

"I would never stand in the way of my patients' education and empowerment when it comes to their mental health." The corners of her eyes crinkle. "Please come through."

I enter a sunny room with blond wood furniture and pistachio walls decorated with framed paintings of benign autumn landscapes. Renatta invites me to take a seat on the microfiber sofa beneath the window as she grabs a legal pad and perches on a leather armchair across from me. Between us is a coffee table with an unopened bottle of water and a box of tissues. I wonder how much you need to cry before your body starts to dehydrate.

"Help yourself." She motions to the water.

"I'm okay, thanks." It's hard not to feel like every statement coming out of my mouth is loaded, with Renatta assessing each word on multiple levels.

She tilts her head and scribbles something on the pad, which I imagine to be: *patient claims she is okay; immediate indication of denial.*

"How are you doing today?" she asks.

"I'm . . ." Normally, I would offer a safe adjective like "good" or "fine," something that would invite no concern and discourage additional inquiry, but I can't bring myself to do that here. After all, what's the point of paying a professional to listen to me if I give her nothing but hollow sentiments? "I don't know how I am. I don't know if coming here was the best idea." I grab a sage cushion and hug it to my chest. "Can I be straight with you about something?"

"Of course." As if she'd encourage me to lie.

"I mean no offense to you or your profession here, but there's something about therapy I don't quite buy. Not in the sense that it doesn't help people—I'm sure it does—but I've always wondered if there was some kind of placebo effect going on. Something that wouldn't work on me."

"It sounds like you're saying you believe you are immune to therapy."

Soothing voice and quick on the uptake. I can work with this. "Exactly. Like how some people just aren't ticklish. That's why I never did this kind of thing before. I never understood how people believe they can talk their problems away. I mean, people talk too much already, and complaining about problems is like the majority of what comes out of their mouths. I'm not saying mental health isn't important, but it seems like a lot of people are this special combo of clueless and self-obsessed. They're so tangled in their own hang-ups and triggers, it takes over their lives. Maybe they wouldn't be so miserable if, I don't know, they shut up about themselves and thought about other people once in a while."

Renatta tucks a strand of her black bobbed hair behind her ear. "Do you see being here as an act of selfishness?"

"Kind of? But that's because I'm not clueless and I don't want to become self-obsessed. I know what's wrong with me but I don't think talking about it is gonna fix anything."

"And yet, here you are." Tilting her head, Renatta gives me a searching look.

"Yeah, that's because of the sleepwalking. It's something I've done on and off throughout my life, but it's sorta gotten worse." I tell her about my al fresco nap by the Witkin.

"Are you currently on any medications?"

"Nope."

"What about stress?"

"Is anybody on the planet *not* under stress?" It's tough to keep the petulance out of my voice.

"Yes, but the levels of stress we experience and our coping mechanisms vary greatly. When we spoke on the phone, you mentioned needing to work through some family issues. Could this be causing you undue stress and exacerbating your sleepwalking?"

I let out a put-upon sigh, sounding like teenage Quinn whenever she felt I was being too smothering. "Pretty sure it is, yeah."

A few jots on the legal pad and Renatta glances up, waiting for me to continue.

Not continue so much as begin. I dig my fingertips into the pillow. Why is it so hard to talk about? Why is *she* so hard to talk about?

"Just about ten years ago, my sister went missing. The theater I woke up in front of, that's where she was last seen. The whole thing is so obvious. I don't know what happened to her, we weren't on the best terms when she disappeared, and her annual candlelight vigil is coming up.

Clearly, my subconscious brain is seeking some kind of impossible closure. It's not that complicated."

"It sounds a *little* complicated."

"Okay, maybe," I concede. In fact, my relationship with Violet is such a knotted mess of resentment, I can't find a single loose thread to pull on in hopes of unraveling this thing. I stare at Renatta's feet, which are encased in black leather ankle boots. Square-toed. Sensible heel. I don't trust women who wear trendy, uncomfortable footwear. "I like your boots."

"Thank you. So, this latest sleepwalking incident . . . Can you think of something specific that might've triggered it?"

"Gosh, let's see. It could be the billions of flyers plastered all over Willow Glen advertising the vigil—it's like they printed ten times as many to mark the ten-year anniversary. Then every day there's an announcement of a new book or TV series or god-knows-what about my sister. And we can't forget the podcast host hounding me to be on his show, along with other media requests, which I can usually ignore. But what's harder to ignore are the fake sightings and photos of my sister." At Renatta's perplexed look, I add, "Did I mention my sister is Violet Volk?"

"Ah." Vague recognition at the name. "You did not." Her face and voice are set to neutral.

"I'm guessing you've heard of her?"

"I'm not closely familiar with her work, but I know who she is, yes." Points to Renatta, for using present tense without my correcting her first.

"Everybody wants to know what it was like to have a famous sister. *Is* like." What the hell? Since when am I the one to slip into past tense?

"And what do you tell them?"

"I say I'm proud of her achievements and that I never would've been able to face the pressures of stardom with the same grace she did." I snort. "Sometimes, to be extra cloying, I'll add that I don't think of Violet as a celebrity. That she's still my sister."

"And what's the honest answer?"

"Honest answers are few and far between when you have a sister like Violet. I lie to keep the peace. She lies because that's who she is."

"What do you lie about?"

My laugh is throaty and dark. "Oh, I'm not gonna take the pin out of *that* grenade just yet."

"That's fine." A quick scribble of notes and she gives me a sympathetic smile. "So your relationship with Violet was turbulent, she unexpectedly vanished, and now there's this sudden abundance of attention on your sister. What is that like for you?"

"There's always been an abundance of attention on my sister. I've grown used to it." Lying *and* playing dumb to my therapist? Tsk-tsk.

Fortunately, she calls me out on it. "I think you know what I'm getting at. You said something about fake sightings and photos."

I clench the pillow in a death grip. "It's just a meme. #violetisback. Something to show off for social media. People are already moving on to eating laundry detergent pods and other dumb crap. None of the posts are actually her. The sightings are bullshit, too."

Renatta adopts a delicate tone. "That may be the case, but there's no way to know that with a hundred percent certainty, correct? Is there a part of you that wonders or hopes—"

"No," I snap. Another lie, but I plow through before impending tears close up my throat. "I don't want to waste my time on false leads."

"Okay. I'm just trying to see the connection between your sleepwalking and everything happening around this anniversary. When did this latest episode occur?"

"A few nights ago."

"Did anything noteworthy happen around that time?"

Gabriel and I were binge-watching the latest season of *Black Mirror*, our phones untouched on the coffee table. It felt good to take a break from my special brand of doomscrolling, splitting my attention among multiple screens, and obsessing about my sister. A couple hours in, Gabriel went into the kitchen for a snack (sour straws or a Granny Smith apple or yogurt—he jokes about having a sour tooth). As soon as he was out of sight, I grabbed my phone. Automatically, as if I'd been waiting for him to leave, pulling up Instagram before I could talk myself out of it, searching that wretched hashtag, though I knew I shouldn't.

The most upsetting #violetisback posts, the ones that make my breath catch in my throat, are the ones that, at first glance, look like they could be her. They never are, so the initial jolt of familiarity is followed by disappointment (a separate type of familiarity).

I looked at only one post before switching my phone off. It was upsetting for a different reason. The photo was of a combat boot in the middle of an empty road streaked with blood. Tagged with: #violetisback #justkidding #violetisgone

"Sasha?" Renatta's voice is like being slapped by a hand in a velvet glove.

"Yeah. Sorry." I grit my teeth. *Don't ask me, don't ask me, don't ask me.*

"Where did you go just now?"

And even though it's the main reason I'm here, the last thing I want to discuss is that photo or my sleepwalking. Inside me, a steel gate is clattering down, locking me in. I am closed for business.

"Let's talk about something else," I say.

The flicker of disappointment across her face is fleeting, but I catch it. "I'd still like to know more about your relationship with Violet," she says. "Maybe you could talk a bit about your childhood?"

This I can do. Some of the early territory is thorny, but not as incendiary as the later years.

"Growing up with Violet was . . . never boring. We had a way of balancing each other out. She had a year on me, but I often felt like the sensible older sister, even as kids. I was more reserved and cautious, she was more outgoing and daring. I was the realist, she was the fabulist, trying to get me to go along with the crazy stuff she'd make up. Like that we were royalty and fled Russia to avoid getting executed like the Romanovs, or that our parents were spies. Or when I started sleepwalking, she tried to convince me that I had special powers and could actually teleport. I didn't believe any of it."

"How old were you when you first began to sleepwalk?"

No no no. That's one origin story she won't get today. "I don't know—it was sometime in grade school." A buzzing in the back of my mind urges me to change the subject, but I can tell Renatta will harp on it if I don't give her more. "It didn't happen a lot, and it wasn't a big deal. One time, after Violet made me watch *Poltergeist* with her, I woke up in the middle of the night in the bathtub. Not all scary movies made me sleepwalk, but I figured out pretty early on horror could be a trigger, so I tried to limit my exposure to it. Of course, that didn't stop Violet, who was obsessed with horror movies, from coercing me into watching that stuff with her. I swear, it's like my job was setting the boundaries and hers was pushing them." Eager to keep the discussion moving away from my nighttime wanderings, I add, "Like whenever we'd go to the beach . . ."

"What happened at the beach?"

"Violet always tried to get us to swim out farther than anyone else. It drove our mother crazy. Mom would be standing on the shore, frantically waving for us to come back in, and yelling at us afterward. Funny thing is, she yelled at me more, even though I was younger, because she said I should know better."

"It sounds like there were expectations early on for you to be the more responsible one." Renatta uncrosses and recrosses her legs.

"Which was fine, because that was the role I gravitated to naturally. I didn't mind Violet being more mischievous, because without her I would've been a dull Goody Two-shoes. But she did have a mean streak. Or maybe it was just a sick sense of humor?"

"Say more about that."

"She was double-jointed and loved to play gruesome tricks on people. Like having them arm wrestle her until she cracked her elbow joint and made it look like they broke her arm. Or pretending to fall down the stairs and contorting her leg, screaming in pseudo-agony until she couldn't help but laugh. The first time she pulled that one on our parents, she played dead at the foot of the stairs instead. When they saw her, Mom fainted, and Dad got chest pains—Violet came close to giving him an actual heart attack. Hilarious, right? But that's not what really bothered me." I pause to take a sip of water and side-eye the box of tissues like they're daring me. "It's funny, talking to you is the opposite of what it was like talking to Violet. With her, it was like a high-speed game of double Dutch; she did most of the talking and I had to find the right second to jump in. My daughter can be like that, too. But you actually give me time to collect my thoughts. It's nice."

"I'm glad you think so. Now, you were saying Violet's dark sense of humor isn't what really bothered you."

"Right." My eyes wander to the bookcase, which displays a vase of sunflowers beside three bronze swans. "I thought having a sister would mean I'd always have a built-in best friend. I don't know if Violet ever saw it that way, because she treated me more like a built-in opponent. What *really* bothered me was her competitiveness. Not toward other people, just me. It's like she had this mental tally of the ways I excelled over her and vice versa, and she'd list it at every opportunity. I was taller and had prettier eyes and hair, but she was more flexible and had cuter feet. Mom liked me better because I kept my room tidy, but Dad liked Violet better because she spent hours watching him and Uncle Slava play cards. I was better at checkers but she was better at Connect Four. It was ridiculous."

"Sibling rivalry is not uncommon."

Maybe that's why I was adamant that Quinn remain an only child. "The thing is, I had no interest in competing. I can't help what kind of hair or eyes I was born with, and if she wanted to win at checkers so badly, I'd let her. But that was no good—she wanted to draw me into battle and make me fight fair so that she could win fair. And when she couldn't win in one area, she sought out a different way to top me. That's probably why she took up magic."

"How old were you at this point?"

"I don't know, seven, eight?"

"Did things between you change when she began practicing magic?"

I shift in my seat. "I'm really holding you to the client confidentiality thing here."

"As long as you are not a danger to yourself or others, anything you say stays between us."

"Okay then. Here goes. I *hate* stage magic. Loathe it. Vehemently despise it."

"Is this since your sister has gone missing?"

"No, I've never enjoyed it. Not even as a kid. I didn't feel a sense of awe or wonder, I felt manipulated and frustrated when I couldn't figure out how a trick was done. Because obviously there's no such thing as real magic. When Uncle Slava taught Violet a few coin tricks, it was different, because she'd tell me how they were done, so I could relax and admire the artistry of, say, her making a quarter disappear and reappear. This was back when I was in second grade and she was in third . . ." I'll need a few deep breaths for this next part. "She started getting in trouble with her teacher and being forced to stay after school. I'd wait for her so we could take the late bus together—we were latchkey kids, our parents never knew what time we got home. One day, she was taking longer than usual, and I was worried we'd miss the bus, so I went looking for her. She was in the bathroom, mummifying her legs in toilet paper." Fuck. The tissues beckon. I grab one and dab at my wet cheeks. "I asked what she was doing and before she could answer, I saw spots of red seeping through the toilet paper on the back of her legs." I blow my nose and reach for another tissue. "Violet looked guilt-stricken and swore she was trying not to be bad, but she couldn't help sneaking a coin into class now and again. I didn't know whether there were rules against teachers hitting children, but I knew it couldn't be right to make a little girl bleed over a *motherfucking quarter*." More tissues, more deep breaths. "She begged me not to tell our parents, but how could I keep something like that from them? I cried the whole way home and was still crying when Mom and Dad got home. It must've been a Friday, because the next time we were back in school, Violet had a sub and the other teacher never returned. I thought Violet would be grateful that I helped get rid of this monster."

"She wasn't?" Curiosity knits Renatta's brow.

"She refused to talk about it. After that, she also refused to tell me how she did any of her tricks. I started hating magic even more then."

Date: February 13, 2018, at 5:15 AM
To: cfrank@sidecarstudios.com
From: checkmate@protonmail.com
Subject: Vanishing Violet

Dear Mr. Frank,

I have some information about Violet Volk that I believe you will find compelling. Nothing I say will be off the record, but if we speak, I do urge you to be circumspect about what you share with your audience. There are safety matters to consider.

I cannot divulge my identity or relationship to Ms. Volk. You may refer to me as Checkmate.

If you choose to speak with me, once you indicate your agreement, I will set up a secure communication channel.

You may ask any questions during our conversation, but you may not respond to this email with anything except for "YES" if you wish to continue our correspondence. If you respond with anything other than those three letters, you will not hear from me again. If you take longer than forty-eight hours to respond, you will not hear from me again.

Sincerely yours,

‡

Date: February 13, 2018, at 8:19 AM
To: checkmate@protonmail.com
From: cfrank@sidecarstudios.com
Subject: Re: Vanishing Violet

YES

Date: February 13, 2018, at 9:04 AM
To: cfrank@sidecarstudios.com
From: checkmate@protonmail.com
Subject: Re: Re: Vanishing Violet

Dear Mr. Frank,

Very good. I must secure a new location for myself, but you will hear from me again soon.

Sincerely yours,

‡

Date: February 13, 2018, at 9:05 AM
To: cfrank@sidecarstudios.com
From: twoods@sidecarstudios.com
Subject: Sasha update

You've had a month now. What's the latest?

—TW
Tobin Woods
Editorial Director & Cofounder
Sidecar Studios

Date: February 13, 2018, at 9:36 AM
To: twoods@sidecarstudios.com
From: cfrank@sidecarstudios.com
Subject: Re: Sasha update

I visited her at the salon just a couple of weeks ago. We had a brief chat. Still looking to set something up after the vigil, maybe late February/early March.

In the meantime, I've just come across an intriguing new lead claiming to have Violet intel. The info is so major, they're remaining anonymous for now.

—CF

Date: February 13, 2018, at 9:42 AM
To: cfrank@sidecarstudios.com
From: twoods@sidecarstudios.com
Subject: Re: Re: Sasha update

We're doing an entertainment podcast here, not bringing down Richard Nixon. Forget Deep Throat and get me Sasha.

Strange Exits

⌒

Episode 3: "Ace Morgan"

CAMERON FRANK [STUDIO]: Harry Houdini, history's most legendary magician, boasted that he could figure out any illusion if he saw it performed three times. That is, until February 1922, when a young magician named Dai Vernon performed a card trick for him. Vernon had Houdini sign the ace of spades, slipped it beneath the top card, and squared the deck. A second later, Vernon turned over the top card, revealing the signed ace of spades. Puzzled at how his card had risen to the top of the deck, Houdini asked to see the trick a second time and a third, and Vernon obliged, adding a fourth and fifth demonstration, to no avail. Dai Vernon became known as "The Man Who Fooled Houdini," and the illusion, dubbed the Ambitious Card, is a staple of the magician's repertoire to this day.

Anyone who's seen a magic show has likely seen a variation of this trick; sometimes the chosen card isn't signed but bent or marked with an *X* and placed in the center of the deck. Sometimes the card isn't marked at all, but instead of resurfacing at the top of the deck, it reappears in a wallet, pocket, shoe, behind a pane of glass, or is even coughed up by the performer. Among magicians, the trick is often used as a type of business card: each puts their own personal spin on it.

When Ace Morgan performed the Ambitious Card at Cyndi Yanoff's eleventh birthday party in 1988, he was upstaged by a fifth grader named Violet Volkov. According to Willow Glen librarian Eleanor Toback, Violet hijacked his routine, making the selected card turn up in Cyndi's birthday cake and then shocking partygoers by levitating a foot in the air.

Was this all truly unplanned? Or was it the inauguration of a decade-long mentorship that had already been in progress?

Today I'll be sharing a conversation I had with magician and creative consultant Ace Morgan. Born Aesop Morgenstern, he grew up in Brooklyn and got an agent at sixteen, booking professional gigs as a magician, at which time he adopted the stage name he still uses to this day. He spent his twenties performing around the United States and Canada, establishing himself as a master of close-up magic. In fact, he won the Platinum Wand in the Close-Up Division of the 1989 International Magic Symposium, one of the most prestigious awards in the world of illusion. If there were an Olympics for magic, Morgan would be a gold medalist.

All of which is to say, when the Yanoffs hired a magician to perform at their daughter's eleventh birthday, they spent good money to hire one of the best.

For much of his career, Ace Morgan didn't receive the level of media attention his contemporaries did and was nowhere near as high-profile as his protégée Violet Volk. That changed in 1998, when he was unmasked as the disguised star of *Magic Secrets Uncovered*, a two-hour television special that revealed how some of the world's most popular effects were performed. While the program received top ratings, it caused outrage in the magic community, where secrecy is paramount. He was swiftly banned from the Alcazar and nearly stripped of his Platinum Wand. Violet Volk was among those who voiced their outrage, because several of her most guarded and well-known illusions had been exposed.

While Morgan's reputation was tarnished among his professional peers, television networks were clamoring to secure him for additional programs in which he'd spill more magic secrets. Soon the trades announced another TV special for Christmas, but a few weeks later, it was scrapped, with no explanation from the network or Morgan, who stated he chose to pursue other projects. He has not performed since then, opting to remain behind the scenes, working as a creative consultant in Los Angeles.

We caught up recently over the phone.

ACE MORGAN: I'm telling ya, I was as shocked as everyone else at that kid's party.

CAMERON FRANK: You'd never met Violet before that day?

ACE MORGAN: No. And to be perfectly frank, I was pissed off when I saw that card come out of the cake. I thought the Yanoffs had hired a second magician—god knows why, I was one of the best in the tristate area. But I never saw a little girl perform like that. When she levitated, I almost pissed myself.

CAMERON FRANK: At the time, you told everyone she was part of the show.

ACE MORGAN: Of course I did. What was I gonna do, say she's some kind of superhero? Invite the news, the government, and religious wackos to put her under a microscope? She was a little girl. And I wanted to see what else she was capable of.

CAMERON FRANK: So you claimed to be her mentor.

ACE MORGAN: I *was* her mentor. From the second I saw her floating in the air like that, I knew I had to . . . I don't know, look after her somehow.

CAMERON FRANK: You've given some conflicting accounts of your relationship with Volk over the years.

ACE MORGAN: It was always strictly professional. No funny business.

CAMERON FRANK: I'm referring to your professional relationship. Which, according to public record, lasted over ten years. You helped her develop her act when she moved to New York and even helped her get her job at Marabou, correct?

ACE MORGAN: All true. I only saw her once in a while when she was a kid—I'd make time whenever I was in the area for a gig. Always under adult supervision, in case anyone has the wrong idea. I was living in

New York back then and told her if she wanted to be serious about performing magic, she'd be better off moving to a city that would offer more opportunities for entertainers. After she graduated high school, I helped her find a place in Brooklyn and offered to hook her up with a waitressing gig at Marabou, since I was friendly with the manager. I warned her, even though the place tried to pass itself off as classy, it was still a titty bar. That didn't bother her. She just wanted to start making money. And as soon as she saw the girls onstage were the ones who got the real tips, she asked a couple of them to teach her burlesque while I coached her on sleights. Before long she was making those big tips, too.

CAMERON FRANK: It sounds like it was pretty easy for Violet to establish herself in New York.

ACE MORGAN: It's easy when you got a sucker like me pulling strings on your behalf. And when you're not afraid to take off your clothes to make an extra buck. In all fairness, she did work hard. Instead of partying with the other girls, she used most of her free time to rehearse her act and hone her sleights. Mind you, she did fool around with a couple of the girls, and I heard a couple others left because she fooled around with their boyfriends, but that was none of my business.

Anyway, no matter how messy her personal life was, the magic always came first. Violet told me she spent at least an hour a day doing finger and hand exercises to improve her dexterity. It showed—I never saw someone get that good that fast. Performing magic was always the ultimate goal, and she saw burlesque as a way to get on a stage and develop her act until she was ready to branch off on her own.

CAMERON FRANK: After the levitation incident at the birthday party, did you ever see her do anything similarly . . . strange?

ACE MORGAN: Like supernatural? Come on, gimme a break. What made her special was how she'd learn something and put her own spin on it. At Marabou, it was often raunchy, like an Ambitious Card routine where the signed card would reappear in her bra or garter.

Look, once you know what to look for, the mechanics of most tricks are pretty easy to figure out. Even levitations, there's a few standard ways those are done. The way Violet did hers . . . sometimes it was puzzling. Her execution, the flair she added, made it hard to pin down her methods. Like she'd make a newspaper float up and burst into flames, then make a glass of water levitate across the room and put out the fire. I never saw anyone else do that.

CAMERON FRANK: Was she difficult to mentor?

ACE MORGAN: Sometimes . . . She liked to push things. Which could be good, because she was a quick learner and always wanted to learn more. But she'd get bored with me after a while. She had to find a way to make things more dangerous, more extreme.

CAMERON FRANK: And how did she do that?

ACE MORGAN: By rigging private high-stakes poker games.

CAMERON FRANK: Violet publicly denied ever doing such a thing.

ACE MORGAN: Is that something you'd fess up to, especially when your bread is being buttered by one of Vegas's biggest casino hotels?

CAMERON FRANK: Did her uncle get her involved in those poker games?

ACE MORGAN: There wasn't a serious backroom card game between New York and Atlantic City that Slava didn't know about. And he was begging that girl to join his racket as soon as he saw her act at Marabou. Though if you ask me, the bigger transgression was watching his barely legal niece strip down to pasties and a thong. I felt like a creep watching her perform and I'm not even related to her. Call me old-fashioned. But apparently, she invited him, hoping he'd see her potential as a ringer.

CAMERON FRANK: It sounds like she was making steady progress in her career at that point. Why get involved in anything illegal?

ACE MORGAN: Why do people go skydiving and bungee jumping? For the goddamn thrill of it. Violet needed a sense of risk or life got really dull really fast for her. There was no room for error with the crowds Slava introduced her to. If she was caught in a false shuffle or crooked deal, she wouldn't get booed or laughed at. We're talking much more serious consequences. And I'll tell you what, she took her card manip to the next level, thanks to those games. Stashed away some good money, too.

CAMERON FRANK: While putting herself in real danger, from the sounds of it.

ACE MORGAN: Real enough that her magic career could've been over in a second . . . She came close.

CAMERON FRANK: She got caught?

ACE MORGAN: I heard about one mishap. There's this routine where you play clean all night until it gets late, then you say something like, "Is it really 5:00 AM?" so everyone looks at the clock. While they're all turned around, you switch the decks. Worked like a charm until the night Violet got careless and didn't notice one guy who didn't turn around. Slava took the blame, told everyone he put her up to it.

CAMERON FRANK: What happened to him?

ACE MORGAN: There's three things those card games always had on hand. Stacks of cash, a case of vodka, and a pair of those scissors gardeners use.

CAMERON FRANK: Pruning shears?

ACE MORGAN: Those are the ones. I knew a guy who worked as a coroner in New Rochelle, had to do autopsies once in a while, and he said pruning shears worked better than bone saws cutting through ribs. Anyway, Slava lost a thumb that night. Violet gave up the poker games after that. Hadn't been at it even a full year.

CAMERON FRANK: Wow.

ACE MORGAN: Oh, Slava got it a lot worse later on. Poor guy couldn't get his gambling under control and "fell" off a fourteenth-story balcony in Brighton Beach.

CAMERON FRANK: Some people believe you and Slava were friends long before you and Violet crossed paths.

ACE MORGAN: What are you saying, that her uncle and I concocted an elaborate scheme to embarrass myself and have his niece make her magic debut at a kid's party? I told you, I never saw her before.

CAMERON FRANK [STUDIO]: I considered skipping the next question, taking into account Ace's increasing annoyance with me, or asking it later on, but I went for it.

CAMERON FRANK: You know that website about Violet that made the rounds a couple of weeks before she vanished? With the anonymous essay?

ACE MORGAN: I don't remember. There's been so much written about her. You think I keep track of it all?

CAMERON FRANK: I'm talking about violetisafraud.com, with that particularly harsh takedown of Violet. She went to a lot of effort to get the site shut down, which only resulted in more press for it. It contained some pretty hurtful and embarrassing assertions.

ACE MORGAN: What are you asking, did I make that website? I'm not good with computers and I'd never write personal crap about her. What kind of scumbag do you think I am? Violet was my protégée; I wasn't out to get her.

CAMERON FRANK: It's odd that you're so protective of her, when at the same time it could be argued that you betrayed her. Things seemed rather contentious between you two in the late nineties.

ACE MORGAN: When I did *Magic Secrets Uncovered*? She was pretty bitter about that one. God forbid a magician get more attention than her for once and she'd have to change up her stale routines.

CAMERON FRANK: But even before the backlash over *Magic Secrets Uncovered*, you were quoted in interviews saying Violet was getting lazy, that her brand of magic was relying more on style than substance, that playing up her personal drama for headlines was tacky . . .

ACE MORGAN: . . . I'm waiting for a question.

CAMERON FRANK: Were you misquoted? If not, what motivated you to say those things?

ACE MORGAN: I damn well did say those things. They were all true.

CAMERON FRANK: You sound angry.

ACE MORGAN: Talking about her always does this to me. She's one of my . . . what do the oversensitive kids today call it? One of my triggers.

CAMERON FRANK: What is it about Violet that's so triggering for you?

ACE MORGAN: She didn't have to stoop as low as she did. All that self-help crap she did later in her career? It might've earned her bigger bucks and made her a bigger star, but she should've stuck to magic. Violet Volk was the real deal. She had everything: natural ability. Good discipline. A sense of showmanship. Agility. A strong persona. But she let her persona overshadow everything else, even before the motivational guru bullshit.

CAMERON FRANK: How so?

ACE MORGAN: Like rarely giving interviews, so she could appear more *mysterious*.

CAMERON FRANK: Some celebrities are press-shy.

ACE MORGAN: [*laughs*] Trust me, that was the last thing Violet was. The way she'd show up at these big events with a guy on one arm and a girl on the other? That ain't shyness. And boy, did the tabloids eat that up.

CAMERON FRANK: Are you saying she played up her bisexuality for the media?

ACE MORGAN: And get the PC police on my ass? No way. I'm just saying, if she was so press-shy, she wouldn't have made herself so . . . let's say *noticeable* to the press. Like, what about all the assistants who kept getting injured?

CAMERON FRANK: I'm not sure what you're implying. There are multiple witnesses who saw the accidents occur and hospital reports to back up the extent of the assistants' injuries.

ACE MORGAN: I'm not saying the injuries were fake. But calling them accidents is a stretch.

CAMERON FRANK: You think she was hurting her assistants on purpose?

ACE MORGAN: Maybe not the first one. But when the accident got media attention and helped ticket sales . . .

CAMERON FRANK: That's a pretty serious allegation.

ACE MORGAN: Good thing she's not around to sue me.

Think about it. However smart and civilized humans may claim to be, deep down, we're bloodthirsty animals. Let me put it to you like this. Say you have a choice of seeing two magic shows, one where the magician has never had a mishap and another where a magician's assistant almost bled out onstage. All other things being equal, I bet you'd sooner see that second show. Because now there's a proven element of real danger.

Tell me something. You ever slow your car down to get a closer look at a traffic accident?

CAMERON FRANK: Actually, no. But I'm not denying it's human nature.

ACE MORGAN: Maybe you're just a better human that the rest of us, huh? I think we *should* be better than that. But most of us aren't. Violet should've been better than that. She didn't need the bells and whistles. She should've cared about her craft more than her popularity. *That's why I did Magic Secrets Uncovered.*

CAMERON FRANK: And you benefited pretty well from it. Why did you scrap the second TV special? Some have speculated Volk's people paid you off.

ACE MORGAN: If they did, I bet they would've also had me sign an NDA to keep my mouth shut about it. But they didn't. I just didn't want to do a second special. Moving on.

CAMERON FRANK: Are there any specific illusions Violet performed that you've never been able to figure out?

ACE: Yes. In the Picture.

CAMERON FRANK [STUDIO]: If there was a single trick Violet Volk was known for, it was this one. In it, she would invite a group of volunteers onstage, and snap a photograph of them with a Polaroid camera. A small glass box would descend from the ceiling, and once the volunteers confirmed it was empty, Violet would place the photo in the box, which was raised just above their heads, connected to a projector screen. Though the audience couldn't see the image as it developed, they could keep an eye on the Polaroid to make sure it wasn't being tampered with.

Meanwhile, Violet would talk about how she's never considered herself to be photogenic, how she preferred to be the one behind the camera instead of in front of it. She'd say the only person she trusted to take a decent photo of her was . . . herself. Remember, this is years before selfie culture and social media.

During her spiel, she'd use a stepladder to peek at the Polaroid in the box, keeping her arms behind her back. Violet spoke about how being in the public eye made it necessary to get over her camera inhibitions, particularly when fans asked for a photo with her. Fortunately, she said, she had found a way to do so. She promised she'd pose for a photo as long as she could take one of just them first.

This is when the box would rotate ninety degrees forward, revealing the Polaroid fully developed. The volunteers would be shown clustered together exactly as they posed for the camera . . . but there would be an extra person in the photo: Violet Volk.

ACE MORGAN: Nobody's been able to figure out how she did that effect. Any magician who's tried to copy it has ended up with a piss-poor imitation. Yeah, I'm still stumped by that one.

CAMERON FRANK: What do you think happened to Violet?

ACE MORGAN: I'm still asking myself. I hope she left by choice. Showbiz has a way of giving you everything while bleeding you dry. If she rigged her disappearance like she rigged everything else, chances are she'll get bored of living under the radar. She could piss me off like nobody else, but . . . it wouldn't be the worst thing, to see her again. Who doesn't love a good comeback story?

CAMERON FRANK: If she did leave by choice, do you have any thoughts on how she could've pulled off such a disappearing act?

ACE MORGAN: Sure I do. But I'm gonna keep those to myself. When I broke my magician's oath before, it was for a good reason. I wanted to shake things up, get performers to stop relying on all the same old illusions and breathe some new life into the craft. Violet did that with effects like In the Picture. She amazed all of us and got the world talking about magic. This time around, there'd be no good reason to break my oath again except to be a dick.

Here's the thing. The older you get, the more you see what a shithole the world is. You lose your innocence and that's it, it's gone. You just keep going down this dark one-way street getting more and more jaded.

That sense of wonder you feel watching a really great magic trick, for me, it's like a weapon against cynicism, the closest you can get to recapturing some of that innocence. Violet's final disappearing act—for all the chaos it created—it's still a great fucking trick. I'm not gonna mess with it. Let the world keep wondering.

[MALE VOICE]: He wouldn't tell you, huh? What a hypocritical prick . . . I'm guessing nobody told you about her secret performances, either . . . Man, there's so much people don't know about her . . .

CAMERON: That's Benjamin Martinez, Violet's former choreographer and ex-husband. He has a lot to say about Violet Volk. We'll hear from him next time.

Sasha

February 13, 2018

"'*Harry Houdini, history's most legendary magician, boasted that he could figure out any illusion if he saw it performed three times. That is, until February of 1922 . . .*'"

I switch off the podcast and put on a Madonna playlist.

It's a Tuesday afternoon in the salon, and Gabriel is sweeping up hair while I'm at the reception desk computer, looking over sales reports from the last month.

"That might be a new record. You made it—what, fifteen seconds into an episode this time?" he teases.

"I don't love Cameron's smug smooth-guy voice, it irks the crap out of me. But can I tell you how much I *do* love this new POS system?" I click between tabs, making a list of hair products to reorder. "I no longer want to kill myself doing inventory."

"How many unfortunate lives might've been saved with the right point-of-sale tools?" He clutches the broom to his heart, then resumes gathering brunette curls into a mound. "Nice to see us in the black again, huh?"

"We've been doing well the last couple of months." Without thinking, I air-spit three times and knock against the side of the reception desk, glad we opted for the reclaimed barn wood Quinn insisted on instead of laminate. Try as I might, some superstitions are ingrained in me. "Between the extra business we've been getting around the vigil and your marketing mojo, we should be able to hire an assistant again soon."

"Why do we need to hire an assistant when our daughter is about to graduate college and have her days free again? We've pretty much homegrown our own assistant. Isn't that the whole point of having kids?" Gabriel's deadpan face twitches, a smile fighting its way out.

"You would think, but apparently parents are supposed to let kids become their own people or some crap." I lock eyes with him, daring him to laugh before I do.

"Seriously? This business of supporting your child's life choices is hogwash."

"Utter malarkey." We simultaneously break into chuckles.

The bells above the front door tinkle as my 3:00 PM enters the salon.

"Sally!" If I could leap over the counter like a cool bartender I would, but since I lack such dexterity, I rush around it instead to ambush the curvy blonde wearing an insane patchwork coat trimmed in what can only be Muppet fur.

"I don't know what you two were just talking about, but you look like you're about to pounce on each other." Her eyes flash wickedly. "I don't mind waiting if you want to have a quickie in the back room."

If it's wrong for a stylist to have a favorite client, I don't want to be right, because Sally Forsberg is mine. She's gregarious, body positive, sex positive, and lets me endlessly experiment with her hair. A good portion of the new clients I get come by way of her recommendations, to the point where I've offered her commissions. She and her best friend, Astrid, own U4ia, a popular local boutique that sells handcrafted items, all made from materials that are upcycled, recycled, or locally sourced (naturally, it's Quinn's favorite place to shop). A divorced self-professed polyamorous pansexual Sally's dating life is as colorful as the coat on her back, and there's no such thing as oversharing as far as she's concerned.

"Is that a new shirt?" she asks as I put on an apron. It's a running joke between us; jeans and a white button-down are my standard uniform. "This one looks less pearl and more . . . alabaster?"

"Good eye. It is new, but it's eggshell. Thought I'd mix it up."

"You're a wild woman." Sally sits in her preferred styling chair ("the other one is too creaky"). As she lifts her hair to let me fasten a vinyl cape around her, a pungent waft hits me like a punch in the face, which can only be her latest foray into amateur perfumery. It smells like limoncello mixed with Pine-Sol and formaldehyde, and it makes my eyes water.

Noticing my recoil, Sally's eyebrows wiggle impishly. "I see you're enjoying my new creation. I would've brought you a sample, but I figured you didn't want to smell like a drunk Christmas tree molesting a rotten lemon meringue pie."

"Okay, I gotta get a whiff of this one." Gabriel, who has a weird affinity for bad smells, comes over. "Yep, it's horrendous." More sniffs to confirm. "Wow. You can wake the dead with that. Hey, what about selling it as 'artisanal smelling salts'?"

"You kid, but I might actually do that." An admiring nod from Sally. "Especially considering how well I did with your last idea. Who knew people would be so into organic bug spray? Still one of my top sellers online. You know, you should probably stop giving me all these ideas for free and make me hire you as a marketing consultant."

"I probably should." Gabriel takes out his phone just as it trills with an alert. "I've gotta meet a vendor right now, but let's talk soon." Turning to me, he waves. "See ya later, wife."

"That's all I get, 'see ya later'?" I feign huffiness.

"Nope, you also get this."

In an instant, his arms are around me, his mouth is on mine, and he's dipping me halfway to the floor.

Once Gabriel leaves, I run a brush through Sally's golden hair and fluff it with my fingers. "So what's the plan for today? Dealer's choice or did you have something specific in mind?"

"Oh, we are going on an adventure today. Are you familiar with a little something called oil slick hair?" She scrolls through her phone and holds up a photo of a black sheared bob threaded with purple, magenta, teal, and blue.

"Being that my vocation requires staying on top of hair trends, I am indeed familiar with oil slick hair. You really wanna go that dark?"

"Dark and short. I'm thinking . . ." Using her fingers as imaginary scissors, she traps a section of hair at chin level.

I look back and forth between my friend and the photo and let out a sigh. "Oh, Sal. I thought things were going well with Kerry and Jerry."

Sally plucks the phone out of my hand, fumbling with it as she puts it away. "Way to read into things. You know I like to be dramatic and change it up."

"And you know I've been doing your hair for the last ten years, and hair in general for over twenty years. God, that makes me feel so old."

"Don't you dare." Clearing her throat, she holds up her right wrist, which bears a silver cuff engraved with: F@AA/F@AW. It stands for *Fabulous at Any Age/Fabulous at Any Weight*, one of the mottos adorning various goods in her shop.

"I mean, god, that makes me feel so fabulous," I correct myself, containing most of my sarcasm. "Anyway, if you don't want to get into it, fine, but let's not pretend I'm not an expert at sniffing out breakup hair."

"There's nothing to get into. Kerry and Jerry decided they wanted to end their open marriage."

"That sucks. I'm sorry."

"It's fine. We got along great, but I knew it wouldn't last. They liked to cook naked, which bugged me, not from a modesty standpoint, more because of how impractical it was. And this is so petty, but . . . their rhyming names creeped me out. Kerry and Jerry Perry. It reminds me of a private detective I hired years ago named Yannis Mannis. I should tell you about that sometime." A weak laugh and her voice cracks. "I thought we made a really good throuple."

"I'm sure you did." I offer her a tissue and crouch beside her. "You got anywhere you need to be for a while?"

Sniffling, she says, "No, I figured the oil slick hair would take ages, so Astrid's watching the store the rest of the day."

"Good." I lock the front door and flip the sign to CLOSED. "Let's head to the back. I've got tea and coffee, unless you want me to run out and get something stronger?"

"Coffee is fine." With a sigh, Sally stands and follows me.

In the kitchenette, I fill a pot with hot water and rummage through the cabinet for a box of cookies or snack cakes. It was something Mom ingrained in me: when you have a guest, you always serve coffee or tea with a sweet treat, even if it goes uneaten.

"Beautiful samovar," Sally says from the doorway, pointing to the end of the counter. "Was that your mother's?"

"Yeah." I cast a contrite look at the thing, which resembles an ornate bronze UFO with handles and a spigot. "She used it to brew tea for her clients. It's mostly decorative now, though I usually hide it in the cabinet." My electric kettle isn't as pretty but it's faster; I don't know how Mom managed to do hair and work such a fussy contraption.

"And what are those?" She points to a pair of filigreed metal glass holders beside the samovar.

"It's called a *podstakannik*. It literally means 'thing under the glass,'" I explain, holding one up. "In Russia, tea is traditionally served in a glass—"

"Because what else would you want to drink a boiling hot beverage out of?"

"Exactly. But some smart Russian must've been tired of getting scalded all the time and came up with this." Tracing a finger over the delicate lacework, I shake my head. "I may not agree with their faulty tea logic, but my people do get points for craftsmanship."

"Sometimes logic is overrated."

That sounds like something my sister would say, but I won't hold it against Sally.

We take our coffee into the reception area of the salon and perch on a banquette.

Unsure of how much she wants to rehash her breakup, I go in delicately. "Do you want to talk about . . . ?"

"The naked chefs with rhyming names who broke my heart? Not particularly. Do you want to talk about all the Violet craziness?"

"No." I glance outside, where three young women in skinny jeans and military jackets pause in front of the salon to take photos. "Speaking of Violet craziness." Their lapels glint with the silver double *V* of my sister's logo (the letters' legs jagged like bolts of lightning), and as they turn around, each reveals a large swan patch sewn onto the back of her jacket. Are swans a new part of my sister's fandom?

"How much are you dreading the vigil next week?" Sally asks.

"So much. More now that Quinn has volunteered as tribute. I'm a wreck just thinking about her onstage in front of all those people."

"I'll be there with extra Xanax if either of you need it."

The women outside take a few more selfies and catch me watching them. Offering nervous smiles and waves, they walk on.

"Is there any part of you . . . um . . . Do you think . . ." Sally begins.

My head whips in her direction. This must be serious. It's not like her to hesitate—she's of the speak now, apologize later variety.

"Do I think what?"

She studies her coffee and lowers her voice. "Do you think it's even . . . a teeny-tiny bit possible . . . you know, with all the hubbub going on . . . that *maybe* Violet . . ."

"Is behind any of it? Is gonna use the anniversary to stage a comeback?" My tone is surly, and I roll my eyes, but it's more to keep them from tearing up. "No way. All the resources she would've wasted having people look for her, all the emotional turmoil she caused . . . It would be a bad PR move and come off as too manipulative, even for Violet. She'd never do such a thing." She wouldn't, right? Coffee sloshes dangerously in my mug and I hold it with both hands to keep it steady. "I don't think she's ever coming back."

"Well, if she does, I'll be the first one to kick her ass for putting you through all this." Her eyes sweep the walls, taking in the photos and posters. "I see you have some new additions to the shrine."

My sister's presence lingers like heavy smoke, impossible to air out or wave away. Countless people have walked into the salon with reverence, like this is a Violet Volk holy site. The first time Sally entered the salon and saw the photos, she said, "Blech, I hate magic. No offense." It was all I could do not to grab her by the shoulders and kiss her on the mouth.

I can't resist asking, "Hey, were you being honest when you said you hated magic? Or were you just trying to get on my good side?"

"Ha, no, I blurted that out and meant every word. Magic is just so . . . cheesy. The vests, the smoke, the melodrama. At the same time, it's boring! If I can figure out the trick, it's stupid, and if I can't, *I* feel stupid. We know people can't really fly or teleport or read minds, so why pretend they can? How can I be entertained by somebody trying to manipulate me and make me feel dumb?" Catching herself in a rant, she slows down; her face grows thoughtful. "But you know, recently I realized it goes deeper than that."

"How so?"

"Setting aside the small subset of magicians who are women, a lot of magic seems to be about the different ways a man can control a woman's body. Think about it. You have the man sawing a woman in half, stretching her out, throwing daggers at her, levitating her . . ."

Is this why all of Violet's assistants were male? As I mentally rifle through her illusions, men are the ones being contorted and manipulated. And whenever something was happening to her, whether she was on fire or bleeding or levitating or disappearing, Violet was doing it to herself. She was always the one in control.

We regard the walls in silence, then each other. I lower my voice. "Can I confess something to you?"

"Is it that you hate magic a little less, knowing your sister subverted a lot of that bullshit?" Our nods are slow, synced, and reluctant. "Can I confess something to you?" Sally counters.

"Is it that you don't want to chop half your hair off and have it look like an oil slick?" Our nods are slow, synced, and punctuated with giggles.

"I do think it's great how willing you are to try new things. I'm such a creature of habit," I say.

"Unlike Violet, no doubt."

"I'm glad she got me out of my comfort zone once in a while. Sometimes I worry being a creature of habit has closed me off from new things. And maybe that's had a negative impact on Quinn. She has more ambition than I ever did, but she's still a nervous kid in some ways. I mean, she got into good schools all over the country but stayed local. She wants to make the world a better place, but she doesn't seem curious about seeing much of it."

"You're not holding her prisoner in Willow Glen."

"Fair enough. But I wonder if my reluctance to branch out made her too insular. Or if she has a whole other life I don't even know about. Quinn can talk to me for hours about what she wants to do to our garden, but I've met maybe two of her friends the entire time she's been in college. And I'm completely shut out of her love life. I don't even know if she has one." Sighing, I rub the spot between my eyebrows, like my mother used to do whenever she caught me frowning. "I just don't want her to end up alone."

"Is this about Quinn not wanting kids? Because that's a valid choice, and she needs to know that. Just look at my fabulous child-free life." Sally makes a flourishing gesture.

"No, I mean . . . I wonder if she's struggling with her sexual identity or gender identity or I don't know what. And she won't tell me because I'm so . . ."

"Cisgender and straight?"

"Yeah." If Violet were around, I bet Quinn would've opened up to her by now. "Does she talk about any of this stuff with you?"

"What your daughter and I discuss is our business." A contemplative pause before Sally continues. "You know, the only time I ever have second thoughts about choosing not to breed is when I'm around Quinn. You did good with her. But you do need to talk to her. *Really* talk." Her mouth forms a sly grin. "Now can we discuss something more important?"

"Like your hair?"

"Like my hair. Since you're all in your head about not trying enough new things, you can live vicariously through *this*." She shakes out her blond mane. "Right now. Go nuts. Try *anything*."

It's dark out by the time her new look is complete and I'm spritzing Sally's hair with finishing spray.

I swivel the chair and hold up a mirror so she can see the full ombré effect in her newly platinum hair: a pastel spectrum of lilac, aqua, and pink.

Sally gasps, laughing in pure delight. "Now this is motherfucking magic."

"You should've been born with mermaid hair."

"Right?" Sitting up straighter, she turns to admire herself from different angles.

When my mother owned this salon and I was too young to do more than sweep up hair, I'd watch for the moment when clients viewed her finished work, when that spark of confidence would appear in their eyes. And it always did. Ninety-nine times out of a hundred, they left the salon looking and feeling better. In the rare case when a client was displeased, my mother still found a way to improve their mood, whether by giving them complimentary beauty products, offering a free follow-up appointment to fix any perceived hair slight, or taking them to the back room, where she'd serve hibiscus tea and ginger biscuits. ("Sometimes it's not the hair they are unhappy with," she'd say, "and having a little snack and chat is enough to cheer them up.") Violet may have made a career of magic, but I experienced more wonder observing the way my mother interacted with people, making them feel more beautiful, lifting their spirits with her perennial smile and quirky Russian expressions, listening to their stories. It's invaluable, having a place to go where you can feel seen and heard.

"You really like it?" I ask again. "Honest?"

Her squared shoulders and raised chin tell me everything I need to know, but it's still nice to hear her say, "I love it. It's exactly what I wanted. And I didn't even know I wanted it."

A warm glow spreads through me. There's that twinge of guilt that pops up occasionally, the voice of my sister that questions whether I could've made a more meaningful contribution if I had pursued medicine. Is there something lacking in me for not setting my ambitions higher? Even if there is, I can't help but find satisfaction in the small ways I can contribute to brightening another person's day. Isn't that what ultimately matters, giving it your best effort and taking pride in your work, no matter the scope?

I smooth the top of Sally's hair and grab my cell phone. "Mind if I take a photo? 'For the 'gram,' as my daughter likes to say."

"You can take a photo, but if you ever say 'for the 'gram' again, we can't be friends anymore."

I walk in a semicircle around Sally and take some snaps as she makes sultry eyes at my phone's camera. Scrolling through the results, I turn the screen around to show her the best one.

"You know what, Kerry and Jerry can suck a bag of dicks. I'm a stone-cold fox." Sally marvels at her image and squints, craning her neck for a closer look. Her eyes zigzag between the phone and a spot over my shoulder. "Did Gabriel come back from his meeting?"

"Nah, he's up in New York and won't be back for a while." I turn around and peer into the supply room: it's empty. "Why, you see a ghost or something?"

"Something." There's a blue tint to Sally's mouth as she hands me back the phone.

"I don't see anything." I examine the picture. "Are you sure—oh shit." The phone slips out of my hand and clatters to the floor. A web of jagged cracks runs across the now-black screen.

But the photo remains clear in my mind. The naughty gleam in

Sally's blue eyes and the candy colors of her hair. The mirror behind her, reflecting the open storage room. And the woman in the reflected doorway dressed in head-to-toe black, her narrow face pale, her glittering red lips smirking.

I swivel my head again to the storage room: it's empty. Back to the broken phone: its screen remains dark. But moments ago, it showed Violet leaning against the doorway, arms folded, her shrewd gaze taking dead aim at the camera.

The Queen of Illusions:
Exclusive Interview with Violet Volk

By Malini Agarwal

JULY/AUGUST 1997

"Could this shoot *be* any more of a disaster?"

The question comes from Violet Volk as one of her numerous pearl necklaces comes undone and scatters along the cobblestones of Fifth Avenue. The cover shoot takes place along the Central Park side of Museum Mile, and with the theme of *Foxxy*'s summer issue being Hollywood Icons, Violet's been dressed as Audrey Hepburn in *Breakfast at Tiffany's*. What seemed like a whimsical idea in concept is proving to be . . . well, Violet's not wrong: it's a disaster.

The black column dress is so tight around her thighs and her stilettos so unstable on the cobblestones, she can take only tiny steps. On top of which, she's walking three leashed huskies, which were supposed to be trained but are unruly, pulling in different directions. Then another pearl necklace snaps. And so does Violet's patience.

"This is ridiculous," she fumes. "Why am I dressed like some dainty sweet movie star? It's not me at all. And it's not even accurate. Didn't Audrey have a cat in that movie? And didn't she wear flat shoes? What is all this bullshit?" As she raises her voice, a small crowd gathers, and a few onlookers stop to take their own pictures. "If you wanted to update Holly Golightly, you could've given me wolves instead of dogs. You could've given me a vinyl dress, a tiara made of barbed wire, cooler hair than this beehive. You could've—" Before she can complete her thought, the huskies jerk her forward face-first into a light stand, leaving her with blood trickling out of the corner of her mouth.

"That's it, I'm done." Violet kicks off her shoes and stalks off to the wardrobe trailer. An assistant rushes off after her.

Fifteen minutes later, she returns, still wearing the column dress but with a hastily cut slit up one side and now paired with Doc Martens combat boots. She's swapped her remaining pearls for a dog collar, her beehive is disheveled, and her tiara is crooked. The opera gloves are gone, and her arms are encased in fishnet, presumably the tights she was wearing when she first arrived.

"It's this or nothing," she says, striking a pose. "You have ten minutes."

The photographer picks up her camera and starts shooting.

A few days later, I get to the Korova Milk Bar in the East Village fifteen minutes before our scheduled meeting time and several hours before it'll be open to the public.

Any fan of Stanley Kubrik's *A Clockwork Orange* would appreciate this dimly lit East Village bar, with its checkered floor, black-and-white-striped walls, and naked mannequins suspended from the ceiling. I order a Frozen Embryo, one of the alcoholic milkshakes the bar is known for, and take a seat on a white leather couch that glows under a strip of black light. The stereo system plays a chorus of Gregorian monks chanting over electronic beats. Not the strangest setting for an interview I've conducted (that honor goes to a museum in the Midwest whose works of art are made entirely out of corn), but it would make the top ten.

It's been two years since Violet Volk's star-making appearance on *Later Tonight with Jackson Cleo*. Considering the sold-out live performances, the hit television specials, which garnered millions of viewers, and the innumerable tabloid articles that followed, you might think talking to the media would've become second nature to the young magician. And yet, Volk has been surprisingly reticent with the press. While countless newspapers and magazines have devoted pages to her meteoric rise to fame, closely tracking her accomplishments and antics, this is the first official interview she has granted since her confident late-night debut.

Volk's elusiveness while remaining in the spotlight has sparked speculation. Is it all part of a strategically crafted celebrity persona? Does she want her actions to speak louder than her words? Is she, in reality, a deeply shy and socially anxious person?

As I wait for Violet's arrival, I can't help but wonder if she'll demonstrate the same volatility she did at the photo shoot or how else her dramatic flair might manifest itself. After all, it's this lack of predictability that gets her invited to the star-studded events at which she's become a ubiquitous presence. There was the celebrity wedding where she made the couple's wedding bands disappear and reappear woven into the bride's updo. There was the awards show where she presented the honors for best special effects and cried buckets of what appeared to be blood. And, of course, there were her memorable red carpet stunts, like the one where she wore a dress made entirely of playing cards and changed their suit from spades into hearts, or when she secretly handcuffed two rivaling action stars, forcing them to make their entrance conjoined at the wrist (by fuzzy pink cuffs, no less), or when she transformed the mink stole of a Hollywood Golden Age actress into an inflatable snake.

Of course, not all of her stunts have been warmly received. The Broadway premiere where she unexpectedly made it rain over the first five rows of the audience did not go over well with the soaked attendees. Her appearance in a Riley Price music video left the set in flames and the pop princess with her eyebrows singed off after a practical joke gone wrong. And the crew of TV's favorite legal drama, *Overruled*, has expressed consternation at Volk's presence in background shots of several episodes—her sparkly crimson mouth conspicuous and distracting—while scratching their heads as to how she made it onto the soundstage without being spotted.

As you might expect, the young woman knows how to make an entrance. One second, I'm sitting alone on a leather love seat, asking a cocktail waitress for a glass of water, and the next, Violet is sitting beside me. It was instant, impossible. I had my head turned for maybe two seconds. Anyone coming in through the front door would've crossed my line of vision, and the sofa was flush with the wall. The end tables were glass, and there were no hiding spots or other entrances in sight. (I did a meticulous inspection of the area after she left, and I still have *no idea* where she could've come from.)

It's so unexpected, the way Violet appears out of nowhere, that I let out a yelp and nearly knock over my Frozen Embryo, but not before some of it splashes onto her black patent leather pants. Do I know how to make a good first impression or what?

Thankfully, Violet laughs it off, taking full blame for startling me. Her choreographer and rumored boyfriend, Benjamin Martinez, hurries over with napkins. A handsome, diminutive man with art-fully disheveled black hair, he dabs at her pants until she murmurs something in his ear, at which point he smiles, nods, and takes a seat across from us.

Once we're settled in, I take a good look at Violet. Petite and wiry, she looks like she could've come from the set of another music video, her leather pants paired with black platform boots and a slinky silver top. "It looks like metal, right? But it's a fab-ric invented by Versace like over ten years ago," she says when I compliment her on it. "It's called Oroton. So cool, right?" Her naturally gray-blue eyes are amped up to bright turquoise with the aid of colored contacts, and her raven hair is piled on top of her head, messy-yet-meticulous, secured in place with rhinestone butterfly clips. And, of course, her lips glitter with all the intensity of a crimson disco ball.

"Wanna see something?" she asks, waving over the bartender and server lurking a few feet away to come closer.

We all exchange excited smiles and nod.

Violet plucks a butterfly clip from a section of hair above her ear and holds it out for us to examine. It's about the size of a nickel and its wings are decorated with iridescent stones. She turns the clip this way and that, and before any of us can react, pops it into her mouth, her eyebrows shooting up like she was taken aback by her own actions. A carousel of emotions plays out on her face over the next few moments. Perplexity leads to apprehension, then curiosity and an escalating sense of wonder. Finally, she opens her mouth, sticks out her tongue, and reveals the living butterfly perched on its tip. Violet holds her finger up to it, and the crea-ture flutters its wings tentatively before exiting her mouth for the makeshift perch. An assistant appears at her side (where did *he* come from?) with a mesh container the size of a lunch pail, which he unzips and coaxes the delicate insect into.

The bar staff and I break into nervous laughter and applause. Violet bows her head in appreciation and gives her assistant a short nod to sit down.

When seeing magic performed so expertly, especially close-up, a mental tug-of-war ensues. The left brain wrestles with logistics while the right brain is caught up in the awe and artistry of the moment. The result is disarming, perplexing, delightful yet oddly disturbing. I have to remind myself that I'm here to do a job and mustn't let myself be charmed and distracted before I uncover a genuine layer of Violet Volk.

Considering the first few minutes in her company, it's clear my work is cut out for me.

Though this bar is known for its boozy milkshakes, Violet orders a club soda and pulls out a slender flask from her back pocket.

"My grandfather made a vodka from peas and passed on the recipe. It's the only alcohol I drink, and nothing is better," she says, sipping from the pewter flask. "Even the top-shelf stuff tastes like nail polish remover by comparison."

Before I suggest she mass-market her grandfather's recipe, she tells me Volk Vodka will hit retail shelves in time for Christmas. No doubt the packaging will be spectacular.

I'm not sure whether to mention the photo shoot from earlier in the week, but Violet is quick to apologize for her outburst.

"I didn't mean to be unprofessional, and I regret losing my patience like that. I hope you got some usable photos."

As a matter of fact, the pictures taken after Violet's self-imposed makeover turned out to be miles better than anything shot before; these were dynamic, lively, and filled with attitude. When I tell her as much, her nod is half modest, half knowing.

It's puzzling, considering the way Violet is able to command a room, that this is her first real interview since 1995.

"You make it sound like I'm a monk coming out of hiding. There are talkers and doers and I'm one of those people who would rather show you what I'm capable of instead of talking myself up. Naturally, press is part of the game I'm expected to play, but I've found it a better use of my time not to bother with all that and work on being the best damn magician I can be. Of course, when you don't play, the media tells whatever story they want to tell. Anybody can make shit up about me, pass themselves off as 'a close source,' and it'll be printed."

And plenty has been printed about the semireclusive illusionist, from rumors of a threesome-gone-bad being the cause of Jackson Cleo's divorce ("he and I hung out, like, three times total, nothing happened, and I never even met his wife"), to whispers of an affair with mentor Ace Morgan when she was underage ("don't be gross, he's like an uncle to me"), to her possessing actual telekinetic abilities ("I fucking wish. I wouldn't be so lazy about brushing my teeth before bed").

Given the tabloids' penchant for misinformation, one might think Violet is looking to set the record straight on other issues, but she's blunt about her desire to promote her upcoming residency at the Kintana Resort and Hotel in Las Vegas.

"I've gotta keep the people in suits who make money off me happy. They built the theater special for my show, so we need to get the hype machine going."

It was Violet's decision to go with *Foxxy*; she cites it as her favorite magazine without a hint of obsequiousness.

"I appreciate the way it doesn't kowtow to celebrities but shows them more as real, flawed people. Like, I'm sure you'll write about my little Holly Golightly meltdown, and that'll make some people see me as a spoiled diva." Though she would prefer they see her "as someone who doesn't put up with derivative crap. I commit myself a hundred percent to being original and creative and putting my personality into everything I do."

Some might argue Volk has capitalized on existing trends to find her own place in the alternative movement. She's following recent successful acts like the Jim Rose Circus's edgy sideshow, pop goth movies like *The Crow* and *The Craft*, and bold music personalities like Courtney Love and Marilyn Manson.

When I point this out, she bristles at the word "trendy."

"I can't help it if what I'm doing fits into a greater pattern of what people happen to like."

Volk has gone from being unknown, performing in a downtown burlesque club, to a multimillion-dollar contract with the Kintana in the span of a couple of short years. But she is not one to sugarcoat her whirlwind success.

"Okay, first of all, it wasn't a couple of short years. I've been working at this since I was a kid—I was probably doing coin manip before I could walk. Second of all, I know you're looking for a cute sound bite about what a fucking fairy tale my life is. Like, golly gee, it's so awesome to have your dreams come true after working so hard, yada yada yada. But it's more like waiting in line at an amusement park, not knowing if it'll ever be your turn to go on the ride. And if you're lucky enough to get on it, like I was, it's thrilling but also faster and scarier than you ever expected. Sometimes you enjoy it and wanna go even higher and faster. Sometimes, it makes you kinda sick, and you wish it would slow down. On top of that, you're always kinda terrified it's gonna end, so you just try to hold on for dear life."

It's far from the sunny gratitude-laden epithets you'd typically hear a newly minted starlet utter, but Volk is not your typical celebrity.

"The truth is, it's actually like being in a hamster wheel whose speed is being remote controlled by a sadistic bastard. On top of that, you have to deal with all these mixed messages. 'Your show is perfect and you're perfect but let's add some new tricks and also, could you make it sexier and do something about your nose?' 'We love your feminist vibe and how teenage girls look up to you, now can you endorse these diet pills, which most of the time don't cause heart failure?' 'It's cute how you're dating your choreographer, but could you pause that to have a fling with this actor so he gets extra press before his opening weekend, and also could you keep the bi thing hush-hush?'"

Since she brought it up first, I ask her if it's challenging being openly bisexual, personally or professionally.

"Oh no, I love it when people assume I have no standards and will sleep with anybody because I like men and women." Her throaty voice takes on a playful lilt, but there are needles beneath the surface. "Getting called a slut is always fun, especially by other women. Like at the one and only magic convention I went to, where I heard a group of Chatty Cathies going on about all the guys *and* girls I must've slept with to get where I am. And then there was the publicist who suggested I play up being bi to boost my sex appeal—let the paps get hot photos of me kissing other women— since so many men fantasize about threesomes."

Violet takes a long swig from her flask, as if washing a bad taste out of her mouth. "You hear about the dark side of showbiz all the time, but I never expected it to be this gross."

After such an unfiltered outburst, most would backtrack and ask it to be kept off the record, but Violet does not. Instead, her face brightens, all traces of disgust eradicated, as if someone pushed a button on a remote control (perhaps the same sadistic bastard controlling the speed on her hamster wheel). She tilts her head and tells me I have something in my hair, pointing above my ear. When I check, I find an addition to the bobby pins holding my bun in place: one of Violet's butterfly clips. Momentarily speechless, I hold it out to return it to her, but she says to keep it. Then she begs me to ask her some questions that aren't "boring or lame." Her face is alert, expectant, silently assuring me that even though I'm conducting the interview, she's the one controlling it. If we were playing poker, she'd be holding aces and I'd be trying to bluff with a pair of twos.

Suddenly, as if spying a card peeking from her sleeve, I see what she's doing. She's provoking me to go bolder with my queries. I sidestep the unspoken dare and instead ask what people would be surprised to know about her.

She blinks in confusion, like she was expecting a grenade and instead I threw a spitball. "I don't know what people might find surprising or unsurprising. My favorite bands are the Beastie Boys and Siouxsie and the Banshees. I watch *The Way We Were* at least once a year and cry like a baby every time. I'm weirdly superstitious. I love hiking. Is any of that surprising? Who are these people we're talking about? How am I supposed to know their expectations before I subvert them?"

It's a good point. Most have come to expect the unexpected from her by now.

"But what does that even mean? If I'm expected to be outrageous and I pull wacky stunts, aren't I giving people exactly what they expect? See, I think I've been assigned a very specific box and am expected to stay within its boundaries. I'm brought in to make things exciting in a safe way, so everyone can forget about their pointless lives for five minutes. And I'm okay with that. That's the contract I've entered into."

Whether or not it's false modesty, it's also reductive, seeing that Volk is regarded as an up-and-coming feminist role model.

"That's not for me to say, is it? I think that comes up because I'm in a section of entertainment where women are typically props and background players. But I'm not on this career path to make some kind of social statement or pave the way for women in magic.

It just so happens that there aren't as many chicks obsessed with this shit as dudes."

That may be a simplified way of looking at it, though, which she concedes. I ask her what it's like being a woman in a male-dominated industry.

"You're a journalist with tits, you tell me."

When I tell her that it can be a challenge, she smirks and says, "That's one way to put it. I'm not saying there's rampant sexism, but . . . well, you know. We've all experienced something like that."

Something like what?

"Okay, so when I first moved to New York, I was told about a weekly meetup for magicians at Dirty Lou's, this dive bar in Hell's Kitchen, open to anyone. So I went, hoping to make some connections, get some tips, learn some new techniques, you name it. The main focus was on card magic."

As if reenacting those days, she pulls out a deck of cards, fans them out, and hands me one facedown, instructing me not to look at it.

"The first few times I went to Dirty Lou's—with a fake ID, since I wasn't twenty-one yet—the only women I saw there were bartenders and girlfriends of the magicians. As you might expect, I got hit on by the guys, and when I wouldn't hook up with them, some tried to recruit me to be their assistant. Thanks, but no thanks. After I showed off a few sleights, they took me a little more seriously, but there was still a condescending vibe about the whole thing. What do you want it to be?" She nods at the card I'm holding.

I stammer out the first thing that comes to mind, the four of clubs, and Violet has me turn over the card. It's the four of clubs. Ignoring my bafflement, she retrieves the card and shuffles the deck as she continues the story.

"Then there were the old-timers and wunderkinds. They'd take over this corner booth in the back of the bar and always had a crowd watching them hold court. You could show them a trick or ask them questions, but only from the sidelines. You had to be invited to sit with them. Fortunately, Ace [Morgan] was always welcome back there, and he got me in with those guys. After a few weeks, I became a regular. I learned a lot about card manip in that back booth." Violet holds out the deck balanced on her palm and tells me to name a card.

This time, I go with the ten of hearts. She has me cut the deck and puts her other hand over it. Moments later, she hisses.

"I can't, it's too painful." Setting aside the cards, she holds up an apologetic hand. On her palm is what appears to be a brand, of the number ten outlined with a heart.

These feats make it tough to focus on interviewing her, which is likely the point, but I press on, urge her to share more about those early days at Dirty Lou's.

"For the first couple of months, it was great. I got so much better at passing and palming, false shuffles and cuts, all kinds of knacky sleights . . . The older guys didn't hit on me as much, but a couple of them . . . they would get handsy in that booth. Two old-timers there were pretty much worshipped by the magic community and the unspoken rule was that you never interrupted them in the middle of a routine. So one day, one of them was show-ing off this complicated shuffle, and I felt a hand on my thigh. On my bare skin, 'cause I was wearing a short skirt that day. I tried to scoot away and muttered to the sleaze to get his hand off, but I was shushed by everyone around me. I couldn't do anything but sit there. It got worse. The hand went up my skirt. The trick seemed to take hours. Finally, it was over, and I got the hell out of there. I threw up right on the sidewalk and never set foot in Dirty Lou's again."

Between Violet's poise and bravado, the bold clothes and makeup, it can be easy to forget how young she is, that for all the time she spent in bars years ago, she's barely above the legal drinking age today. When she shares this harrowing experience, there's a mo-ment where all I see in front of me is a vulnerable young girl searching out a place for herself as larger forces try to control her.

But a moment later, the smirk returns to her sparkling mouth and her eyes flash with mischief.

"I think you'll like this one," she says, reaching for my empty glass.

She removes the drinking straw, folds it in half, places it in her mouth, and transforms it into a cigarette.

"Got a light? Never mind, I got one right here." She fishes a milky ice cube out of my glass and holds it flat in her palm at chest level. With her other hand, she snaps her finger, and the cube ignites like a lighter being flicked on. It slowly levitates upward and lights her cigarette.

Violet takes a few drags off the cigarette, then throws it over my head. I turn to see where it landed, but the cigarette has seemingly vanished. And when I turn back around, Violet is also gone, leaving traces of smoke in her wake.

Strange Exits

⌒

Episode 4: "Benjamin Martinez"

CAMERON FRANK [STUDIO]: While Violet Volk never spoke publicly about her love life, media coverage indicated a complex history of paramours and romantic encounters. Then there was her marriage to Benjamin Martinez. That's who we're talking to today.

The first thing you should know about him is, he doesn't do nicknames—nobody calls him Ben or Benji, only Benjamin. Now in his early forties, he's been working in the entertainment industry for twenty-five years. A former skateboarder and break dancer, Benjamin quickly parlayed his agility and charm into a career as a performer, choreographer, and television personality, known best for being one of the original judges on the hit reality dance competition *You Got Da Moves*. These days, he lives with his wife and three children in Saratoga, California, where he runs his own dance studio.

CAMERON FRANK: Thank you for joining me on the show, Benjamin. Tell me about how you met Violet.

BENJAMIN MARTINEZ: We're going back to the mid-nineties here. I was doing choreography for a Riley Price music video—the one with all the scorpions and Plexiglas scaffolding, though now it's known as the one where Violet set Riley Price on fire. Anyway, I first saw Violet on the set, but I didn't know who she was.

CAMERON FRANK: Wasn't she pretty famous at that point?

BENJAMIN MARTINEZ: Yeah, but she wasn't all done up, so I thought she was some random nerdy goth girl.

Anyway, it was the first day of the shoot and everyone on the set was rushing around, except for her. She was sitting on the floor in front of this giant stack of folding chairs, painting her Docs with red nail polish. When I walked by, I made a wisecrack about her being too lazy to unfold one of the thousand chairs behind her. At first, she looked at me like she recognized me, but then her face went blank, totally unimpressed, and she went from painting her combat boots to painting the nail on her middle finger, which she held up for me.

CAMERON FRANK: How did you react to that?

BENJAMIN MARTINEZ: For some reason, I said the first thing that popped into my head, which was, "So that's how it's gonna be, huh?" Then I took the nail polish, drew a red circle on the tip of her nose, and handed it back to her. She laughed and said she'd get me back for that. A couple hours later, I was introduced to Violet Volk. She was in full costume and makeup, so I still didn't make the connection. Not until she pointed to her nose, then made a motion like she was slitting her throat.

CAMERON FRANK: So the practical jokes between you started early on.

BENJAMIN MARTINEZ: Yeah, and I almost got fired from the shoot for it. A few hours into that first day, my watch went missing. Turns out Violet swiped it off my wrist and hid it in the scorpion tank. I waited until the next day to retaliate. Riley and Violet were about to film a scene where they got into a laser gun fight. The guns were actually empty water pistols, and when I saw Riley's lying around, I thought it would be funny to fill it up—with any luck Violet would get a face full of water. Only the director had Violet and Riley swap guns at the last minute, and the Evian bottle I used to fill it up was actually somebody's secret vodka stash, and the scaffolding was covered in candles, so . . .

CAMERON FRANK: Hang on, are you saying it was your fault Riley Price was set on fire? Violet took the blame for that. There were rumors that she and Riley were romantically involved and that incident broke them up.

BENJAMIN MARTINEZ: There were rumors Violet was romantically involved with any person she came within two feet of. It's not my place to comment on that any further.

CAMERON FRANK: Why do you think Violet took the blame for something you did?

BENJAMIN MARTINEZ: I guess she liked me. She did also promise to plot sweet revenge, though she said it wouldn't be as bad if I showed her around LA—she was new to the city. So I played tour guide for her the next day, and over dinner, she asked me to join a new show she was putting together, her biggest yet. I was mostly doing choreography at that point, but she wanted me to perform, too, because of my background in gymnastics and breaking. Suddenly, I wasn't sure if this was a date or a business meeting. I tried to keep those two worlds separate, so I agreed to join her show on the condition that things stay platonic between us.

But Violet is one of those people who draws you into her orbit, no matter how much you try to fight it. Who would've thought a month later I'd end up as her date to the Grammys, with people laughing at the white handprints all over the back of my tux? That's how she got back at me for the Riley Price fire. She had a dress specially designed with hidden pockets, which she filled with baby powder, just to mess with me on the red carpet. [*chuckles*]

CAMERON FRANK: It sounds like there was an instant connection between the two of you.

BENJAMIN MARTINEZ: And instant red flags.

CAMERON FRANK: Such as?

BENJAMIN MARTINEZ: Working with and dating someone so volatile. It would be a lot to handle one of those situations, and I was doubling down on trouble. Then there was her insistence on having an open relationship. Her bisexuality wasn't an issue for me, but I'm more the monogamous type. The thought of her being with someone else while we were involved, regardless of gender . . . I wasn't sure I could handle it. But I said I'd try.

CAMERON FRANK: Why not cut your losses at that point and focus on the business relationship?

BENJAMIN MARTINEZ: I was already too into her. That's always been a problem for me, falling in love too quickly. I guess I thought, eventually, the feeling would be mutual, and she wouldn't want to see anyone else.

    We had a lot of good times those first few months in LA. Some of our dates were more low-key—we did a lot of hiking—but I got the sense that she wanted to be where she would be seen. Like, at first, she loved the trails in Topanga, which were more remote, but soon she was all about Runyon Canyon, where people go to spot celebrities. She started getting recognized more and more when we went out. Then the Kintana deal happened, and things got hectic fast. There was the move to Vegas, two months of rehearsals, previews, and—BAM!—*Ultra-Violet* is the hottest show on the Strip. Around that time, her next TV special aired, and it was huge—it seemed like overnight everybody knew who she was.

CAMERON FRANK: Was that new for you, dating someone in the public eye?

BENJAMIN MARTINEZ: I'd worked with celebrities, and even partied with them once in a while, but yeah, I'd never dated someone famous before. I was used to my private life being private. Now, all of a sudden, something that should've been simple, like going out to dinner, became a big production. There was all this coordination with bodyguards, drivers, restaurant staff. But there were times she'd put on a ball cap and sunglasses, ditch her security detail, and walk around the mall without being recognized. I wondered why she couldn't do that with me, why every date had to turn into a photo op. I thought things might get better when we moved to Vegas, which isn't a big paparazzi town like LA. But Violet and I still got swarmed with photographers all the time.

CAMERON FRANK: Did it feel like you were in two relationships, the public one and the private one?

BENJAMIN MARTINEZ: Kind of, yeah. When we were alone, she was sweet, goofy. On hikes, she'd be like a little kid at Disneyland, pointing out animals and pretty scenic spots. Or at home, she'd put on a Run-DMC album, crank it, and start dancing and jumping on the bed until I joined her. And she could surprise you in the nicest ways. Our first Christmas together, she got me a signed Caballero skateboard deck—I never even told her Steve Caballero was one of my personal heroes. She had an open offer for anyone working on the show who was willing to adopt a pet from an animal shelter, promising to cover food and vet expenses for a year. That's something I really appreciated about Violet: when she was being generous, she was real thoughtful about it.

But Violet in public was different. It's like she couldn't make it through a night out without creating drama. If it wasn't showing off a crazy outfit, it was demonstrating a new trick in public, or picking a fight with me to cause a scene. God forbid twenty-four hours went by without people talking about her. I was happier staying in, ordering food, and watching a movie. I think she was happier doing that, too, but she kept pushing herself to go out all the time.

CAMERON FRANK: It's odd that she'd crave so much additional attention when she was already receiving plenty of it through her TV appearances and stage show. She was performing for thousands, night after night.

BENJAMIN MARTINEZ: It wasn't enough. What's really odd is, she hated big crowds, she just had a need to be seen. Violet jokingly referred to herself as a shy attention whore. Her plan was to get as big as possible, put away millions, and then get some farmland in California, retire early, and live what she called our "real life" in luxury. It sounded like a good plan, so I went along with it. And I went along with other things . . . some of which I don't feel so good about looking back.

CAMERON FRANK: What sorts of things?

BENJAMIN MARTINEZ: It started small. She got me this Beastie Boys ringer T-shirt and wanted me to wear it all the time. The Beastie Boys were not really my thing—I was more into old-school hip-hop and punk—but she said I looked sexy in it, so I wore it for her. Same with the red Chuck Taylor high-tops she got me. Then there was my hair. I wore it down to my shoulders back then, but she thought it would look so much better short on the sides and shaggy on top. So, I cut my hair, wore the clothes she bought for me, and continued being her arm candy.

At some point during that first year, her uncle died, and she asked me to fly out to Jersey with her for the funeral. I hadn't met her family before, and it was . . . kinda weird.

CAMERON FRANK: Was there tension between Violet and Sasha?

BENJAMIN MARTINEZ: Not at first. Violet was pretty broken up about losing her uncle—this was on top of her dad dying the previous year—but it had been a while since the sisters had seen each other, and they seemed happy to be reunited. Sasha was welcoming but gave me a couple of funny looks when she picked us up from the airport. It wasn't until we got to Willow Glen and I met her husband that I understood why . . . It wasn't quite like looking in a mirror, but Gabriel could've been my long-lost brother. We even had the same haircut.

The day after the funeral, Violet and I met up with Sasha and Gabriel for breakfast before we headed to the airport. You know that ringer Beastie Boys shirt Violet got me? I wore mine to the diner . . . and Gabriel showed up wearing his. And both of us wore red Chuck Taylors. We all had a laugh about it, but I caught Sasha glaring at Violet.

CAMERON FRANK: What was going through your head at the time?

BENJAMIN MARTINEZ: That Violet and Gabriel had some kind of history and she was obviously trying to get me to look more like him.

When I confronted her about it, she said she'd been friends with Gabriel since they met at magic camp, but it was never anything more than that. She denied ever having feelings for him—she just thought he had a really cool style.

CAMERON FRANK: Did you believe her?

BENJAMIN MARTINEZ: Back then, I kinda had to? Or it wasn't gonna work between us. Years later, after we divorced, when that website came out ripping her to shreds, I did wonder if the stuff about her and Gabriel was true.

CAMERON FRANK: I was actually going to ask you about violetisafraud .com. A lot of people suspect you wrote that takedown. It felt personal, and since things did end on a sour note between the two of you . . .

BENJAMIN MARTINEZ: Come on, man, that wasn't me. I don't go for such petty bullshit.

CAMERON FRANK [STUDIO]: Normally, I might press the issue, but my years as a journalist have made me pretty good at sensing when someone is hiding something. I didn't get that feeling from Benjamin. There might have been topics he didn't want to discuss in detail, but he struck me as an honest, upstanding guy. So when he said it wasn't him, I believed it.

I asked him to tell me more about those early days in Vegas.

BENJAMIN MARTINEZ: I was too busy working and falling in love to notice how orchestrated it all was. *Ultra-Violet* was a huge hit, we were living in a sick penthouse suite, and we got VIP treatment twenty-four/ seven—it was easy to get caught up in it.

Violet had this warehouse built out for her off the Strip to develop new effects with a team of consultants, and she started spending more time there. It was confusing—we lived together and worked together, but by November, I felt like I hardly ever saw her.

I told myself it was temporary. After all, we had a couple weeks off in January, and talked about taking a vacation somewhere in the Pacific islands. I figured we'd get some quality time together soon. Plus, one of my sisters was about to have her first child, and I planned on finally introducing Violet to my family.

Of course, it didn't work out that way.

CAMERON FRANK: What happened?

BENJAMIN MARTINEZ: Right after Thanksgiving—which we spent in Vegas, working—Violet was offered a booking to do a week at some private retreat in January. I don't remember where—maybe off the coast of Peru? Some exclusive getaway for rich and important people. The money was so good, Violet couldn't really say no. And she couldn't take me with her; this was a solo deal. There was so much secrecy around the whole thing, she couldn't tell me much about it.

I was livid. We finally had some time to spend together, and she was going somewhere else without me? When I asked her not to go, she accused me of being controlling and said I needed to trust her. We were arguing about it by the pool in our suite, and at one point, she got so mad, she pushed me in. That made us both laugh, and Violet jumped in after me, fully clothed. Then she got all sweet and told me how much she loved me and would marry me that very day if it would put my mind at ease.

I actually planned on proposing to her after she met my family—already had the ring and everything. Since she brought up the subject first, I went and got the ring, and got down on one knee, right by the pool. She said yes. On the condition that we get a confidential marriage license, have a private civil ceremony, and keep our nuptials secret for the time being.

CAMERON FRANK: That's . . . not a typical response after being proposed to. How did you react to that?

BENJAMIN MARTINEZ: I was happy she wanted to marry me but found the rest ridiculous and a little insulting. What was I, some dirty little secret? And after all her media whoring, a private civil ceremony? How could I get married without my family there, without being able to tell anybody about it? What was even the point of getting married?

CAMERON FRANK: How did Violet justify it?

BENJAMIN MARTINEZ: Oh man, she was clever. Damn clever. All the complaining I'd been doing about the paparazzi, living under a microscope—she turned it around on me. Said getting married was something she didn't want to cheapen with public scrutiny. Said it was too important. I was such a sucker for buying into her bullshit. Still, I went along with it. When she threw in a prenup, I went along with that, too. We got married in California, in secret, just like she wanted, in December of '98.

CAMERON FRANK: Was there much of a honeymoon period?

BENJAMIN MARTINEZ: We spent a long weekend in Palm Springs after the civil ceremony, then went back to work. But in the broader sense . . . I mean, I don't know what was going on in her head, but I guess I felt closer to her. Violet seemed to feel bad about excluding my family from the wedding—she didn't get to meet them when we were in Cali—so she cut down on the partying and made an effort for us to have more quiet time together. It was nice. It almost started to feel like a normal life. Then she had to leave for Peru.

Violet swore she'd be safe—private plane, bodyguards, the works—but she could have no outside contact while she was away. The whole thing sounded sketchy, but what could I do?

CAMERON FRANK: What did you do?

BENJAMIN MARTINEZ: I tried to put it out of my head and not think the worst, which was that it was some kind of ruse to have an affair. Up to that point, Violet had been out on a few dates, but she always told me about them, and it was nothing serious. I had no choice but to trust her and trust that this was just business. I visited my parents and sisters, met my newborn nephew. Came back to Vegas and drank a lot until my wife came home.

CAMERON FRANK: And how were things after that?

BENJAMIN MARTINEZ: They felt . . . off. Violet acted like she was trying to be on her best behavior with me. Or the version of her she thought I liked the best. She stopped baiting me into stupid arguments and playing practical jokes. It was a little Stepford Wife-y. The most she'd say about the trip was that everything went smoothly.

It still seemed like something was bugging her, though. She was definitely more preoccupied. And a lot more fidgety. It used to be that we could watch a movie as long as she had a deck of cards to keep her hands busy. After the trip, she couldn't sit through a half-hour show without needing to get up, walk around, do something. Days off were the worst for her, so she started booking TV guest spots and film cameos, mostly in LA and New York. Sometimes I went with her, but the extra travel wore me out after a while. So did the late dinners, parties, and clubs, which I skipped out on more and more. I suggested we start hiking again, but she said she was tired of all the same old trails, which wasn't like her at all. Then she decided the nightly performances weren't enough for her. She wanted to do a smaller, more intimate show, but to keep it off the books. Her contract entitled her to have additional suites reserved for her, at the Kintana and affiliated resorts, so she started using them for secret close-up shows.

CAMERON FRANK: How involved were you with those?

BENJAMIN MARTINEZ: Not at all. Close-up magic is more a solo operation. I didn't get why she needed to do it. I wanted a life outside of performing, whereas performing *was* Violet's life. She said it was about putting away enough for us to have a secure future, but once you're earning millions, how much more security do you need? And the pace she worked at seemed unhealthy. She couldn't have been sleeping more than a few hours on nights when she did the close-up shows, which were happening more and more often. And during the day, she was holed up in her workshop. Or off filming another "special appearance." I barely saw her.

CAMERON FRANK: Were there any more mysterious trips?

BENJAMIN MARTINEZ: There were. A couple months after that first one, she was summoned again. This time, to somewhere in the Caribbean, another one of those off-the-radar things. At that point, she was so overworked, I thought she was headed for burnout, so I hoped it could also be a vacation of sorts for her. Part of me still wondered why

I couldn't join her, what she might be hiding. One time, I walked in on her arranging stacks of cash in a suitcase.

CAMERON FRANK: What was that about?

BENJAMIN MARTINEZ: As if I'd ever get a straight answer. Here she was, looking like she'd just robbed a bank, telling me not to worry, to pretend I didn't see anything. She left with the suitcase, came back a few hours later and refused to say a word about it. If I tried to bring it up again, she'd either blow up at me or give me the silent treatment. I stopped asking about it. But all these things, they added up. Everything she did behind my back chipped away at the trust between us. At the time, I thought it was a rough patch, something all marriages went through. But things only got worse and worse. Violet's nervous energy increased, to the point where I wondered if she had a drug problem.

CAMERON FRANK: Did you discover any substance abuse issues?

BENJAMIN MARTINEZ: Here's the crazy thing. I never saw Violet take anything besides vitamins. But her whole thing with vodka . . .

CAMERON FRANK [STUDIO]: Violet Volk claimed to not drink any alcohol except for vodka, and not just any vodka, but a special home brew she carried around in a silver flask with a diamond-encrusted double *V*. It was from a recipe passed down several generations, unique in that it was brewed from peas instead of potatoes, and Violet quickly negotiated a deal with a craft vodka distillery on the Jersey Shore. Volk Vodka remains one of the top three vodka brands today, with all proceeds going to support wildlife preserves.

BENJAMIN MARTINEZ: It was a quality product, but Violet's pretension around it drove me crazy. That flask was too much. After she started taking those shady business trips, there were a couple of times I checked her purses, pockets, drawers, for any sign of drugs. I didn't find a thing, but of course I had to get to that flask. I wasn't even slick about it, I just snatched it out of her hand at some club one night and took a swig. It was goddamn water. She tried to brush it off, saying she ran out and refilled it in the bathroom, but I did the same thing to her a couple of nights later on our way to dinner—so the flask should've been full of vodka—and again, it was water. Turns out, Violet didn't even drink. We got into a huge fight about it. She was pissed because I'd invaded her privacy. I was pissed because it was yet another thing she'd hid from me . . . [*sighs*]

I used to wonder if you can get temporary insanity from a person. That's the effect Violet had on me—she made me go out of my head. In the beginning, it was exciting, *she* was exciting. Even I got dazzled by her tricks. But it was like being in a flashy sports car with your foot on the gas. You get so caught up in the thrill of the ride, you forget to keep your eyes on the road . . . and it's only a matter of time before you crash.

CAMERON FRANK [STUDIO]: Let's fast-forward to 1999. Las Vegas is about to experience a turning point. Where it was dominated by the gaming industry, the city is undergoing a transformation to broaden its appeal beyond a hedonistic mecca for partiers and gamblers. The plethora of live shows, nightclubs, and pool parties, along with an already thriving restaurant scene, are drawing a broader tourist crowd. In fact, 1999 will mark the first year nongaming entertainment brings in more revenue to the city than gaming. Some attribute this to the enduring success of *Ultra-Violet*; after two years, Volk's show continues to draw steady patrons to the Kintana. But there are several noteworthy resort hotels brightening up the Strip, including the highly anticipated Bellagio, the Venetian, Mandalay Bay, and the Paris.

BENJAMIN MARTINEZ: It made her crazy, watching how much attention the shows at these new hotels were getting. She checked in with the box office every day to see if we were sold out, and I could tell if we weren't by glancing at her face. On those days, rehearsals would be miserable. Even if we had a clean run, she'd find things to criticize. She'd make constant minor changes, then freak out if we were off on the timing. Suddenly, everything about the show felt stale. She wanted the effects updated, the music, the costumes, the choreography—everything. Her contract allowed for some modifications, but she started asking for bigger things. A new lighting rig. More background performers. The Kintana bigwigs gave in to some of her demands when it was justified—like when she had to replace some effects after Ace Morgan's

TV special—but they didn't want to risk a dip in profits by changing things up too much. And they drew the line at some of her more outrageous demands, like half a million dollars for Nesting Dolls, this custom illusion she wanted constructed.

CAMERON FRANK: The way you talk about it almost makes it sound like a hostage negotiation.

BENJAMIN MARTINEZ: That's exactly how it felt, like she was taking the show hostage. She may have been the star, but over fifty people were involved in putting on *Ultra-Violet*. So when she went AWOL for two days after her revised costume budget was rejected, that's two days those people didn't get paid.

It was a dangerous game, because if the Kintana execs weren't happy, they could've used behavior like that to void her contract. Which could've been what Violet was hoping for, since her manager was pushing her to do more TV and film. Maybe that's why the accidents started happening.

CAMERON FRANK: Let's talk about those incidents. When I spoke with Ace Morgan, he claimed they were coordinated efforts to draw publicity.

BENJAMIN MARTINEZ: Ace was a purist who valued sleight of hand above all else. He didn't see the artistry in feats of endurance or big showy gimmicks—you know, the stuff that usually gets magicians attention. No matter how good you are at what you do, you always gotta do newer and bigger things or you'll lose that attention. But to imply that Violet would willingly and methodically hurt people for her fame . . . she's narcissistic and shrewd as fuck, but no way would she be capable of something like that.

CAMERON FRANK: So you're saying all those accidents were what? A series of careless events?

BENJAMIN MARTINEZ: You know, even after all these years, however I look at it, I still don't know what to believe.

When it came to Violet offstage, she was a mess. Living with her was like living with a small tornado. She left disaster areas wherever she went—clothes, makeup, playing cards, hair clips . . . She couldn't resist buying every trick she could find—even the cheap ones for kids—to tinker with them, and she left those all over the place. There was always glitter and confetti in the carpet. When it got really bad, I was too embarrassed to let housekeeping in and cleaned the place myself, but it didn't matter. As soon as Violet was home, within an hour, it looked like a kid's birthday party had exploded in our suite. Calling her a slob would be an insult to slobs.

But in the theater, she was a different person.

I've worked with hundreds of performers during my career, many of them driven and hardworking, but none as . . . *meticulous* as Violet. She kept track of every last detail of the show. If a lightbulb went out, a costume was torn, a music cue slightly off, she noticed it before anyone else. One small misstep could send us into hours of extra rehearsals. That level of perfectionism could be annoying, but she held herself to those same high standards.

CAMERON FRANK: Right, but if Violet was a perfectionist, technically those incidents wouldn't be mistakes. They would've been planned.

BENJAMIN MARTINEZ: Come on, as if we practiced stabbing and crushing our assistants. The whole point of so many rehearsals was to make sure things like that *didn't* happen because some of those tricks were seriously dangerous.

CAMERON FRANK: There were quite a few mishaps on *Ultra-Violet* before the night Dominic Puglisi was killed. One assistant broke his foot after a harness malfunctioned. Another had his fingers crushed by a heavy crate. A third got impaled by a dagger—actually, the knife-throw routine went badly twice, right? Once where the assistant was stabbed through his palm, the other time his shoulder. Can you talk about what went wrong during those performances?

BENJAMIN MARTINEZ: Like I said, these things happen.

CAMERON FRANK [STUDIO]: Since Benjamin remained reticent on the subject, citing the unusually robust NDA Violet required, here's a quick rundown of what happened with Dominic Puglisi.

The effect—called Heart-Shaped Box in Violet's show, but typically called the Sword Basket Illusion—is one you're probably familiar with. A basket or box barely large enough to fit a person is brought out, someone climbs inside, the basket or box is closed and is then impaled with a number of swords. Sometimes the magician is the one inside dodging swords, other times the magician is the one outside wielding them. In Volk's version, the box was shaped like an anatomical heart—a heart-shaped box, get it?—and it was minuscule, seemingly the size of a microwave. It was hard to believe the assistant could contort his entire body into such a container. Instead of swords, Volk used these vicious-looking razor-sharp barbed arrows. The total effect, of a man trapped inside an impaled heart, which would then pump out fake blood, was stunning.

Here's the way it works: the box has a false bottom and is placed on a hollow stand, which provides the assistant with extra room to maneuver. That night, the hatch to the false bottom got stuck, and Puglisi couldn't position himself in a way to avoid all the arrows. When Violet heard him scream, she immediately stopped the illusion to let him out.

But one of the arrows had sliced across Puglisi's abdomen so deeply, when he stood, he had to hold his stomach with both hands to keep his intestines from falling out.

BENJAMIN MARTINEZ: Here's what I can say about the whole thing. I only saw Violet cry twice. Once was at her uncle's funeral. The other time was when she found out Dominic didn't make it through the surgery.

Ultra-Violet closed for a week, and there was a ton of press, but this wasn't the kind that helped ticket sales. Somebody died, and Violet was being blamed for it. Unfairly, because there's no way you can control every aspect of a show, as much as she tried. A few assistants quit before we reopened, but everyone else rallied around Violet. We told her it wasn't her fault. I still believe that.

CAMERON FRANK: Considering some of the unpleasant things you've said about her over the years, I'm surprised you're coming to her defense.

BENJAMIN MARTINEZ: Let's be clear: I'm defending her work, not her as a person. We've reached a point where society refuses to distinguish someone's creative work from who they are. A lot of great art has been made by shitty people. Is it disappointing when someone you admire turns out to be a scumbag? You bet. But if I don't keep the work separate, there's a hell of a lot less of it for me to enjoy. What Violet did was a form of art, and I still respect that, even though she may not have been the best person. She was definitely a crappy wife. And before you ask, it wasn't just the polyamory, there were a lot of reasons our marriage failed. I'm not gonna bag on a lifestyle choice that works for other people. It wasn't for me, that's all.

CAMERON FRANK: When did things between you and Violet really start to sour?

BENJAMIN MARTINEZ: If I really think about it . . . actually, before we got married. It was like . . . I was the frog, and she was the pot of water getting hotter and hotter, and I didn't notice until I was being boiled alive.

It's funny, she did this interview right before we opened in Vegas and was disgusted at the idea of using her bisexuality as a way to get more publicity. But when Violet invited a lingerie model to be our date to some high-profile event, she sure didn't mind using it as a photo op.

CAMERON FRANK: So she was actually dating this woman? Or were you seeing her together?

BENJAMIN MARTINEZ: [*clears throat*] Look, I'd like to keep the details of my past exploits private. But yeah, it began with her bringing in women we both liked. It was . . . fun?

CAMERON FRANK: You don't sound convinced.

BENJAMIN MARTINEZ: I'm just, uh . . . realizing what a hypocrite I am. Because Violet wasn't the only one who liked the attention. It was awesome, being seen as this ladies' man. Behind closed doors, it was less awesome. For me, it was kinda awkward. After a while, I kept posing for the photos but didn't participate in any of the other stuff. I only wanted Violet, so I waited for her to . . . I don't know, get other people out of her system, I guess.

CAMERON FRANK: She dated quite a few other men, too, right?

BENJAMIN MARTINEZ: Yeah, but some of that was PR setups. Not all, but some. I won't name names.

I'll tell you something, in our industry, it's not easy to stay monogamous. You're surrounded by gorgeous people in the best shape of their lives, you work with them day and night . . . I wasn't tempted, but that's me. When she went out with other people, I—I guess I found a way to compartmentalize and not think about it. I tried going on a couple of dates with other women, but . . . I wasn't into it.

It wasn't an ideal situation, but I didn't want to lose Violet, so it was another one of those things I went along with.

CAMERON FRANK: It doesn't sound like you were cool with it, though.

BENJAMIN MARTINEZ: I mean, of course I hated the idea, but Violet made it out like we were getting one over on the press, exposing the "reality" of relationships. Society dictates monogamy is the standard, but so many couples, in showbiz and everywhere else, don't follow those rules. They have threesomes, open relationships, or they just cheat.

Violet thought it would be refreshing for us to publicly show off our open relationship, even though our marriage was still under wraps. Weird how she wanted to expose society's lies and hypocrisy with more lies and hypocrisy, huh?

CAMERON FRANK: Between the troubles with the show and tensions in your marriage, I could see how a breaking point was inevitable.

BENJAMIN MARTINEZ: Yeah. Her name was Mayuree.

CAMERON FRANK [STUDIO]: Mayuree Sakda is a photographer known for her unconventional and memorable celebrity portraits. She declined all requests to participate in this podcast.

BENJAMIN MARTINEZ: They met on a magazine shoot in New York and hated each other at first. Then they met again in LA a couple years later and started an on-and-off thing. They might've been together when

Violet and I met, she never told me for sure. Mayuree traveled a lot on assignment—who knows, maybe some of those "confidential" business trips Violet took were to see her. Anyway, our last year in Vegas, all of a sudden Violet hires her own private photographer, though Mayuree insisted on spending half her time in LA.

CAMERON FRANK: Did you have any sense that this was different from the other times Violet dated other people?

BENJAMIN MARTINEZ: She was always upfront about who she was seeing, what she was doing with them, and how she felt about them. Love was never part of it, and most of those side relationships didn't last more than a couple of weeks. When those weeks turned into months and Violet was still seeing Mayuree—this was before I found out their history together went even further back—I started to worry.

Before I could talk to her about it, the thing with Dominic happened. A week after his funeral, Violet sat me down and told me she still loved me and wanted to be with me, but she was in love with Mayuree.

I filed for divorce the next day. And since she was so hungry for press coverage, I sent a copy of the paperwork to a few tabloids as my parting gift to her. She was already getting headlines for Dominic's death and her "steamy romance" with her personal photographer, and she got a shit-ton more for her divorce from her "secret husband." Then a porn actress came forward and claimed I'd been having an affair with her for years, so the narrative became that my cheating sent Violet into these other relationships. I wouldn't be surprised if Violet or her people paid off the porn star to say all those things.

CAMERON FRANK: And meanwhile, you and Violet were still doing a show together.

BENJAMIN MARTINEZ: Exactly, though I moved out right away. I was in a rage for maybe the first week or two, and then I felt nothing. I was over it. Like that [*snaps fingers*]. I started counting down the shows until my contract was up. Those were some *long* months. I couldn't wait to come home to LA.

Once I got settled in with a new place and steady work, life became predictable again. Which was great. I didn't have to deal with Violet's moods or secret trips or publicity stunts—or her superstitions. Jesus, she was so annoying with those, tugging on my ear all the damn time when I sneezed, not letting me whistle indoors, all kinds of other crazy Russian stuff. Oh, like we couldn't kiss while standing on opposite sides of a threshold because it meant we'd get into a fight.

In the early days, I thought it was cute. When you fall in love with someone, their quirks are charming. Once the novelty wears off, you tolerate them. But when things got rotten, the same quirks I used to find cute made me want to kill her. Toward the end of our marriage, I'd sometimes whistle indoors just to piss her off. I'd cover my ears after sneezing so she couldn't pull on them.

It's funny, not long after it ended, I found myself wondering if we'd ever kissed across a threshold without noticing and put some kind of cosmic black mark on us.

CAMERON FRANK: What do you think happened to Violet when she disappeared in 2008?

BENJAMIN MARTINEZ: I think she carefully orchestrated her escape. There was bad shit coming for her.

Violet was more than a skilled performer. She was also very rich and very famous. And when you're that extraordinary and getting a lot of attention, it can trap you in a circle. Sometimes that circle is a spotlight and sometimes it's a bull's-eye target. Sometimes it's hard to tell the difference.

I think Violet's circle was closing in on her and she had to step away from it, for good.

I have no idea where she is, but I don't expect any of us will ever see her again.

Sasha

February 16, 2018

"If I were the only one who saw that photo, I would've been asking you to fit me for a straitjacket," I say to Renatta in our next therapy session, holding on to a throw pillow like I've just fallen out of a plane and it's my sole flotation device. "But Sally saw it first. Of course, when I asked her about it later, she flip-flopped and said it was probably a shadow. But shadows don't wear red lipstick! I'm so mad I dropped my phone like an utter dumbass. Damn thing wouldn't even switch on again. It was old, and that's all it took to kill it for good. Good thing my photos back up to the cloud automatically, right? Except, the salon Wi-Fi is spotty, so that didn't happen."

We go silent as Renatta waits for me to say more. I stare at her brown oxfords, marginally comforted by her continued selection of sensible footwear, until eventually, she asks, "Did you try any other methods to recover the photo?"

"Of course. I googled the shit out of it when I got home. Downloaded some kind of data recovery software, hooked up a USB cable to my laptop, but guess what?"

"It didn't work?"

"It might've worked, but when I went to get my phone out of my coat, it wasn't there. I turned the house upside down, retraced my steps to the salon, checked every inch of the place . . . nothing. Quinn tried to find it using some app . . . no luck. I was so desperate, I even called out this superstitious phrase my parents used to recover lost objects: *Devil, you played with it, now give it back.* Still nothing." There's a sour taste in my mouth and an unexpected sting in my eyes.

"That must have been frustrating."

"God yes. I wanted to break things, but trashing the salon would've been pointless, so I did what I always do—I went for a long run. I'm so mad at myself about that phone. The last thing we need is another unnecessary expense."

"But it's not so much about the phone itself, is it?"

"Nope." I breathe through my nose and give my nemesis, the Kleenex box, a dirty look. It won't get me this time. "Gabriel thought it was silly for me to get so worked up about it, but I couldn't tell him what really happened."

"Why not?"

"For the same reason I haven't told him about the other weird stuff that's been happening." My foot wiggles, demands more motion from the rest of the body, so I get up and pace the carpeted office. "Stress makes me lose my appetite and I enjoy running. It's not that compli-cated. But Gabriel makes it a bigger thing than it is, which is what he'd do if he knew about the sleepwalking or the number patterns." Wait, did I already tell her about the twos?

Renatta's pen goes into hyperdrive taking notes. "What kind of number patterns?"

Shit. Guess not. Pausing in front of the bookcase, I aim my re-sponse at the vase of sunflowers. "It's not important. I didn't mention it earlier because of how unimportant it is." A sudden glint diverts my attention to the bronze swan figures and I'm unable to resist the urge to touch them, one, two, three, running a finger down the curve of each cool neck.

"Since you brought it up now, humor me." Her tone is casual but her penetrating gaze says I have no chance of evading the subject.

I sit back down, push the tissues to the opposite end of the coffee table, and tell her about the twos.

"It's so stupid," I conclude. "I know it doesn't mean anything, that it's my subconscious way of creating order out of chaos, yada yada yada."

When I stop there, Renatta makes a beckoning gesture. "Sounds like there's a 'but' coming."

"*But* . . . it's still a little weird. Our house number is 233, but all of a sudden, we're getting mail for 222 Persimmon Drive. All the time. That's never happened before. Whenever I look at a receipt or inventory number, it seems like it always ends in triple twos. It's the type of synchronicity bullshit my sister would've made a big deal of, but I have no time for it."

"It sounds like you were irritated by Violet's penchant for magical thinking."

A dry chuckle rattles out of me. "Magical thinking, I see what you did there." A hint of a smile but Renatta says nothing. Jesus, this woman is diversion-proof. "It wasn't just Violet. It was my whole family and their obsession with superstitions. Here's an example. We were forbidden from giving sharp objects—scissors, knives, safety pins, et cetera—to anyone. We couldn't receive them from others, either, because according to lore, you'd take on their troubles. So when Gabriel and I got a set of steak knives as a wedding gift, my mother was beside herself until we mailed the sender a dollar bill—apparently, paying for sharp objects protects you from being cursed by them." My eye-roll would surely rival one of Quinn's best. "As if all the Russian nonsense wasn't bad enough, Violet added American superstitions to her repertoire, and she could get . . . extreme about it."

"How so?"

"She hated the number thirteen. Wouldn't even stay on the fourteenth floor of any hotel, because it was technically the thirteenth. Refused to schedule any performances or travel that fell on a Friday the thirteenth. It could be maddening. When our father had a stroke that put him in the ICU, it was on a Thursday. Violet was doing a show in Toronto and couldn't get a flight out that night. But the next day was Friday the thirteenth, so she booked the earliest Saturday flight to Jersey. He died Friday night, and she didn't get to say goodbye because of her stupid fucking superstition. If anything, him dying on Friday the thirteenth further affirmed her belief that it was an unlucky day." My jaw clenches as I remember those first hours of loss and confusion, putting any personal needs for solace aside to tend to immediate logistics and my hysterical mother. "I would've lost my mind if I hadn't had Gabriel, but it would've been nice not waiting an extra day for my sister." I blink at the ceiling, refusing to cry. "Not that Violet was of much use. She argued over everything, from where to bury our father to what to do with all his clothes—and she left the morning after the funeral. Had to get back to Canada because she couldn't afford to cancel any more shows. She couldn't even help much with funeral expenses, because she said she wasn't getting paid more than a per diem until the end of her tour." Sucking in a long breath through my teeth, I shake my head. "I guess I had bigger things to get mad about than her superstitions. But sometimes the smaller shit is easier to focus on, you know?"

"Sometimes the smaller things have a larger meaning than you'd expect," Renatta points out. "You mentioned the whole family followed these superstitions. Were you the only one who didn't?"

"What are you getting at, that I was somehow left out of the family because I rarely joined them in yanking on each other's ears and spitting to ward off jinxes?" Even though my tone is mocking, I tense up. I've hit enough nerves with all this poking around.

"Is that how it felt?"

"No . . . it felt more like a hobby they all shared that I wasn't a part of. Which was fine. They were all fooling themselves, anyway. Except when Violet was trying to fool me."

"Was it possible that was Violet's way of including you?"

"By trying to make me believe that she and I were princesses, and Mom and Dad were spies? Or that she could make objects float and I could teleport? Yeah, no thanks. I was fine being left out of that bullshit." Before Renatta can challenge me, I hurry to add, "But let's get back to this Violet photobomb. I need to know if I might be . . . there's a Russian expression for when you're questioning your sanity, *maya krisha poyekhala*. It translates to 'my roof is slipping.' Should I worry my roof might be slipping?"

"Have you been hearing voices or having hallucinations?"

"No and no—unless that picture of Violet counts. Does it?"

"You mentioned your client saw something in the image, too."

"Yeah, but she seemed less sure of it after. I thought maybe I clicked on Instagram and pulled up a #violetisback image. But it was definitely Sally in that picture. Who knows, maybe it was that shared delusion thing—what's that French term for it?"

"Folie à deux. Do you think it was a shared delusion?"

My head feels like it's being flooded with ink, blacking out rational thoughts. "I don't know. This kind of thing happens to me and I think I'm losing it. But then I read something batshit about my sister online or listen to a podcast where her ex-husband goes into all the insane things she put him through—and I think I can't be the crazy one. At least, not *as* crazy. Nowhere near."

"Have you had any additional sleepwalking occurrences since our last session?"

"No, so at least I have that going for me."

"And this podcast you mentioned, is it the same one you were so distraught about in the last session?" A faint rustle as she flips through the pages of her legal pad. "*Strange Exits*?"

"That's the one."

"Let's talk about that."

"Do we have to? Seems like everyone else in the world is already going on about it."

"In earlier sessions, you seemed pretty adamant about not listening to it. What made you change your mind?"

I give her an isn't-it-obvious glare but she lobs a patient half-smile back at me. "It's kind of unavoidable. At first, it was the local papers and some true crime bloggers mentioning it, and I told myself I wouldn't listen because I didn't want to give it any importance. But now it's blown up—people are calling it the next *Serial*. So if I ignore it, I come off like I don't give a shit about Violet, which might piss off her precious Wolf Pack. I do give a shit. It's about my sister—how could I *not* listen? On top of that, my daughter is getting more fixated on her dear aunt Violet. She tells me she's working on her thesis when I know she's working on her speech for the vigil or going down another #violetisback rabbit hole . . ." A sudden urge to curl up under the coffee table. "There's no escaping it. No escaping *her*. When Violet was alive—I mean, around, among us, whatever—it was like living next to the train tracks. There'd be periods of stillness, but then she'd pass through and rooms would get noisy and the walls would rattle and occasionally something would break. After she disappeared, it felt like she left behind an echo. Like the walls would never stop shaking, the ground would never be steady beneath my feet, the residual din resonating forever in my head. It took years, but things finally got quieter. Until Violet Mania. And the podcast. And the sleepwalking. And the numbers. And the photo."

"Sounds like things are getting pretty noisy for you again."

The compassion in her voice makes me tear up once more. "They are. Which makes me wonder"—the rest comes out in a strangled whisper—"if I'm losing my mind."

Renatta rests her elbows on her knees and interlaces her fingers, fixing me with an intent stare. "I am less concerned about whether you're losing your mind and more concerned with what your mind is trying to tell you."

"I know what it's trying to tell me. My brain is about as subtle as a pink neon sign spelling out SISTER ISSUES. I thought I had a handle on all that. I've gone through the whole spectrum you're supposed to when you lose someone: anger, fear, bargaining, acceptance—it's five stages, right? So I'm missing one . . . Oh, the obvious, sadness. I was plenty sad. I'm over it. But no matter how much I'm done with the Violet drama, it won't be done with me."

The way she frowns and scribbles in her pad makes me feel like I'm tanking a job interview.

"We've got a few things to unpack there," she says. "If you go by the Kübler-Ross model, yes, there are five stages of grief, though not everyone experiences each one, and the order can vary. In your case, you're also coping with ambiguous grief in reaction to a loss with no closure. This comes with added levels of stress, which can leave you stuck in any one of these stages. What I find interesting is that you listed fear as one of them."

"Anger, sadness, bargaining, acceptance . . . Fear isn't one of the five? Are you sure?" Her expression asks me if I'd like to revise my answer, but I can't think of what else it could be. "I have no idea. What's the right one?"

"It's denial. But it's not a matter of right and wrong—there's no such thing when it comes to your emotions. It's not about what you should and shouldn't feel as much as identifying what you *are* feeling."

"So what does it mean, I swapped fear for denial? I'd argue fear is the healthier reaction. Having your sister go missing is fucking scary. I never pretended it didn't happen. I faced the reality of that shitstorm head-on. Isn't that better than denial? Or at least more productive. Unless you think I'm in denial over something else?"

"Like what?"

"Isn't that where you're supposed to come in?" Only I want Renatta to stay where she is. It's like we're facing each other in a dark tunnel—she's armed with a flashlight, and I keep retreating as she moves forward, waving around the light. Aren't I here so she can help my stumbling around? And yet, I want her to stop moving toward me. Stop trying to illuminate things.

"Let's go back to the fear then," Renatta says. "What role has fear played in your grieving process?"

"I guess . . . I was scared she was in danger."

Renatta narrows her eyes and I imagine her zooming into my brain. "How so? There's more you're not saying."

"There always is. That's kinda my thing." But my quips won't erode this woman's patience. "Okay. I'm scared of being wrong about Violet. I mean, I'm scared because there's no right way to think about her disappearance. I get angry because usually I'm sure she left for selfish reasons—avoiding bad press, lawsuits, the IRS—but if it turns out she was being threatened or was actually harmed in some way, I'll be devastated. Then again, if I mourn her like she's dead, and it turns out she staged all of it, I'll be devastated in the other direction." I throw up my hands. "Who the fuck even knows? I guess I'm scared of believing the wrong thing, feeling the wrong way. It's a lose-lose situation: either somebody willfully hurt Violet or Violet willfully hurt me. It's probably the latter, but there's no way to know for sure. I keep looking for a way to feel that makes sense, but . . . deep down I know I won't ever get a satisfying answer. And that lack of resolution—the inevitable *persistence* of it—that's the scariest thing of all." That's still not all of it, though. What's even scarier is this tiny seed of hope germinating in me that I might see her again.

"It must be unsettling living with that much uncertainty. Apart from her disappearance, what do you feel is unresolved about your relationship with Violet?"

"Um . . . all of it?" I rest my head on the back of the sofa.

"Drill down a bit."

"There's a lot I never told her—or told her off about. Things I downplayed for the sake of keeping the peace. As we got older, the more honest our conversations were, the more we'd end up yelling at each other, and the louder you yell, the less the other person wants to hear. It got to a point where it was easier to leave certain things unsaid."

"How did you deal with those unspoken things?"

"Sometimes I vented to Gabriel, but mostly I sucked it up."

"Did you have any other outlet, like a diary?"

"No, I found it pointless to keep track of my inconsequential life." A bitter laugh escapes me. "I used to write her when she was on the road, because she begged me to. Her manager would fax me her travel itinerary and whenever I could grab a few free minutes, I'd rack my brain for a way to update her without saying anything negative about Mom's illness or our money problems. Once in a while, Violet sent us a postcard from the road." I cross my legs and notice a loose thread at the inside seam of my jeans. "A more decent person would've made an effort not to glamorize things—brag about media coverage, celebrities she met, gifts she got from admirers, but we're talking about Violet, who always fell short in the self-awareness department." Fuck it. I tug at the thread and it comes loose in my fingers.

"What do you wish your sister had been more aware of?"

"How hard it was, for all of us." My voice is louder and sharper than I intended. "It was her choice to leave, so her complaints of being homesick felt . . . I don't know, trite somehow. Like she never understood what a luxury it was for her to be out there, chasing her dreams, when I was here struggling with basic survival. Paying bills, taking care of family, trying to keep everyone happy. There's so much she took for granted . . ." My eyes rove the bookcase, settling on the bronze swans. Why are they so oddly reassuring? "And there are so many ways she hurt me, which I've mostly kept quiet about. But they're still up here." I tap at my temple. "Crowding my brain for years."

"Give me one example."

"Just one? What am I, Meryl Streep in *Sasha's Choice*?"

The giggle-snort Renatta rewards me with makes me open right up.

"There was the time in tenth grade Violet and I went to Wei Zhang's for a sleepover and I woke up with gum in my hair. It was just the three of us, and it couldn't have been Wei, because she was the nicest person you ever met. Plus, she wore braces. When we couldn't get the gum out with peanut butter, my sister was quick to 'help' by lopping off all my hair. Coincidentally, this was just a few days after I mentioned how much Gabriel loved my long hair. I was devastated at how short it was, but I downplayed it. And I didn't call her out on it, but I knew it was one of Violet's spiteful schemes, no matter how much she denied it. What a petty bitch, huh?" I try to keep my voice flippant, but the animosity cuts through. "Then there was the time I got a headache as we were getting ready for junior prom, and Violet 'accidentally' gave me a Benadryl instead of aspirin. She completely ignored her date to flirt with Gabriel all night as he tried to keep me from passing out on the bleachers. The maddening thing about my sister was how she did shitty things with just enough plausible deniability. How she'd try to walk back the worst things she said, like it was a bad joke I didn't get. This went beyond the high school crap."

As much as I want to stop there, this tirade is shaking loose something long dormant in me, something that wants out.

"Here's what happened when I told my sister I was pregnant. Bear in mind, I was scared shitless. Nineteen, working as a hairdresser, living with Gabriel and my parents, trying to take care of my sick mom. Part of me wondered if having a kid so young wouldn't only wreck my life, but also Gabriel's—by foisting parenthood on him—and my future daughter's, by me being a woefully unprepared mother. Sure, Gabriel and I were madly in love—still are—but I worried he'd be staying out of a sense of duty more than anything else and eventually, he'd resent me for derailing his life. At the same time, I couldn't imagine a scenario in which I didn't keep this child. So that's what was going on in my head when I called Violet to tell her the news. You know what was the first thing she said? 'You sure you ready for a kid after what happened with Dolly?' If I could've reached through the phone to strangle her, I would have."

"Was Dolly a . . . childhood pet?"

"A salamander we caught in Brigantine, at the very end of the summer. I think we were nine and ten? We put her in a shoebox—deciding it was a girl, even though we didn't know for sure—and spent the entire ride home arguing over whether to name her Dolly, like she wanted, or Yentl, like I wanted. Mom suggested Fanny Brice, since *Funny Girl* was our favorite movie back then, which was the perfect solution, but we dismissed it and kept arguing until Dad had enough and threatened to toss our new pet out the window if we didn't stop. We never did agree on the name, so Violet called her Dolly and I called her Yentl, and it seemed like every day one of us was measuring the wall between our rooms to make sure the table with her tank was exactly thirty-one-and-a-half inches away from each of our bedrooms.

"I don't know why we couldn't compromise—we both would've been happy calling the salamander Fanny Brice, and we would've enjoyed taking care of our first pet so much more. And after Yentl died, we could've mourned her with dignity and a single grave marker, instead giving her two over-the-top headstones made of glitter and Popsicles. Oh, and it was my fault she died. I used to take her out of her tank at night after Violet went to bed and put her in my retainer case, so she could sleep near me, sneaking her back early in the morning. I did that for a few days until I woke up to find Dolly/Yentl dead. I don't know if I didn't punch enough holes in my retainer case or if it got too cold at night or what. Dad told us she died in her sleep, but I think Violet knew I was the one who killed her. That's why she took that dig at me when I told her I was pregnant. I couldn't even keep a salamander alive, how did I expect to raise a child? So much for trying to get any reassurance from my sister. She never knew how much that wrecked me."

Renatta steeples her fingers under her chin and goes for the million-dollar question. "Why didn't you tell Violet how you felt?"

"Because one of us had to be the nice one." I rub the back of my neck; how heavy this crown of self-righteousness.

"That reminds me of something you said about your sister in our first session. About how Violet turned your relationship into a competition."

"I never said that."

"You did." Checking her notes, she quotes from them. "You said you viewed sisterhood as the chance to have a built-in best friend, whereas Violet treated you more as a built-it competitor."

"Yeah, like it was a race to see who can have the bigger, more fabulous life. I didn't want to compete because I'm fine with my smaller, less fabulous life. She can have that win."

"Is it possible you set up your own competition for the two of you, one you got to win by taking the moral high ground?"

I recoil from her analogy. "You're making it sound like I'm a sociopath for being nice. Like I have an ulterior motive for being a good person."

"I wonder why you equate restraining your true feelings with being good."

"It's not about restraint, it's about putting other people first. *That's* what I equate with being good. Violet led a selfish life and was *praised* for being bold and raw and speaking her mind. But if I speak my mind, I get slandered, my family gets threatened, and my business is vandalized." How much longer do I need to sit here? I pull out my new phone to check the time. "Oh, surprise, surprise. It's two twenty-two. We went two minutes over."

A hint of puzzled awe as she smiles in slow motion. "I must've lost track of the time. Any thoughts on—"

"The terrible twos? Nope." I get to my feet. The clock's run out on introspection and I have no desire for any overtime.

September 12, 1995

VV,

I hope you'll see this letter in the mountains of fan mail you must be getting.

Seriously, though, you rocked Jackson Cleo's show, and you're gonna rock this world tour. It must be awesome to finally get recognition for being the magic genius we always knew you were. All us little people in Willow Glen are super proud, and you're already becoming a local hero around here. Sasha and Regina put a huge framed photo of you in the salon window, the *Finchley Free Press* is doing weekly write-ups on you, and Benny's Deli just named a new hot hoagie after you, the "Violet V.I.P." (Unfortunately, the *V* stands for veal, and none of us have the heart to tell Benny you don't eat meat.) For all the "overnight success" stories being written about you, I know how long you've hustled to get where you are. Congrats.

In less happy news, Sasha was crushed when she got your RSVP. You know your sister's not the type who's gonna guilt trip you over it. But come on, V. You can't miss our wedding.

Nobody wants to stand in the way of your stardom, and it's amazing that you're doing this big tour, but there has to be a way you can move some things around to be here when we get married.

It's not gonna be a big thing—you saw the invite, a city hall ceremony and an early dinner reception after. Sasha even picked Angelica's because they had the best veggie options for you. It'll be thirty people max, though your absence would be noticed even if we had three hundred coming.

Between you and me, Sasha kinda wonders if you're doing this to get back at her for missing your Jackson Cleo taping in Chicago. I keep telling her that's ridiculous, that you'd never be that vindictive. You know we had the plane tickets booked and would've been there if it wasn't for Regina's relapse. Whether or not Sasha should've told you about that before your taping is something I won't get in the middle of. I could see why you'd be pissed at her plumbing emergency excuse, but Sasha didn't want to mess up your big break.

Look, I know nothing is easy when it comes to you and Sasha. Bottom line: you love the shit out of each other. You can't miss seeing her get married. Do us a solid and come to our wedding, before you become such a big superstar that we hardly get to see you at all.

—G

October 2, 1995

Dear Violet,

I can't believe you came.

It doesn't matter that the food got cold or that Gabriel's dad and Uncle Slava got too drunk or that I muddied the hem of the wedding dress Dad made me. What really matters is that you were there.

Thank you for coming to my wedding.

222,
Sasha

Date: February 17, 2018, at 5:45 AM
To: cfrank@sidecarstudios.com
From: checkmate@protonmail.com
Subject: soon

Dear Mr. Frank,

My deepest apologies for the delayed response. I have been on the move, but I have not forgotten you.

I have asked a trusted friend to send you a package. It will be a small black box with a white rook chess piece printed on it. When you receive it, DO NOT OPEN IT. Instead, notify me via this email address, and I will provide next steps.

Please confirm your receipt and acknowledgment of these instructions.

Sincerely yours,

‡

Date: February 17, 2018, at 8:06 AM
To: checkmate@protonmail.com
From: cfrank@sidecarstudios.com
Subject: Re: soon

Confirming receipt but not without reservations. How can I be sure this package will not contain something harmful to me?

Cameron

P.S. If you're the rook, does that make me the pawn?

Date: February 18, 2018, at 8:17 AM
To: cfrank@sidecarstudios.com
From: checkmate@protonmail.com
Subject: Re: Re: soon

Dear Mr. Frank,

Trust me or don't trust me. All I can tell you is that my personal safety is at much greater risk than yours.

If you will adhere to my terms, respond with "ONWARD" within the next twenty-four hours. If you do not wish to move forward, send any other response or no response at all.

You are nobody's pawn; you may move across the board as you wish.

Sincerely yours,

‡

Date: February 18, 2018, at 8:20 AM
To: checkmate@protonmail.com
From: cfrank@sidecarstudios.com
Subject: Re: Re: Re: soon

ONWARD

Strange Exits

⌒

Episode 5: "Vanishing 101"

CAMERON FRANK [STUDIO]: When looking at the disappearance of Violet Volk, we are left with two options: Violet went missing either involuntarily or voluntarily.

Let's look at that first hypothesis. What are the ways she could have gone missing involuntarily? Again, there seem to be only two options: misadventure or foul play.

An accident is unlikely. She was performing in a theater, in front of thousands of people, not hiking solo in a treacherous forest. If she suffered a fall or some other calamity in the middle of an illusion, somebody would've seen or heard something. If nothing else, she would've certainly been found somewhere in the building shortly thereafter.

What about foul play? We cannot one hundred percent rule out the possibility of kidnapping, right? Of course, the timing seems unusual. This was Violet's big return to stage magic. That night, she was arguably the most visible she'd been in years. Consider the sheer number of potential witnesses, the security presence, the crowds gathered outside the theater who hadn't been able to get tickets but hoped to catch a glimpse of Violet . . . I don't know about you, but those don't seem like ideal kidnapping conditions. It makes about as much sense as trying to kidnap Janis

Joplin in the middle of her set at Woodstock. Or, for the younger listeners, trying to kidnap Beyoncé in the middle of her Super Bowl halftime show. It's beyond ludicrous.

While an accident or foul play aren't impossible, at best they're highly improbable. Common sense dictates Violet Volk went missing voluntarily. This is the most popular theory, and plenty of conjecture has been devoted to the why. Whether it was legal, financial, familial, or romantic troubles, the why has received plenty of scrutiny.

In this episode, I want to look at the how.

My guest today is John Arno, an esteemed lecturer, investigator, and privacy expert. He's the founder of JPS, Inc., a company offering privacy and security services. JPS is also John's personal nickname, a play on GPS, because of his remarkable track record locating people. Over the course of his career, which spans four decades, he's helped find thousands of bail jumpers, deadbeat parents, runaways, insurance scammers, kidnapping victims, even celebrities.

Arno himself offers an additional service to a select clientele: using his unique expertise, he helps people disappear.

CAMERON FRANK: John, thank you for joining me. To begin, I'd love to know how you ended up doing what you do today.

JOHN ARNO: I started out in law enforcement but quickly decided I wanted to be my own boss. So I went the PI route. I didn't care for the infidelity cases so much—I focused more on investigating insurance fraud and locating missing people. I also dabbled in bounty hunting but didn't enjoy rounding up the criminals myself. I preferred skip tracing, so I stuck to that.

CAMERON FRANK: For those of us unfamiliar with the term, could you explain what skip tracing is?

JOHN ARNO: A skip tracer collects private information about an individual. Could be phone records, banking info, addresses, anything. Usually, this info is used to locate people, though unlike bounty hunting, it doesn't necessarily have to be a criminal. Tabloids have used skip tracers to hunt down celebrities.

Anyway, a few years in, I had a case that changed everything. A guy hired me to track down his missing wife, and when I found her—took me three days—it turned out the sonofabitch was beating on her, and that's why she took off. One look at this woman's busted face and I knew there was no way in hell I was gonna tell her lowlife husband where to find her. But I couldn't rely on the next guy who went looking for her to be as kind-hearted. I needed to make sure this woman covered her tracks so well, nobody'd ever go looking for her again. So I helped her fake her death. It worked. The husband bought it and stopped the search—dropped dead of a heart attack a year later. I hope he's still rotting in hell.

That case got me thinking: lots of folks out there need to disappear. Maybe they're in danger, maybe they've been let down by the legal system, or maybe they just want a fresh start. They might try to run off, but they won't know how to do it right. Ninety-nine times out of a hundred, a guy like me will find them. Some of these people have the right to go missing and stay that way.

To be clear, I'm very selective when it comes to who I help disappear—I won't help insurance fraudsters, money launderers, deadbeats, or any other type of criminals or parasites avoiding justice. I'll gladly keep hunting those unsavory types.

CAMERON FRANK: Aside from the more unsavory types, are there many people out there looking to walk away from their lives and start over?

JOHN ARNO: You'd be surprised. Sadly, some feel like they have no choice. Not only domestic violence survivors, but also stalking victims, whistleblowers—there's all kinds of circumstances that could make you feel unsafe. Not all go to the extreme of faking their death. Sometimes a new identity and a change of scenery is enough. Not all want to or need to give up their identities, either. I work with lottery winners looking to protect themselves from scammers and greedy family members. I get a ton of clients whose lives got blown up by something stupid they posted to social media, and now they can't get a job or a date because googling them brings up the scandal. In those cases, it's more about adjusting their digital footprint, erasing or smudging what we can while adding other footprints leading nowhere. That makes it possible for those folks to go on with their lives without being tormented because of something lucky or unlucky that happened to them, or because of a momentary lapse of judgment and a hypersensitive online environment. Cancel culture is a disease, but I can't deny it's been good for business.

CAMERON FRANK: To go back to something you said earlier, you mentioned helping tabloids track down celebrities.

JOHN ARNO: Not the work I'm proudest of, and I don't do it anymore, but back then I figured anyone who plays the fame game relinquishes their right to privacy.

CAMERON FRANK: Did you ever help track down Violet Volk, before she disappeared?

JOHN ARNO: A number of times, when she was on the road. She was a strange one—most of the time, she was buddy-buddy with the paps and invited them to capture her every move. But once in a while, she'd go off the radar and become very difficult to locate. You know, I listened to the other episodes of your show, and it's too bad her ex-husband never employed my services—he might've gotten some peace of mind.

CAMERON FRANK: How so?

JOHN ARNO: The times I went looking for her, I found nothing suspicious in her activities. Mostly it was international corporate gigs. Probably she wanted it private the way celebrities used to go to foreign countries to quietly shoot commercials while keeping their credibility with their domestic fan base. A few of the trips were to national parks, wildlife preserves. She liked to go hiking and camping on her own.

CAMERON FRANK: Wait, what? How come we never saw any of that in the tabloids?

JOHN ARNO: A couple of reasons. First, unless she's out in the forest smoking crack or canoodling with some new lover, it's not gonna be worth anybody's time to schlep to the middle of nowhere for photos of her and some trees. Second . . . [*clears throat*] Uh, Ms. Volk actually busted me spying on her one time.

CAMERON FRANK: I imagine that's a rare occurrence.

JOHN ARNO: You got that right. It happened in Peru, on the Inca trail to Machu Picchu. It was just her and her porter, and me and my porter got a little too close. She didn't believe I was a tourist because she recognized me from watching her other times. I was embarrassed . . . but also impressed because it's rare for people to be as aware of their surroundings as she was.

CAMERON FRANK: So what happened next?

JOHN ARNO: She offered to pay me double for keeping her whereabouts private. I made her a counteroffer: pay me double *that*, and I'll teach you how to evade creeps like me.

CAMERON FRANK: I'm guessing she took you up on the offer?

JOHN ARNO: If she did, would we be having this conversation right now? Wouldn't I be violating the terms of my agreement with Ms. Volk?

CAMERON FRANK: But if she didn't, there would've been some media coverage of her sneaky camping trips at some point. You're more of an expert on tabloid practices than I am, but I call bullshit on paparazzi not being willing to "schlep to the middle of nowhere." Considering the effort they make with helicopters and telephoto lenses to get celebs on yachts, private beaches, you name it—they would've made the effort to follow Violet wherever she went, especially if it was somewhere as unexpected as a wildlife preserve.

JOHN ARNO: You can believe what you want, but I can neither confirm nor deny.

CAMERON FRANK: Okay, then how about this. Were you involved in the search for Violet Volk?

JOHN ARNO: In a manner of speaking.

CAMERON FRANK: Was this in an official capacity, like working with the feds, or helping the family on a separate investigation, or . . .

JOHN ARNO: Or what? Looking for her like it's a hobby of mine? Like in my spare time I enjoy golf, crosswords, and looking for Jimmy Hoffa and Violet Volk? Some TV show hired me years ago. They were covering cases where people had faked their deaths. Wanted me to take them through the logistics of how Violet could've done it. There were some problems with the production and the whole thing was shut down before we finished filming. Never even aired.

CAMERON FRANK: What information did you present on this show?

JOHN ARNO: I was able to map out a feasible way she could've escaped the Witkin Theater without being spotted. When that place was a private estate, it was built with multiple secret passages and staircases, presumably for the servants to move around without causing disruption to the Worthington family. Some of these passages are still used today by the theater staff, and I found two others, both near the backstage area, which had been sealed and unused prior to the night of Volk's final performance. Unfortunately, it was never determined whether these passages were unsealed by investigators, panicked staff searching for Violet, or somebody else, but they provided direct access to the subbasement. This subbasement was connected to the Finchley Mines tunnel network, which offered any number of exit points from Willow Glen and several neighboring towns.

CAMERON FRANK: Hypothetically, what would happen next? She has a getaway car near one of these exit points?

JOHN ARNO: Most likely. If she's smart, she takes a nonlinear journey to where she wants to go and uses public transportation to get lost in the crowds at airports, train stations, bus terminals.

CAMERON FRANK: And how does this happen without her being recognized? Especially in the days that follow, when everyone is looking for her?

JOHN ARNO: Without her crazy makeup and outfits, she was pretty nondescript. A celebrity like, I don't know, Angelina Jolie or Sarah Jessica Parker would have more trouble going unrecognized because they have such distinct facial features, but Violet was ordinary-looking. She would've had no problem being incognito.

CAMERON FRANK: What about the other logistics involved in something like this? It's hard to believe anybody could voluntarily vanish in this day and age, with all the technology we have: cameras, GPS tracking, facial recognition software. It might not have been as prevalent ten years ago, but I can't imagine it would've been easy to go off the radar back then, either.

JOHN ARNO: Is it tough to disappear in this day and age? Absolutely. Participating in modern society demands you sacrifice your privacy for the sake of ego and convenience. Not to mention, the government finds more and more ways to keep tabs on you every day. At this point, you hand over those liberties willingly. Whether it's online banking and shopping, navigation systems in your car, location tracking on your phone and fitness devices, social media sites, the more you use these tools, the more visible you make yourself and your personal information. When a person decides to abandon these conveniences and start a new life, there are a lot of connections to sever. It's a process that can take months if you want to ensure you won't be found again. But it *is* possible, even today.

CAMERON FRANK: Is it legal?

JOHN ARNO: There's no law against dropping out, cutting yourself off from everyone you know, and moving somewhere new to start over. It's well within your rights to engineer a more discreet life for yourself. Just as long as you aren't evading legal prosecution or breaking any laws in securing this new life for yourself, like committing identity fraud.

CAMERON FRANK: Don't you pretty much need a new identity to successfully disappear and start a new life?

JOHN ARNO: That is illegal, and I don't condone or assist people in breaking the law. Sure, aliases are helpful, but there are ways around that. There are gray areas you can play with when muddying your trail, like going through all the accounts that have your personal details and "accidentally" updating your contact info with incorrect information, maybe misspelling your name or changing around the numbers on your address. That's one part of a much more involved process.

CAMERON FRANK: Going back to what you said about not helping unsavory types . . . Couldn't you argue Violet fell into that category because she was evading lawsuits and investigations into her finances?

JOHN ARNO: Who said I ever helped her?

Besides, if that was her motivation, her best bet would've been to fake her own death definitively, not vanish in such an open-ended way that would keep people looking for her. Stage a kayaking accident, something along those lines. You do that in a place like the Philippines and pay the right people, you can even get a body and a death certificate, which makes it easier to get a life insurance payout.

If Ms. Volk was looking to avoid legal repercussions, this would be a better way to disappear, after making sure all her money was stashed away in offshore accounts. Instead, for all the rumors of her undeclared income and cash hoarding, she left enough in her estate to pay off outstanding debts and settle lawsuits, with plenty left over to give to charitable organizations, who were also the beneficiaries of her life insurance settlement. If the money had gone to friends or loved ones, I might be suspicious she was in on a fraud scheme.

No matter which way I look at this case, I have trouble classifying it as a pseudocide, even though Volk was eventually declared dead. The only conclusion I can reach is she wanted to start a new life.

CAMERON FRANK: Also, statistically, pseudocide is committed by men far more often than women, right?

JOHN ARNO: That's a tricky stat, because the only data you can use is based on people who've been caught. There may also be cases that go unreported. Using the data available to us, yes, men are more likely to fake their own death. It's possible women don't do it as much because they're more rooted to their families and communities and feel a stronger sense of responsibility, particularly if they're mothers. It's also possible women just don't get caught as often. Could be they're better at disappearing.

CAMERON FRANK: And if Violet chose to willingly disappear, do you think she'd be good at it?

JOHN ARNO: No. [*dry laugh*] She would be the goddamn best.

Sasha

February 21, 2018

I can't get comfortable. My hips and shoulders try to dig into the mattress, but there's zero cushioning and—

I wake up but keep my eyes closed.

Please please please let me be on my kitchen floor or my bathroom floor or the floor of any room of my house.

I open my eyes.

Shit.

As I adjust to the darkness, I can't bring myself to my feet, not yet.

This isn't any room of my house. In fact, my entire house could fit into this room. A chandelier the size of a school bus is suspended from the multistoried ceiling of this room, and the red emergency EXIT signs in the back look like they're a mile away.

Oh Jesus, so now I'm *inside* the Witkin Theater? I get to my feet.

Just like last time, I'm in nothing but pajamas, but at least this time I'm not outside in the cold. So that makes it . . . better?

On either side of me are roped-off curtains. Oh, cool, center stage. A few more feet and I would've fallen into the orchestra pit. Above me, a lighting rig. Farther out, I can make out balconies with elaborate gold leaf trim.

No, this is worse than when I woke up outside. Definitely, definitely worse. I can think of three reasons why off the top of my head.

One: The trespassing factor.

Two: The embarrassment factor if someone finds me.

Three: Sleepwalking once beyond the confines of my home is a fluke. Twice means it's becoming a pattern.

"That's so inconvenience stores," Violet would say, referencing a *Far Side* cartoon we both loved. In it, a retailer kept his merchandise stocked on shelves along a high ceiling, way out of reach. When Quinn was three, we visited Violet in Las Vegas and saw her show at the Kintana. Afterward, we went backstage, and it made me smile to see the cartoon taped to her dressing room mirror.

Pounding footsteps in the distance snap me back to the Witkin.

"Is somebody in here?" A flashlight beam zigzags down the center aisle.

Crap. I need to get out of here.

I turn around and make my way upstage as quickly and quietly as possible. In my haste, my body collides with a heavy curtain. I claw at it, trying to find an opening. It's like swimming through fabric and I get more and more tangled up in it until I break free only to run headfirst into another curtain and lose my balance. I fall onto the stage, landing with a thud.

From the direction of the orchestra pit, a male voice shouts, "Come out before I call the police!"

Oh hell no. I crawl around in search of an exit and my fingers brush against some kind of braiding. It's the hem of the curtain. Great, I'll just follow this into one of the stage wings—only I'm hyperventilating because tight, enclosed spaces are not my favorite, and I'm cocooned in heavy curtain right now and it brings back terrible memories of being trapped in a mining tunnel as a kid, memories I don't care to revisit now or ever. I clutch the braided hem and do my damnedest to slow my breathing. It's not going well.

Fortunately, the shouting man sounds farther and farther away.

Unfortunately, because everything around me is already dark, I don't realize I'm blacking out until a split second before I hit the floor.

It's light out when I open my eyes. How did I get back here, back in my own bed?

Did I sleepwalk offstage, out of the theater, and back home?

That doesn't seem plausible. Instead, it could be I'm remembering a dream for the first time in my life.

Except, when I sit up and swing my legs out of bed, a piece of gold braiding falls to the floor.

Behind me, Gabriel asks, "Where did you go last night?"

I sweep the braiding under the bed with my foot and turn around to find my husband watching me with solemn professional detachment. It reminds me of the time a police officer came by the salon to ask about a nearby break-in. I had no connection to the incident and no helpful info to offer, but I felt an undercurrent of fear and guilt the entire time he questioned me. As if he were going to reveal I perpetrated a crime I had no knowledge of.

That's how I feel now as I urge myself to stay calm and neutral, as I mentally draft an appropriate response. Meanwhile, Gabriel has more to say.

"It used to be, I'd wake up in the middle of the night, and if you weren't in bed, I could search the other rooms of the house and find you crashed out on a sofa or armchair, once in a while at the kitchen table. But last night, when I saw you weren't in bed, I couldn't find you anywhere in the house." He rubs a spot in the center of his forehead where he gets stress headaches. "I checked the backyard, but you weren't out there, and you weren't wandering the front yard trying to get back into the house either—yeah, Quinn told me about that. You shouldn't have asked her not to."

Annoyance at Quinn for not keeping my secret is quickly superseded by shame at asking her to keep it in the first place. I open my mouth to speak, still unsure of what to say, but Gabriel puts up a finger. He's not done yet.

"If you left the house, it would've made sense for you to take your car keys or wallet or phone, but those were all here. I didn't know what I should do. Wake up Quinn to see if she knew where you'd gone? Search the neighborhood? Call the police? I did another sweep of the house, this time checking the basement and closets. You weren't there. So I went back upstairs, intending to get dressed and drive around until I found you, or go to the police if I didn't. Wanna guess what happened next?"

I shake my head, a nameless turmoil scrambling my thoughts.

"I found you." A lifeless laugh as he rakes his fingers through his hair. "In bed, like you'd never left. Fetal position, blankets thrown off you, dead asleep."

"Oh." My surprise ushers in no relief.

"I know, right?" he says, as if I've just delivered an insight-filled soliloquy. "How could I not have seen you coming back to bed? Our house isn't that big and the floors creak like a mofo, so it shouldn't be possible. And yet . . ."

And yet.

"I don't know what happened," I say. "I must've been sleepwalking. And the other week, too, when Quinn found me outside."

"There's more to it. More you're not telling me." His gaze intensifies, and I have to peer closely to find the flecks of amber hiding in his dark eyes. "Obviously tomorrow's vigil is fucking you up, but I wish you'd . . . I don't know . . ."

"Tell you the nitty-gritty of exactly *how* it's fucking me up?"

"Kinda, yeah."

I can't keep withholding, but I can't tell him the full story, either. "It's all these pictures of pseudo-Violet everywhere. I saw one the other day . . . and I could've sworn it was really her." Unsure if I should be impressed or repulsed by my double-talk, I aim for more sincerity. "But it's more than that. I'm worried about Quinn speaking at the vigil, but it's more than that, too. For the last few years, it seemed like we were finally settling into a rhythm. Sure, the weeks around the vigil would suck, but then we got to carry on in our post-Violet lives. Now, with the whole world obsessed with my sister again, everything seems so much more chaotic."

"Do you think it might be time to—"

"Get professional help? Already on it. I recently started seeing a counselor. From the looks of it, she and I will have plenty more to talk about in our next session."

Most of the storm has cleared from his face, but a few dark clouds keep his eyebrows knitted together. "I'm not a fan of you hiding things from me. It's one thing for us to choose to protect our daughter from certain unpleasant realities, but I'm your husband. I thought we had that whole trust-and-open-communication thing going that's supposed to keep marriages healthy."

"We did. We do." Tears spring to my eyes and I blink hard, furious with myself. "I thought I could handle this on my own, without burdening you."

"Well, knock it off." Gabriel grabs the nearest pillow and swats me with it. "I've burdened you plenty with my crap over the years." He counts off on his fingers. "Alcoholic dad, absent mom who only reappears when she needs money, celebrity sister who went missing—oh wait, that one's yours."

We exchange crooked smiles.

"Nice try comparing baggage," I say, "but I know mine still outweighs yours."

"Sweetheart." He gives me a tender look, leans in, and touches the side of my face. "There's no question you have more baggage. It's not even a contest. I was just trying to make you feel better 'cause I'm a fucking nice guy."

When I roll my eyes and make to get up, he pulls me back to him, all irony gone from his face. "I don't really know what to do here, Sasha. I always feel like I'm either getting too involved or not involved enough when it comes to the sister drama. I've been hanging back lately, but only because I overstepped my boundaries before."

"You were just trying to keep us happy. Both of us, but especially me. Things would've been way worse without your interventions. At least I have some good memories of her, thanks to you." Though some of the best ones are tainted, knowing how much Gabriel had to strongarm my sister behind the scenes.

"What about all the money I had us sink into looking for her?" A wince puckers his mouth. "That last private investigator almost tapped us out completely."

He's not wrong. Printing flyers, renting billboards, and especially hiring investigators—it all adds up. We're still paying off the second mortgage and extra line of credit we took out. "You know what?" I say. "Despite all that, I can rest easy knowing we did everything to try to find her." Even if she didn't want to be found.

"What can I do to help you? There has to be something."

Don't question my sanity. Don't lock me up. Don't give up on me.

"This. You're already doing it. The rest is up to me to sort out. Whatever this insanity is, I'm sure it's temporary." My voice is so assured and emphatic. If only I could believe it myself.

May 8, 2001

Dear Violet,

I wish you didn't have to leave so soon. Even though you only planned to be here a week, part of me hoped you'd stay in Willow Glen longer while you figured things out. With everything you're going through—the divorce, the Vegas bullshit—you should be closer to the people who'll support you the most, and if Gabriel and I aren't at the top of that list, I don't know who is. Plus, can't you write a book pretty much anywhere? But I won't be pushy. If LA is where you need to be right now, do your thing on the west coast, and we'll keep cheering you on back east.

By the way, Quinn cannot stop talking about you. She's obsessed with the philodendron you got her (I've never seen a kid prefer plants over toys—how weird-but-cool is that?) and you have no idea how much you dazzled her with your sleight-of-hand. The other night, we were watching *Sabrina, the Teenage Witch* (she's a little young for it, but it's her favorite show), and she asked, "Is Aunt Violet a witch, too?" I told her you weren't a witch but a magician. Her first-grade teacher said she's been bragging "my aunt Violet is magic" to the class ever since. Quinn keeps asking when you'll come over again, and I tell her I don't know, but I hope it'll be soon, and that you're always welcome here.

I mean it, sis. You always have a home here. And if you need me to come to you, I'll be on the first flight over.

222,

Sasha

May 10, 2001

Violet,

I appreciate you keeping your word and not mentioning anything about that night at the bar to Sasha. You have no idea how happy she was to spend time with you and watch you bonding with Quinn. They're dying to visit you in LA this summer.

I won't be coming with them. It's better if you and I have some distance for a while.

I don't want to kick you when you're down, but what happened last week was unacceptable. I can see how you might be in a place where you're reassessing your life. If you actually decide to have children and apply the same tenacity to motherhood that you have to magic, I'm sure you'll be a great parent.

That said, I never want to hear a proposition like that from you again. Please don't insult me by continuing to insist it was a joke, you were drunk, etc., and let's not pretend this was about getting a sperm donor. I saw how you looked at me when you asked. I've seen how you've been looking at me all these years. And I saw what the guy you married looked like.

I'm not gonna apologize for feeling a certain way about Sasha instead of you, but I am sorry for any pain it's caused you. Maybe trying to maintain a friendship between us wasn't the best idea. I tried to be sympathetic, and I let a lot of things go, but I'm gonna need some time for this one.

You've seen how we live: our house is comfortable, but there's always something in need of repair. Same with our cars—one of them is always in the shop. You helped with your mother's funeral costs, but you have no clue how much we spent on her hospital bills. And sure, you can be very generous with gifts, but it's hard to enjoy something like a five-hundred-dollar pair of sunglasses knowing that money could've been put toward a new set of tires or replacing our broken hood dryer at the salon. We'd never come out and ask you for anything, but you can't be so oblivious to our situation.

Aside from the obvious, that's why your little "joke" bothered me so much. You offered two million dollars for my sperm like you were offering to buy me a beer. Like it was nothing for you to part with that much money.

You crossed a line, and I don't know what this means for our friendship. Maybe it's better if we don't have one for a while.

—Gabriel

Strange Exits

⌒

Episode 6: "The Vigil"

CAMERON FRANK [STUDIO]: It's February twenty-second, 2018. As the sun begins to set in Willow Glen, thousands have gathered in front of the Cordova Park bandshell, a mile from the theater where Violet Volk was last seen. The weather has been unseasonably warm for late February, with clear skies and temperatures in the high fifties. While it's a relief that no precipitation will disrupt the event, one can't help but hope the impending darkness will bring a chill to the air. Just enough to honor the somber tone of these proceedings.

They've been coming every year on February twenty-second— the date of her final performance—for the last ten years. The candlelight vigil is organized by members of the Willow Glen community, who spread the word locally, and the Wolf Pack, who spread it everywhere else. A month beforehand, seemingly overnight, Willow Glen is papered over with flyers announcing the event, followed by posts on social media. Attendees are encouraged to bring their own candles.

This year, people have come from all over the world to honor Violet on the ten-year anniversary of her disappearance. Hotels in the area have been booked for months, and locals have listed their spare bedrooms on Airbnb to accommodate the influx of visitors.

The program varies from year to year, though there's usually at least one well-known name on the roster. Two years ago, Riley Price performed an acoustic set. Last year, Jackson Cleo gave a touching speech. This year's lineup includes half a dozen participants, including a special tribute by Viva Vox and a highly anticipated last-minute addition, Quinn Dwyer, Violet's niece. It will be the first time anyone from the Dwyer family has formally addressed the crowd, apart from the quick thanks Sasha offers the attendees.

I've arrived at the vigil two hours early and it's nuts how many people are already here. You'd think U2 was giving a free concert in Cordova Park tonight.

[MALE VOICE]: Check one, two. Check one, two. [*electronic screeches*] [*faint howling*]

CAMERON FRANK [STUDIO]: That howling over the sound check is from self-identifying members of the Wolf Pack announcing themselves to each other. You can also spot them by their silver pins bearing Volk's double-*V* logo. While paraphernalia bearing the logo is ubiquitous among this crowd, the superfans wear two pins side by side, so that the *V*s form a *W*.

One thing I've always appreciated about Volk is her diverse audience; to this day, it transcends age, race, gender, and nationality. In other words, there's really no such thing as a "typical" Violet Volk fan.

The reason I'm here early is to get sound bites from some of the attendees, and I certainly have my pick.

[MALE VOICE 2]: Do I have to give my name? No? Okay, then yeah, I got something to say about Violet. I wouldn't be alive today if it wasn't for her. Bro, I'm not even kidding you. I had a loaded gun in my hand, ready to put into my mouth. I accidentally sat on the remote and the TV came on. All of a sudden, there's an angel on-screen. When you're about to blow your brains out and an angel appears right in front of you, even if she's just a girl wearing wings, that's deep. I put down the gun and watched the rest of her show. The next day, I got her book. A week after that, I got rid of the gun.

[FEMALE VOICE 1]: My brother was really into the escape stuff she did, only he wasn't so good at it. He dislocated his shoulder like four times trying to get out of a straitjacket. The first time he tried her routine with the fishing nets in our swimming pool, he almost drowned—the dumbass didn't realize you have to train yourself to hold your breath underwater for . . . well, way longer than he could. When he got up to two minutes holding his breath, he tried it again, but the net got caught in a drain. This time he did drown. Yeah, that sucked. He was so obsessed with Violet, sometimes I kinda think my brother would still be alive today if it weren't for her. Then again, he was also high at the time, so a lot of bad choices factored into his death . . . No, I still think she's awesome. I can't help it. Does that make me a terrible person?

[MALE VOICE 3]: Are we still questioning whether VV had supernatural powers? Because duh! Ever hear the phrase "hiding in plain sight"? Being a stage magician is, like, the most brilliant way to hide your real magic powers! She even tried to teach the rest of us how to do it, writing not one but two books and spending years touring the planet for them! Somebody once said, If humans could fly, they'd consider it exercise and never do it.' Same scenario here. Violet wanted everyone to fly, and everyone chose to Netflix and chill instead. Not me, though. I attended dozens of her motivational seminars, and I know both of her books by heart. I've been practicing every day, and I'm gonna meet her on that higher dimension . . . Yeah, of course that's where she is. Why would she hang around on this lower dimension with us losers? Nobody wanted to fly with her, so she flew away alone. Wait for me, Violet—I'll be there soon!

[FEMALE VOICE 2]: I saw her just last week. We were both at the same hot spring, and in my head, I was all, "Hey, isn't that the magician lady from the nineties?" I didn't, like, talk to her, because I thought it would be rude to bother someone who went to the trouble of fak-ing their own death—or disappearance, or whatever. My momma raised me better than that . . . Oh yeah, I don't mind saying where, this was in Iceland . . . Believe me or don't believe me, but I know the woman I saw was Violet Volk . . . How sure am I? At least thirty-seven percent.

CAMERON FRANK: I might have to put together an entire mini-sode of these sound bites. Oh, here comes Sasha Dwyer with her husband and daughter.

SASHA DWYER: Thank you to everyone who has come out to pay their respects to Violet. Our family appreciates the ongoing support.

CAMERON FRANK: And there she goes. I wish I could describe her facial expression, but she's wearing huge sunglasses, as she typically does at these gatherings. Is she hiding tears? Anger? Indifference?

I've been to every one of these vigils, and I'm always drawn to Sasha, wondering what she's thinking and feeling as everyone pays tribute to her sister. Is it a comfort to know Violet's memory and positive influence live on, or does it open old wounds?

It's one thing for us to lose a beloved performer under mysterious circumstances. It's another to lose your sister that way. To be in a perpetual state of limbo, unable to know what emotions to channel into the void. Should Sasha be mourning a death and fighting for her sister's abductor and killer to be brought to justice? Or should she be recovering from the cruelest trick of all—pseudocide—and coming to terms with Violet faking her own death? Or could there be an even more outrageous alternative?

I can't imagine what it must be like to live with that kind of ambiguity. Do you double down on looking for answers or make peace with the question marks? Do you create your own scenario to offer a kind of false closure? If so, is Violet alive in that scenario or has she passed on? Or does she exist in a state where she could simultaneously be considered both alive and dead, a Schrödinger's sister of sorts?

These are only some of the things I wish I could ask Sasha.

[FEMALE VOICE 3]: Is that a bee? Why the hell is there a bee buzzing around in February?

CAMERON FRANK [STUDIO]: A cluster of local news vans dot the edge of the park and I walk by a petite blond anchor being filmed in front of the crowd, dodging and waving around her free hand.

[FEMALE VOICE 3]: Sorry, could we take that again? I need to get away from this bee, I'm deathly aller—fuck! I need my EpiPen!

CAMERON FRANK [STUDIO]: I don't know if it's just me, but something has felt off-balance ever since I got here, and seeing this anchor in distress only heightens my uneasiness.

Rattled, I make my way through the crowd, searching for a spot where I'll be able to grab a decent recording of the event.

But then things get truly crazy.

[FEMALE VOICE 4]: Hey, bitch, you think dripping candle wax on someone's hair is funny? How about I set your head on fire and see if you find that funny?

CAMERON FRANK [STUDIO]: Just before the first speaker goes on, a shoving match breaks out between two twenty-something women—one tall and gangly, the other short and full-figured.

The short one lunges for the tall one just as a pair of security guards hooks each woman under their arms. Their legs flail as they're dragged apart.

Sasha happens to be a few feet away from the fighting women, and I check her for signs of dismay, but instead I swear I see a smirk flash across her face.

The first speaker is national poet laureate Obi Akinde, and the microphone screeches when he greets us. This is followed by an electrical pop and the mic cutting out entirely. It takes ten minutes for the sound guys to get a mic working again, but there's a background hiss they can't resolve, so I'll spare you the audio. Needless to say, it makes for a distracting reading. Though not as distracting as what happens next.

A middle-aged woman gets up onstage, prompting looks of confusion between the mayor, tonight's host, and a stagehand with a headset and clipboard. The woman has sandy curly hair piled on top of her head, round wire-rimmed glasses with blue lenses, and layers of skirts pinned up at various lengths. The total effect is a cross between a bohemian cancan dancer and something Helena Bonham-Carter would wear on the red carpet.

Eyes darting around like she knows her time is limited, the woman grabs the microphone and speaks in a low, breathless voice.

[FEMALE VOICE 4]: My name is Antoinette Stranger, and I believe I've had contact with Violet Volk.

CAMERON FRANK [STUDIO]: As a security guard marches across the stage, Antoinette quickens her words.

ANTOINETTE STRANGER: Sasha, I know you've got no reason to believe me, and I haven't spoken to her face-to-face or on the phone or via any other conventional methods, but we have communicated. I believe she's well and you may see her again, Sasha. I can show you how you can contact her. Your sister wants to hear from you. She told me to tell you, pay attention to the twos. Follow the twos.

CAMERON FRANK [STUDIO]: The host takes the mic from her hand as the security guard steers her offstage.

ANTOINETTE STRANGER: I'm going, I'm going.

CAMERON FRANK [STUDIO]: Now here is my dilemma. Do I stay to record the rest of the vigil or do I follow Antoinette and see if she'll grant me an interview?

But then Quinn Dwyer's name is called. For me, she's the main event.

QUINN DWYER: Um, hi, everybody.

[SOUNDS OF ROARING APPLAUSE]

CAMERON FRANK [STUDIO]: As she waits for the applause to die down, Quinn hunches over the mic, gripping it with both hands, hiding her face. She remains in that position and says nothing, even when the crowd goes quiet.

The extended silence lasts over a full minute, punctuated by the faint smack of Quinn's chewing gum and occasional hoots from the audience encouraging her to speak. She finally does.

QUINN DWYER: [*whispers*] I'm sorry. I thought I . . . but I . . . sorry.

CAMERON FRANK [STUDIO]: Her voice breaks and she rushes off the stage.

A disappointed murmur buzzes through the audience, and I look over to where Sasha was standing earlier. She's gone. Curious as I am to know what happened, it would be in poor taste to approach the Dwyer family right now.

Instead, I turn around, search the crowd, and catch sight of Antoinette near a gazebo, being escorted out of the park by a security guard.

Maybe Antoinette is the actual main event here. She may be a kook, but I've spent much of my podcasting career giving kooks a voice and it's taught me some things. Just because someone says something crazy doesn't mean it's not true, at least to them. There's so much in this world that's unexplained, sometimes I wonder if certain explanations exist but don't gain mass acceptance because they're outlandish. What if we have more solutions at our fingertips than we realize? What if Antoinette has answers about Violet that nobody else does?

The only way I'll find out for sure is if I talk to her.

I reach Antoinette at the edge of a gravel path that leads to the parking lot. The guard escorting her out still has a hand clamped around her arm and quickens his pace. She winces, taking hurried steps to keep up with him.

ANTOINETTE STRANGER: Could you slow down just a touch, sir? Gravel is tricky to navigate in heels. Granted, these boots were a bad choice, but your legs are twice as long as mine. Good gravy, was your mother a praying mantis?

GUARD: You're lucky you're not being arrested.

ANTOINETTE STRANGER: Aren't you going to be late for your security shift at Walmart?

CAMERON FRANK [STUDIO]: Before she can get herself into any more trouble, I take a chance and step in.

I call out Antoinette's name and tell her I've been looking everywhere for her.

They both turn to me, doubt clouding their faces. They speak at the same time.

GUARD: You know this woman?

ANTOINETTE STRANGER: Who the hell are you?

CAMERON FRANK: It's your son-in-law, Cameron. Don't you recognize me? Linda and I have been really worried about you.

CAMERON FRANK [STUDIO]: Antoinette is quick to catch on to what I'm doing and wrenches her arm free. The wind whips pieces of her curly hair, making her look like a cinematic witch about to cast a spell.

ANTOINETTE STRANGER: Oh, Cameron, I think I'm having one of my episodes. Could you be a kind dear and take me home?

CAMERON [STUDIO]: She looks around like she's coming out of a bad dream and links her arm through mine. I lead her away from the guard, who remains dubious but doesn't move to follow us.

ANTOINETTE STRANGER: So what's this little rescue operation all about? I would've been just fine, you know—it's not like he was taking me to a gulag.

CAMERON FRANK: Could we find someplace quiet to talk? I was hoping I could ask you some questions about Violet Volk.

CAMERON FRANK [STUDIO]: I introduce myself and explain about my podcast and my personal interest in missing persons cases and general high strangeness.

CAMERON FRANK: My hope is for *Strange Exits* to also serve as a forum for various ideas to be discussed with an open mind, since some disappearances defy rational explanation.

ANTOINETTE STRANGER: Like all those people in national parks being kidnapped by Bigfoot?

CAMERON FRANK: There have certainly been unusual cases of people vanishing in parks. I've covered the Missing 411 phenomena in the last podcast I hosted, *Theory X*. Cryptozoology was featured in several episodes, too.

ANTOINETTE STRANGER: And do you have a cat named Scully?

CAMERON FRANK: Why, because *Theory X* is so obviously an *X-Files* reference? You got me there, but actually, I'm more into *Fringe*, so my cat's name is Olivia.

CAMERON FRANK [STUDIO]: At this, Antoinette breaks out into a slow smile and hands me her business card.

ANTOINETTE STRANGER: Why don't you give me a call next week. Oh, and I also prefer *Fringe*. Don't get me wrong, I respect its predecessor . . . but parallel worlds are so much more *fun* than aliens.

CAMERON FRANK [STUDIO]: With a jaunty wave, she walks off.

It's getting dark out at this point. I return to Cordova Park in time for Viva Vox's performance, and then we all light our candles.

Whatever disturbed energy or strange anticipation there was hanging over us earlier, it's gone. The mood now is somber, melancholy, deflated.

[MALE VOICE 4]: At this time, we will observe a ten-minute moment of silence.

CAMERON FRANK [STUDIO]: Every year, a minute is added to represent each year Violet has been missing. Usually, the crowd thins during the final few minutes, but this time, nearly everyone remains quietly standing in place for the duration, holding their candles. The only noise is the juddering blade slap of news helicopters flying overhead.

As we observe the moment of silence, I look around me. Some people have their eyes closed. A few are crying. Many, like me, are gazing around, perhaps searching for that elusive familiar face, hoping it finally emerges from the darkness. Knowing deep down it will not.

The footage broadcast later is stunning, a sea of illuminated faces growing smaller as the camera pans out, until all that remains is an expanse of golden lights, each dot representing a life touched by Violet Volk.

Sasha

February 22, 2018

The last time I saw my daughter in distress onstage, she was thousands of miles away, and I was unable to come to her immediate rescue. The emerging horror and ensuing helplessness were unbearable.

This time, Quinn's distress is unbearable not because I'm so far away from it, but because I'm so close to it, mere feet from the bandshell where she stutters into the microphone, her knuckles white from gripping it so tightly. When she goes silent and bows her head, I'm ready to launch myself forward and get her off that stage, but Gabriel's hand at the small of my back stops me.

"Give her a minute," he says in a low voice.

"Seriously?" I hiss back.

"Don't think this isn't killing me. But, if we try to help her too soon, she'll take it the wrong way."

Sally, who's standing in front of us for a better vantage point, turns around and adds, "He's right. You need to wait in case she gets it together."

So we wait, each second a glacial torture, but Quinn does not get it together. When she finally flees the stage, the three of us follow her to a thicket of trees behind the bandshell. I reach her first, her body trembling as she presses her forehead to the trunk of a red oak.

"Devil, you played with her, now give her back," she whispers, and goes mute as Gabriel and Sally rush over.

We all form a protective barrier around her, murmuring platitudes.

"Do you want to go home?" I ask.

"No, but I do want to get out of here," she says, wiping tears from her eyes.

This is the first time she's wanted to leave the vigil early. Up until a few minutes ago, it was the first time I wanted to stay for all of it.

"Are you absolutely sure?"

Even though the question comes from Gabriel, she directs her reply at me. "I'm positive. This is over. Whatever I thought might . . . yeah, I'm sure."

For weeks, a low-grade hope had been humming through me. In that moment, it becomes muted. She's right. This is over. Nothing miraculous will be happening here today.

Sally gives Quinn a sympathetic arm squeeze. "If you want to go home, I totally understand, but there's gonna be nobody at the diner right now, and you should never underestimate the healing power of blueberry pancakes."

A pause while Quinn considers and then, "I could go for some pancakes."

The four of us say little on the short walk to the diner. Once inside, we take a curved corner booth farthest from the door, where we're least visible.

"I didn't even last a minute up there. I'm such an embarrassment." Quinn slumps over the Formica table, her groans muffled as she buries her head in her arms.

"You are not." I reach over and stroke her hair with one hand, using the other to politely shoo away the approaching waitress. "The fact you even tried to put yourself out there like that is a big deal." The fact that she fled was my sister's fault. If it weren't for Violet, Quinn wouldn't have been so shell-shocked facing an audience. Not that she remembers much of what happened before, outside of what the video cameras captured. Only the aftermath, of being yanked away from the glamorous clutches of her precious Aunt Violet, which was only meant to punish one of them yet somehow ended up punishing all of us.

She grunts and remains facedown.

Sally, who's sitting next to Quinn, leans over her. "Listen to me,

Queenie," she says, using the nickname she coined that my daughter pretends to hate but secretly loves. "You have to stop underestimating yourself. What you did just now was put on a parachute, get in an airplane, and fly miles above the ground. It's okay that you didn't jump. Lots of people would've never even strapped on the chute or gotten on the plane. It doesn't only take guts to do the brave thing. It also takes guts to *try* to do the brave thing."

At that, Quinn raises her head, the desolation in her face softening. "You think so?"

I try not to take it personally that my friend is better at reassuring my own daughter than I am.

We all agree emphatically, just as the waitress returns.

Once our orders are in, Sally gets to her feet. "Oh, I almost forgot." Winking, she rummages around in the pockets of her coat hanging beside the booth. Tonight's outerwear, a black pleather trench, is more subdued than her usual rainbow attire.

"What did you forget, to return Catwoman's coat?" Gabriel says. "She might get chilly during her heists without it."

"Gabriel Sebastian Dwyer, you are a riot." In addition to coining nicknames, Sally is fond of doling out fake middle names. "Here it is." She pulls out a small round tin and hands it to Quinn. "I didn't get a chance to label it, but it's the juniper/yuzu balm you like so much."

Perking up, she thanks Sally and immediately applies the balm to her wrists. By the time our food arrives, Quinn is back to normal, and throughout the meal, she does most of the talking: about local gossip she picked up tonight, how odd she found this year's proceedings, and her thoughts on how to make the salon more environmentally friendly.

"We've been recycling for years," I point out, avoiding Gabriel's less-than-surreptitious glances at my untouched salad. "And we even made the switch to bamboo toilet paper like you suggested, at home and at the salon."

"Which is great, but there's even more you can be doing."

Just what every parent loves to hear.

"Natural hair dyes *are* worth looking into, and you could recycle more than paper and plastic."

Et tu, Sally? She holds back a laugh at my murderous glare.

"That's right. There's a company where you can send foils, gloves, dye, and even hair scraps to recycle," Quinn preaches in between bites of her grilled cheese and tomato. "Plus, how awesome would it be to have a Certified Sustainable Salon?"

"So awesome I can hardly stand it." I spear a chunk of grilled chicken, wave my fork at my husband, and make a big show of chewing the meat.

Gabriel sighs and turns back to his burger. "I actually think Quinn's on to something."

"Because it would be a smart marketing move, too, right? See? Dad knows what's up."

When did our little girl develop business savvy?

"It would be good for the salon, and it would be nice to leave you with a planet that's a little less of a trainwreck. Even if our lineage must end with you," says Gabriel, a hint of wistfulness in his voice. "Though I'll never understand why you care so much about Earth's future if you have no plans to extend its population." He takes a light touch with the subject but welcomes any opportunity to sway Quinn in favor of having children one day.

"Slow down, breeder. You seriously gonna guilt trip her like that?" Sally's doll eyes go even wider.

It's not like we want Quinn to follow our route of early unplanned pregnancy—but she's been adamantly opposed to the idea of having kids since middle school. Hard not to wonder if it's a subconscious response to my life choices. I mean, sure, she's my greatest accomplishment and I do hope she changes her mind when she's older (but not *too* old). At the same time, Violet got hassled by our mother for not settling down early like I did, even as her magic career was taking off. I never want Quinn to feel diminished that way.

"Just because I don't want to procreate doesn't mean I shouldn't want to leave a positive mark on the world," Quinn scoffs. "Sally has no kids and she's all kinds of happy and fulfilled."

"A-fuckin'-men." Vehement nods from Sally.

My daughter can't resist another dig. "Plus, Aunt Violet didn't have kids and look how much she accomplished."

I swallow hard. Gabriel won't meet my eyes but links pinkies with me under the table. "Violet didn't have children, but that doesn't mean she never wanted them," I point out.

"Maybe for like five minutes when she was with Benjamin, but she obviously came to her senses," Quinn shoots back. "Why else would she dedicate a whole chapter in *You Are Magic* to railing against people who use kids as an excuse not to form their own identities?"

Ah, yes, that little gem. I was so proud of my sister when her first book came out. Then I read it and felt like I was being slapped in the face for two hundred pages. That chapter was particularly rough. The way Violet admonished people who claim to be selfless by sacrificing everything for their children, when they're actually cowards who selfishly divert their own dreams onto their children because it's easier than pursuing those dreams directly. Leave it to someone who's never raised a child to claim there's anything easy about it.

Besides, I didn't divert my dreams so much as adjust them. I had to forgo the hope of working in a hospital for the reality of my mother's salon, but I still get to apply my scientific curiosity to coloring hair, and I offer people a different kind of caregiving. I never pushed Quinn to live out my dreams. On a whim, I did get her a chemistry set when she was eight, but when she turned the plastic vials and beakers into miniature flower vases, Gabriel and I marveled at her evolving persona and bought her a child's gardening kit, letting her run with her own passions. So, screw you, Violet.

Gabriel gives my pinkie a squeeze and jumps into the fray. "Did Violet have strong opinions when she wrote that book? Sure. But opinions can change. Look at how much you hated the color brown when you were a little girl. Now you're all about the earth tones."

"I'm not a little girl anymore, and Aunt Violet wasn't one either when she wrote the book. Beliefs about procreation aren't the same as having a favorite color. So if you're waiting for me to wake up one day and decide I'm now *all about* having babies, that's not gonna happen."

"Nobody's pressuring you to procreate, Queenie," Sally says. "Your folks just can't help being biased about it because they had a stellar kid like you."

A reluctant cease-fire follows and our booth falls into uncomfortable silence.

I break it by sneezing into my salad.

From either side of me, my husband and daughter reach over and pull my ear, one upward, one down. "Both of you? Seriously?" I ask. "You do realize how ludicrous these superstitions are, right? I mean, there is no rational connection to whistling indoors and losing money. And no logical reason to tug on somebody's ear when they sneeze."

"Only if you're thinking of someone who died," Quinn says.

"Or death in general. Otherwise, it would make no sense," my husband adds with a wink.

"Gabe, you're not even Russian. Don't you have any crazy Filipino superstitions you can adopt instead?"

"Sorry, I happen to like your crazy Russian superstitions."

There's a wounded note in his voice and I'm flooded with guilt. Gabriel is sensitive about his adoptive parents shunning his native culture, despite the mother who raised him being half-Filipina herself. "No, *I'm* sorry. That was a shitty thing for me to say."

"How about we officially declare this dinner the worst and just get the check?" Quinn asks. "I'm meeting someone for coffee at eight and gotta get going."

I tilt my head. "Someone?"

"A friend from college who happens to be local. Don't make it weird."

"Nobody is making it weird. Go have fun with your friend." The cringe Sally gives me confirms it came out sounding even lamer than it did in my head.

Pushing her plate to the center of the table, Quinn scoots out of the booth. Hesitation crosses her face as she's about to leave. "Mom, can I ask you something?"

"Sure." The somber note in her voice tells me it's going to be about Violet.

"Are you sure you don't know who that woman is? The one who interrupted the vigil? Antoinette?" Her gaze begs honesty.

Thankfully, that's something I can give her. "I really don't know her, hon. I've never seen that woman before, and she seemed kind of . . . troubled to me. If we ever crossed paths before, I don't remember." It feels good to be able to speak freely with Quinn. "For all I know, she might be one of those so-called psychics who tried to reach out to me." After the first three were duds, I started ignoring the rest. "If I knew who she was, I would tell you." All right, let's not ruin it with a potential lie.

Her "hmph" is reluctantly convinced. How sad to be overcome with relief that my daughter believes me when I'm speaking the truth. When did the trust between us become so tenuous?

She's not done testing it, though. "And that thing she said about the twos? Do you have any idea what that means?"

Damn it. I can't get into it, not here, not now. All I can do is I scrunch up my face, mimic her bafflement, and say, "No clue."

Her nod is accompanied by an uncertain squint. I don't know what's worse, that she might not believe me or that she has every right not to.

"Anyway, I'll probably be an hour or two," she says. "In case you want to—do whatever naked stuff it is you do when I'm not around."

Cackles erupt out of Sally, and Gabriel says, "Quinn, this happens to be the woman I love. Don't make it weird."

Quinn breaks into a full grin, showing off the crooked front tooth she typically tries to hide. "Nice callback." With a playful salute, she heads out.

Once she's gone, Sally looks at us with admiration. "That is one resilient kid you have. If I bombed like that in front of a crap-ton of people, I'd still be curled up in a ball somewhere."

"I'm more surprised she wanted to leave early," Gabriel says.

"After all that, could you blame her?"

"She didn't leave early out of embarrassment," I interject. Their heads swivel in my direction. "The thing about Quinn and these vigils . . . I think part of her hopes she'll see Violet again at one of them. And with all the extra hoopla this year, and speculation whether it might lead up to Violet's grand return . . . I wouldn't be surprised if Quinn had even higher hopes this year . . ." It's tough not to project my own feelings here.

"All the more reason I would've thought Quinn would stay for all of it," says Gabriel.

"There was no point." Understanding softens Sally's furrowed brow. "If Violet was there, she would've never let Quinn go through that."

I swallow down the lump in my throat.

Sally's phone trills. "Damn, I thought this was next week. I have a date with a tattoo artist. I can reschedule."

"No need," I reassure her. "If Quinn's fine, I'm fine. You don't know anything about who she's seeing tonight, do you?"

"I do not," she says, her mouth quirked in reproach as she puts on her trench. "But I bet you could find out by—oh, I don't know, *asking* her? Dinner's on me, by the way."

Ignoring our protests, she blows us a kiss and leaves.

"Why do I feel like I just survived a hurricane after every time I see her?" Gabriel asks.

"Because Sally is a force of nature, duh." I rake my fork over my salad like it's fall foliage, sweeping it into two neat piles. "I was so tempted to tell her tonight. Not Sally, Quinn."

"Yeah, I could see that. Which part?" Gabriel asks.

"All of it."

"That would be . . . a lot."

I wipe my mouth and toss the napkin onto my plate, and we both pretend I'm not trying to cover up my uneaten food. "We're not the absolute worst parents, right?" I ask. "I mean, we don't beat her or starve her or neglect her, so empirically speaking, there have to be parents out there way worse than we are."

"Oh, way worse. I would say we're probably not even in the top ten. If we're talking top hundred, maybe we should worry—or would that be bottom hundred?" Gabriel nudges me with his shoulder. "Which makes it a total mystery how we ended up with the absolute best kid."

"She really is the best. In spite of us. At least me."

"Or because of us." He'll take my self-pity bait, but only to a degree. "We made a choice to keep certain things from her, but only in her best interest."

"What about other choices we made?"

"Which ones?"

"Like when my sister *Indecent Proposal*-ed you." I lay down my fork in the center of the plate. "Do you ever wish . . . ?" My hand makes a floundering circle to fill in the rest.

"Do I ever wish I let Violet buy my sperm? Are you really asking that?"

"We wouldn't be worried about money all the time. We wouldn't feel guilty that we can barely help Quinn pay for school." Never mind that my sister put a price tag on Gabriel's loyalty to me—a value my practical mind knows I'm not expected to live up to, but one that pokes me every so often in my bleaker moments. "Who knows, if Violet had a kid of her own, maybe . . ." I stop myself from saying more, but Gabriel infers the rest.

"Maybe she wouldn't have disappeared, and Quinn would have a half-sibling—who's also her cousin—and we'd all be one happy fucking family?"

"You never know."

"Oh, I'm sure having sex with your sister—under the guise of procreation, of course—would've had absolutely no lasting impact on our marriage. Not to mention my *impregnating* your sister. Or how she would've managed to turn motherhood into a twisted contest between you two. Yeah, those family dinners wouldn't have been awkward."

"So, you don't regret saying no?"

"Are you out of your mind? Never. I swear, it's a good thing the two of you weren't twins, 'cause I would've been paranoid she'd kidnap and/ or kill you and then try to pass herself off as you."

"Wow. Dark."

"Well, your sister wasn't exactly made of sugar and spice and everything nice."

"More like arsenic and wasps and everything conniving."

Gabriel scrunches his nose. "Come on, at least make an effort to rhyme. Like . . . arsenic and lies and Monarch butterflies."

"Really? She gets to be a butterfly?"

"Monarchs are poisonous."

"I'm so happy I married a trivia nerd."

"You just keep me around so you can win pub trivia nights."

"Marriages have survived on far less." Even though I'm smiling, my eyes well up. "Hey, I really am sorry about what I said earlier."

"What did you say earlier?" His confusion is momentary. "Oh right, when you were insensitive about my being adopted and raised in a culture vacuum."

"I was. I didn't mean it." I stroke the back of his neck. "For what it's worth, culture can be overrated. What did I grow up with? A language that sounds like it's mad at you, absurd superstitions, and food that's bland and starchy when it isn't being drowned in dill."

"Hey, borscht is delicious."

"Borscht is disgusting." I flick a balled-up straw wrapper at him and go still, my attention diverted by a TV screen behind him. It's showing local news coverage of the vigil.

There's a shot of the crowded bandshell, followed by a male newscaster standing at the edge of the park with a familiar tall blond man.

"I'm here with Cameron Frank, journalist and host of the breakout hit podcast *Strange Exits*, which traces the life and disappearance of Violet Volk," says the reporter. "Cameron, you've been following the Volk saga closely for a while now. What do you think it is about her that still resonates with people all these years later?"

I slouch down in the booth, stopping short of sliding under the table. "It's never going to end, is it? If this podcast gets any more popular, I may finally let you talk me into moving."

"Are you serious?" Hands up in shock, he leans away from me. "Like, to a different town?"

"A different town, a different state, a different hemisphere. What's that place where everyone's supposed to be so damn happy? Bhutan? We could go there. I don't care."

"You've never left the country but now you'd move to the Himalayas?"

Before I can answer him, his phone buzzes with a text.

"Quinn says not to wait up." He shows me his screen.

"Are you playing it cool or do you genuinely have no reaction to that?"

"I'll react when there's something to react to."

"Come on. Doesn't it bother you that we've never met anyone she's dated? Do you think she's been on dates? Or hooked up or whatever kids today are calling it?"

"I don't know. She's twenty-one. There's time for all that."

"Yeah, but she's *twenty-one*. Shouldn't there have been someone by now? I hope she knows she can love whoever she wants and be totally herself with us."

"She knows. Could be she's still figuring that out for herself."

"Or figuring it out with Sally's help."

"Either way, let her come to us when she's ready."

"Fair enough." I exit the booth and give him a sultry pout. "Wanna go home and do that naked stuff we do when Quinn's not around?"

"If only she knew we sometimes do it when she is around." His lusty murmur makes me want to pull him into the diner bathroom instead of waiting to get home.

It's funny how you can carry around a burden indefinitely without realizing it. Sometime between the vigil and now, the vague dread weighing on me for god-knows-how-long has lessened. I still don't know what to make of the number synchronicities or the sleepwalking or that photo of Sally with my sister in the background. But I can only let these things torment me for so long. The Violet saga isn't over—in fact, it may be perpetually open-ended—and I have no control over any of it. All I can do is not let it rule my life. Regardless of what that curly-haired crackpot said, I will not be following the twos, and I know I won't see my sister again. And in this very moment, I'm okay with that.

As we head out, I glance up at the TV one more time, just as the lottery drawing is wrapping up. The five white balls have been chosen and only the red Powerball number remains.

On screen, a man in a gray suit says, "All right, now, for your winning Powerball number, it is twenty-two tonight, and that Power Play multiplier is two."

Damn it.

Date: February 23, 2018, at 12:30 PM
To: cfrank@sidecarstudios.com
From: quinndwyer@sju.edu
Subject: don't hate me

Cameron,

Thanks for coffee last night. And for filling me in on your plans for *Strange Exits*. It's already getting so much buzz—did you see it mentioned in *Pop Ark*'s latest podcast roundup??

Ugh, I hate this part. Letting people down sucks a big D.

You're obviously working super hard to figure out my aunt and what happened to her, and since my mom would rather [insert painful/gross thing here] than go on your show, I'm your only chance of getting a close family member's perspective. I really, *really* wish I could give it to you. But Mom is already so weird about anything remotely to do with Violet, if I do your podcast . . . I hate to think how much it would hurt her. As much as I bag on her for being so closed up, she did go through a lot of shit with losing her uncle, parents, and sister. I don't want to make things harder on her. Also, after my craptacular performance at the vigil, you shouldn't trust me with being on your podcast, anyway.

So yeah, I'm gonna have to pass. For my mom's sake. She might be a neurotic mess sometimes (<—that is OFF THE RECORD!), but she's still the best.

Quinn

Strange Exits

Episode 7: "Antoinette"

CAMERON FRANK: Today, we're going to hear from the aptly named Antoinette Stranger. Regular listeners might remember Antoinette from her memorable appearance at the recent candlelight vigil for Violet Volk. While the security team there may not have been receptive to her interruption, I was eager to hear more of what she had to say. This woman has ideas and theories that some of you may find a bit . . . far-fetched. It's easy to write them off as delusional or crazy, and I understand the temptation to do so. Do me a favor: keep an open mind as you listen. I'm not asking you to agree with her theories, only to give them fair consideration. Leave the door open to what may be possible, even if it strikes you as unlikely.

When I asked Antoinette how she'd like to be introduced—what occupation or other identifiers to mention—she said she'd prefer to have listeners form their opinion of her based on what she has to say, rather than on any preassigned labels. She also encouraged me to be forthright with my own impressions of her, so here they are.

There's something about Antoinette that is at once reckless and deliberate. Her clothes, her gestures, her way of speaking—every part of her feels like it's oscillating wildly yet part of a finely tuned machine. She's not an easy person to read or feel comfortable around. It can be tricky to gauge whether she's being flirtatious or condescending, hostile or solemn. Some of the things she says are downright outrageous, but there's no denying the conviction behind her words. Of course, how much you choose to believe is entirely up to you.

CAMERON FRANK: Thank you for sitting down with me. You made quite an impression at the Violet Volk vigil.

ANTOINETTE STRANGER: I wouldn't normally take such dramatic measures, but Sasha never acknowledged my correspondence, and I needed to be sure my message reached her.

CAMERON FRANK: It sounded more like you were passing on her sister's message. You told Sasha that you'd been in contact with Violet. How so? And what did you mean when you said to pay attention to the twos?

ANTOINETTE STRANGER: How about wining and dining a girl a little? We'll get to all that. But let's ease into it. You could at least pretend to be interested in who I am as a person before probing my inner depths.

CAMERON FRANK: Sorry, I didn't mean to—of course I'm interested—I have a tendency to jump right in.

ANTOINETTE STRANGER: I wonder how your ex-wife felt about that.

CAMERON [STUDIO]: When she said that, I felt this eerie sense of unease. Less because she was joking about a sensitive subject, more because I hadn't told her I was divorced.

ANTOINETTE STRANGER: Oh, darling, don't look at me like I can read your mind. You have a tan line and indent on your ring finger.

CAMERON FRANK: [*nervous laugh*] Right. For a second, I thought you were going to use this as proof of being psychic.

ANTOINETTE STRANGER: This is what we need to be careful about in our line of investigation, overlooking the rational explanation in a rush to classify something as paranormal. My ideological Venn diagram is made up of science, philosophy, and intuition. I try to inhabit the area where all three overlap.

CAMERON FRANK: Fair enough. Why don't we begin with you sharing a little about your background?

ANTOINETTE STRANGER: I studied mathematics, physics, and software engineering at a respectable school where I earned a graduate and postgraduate degree. I worked for a number of years at companies specializing in GPS technology. When I realized my credentials would never qualify me to work anywhere with a more ambitious scope—I was getting bored toiling away on radio navigation systems, NASA wouldn't be calling anytime soon, and SpaceX was in its infancy—I plotted an exit strategy. Went freelance. This freed me up to pursue more experimental and far more fulfilling projects, even when they're less lucrative.

CAMERON FRANK: Looking at your more recent credentials, I see you've consulted and appeared on various cable TV shows that cover different areas of high strangeness. Would you consider yourself to be a paranormal investigator?

ANTOINETTE STRANGER: That's a label I find to be both reductive and an open invitation to derision. I am part of a collective that respects the scientific method while aggregating and analyzing cases that defy conventional logic.

CAMERON FRANK [STUDIO]: I tried to coax her into saying more about this "collective"—I don't know about you, but when I hear about a secretive close-knit community, I immediately think "cult"—but she would say nothing further about it, other than to emphasize that this group doesn't seek out publicity, nor do they do any active recruitment. No recruitment does make it sound less cult-y, but I'm still curious. Maybe there's something there for season two of *Strange Exits*? Anyway, back to the interview.

CAMERON FRANK: What sort of cases do you analyze?

ANTOINETTE STRANGER: We all have our areas of special interests and expertise. Mine is unusual disappearances.

CAMERON FRANK: Ah, so you do follow the Missing 411 phenomenon.

CAMERON FRANK [STUDIO]: For those unfamiliar, Missing 411 is a body of investigative work from David Paulides, a former police officer who's collected cases of disappearances, primarily from national parks, that defy logical and conventional explanations. Examples include hiking groups in which a single member vanishes without a trace, never to be seen again despite exhaustive searches, or found in an area searched multiple times (sometimes dead, other times with no recollection of where they'd been). While the phenomenon has its share of detractors, who are quick to dispute the data and minimize Paulides's credibility due to his prior work related to Bigfoot, the sheer volume of what he's collected is impressive—we're talking thousands of hours of research compiling over fourteen hundred Missing 411 cases.

ANTOINETTE STRANGER: Paulides has offered a few examples I find compelling, but I don't always agree with his methodology. He casts a wide net, whereas I prefer to use a smaller sample size and investigate specific occurrences in greater depth.

CAMERON FRANK: One of those occurrences being Violet Volk's disappearance?

ANTOINETTE STRANGER: Indeed.

CAMERON FRANK: What drew you to this particular case?

ANTOINETTE STRANGER: *Cases.* Plural. I don't think you can look at Volk's case without also considering the 1917 disappearance of Analise Margolis. Each would be intriguing on its own, but seeing that both women vanished—suddenly, strangely—in the same specific area makes them doubly so.

CAMERON FRANK [STUDIO]: I must confess, until I did additional research after this interview, I wasn't familiar with Analise Margolis, who mysteriously vanished from a private estate that later became the site of the Witkin Theater. I've linked to a couple of stories in the show notes that offer a brief overview on Margolis and the estate's history.

CAMERON FRANK: Where has your research into these cases led you?

ANTOINETTE STRANGER: To Willow Glen, naturally. In all seriousness, I've read everything I could find related to the disappearances, with special attention given to architectural and geographical records. I've paid numerous visits to the Witkin Theater—formerly the Worthington Estate—but, unfortunately, I've only been able to do limited investigations of the grounds and the theater's interior before being chased off. The numerous requests I've made to inspect the backstage and basement areas of the building have been denied.

CAMERON FRANK: It's unusual that you've done a deep dive into the "where." I feel like most would focus more on the "why."

ANTOINETTE STRANGER: I don't believe the "why" is the right avenue to explore here. I've gotten ahold of partial police reports, both of which eliminate suspicions of foul play and conclude the women disappeared of their own volition. Both had reasons to do so. From what limited records I could find, there were reports that the Margolis patriarch forbade Analise from marrying a mine foreman she'd fallen in love with. And Violet Volk's looming lawsuits, IRS audit, and money laundering suspicions were common knowledge. Nevertheless, whatever each woman's motivations may have been, I find it more useful to study the "where" and "how."

CAMERON FRANK: Right, so in terms of architecture and geography, what are you looking for? Secret passages that may have been overlooked by other investigators?

ANTOINETTE STRANGER: In a manner of speaking. But there's more to it. I've been trying to determine whether Willow Glen might contain what I refer to as a liminal vortex.

CAMERON FRANK: I can't say that's a term I'm familiar with.

ANTOINETTE STRANGER: Let's start more simply. You know about ley lines?

CAMERON FRANK: It's the notion that certain important ancient structures are aligned along the same paths, right? Like Stonehenge, the Great Pyramids of Giza, Chichen Itza . . . And if I'm not mistaken, ley lines are believed to contain unusual electromagnetic energy, forming this invisible power grid . . . Am I close?

ANTOINETTE STRANGER: You've got a handle on the basics.

CAMERON FRANK [STUDIO]: In all fairness, ley lines are considered a pseudoscience, since there's no accurate way to find and measure them. Some might call it the astrology of geography. But Antoinette does not appreciate such a dismissal.

ANTOINETTE: That term, "pseudoscience," it really burns me up. Pseudo is fake and what we do is not fake. There *are* effective tools that can identify ley lines, they are just more . . . subjective tools. But subjective is not the same as pseudo.

CAMERON FRANK: By "subjective tools," do you mean something like dowsing rods?

ANTOINETTE STRANGER: Dowsing rods are a good example. Let's say you want to build a well and I tell you we can find a water source using dowsing rods. You try it and pick ten spots with the rods—none of them contain water. I have a go at it and find ten other spots, nine of which point to a water source. Wouldn't you say in my hands, the dowsing rods are an effective tool? Subjectivity notwithstanding, wouldn't it be narrow for the scientific community to dismiss such a tool?

CAMERON FRANK [STUDIO]: I was trying to be objective and open-minded here, but this was a tough one for me. There is zero scientific support that twigs or copper rods can be used to find water, metal deposits, earth energy lines, your wallet, or any other hidden items. All the reported success stories are anecdotal with no controlled scientific tests to back them up. I didn't want to disrespect Antoinette during our conversation, but it's frustrating to hear a scientist defend pseudo-science this way.

CAMERON FRANK: Subjectivity isn't exactly part of the scientific method, though.

ANTOINETTE STRANGER: Subjectivity colors everything we do, even when we try to adhere to rules and formulas. Consider the double-slit experiment in physics, where observing whether light will behave as a particle or wave affects any predictability because light behaves as *both* a particle and a wave, and observation actually affects the outcome. Sometimes traditional scientific methods can actually limit our understanding, particularly in matters of space-time.

CAMERON FRANK: I'm guessing this connects to what you were calling a liminal . . . ?

ANTOINETTE STRANGER: Liminal vortex, yes. Certain locations in the world contain unusual energy properties. They're often found in conjunction with ley lines, but are far more concentrated—energy hot spots, you might say. Places where the fabric of space-time is thinner and may behave differently. These hot spots usually have documented cases of perplexing disappearances. Crater Lake in Oregon. The Bennington Triangle in Vermont. Mesa Verde in the Four Corners. And I'm not simply talking about hikers getting lost in the woods. In one case, a man disappeared from a moving bus. Another disappeared from a well-trafficked quarter-mile hiking path that was scoured by helicopters and dozens of searchers.

CAMERON FRANK: Just so I'm clear on this . . . are you suggesting that these disappearances are due to a liminal vortex? That these people passed through some kind of . . . energy portal?

ANTOINETTE STRANGER: It's a theory worth considering.

CAMERON FRANK [STUDIO]: Yes, but how seriously? As utterly fascinating as I find these cases, disappearances in natural settings bring out my inner skeptic. Forested areas are notoriously difficult to search, and a person who meets an untimely end in the woods could easily be camouflaged by vegetation. Crater Lake is the deepest lake in the United States; is it so shocking that a high number of people go missing by a large body of water that is nearly two thousand feet deep? I'm just saying, an energy portal in that kind of setting is a tough sell for me.

ANTOINETTE STRANGER: These areas have been searched to no avail and I've measured temporal anomalies in many of them.

CAMERON FRANK: What kind of anomalies?

ANTOINETTE STRANGER: Take the Witkin Theater, for example. There are certain spots in and around the building where the passage of time is slower by several milliseconds compared to its surrounding areas. I've also recorded electromagnetic disturbances in specific locations: compass needles spin wildly, radio signals get interrupted, electronic devices malfunction.

CAMERON FRANK [STUDIO]: Personally, this is where I perk up. When you have a man-made stationary structure, there are a finite number of searchable locations. Add time dilation and electronic disturbances to the mix and you have my full attention.

CAMERON FRANK: So, supposing the site of the Witkin Theater contains a liminal vortex and somehow Violet Volk passed through it, as did Analise Margolis nearly a century earlier . . . where did they go? Are we looking at some kind of multiverse scenario? Are they in a different dimension?

ANTOINETTE STRANGER: That is the hypothesis I am developing, yes.

CAMERON FRANK: Why haven't there been more people disappearing into this portal, then? Can we go there? What does "there" even look like? Is it possible to return?

ANTOINETTE STRANGER: From what I've gathered, it's not an opening that anyone can pass through. It's more like a security door that's unlocked with a special code, which I'm still trying to crack, whereas

Analise and Violet may have inadvertently—or even deliberately—cracked the code.

CAMERON FRANK: How could either of them have done it?

ANTOINETTE STRANGER: Like I said, there is minimal documentation pertaining to the Margolis case, but I've found some information that suggests her family was involved in the Spiritualist movement. It's not clear to what extent, but they did host and participate in séances. Back then, there were countless hucksters preying upon people who wished to communicate with the dead—there still are, to be frank, but from what I've gathered, the Margolises took a sincere interest in supernatural matters. It's possible Analise developed certain sensitivities as a result.

As for Violet . . . it's a shame her talents were recognized on such a superficial level, because she was truly extraordinary. Violet Volk didn't merely practice magic. As others before me have stated, she *was* magic.

CAMERON FRANK: That is a pretty bold claim. I can't help but think of the Sagan standard.

ANTOINETTE STRANGER: Yes, yes, "extraordinary claims require extraordinary evidence."

Volk's stage shows were magnificent, but I realize they were mostly—*mostly*—the work of skilled performers and engineers.

The close-up shows were a different story. These were sporadic, unpublicized, exclusive . . . and utterly mind-blowing. I was fortunate enough to attend one in 1998, and I'm convinced what I witnessed was more than mere sleight-of-hand.

CAMERON FRANK: Which I imagine is the desired effect. Yet a professional illusionist would have a more practical take. In fact, there have been magicians who claimed to know her secrets, and in the case of Ace Morgan—

ANTOINETTE STRANGER: Ace Morgan never revealed how she performed these specific effects. All the illusions he exposed were part of Violet's stage act. You have a more controlled environment in a theater, more access to rigs and pulleys and elaborate methods of distraction. You have yards of space separating you from the performer. In a hotel suite, high-tech options are more limited. When you're standing mere inches away from your audience, it takes great skill to fool them. Or, in my case, to convince them.

Also, In the Picture was never solved, despite other magicians' claims to know how it was done. They called it one of the best illusions ever crafted and insisted on defending its secrets, but why has nobody ever performed it identically?

CAMERON FRANK: Magicians are always borrowing ideas from each other, but they prefer to iterate on popular tricks, stamping each with their own signature. Like with the Ambitious Card. In the Picture has been performed numerous times in the last ten years.

ANTOINETTE STRANGER: With a key difference. The other magicians who try it never let anybody keep the photograph after. Violet always gave the photo to one of the volunteers at the end of the trick. Nobody has been able to pull off In the Picture in the way Violet performed it, and not because they're taking creative license. They *can't* perform it like she did.

Those Polaroids were analyzed—including one I was given at a private Vegas performance—and shown to have no external tampering. Later on, when she updated the trick to incorporate webcams and cell phones, photo and technical experts studied the images but concluded there was no digital manipulation and no representational materials involved. This debunked the cardboard cutout and special effects theories that had been long prevalent. If that's not extraordinary evidence, I don't know what is.

CAMERON FRANK: So, you believe that proves Violet . . . actually possessed extrasensory powers? And these powers enabled her to . . . disappear into another dimension?

ANTOINETTE STRANGER: I know how it sounds when you lay it out like that.

The collective I belong to *does* maintain a degree of skepticism when investigating high strangeness. We do our due diligence. We're thorough with our research, careful in conducting our own interviews, and employ boots on the ground whenever possible. Something we've learned in our years of doing this is, the loud ones making outlandish claims are usually easy to discredit. The authentic ones do not seek out recognition; in fact, they often go out of their way to avoid the spotlight. There's a musician who recorded an album of eerily prophetic songs, an artist who painted vivid scenes out of strangers' lives, an author who's been published under numerous pen names over the last century and is believed to be immortal. All were careful to maintain a low profile despite their impressive body of work. You've probably never heard of most of them.

CAMERON FRANK: I have heard of a certain magician named Violet Volk, though. She hardly maintained a low profile.

ANTOINETTE STRANGER: Ah, but she never made outlandish claims—her singularity played out behind a veil of entertainment. When she performed a disappearing act for an audience, nobody actually believed she had dematerialized into the ether and rematerialized in a different part of the theater.

CAMERON FRANK: But it sounds like you believe she *could* do such a thing.

ANTOINETTE STRANGER: I'm not the only one who believed it. After I saw one of her private performances in Las Vegas, I created a case study on her and brought it to the rest of the collective. Enough members were swayed to pool our resources to attend another one of Violet's private shows. We made special arrangements for her to perform solely for members of our group, offering a generous bonus to do a meet and greet with her afterward.

CAMERON: What was the purpose of that meeting?

ANTOINETTE: To propose Violet join us for an informational exchange of sorts. We'd provide her certain resources to expand her knowledge of that gray area between the physical and metaphysical, which could potentially benefit her stage act. In turn, we asked her to teach us certain things.

CAMERON: Teach you what exactly?

ANTOINETTE: [*laughs*] How to . . . influence our reality. Not by way of the standard subterfuge an illusionist employs, but her innate abilities extending . . . beyond.

CAMERON: And how did that meeting go? Did she agree to this exchange?

ANTOINETTE: It was . . . a privilege to see Violet perform again, and to speak with her afterward. She was open to our ideas and materials, which we intended to give her regardless, but expressed trepidation at being studied in any way. She cited the need to uphold the magician's code, though she knew we were getting at something deeper. Ultimately, she said she was not in a position where she could teach us anything. Funny how she would go on to do just that by way of her books and motivational seminars in the years that followed.

CAMERON FRANK: Right, but at that point, Violet was using magic more as a metaphor for self-empowerment. Not as any actual metaphysical instructions.

ANTOINETTE STRANGER: And yet, while I am still working on a larger hypothesis connecting these ideas, I'd argue there's a stronger subtext in Violet's contribution to personal development that states those metaphysical capabilities lie within all of us.

CAMERON FRANK: That sounds like a whole other conversation, and I hope we can have it at a later point. I'd like to return to the topic of the vigil. Provided you feel sufficiently wined and dined at this point.

ANTOINETTE STRANGER: I do.

CAMERON FRANK: What did you mean when you said you've communicated with Violet?

ANTOINETTE STRANGER: I heard her and sensed her while meditating, though I didn't get a clear image of her. It was . . . not a situation where

I would've been able to reach out and physically touch her. At the same time, it was not a figment or dream.

CAMERON FRANK: Could it have been some version of an afterlife?

ANTOINETTE STRANGER: There is no afterlife, there is only *life*, in perpetuity. What I saw was not Violet's ghost; it was Violet herself. She told me to keep following the road I'm on. To help navigate Sasha. To tell her sister to follow the twos.

CAMERON FRANK: What does that mean?

ANTOINETTE STRANGER: It all comes down to patterns. The universe has its own language, and most of us don't have even a basic grasp of it. In the grand scheme of things, the most intelligent and enlightened of us are still learning the alphabet. As helpful as it would be to discover an existential Rosetta stone, in the meantime, our most effective strategy has been to collect information and study patterns.

CAMERON FRANK: Are you referring to mathematical properties? Like how the Golden Ratio and Fibonacci sequence appear in nature?

ANTOINETTE STRANGER: Yes, but it goes beyond sunflowers and seashells. Quantum immortality and the multiverse are closer to what I believe, which is that we exist in an infinite and malleable reality. That there are levels of science and philosophy light-years beyond anything humanity in its current form can comprehend. That our mission is to discover and decipher as much as we can, to push at our imposed *Homo sapiens* boundaries.

CAMERON FRANK: And we do that by studying patterns? Like the number two?

ANTOINETTE STRANGER: Everyone has their own starting place. The twos are Sasha's.

For others it might be noticing whenever the clock reads 11:11, or learning something obscure and seeing multiple subsequent references to it, or countless other synchronicities or manifestations. People dismiss these overlaps as coincidences, but they are better interpreted as sign-posts. I like to think of it as the universe waving at you, trying to direct you down a certain path or confirming the path you're currently on. Whether or not you choose to recognize these arrows and follow them is up to you.

CAMERON FRANK: Getting back to Violet, do you believe she's still alive?

ANTOINETTE STRANGER: In some form or other, yes. I believe the human soul is immortal.

CAMERON FRANK: But what about in the conventional sense? Is she breathing and is her heart beating, on this or any other dimension?

ANTOINETTE STRANGER: I think so. Though I can't say exactly where or on what plane of reality. The person who has the best chance of discovering that is Sasha.

CAMERON FRANK [STUDIO]: The day after we spoke, I received a call from the Curiosity Network about a new show they're launching called *Off the Beaten Path*. One of their first episodes will be centered around the Witkin Theater.

I've been asked to be involved with the production, and at my recommendation, Antoinette has also been included. We'll provide commentary on the theater and the disappearances, and also participate in on-site investigations. In fact, we're doing the first of several shoots at the Witkin in the coming weeks.

I'll be sharing some of the behind-the-scenes moments in a future episode.

Reward Up for Missing Willow Glen Woman

MARCH 8, 1917

Stricken with worry and grief over the disappearance of his daughter Analise Margolis two weeks ago, Finchley Mining Company president Salvatore Margolis is distressed that search efforts thus far have been unsuccessful.

"She is a steadfast girl with a happy, stable home," Mr. Margolis said. "It would not be merely out of character for her to run off, it would be downright unthinkable."

The nineteen-year-old was last seen at the Worthington Estate four days ago, where a modest gathering was held to celebrate patriarch Jeremiah Worthington's sixtieth birthday. Margolis was last seen with the other thirty partygoers getting a tour of the wine cellar.

"One moment, she was beside us, and the next she was nowhere to be seen," said matriarch Gertrude Worthington. "We searched every inch of that place, but it was as if she vanished into thin air."

Mr. Margolis has offered two hundred dollars for information leading to the discovery of his daughter's whereabouts.

Flower Tycoon Buys Historic Willow Glen Estate

By Rhonda Breslin

APRIL 11, 1978

In 1902 Jeremiah Worthington, who made his fortune in iron at the helm of the Finchley Mining Company, commissioned a private residence to be constructed for his family in Willow Glen. The palatial property, situated on six gated acres, became known as the Worthington Estate and was considered one of the most lavish homes in Southern New Jersey in subsequent decades. That was until March 1975, when the Finchley Mining Company declared bankruptcy, two months after a tunnel collapse resulted in the death of seventeen miners and led to an investigation into mining safety regulations. Shortly thereafter, the Worthingtons fled the country, abandoning their estate, which has remained vacant ever since. While it has been a challenge to secure a buyer for such a sizable property, it was recently sold to entrepreneur Thurman Rex Witkin.

Witkin is the founder and president of TRF, one of America's largest importers and manufacturers of artificial flowers. Originally from Willow Glen, he is eager to return to his hometown and give back to the community. Local permit registrations show plans for part of the property to be converted into a theater.

"I am committed to advancing local enrichment in South Jersey," Mr. Witkin said in an official statement, "and the former Worthington Estate is an ideal property to develop into a performing arts center. Instead of benefiting one wealthy family, this space can serve as a local cultural hub, benefiting Willow Glen and its surrounding communities through arts education and outreach programs." Witkin has also been named chairman of the Atlantic County Historic Society and intends to preserve much of the estate's architecture.

Renovations on the property are scheduled to begin this summer and the theater's opening has tentatively been announced for the fall of 1979.

Date: May 24, 2003, at 8:35 AM
From: leannakinkaid@popark.com
To: stanheslin@popark.com
Subject: Volk interview

Stan,

Violet's publicist reviewed your VV interview and she'd like you to cut a few sections. Frankly, I found the whole thing fascinating, but there are concerns that Violet may come off as "too boring or too batshit." Agree to disagree, but we made concessions to get this Volk exclusive, so we have to play nice. If that means a shorter cover story, so be it.

Please see attached. I've highlighted the sections that need to be cut.

Nice job on this one. Wish we could publish as is.

LK

Leanna Kinkaid

Editor in Chief, *PopArk Magazine*

NOW YOU SEE HER:
THE REAPPEARANCE OF VIOLET VOLK

By Stan Heslin

APRIL 2003

Let's be honest: historically, magic has not been considered the highest form of entertainment. It's fine for children's parties and cruise ships, but generally, magicians have been a step above mimes in public perception. That is, until the mid-1990s, when a young woman came out of seemingly nowhere and elevated magic to a bona fide art form.

Though Violet Volk was frequently in the public eye and maintained a high level of fame, for better or worse, she's avoided giving any interviews since 1997. It's a rare feat for a performer to remain so popular while fielding so few media inquiries, but Volk has done it. While she revolutionized stage magic, she also faced her share of controversies over the years. Plenty has been written about Volk's insanely popular but tumultuous tenure at the Kintana Resort and Hotel, as well as her colorful love life, so we won't rehash it here.

Instead, we'll fast-forward to early 2001, when Volk returned to Los Angeles. A smattering of movie and television appearances followed, then she once again did something unexpected: she stepped away from the spotlight entirely. There have been few public sightings of the performer in over a year: no impromptu appearances at weddings or birthday parties, no masquerading as an extra on film or television sets, not even any award show antics [insert "shrinking Violet" pun here].

Volk broke her silence in three surprising ways. She wrote a self-help book, *You Are Magic*, she announced an extensive tour (billed as "an evening of magical inspiration"), and she agreed to sit down for her first proper interview in five years.

After two flights and an extended rental car drive, I'm nearing Violet's current residence. She won't let me name the California town where she currently lives, though I'm allowed to mention it's a bucolic coastal enclave with stretches of rocky shoreline. It's on few tourist radars and its residents would like to keep it that way. This place is a far cry from the neon, heat, and hustle of the Vegas Strip. The stone cottage I approach wouldn't be out of place in Middle Earth and looks more like a guest house or servants' quarters.

As I pull into the gravel driveway, I find Volk on her front porch, feet up on the railing. She's poring over a thick stack of papers and greets me, hugging the manuscript to her chest like a shield.

I ask what she's reading, and her face takes on a reverent look. "It's not coming out until next year, but my editor got me an advance copy." She rifles through the stack to find the title page: *Higher Dimensions: A Journey Through Quantum Immortality, Elevated Consciousness, and Parallel Worlds.*

"Just some light reading, then," I say. Considering physics is the only class I ever failed in high school, it looks like something that would give me a headache if I tried to read it. I tell her as much.

"I could never get my head around physics, either, but this doesn't feel like homework, it's more like you're sitting next to someone brilliant at a dinner party, and he's blowing your mind. Anyone who's ever watched *Star Trek* or *Doctor Who* could get into it."

Before I can verify whether Volk is a Trekkie and/or Whovian, she continues her impassioned rave.

"I'll be honest: the philosophical/existential stuff in here is easier for me to grasp—that we're all part of an infinite chain of energy expansion and reallocation. The more scientific ideas tie my brain into pretzels—in the best possible way." She laughs. "I get the concepts on an instinctual level, but it still frustrates me how much we don't know. Like dark matter. Do you know about dark matter?"

Much as I wish I could answer affirmatively, I confess I do not. "Let's go around back and I'll tell you all about it."

It's ten in the morning and I wasn't expecting a conversation about theoretical physics with Violet Volk.

While I'm curious to see her downsized digs, she doesn't offer a tour, and instead leads me around the side of the house to a canopied terrace overlooking the water, where we take a seat at the picnic table. She sets the manuscript off to the side and tosses a sweatshirt over it as a makeshift paperweight.

If it wasn't for her signature glittering red lipstick, I wouldn't recognize the woman sitting before me as Violet Volk. Not that I expected her to show up to the interview in a sequined catsuit, but even in tabloids, I've never seen her wear something as casual as a sleeveless white T-shirt and black jeans. Her combat boots have been swapped for a pair of Chinese mesh slippers, her elaborate updos ditched in favor of a sloppy bun, and her typical smoky eyes are makeup-free, though eclipsed by sunglasses for the majority of our conversation. You could mistake her for a cute barista or art teacher before registering her as one of Generation X's favorite pop culture icons. The pared-down look makes her appear even more youthful than her twenty-eight years, and there's something different about her demeanor. Something less tightly wound and more relaxed and contemplative.

Her husky voice fills with enthusiasm as she returns to the topic at hand. "Okay, so dark matter. It makes up the majority of our universe—like ninety percent—but we can't see it and don't even know what it is. It's just this big sphere of . . . *something* that weighs ten times more than our galaxy. How do we know it's there? Because our galaxy spins so damn fast, it would be blown apart if dark matter wasn't there to keep it together. What's it made of? One theory says dark matter is made up of sparticles, which sounds like something you'd call a doo-wop band in ancient Rome, but they're actually subatomic super particles. Did I mention these particles are also *hypothetical?* I know, it's insane, and we haven't even gotten into supersymmetry and string theory, which hint at other layers of reality. Now we get to the good stuff. As soon as parallel worlds are mentioned, I'm all, 'Hurry up and figure out a way we can visit them.' The bummer of it is, only gravity particles can travel between universes, not light or matter, so neither of us are getting on that guest list. At least, that's what physicists claim, but this book suggests there's a way to tap into a universal consciousness and actually explore other dimensions. Though I still don't think it's giving up the full story."

The armchair psychologist in me wonders if this interest in alternate realities is Violet's way of coping with the personal and professional setbacks she's faced in this one. When I ask where this newfound curiosity has come from, she's quick to correct me.

"It's not new, it's something I've been interested in for years. Anyway, you didn't come to hear me babble on about this stuff."

I didn't, but I'm not sure I want her to stop.

Despite being more easygoing, there are still topics she will not discuss, namely, her personal life. Any questions about her family or romantic relationships are off-limits.

"This one's lemonade and this one's water. Which would you like?" She points between two silver pitchers laid out between us, along with two ceramic mugs. I go with water, and before I can inquire if this is part of a new act, she quips, "I'm not practicing material on you, I'm just offering you a drink."

We laugh politely, and I'd be lying if I said I wasn't disappointed. I've never had the pleasure of witnessing Volk's conjuring live, so it would've been something special to experience, especially close up. If, say, she turned the lemonade into iced tea or filled the water with fish. Maybe there's a parallel universe where I get to see some of her impromptu magic today.

"That's the problem doing what I do," she says, pouring our beverages. "I made such a point of turning small, everyday moments into a spectacle, people got used to it. It got so I felt like it was my job, even when I was off the clock. I mean, these were the people who gave me everything I have—they came from all over to see me, they watched me on TV, they bought my merchandise. They showered me with more love and attention than I ever deserved. I got into this mindset where I felt obligated to give everyone I came into contact with a special moment of wonder, and thought I was letting people down if I didn't. But holy crap, is that an energy suck. Sometimes I just wanted to buy some tampons or eat a hot dog, without having to perform. Not that I'm complaining, I did it to myself. Problem is, I overdid it."

You hear the word "exhaustion" thrown around a lot in the world of showbiz. Work schedules and social pressures can be grueling, and burnout is not uncommon. Other times, exhaustion is code for drug addiction, mental illness, eating disorders, and a myriad of other ailments celebrities would rather keep private. When Volk left Vegas in 2001, she, too, cited exhaustion, as people speculated about the "real" reason the show was being shut down. Rumors of alcoholism and substance abuse abounded, though they were unsubstantiated. Ditto the rumors of emotional break-downs.

There were other types of rumors, too, nicer ones. Of perfor-mances at children's hospitals and senior centers. Of multiple USO tours. All done using a pseudonym and disguises, with great effort to minimize the publicity surrounding them. These rumors are more substantiated but rarely covered in the press.

I'm more inclined to take Violet's exhaustion at face value. Especially right now, sitting across from her, as her immaculate posture momentarily deflates. When she briefly removes her sun-glasses to clean them, a closer inspection reveals colored contacts lending an artificial azure brightness to her eyes, which are other-wise bloodshot, with faint dark circles beneath them. It could be that I'm catching her after a bad night, or it could be that, success notwithstanding, recent years have taken their toll on her.

"Please don't write that I look all strung out," she says, making me wonder if the next area of magic she plans to master is men-talism. "I was up late and didn't feel like waking up early to glam myself up. Don't take it personally."

"Up late?" I echo. Despite the anecdotal warnings I've received about how intimidating Volk could be, I never believed it until now. For some reason I'm more nervous talking to her than I was interviewing a serial-killer-turned-poet I profiled last year (and that guy was twice my size and strangled eight people with his bare hands).

"I was working out tour logistics. Though based on your judgy stare, let me state for the record that I never had a drug or alcohol problem, and I am not mentally ill. The tabloids sell more copies saying I'm in rehab or a mental hospital than they would if they printed the truth, which is that I needed to step away and chill for a while. Yeah, things were rough coming out of Vegas, but working on *You Are Magic* helped me find my spark again. That's not as exciting as me battling addictions or nervous breakdowns, though. It pisses me off when the media insinuates all this bullshit drama."

Again, this woman is an epic mentalist in the making.

She seems irritated, so I offer an easy question in the hopes of getting back in her good graces, asking why she's avoided giving interviews in the last few years, and why she's giving one now.

"I got in trouble for that *Foxxy* piece. The industry doesn't like it when you show how the sausage is made, and my 'people' were not thrilled with some of the things I said. In other words, I was too honest. And apparently, I'm 'too volatile' to be one of those calculated tell-it-how-it-is celebrities. Since my big mouth was considered a liability and I refused to play a sanitized version of myself to journalists, we decided I'd shut the hell up and create more of a mystique around doing spontaneous appearances and cameos, but no formal interviews. I used to think it was a requirement of being famous, but I'm not the only one who avoids them. I mean, look at John Malkovich—not doing interviews hasn't hurt his career. Oh god, please don't call this article 'The Malkovich of Magic.'"

I give her my word and ask why her mouth is no longer considered a liability.

"I guess it's a risk my publisher is willing to take. They actually seem to like who I am and what I have to say, which is why I signed with Empirical Books. And since they were nice enough to give me money to write a book, I'd like to return the favor by helping them promote it.

"But I also wanted to set the record straight about a few things." She holds up a finger while she takes a long sip of lemonade, though I had no intention of interrupting her.

"The accidents. Obviously, I should've said something about them sooner—I mean in a real way, not through carefully worded press releases. People will interpret that however they want, anyway. If they like me, they'll appreciate my being real. If they don't, they'll see it as yet another publicity grab, to get more book sales. Though in all honesty, I think *You Are Magic* is gonna do just fine with or without my hyping it up."

She's probably right. In fact, the hype began early last year, when Volk got a reported seven-figure advance for *You Are Magic*, after a frenzied auction among eight publishers. While early reviews for the self-help title have been mixed, the book is already in its fourth printing and the publication date was moved up three months (from September to June) based on high demand. A publishing industry insider confided *You Are Magic* is expected to become an instant bestseller based on preorders alone. And while many raised an eyebrow at a motivational seminar—ahem, "magical inspiration"—tour in support of the book, every announced date has sold out.

Which lends credence to Volk's sincerity about wanting to clear the air.

"I can't control other people's opinions. I also can't control every single aspect of a stage show that requires dozens of people to make it work. It's not for lack of trying—I'm one of the bossiest bitches you'll ever work with. But I can't do every person's job for them. If I could, there wouldn't have been any accidents. I had the hottest ticket in Vegas and didn't need to endanger lives to pack the house. Even if that wasn't the case, I would never, *ever* willingly put someone in harm's way for attention. I never claimed to be an angel, but I'm not that level of asshole, either.

"Some magicians safeguard their shows more than others. For example, our saws had modified chains with no teeth . . . not everyone uses them, and it can go badly, like one guy who accidentally sawed through his wife's neck and killed her. Then there are effects that are gonna be dangerous, no matter what. The Bullet Catch goes smoothly ninety-nine times, and the hundredth time you can still get shot in the face. Do all the risk management you want, but you'll never get it to be a hundred percent safe. Accidents happen even when you're a pro."

This is true. Stage magic has its share of hazards and tragic stories of lives lost while practicing or performing. The deadliest trick in all of magic, the aforementioned Bullet Catch, has claimed the lives of at least twelve magicians and has also killed or injured countless assistants and spectators. Other magicians have died from suffocation while being buried alive, drowning before they could escape a water tank—back in the day, one magician even died from accidentally swallowing a straight razor.

All of which is to say, Violet Volk's magic show wasn't the first to bear a fatality and, sadly, will likely not be the last.

"I can give you two reasons why accidents kept plaguing my show, neither of which has to do with grabbing headlines.

"Reason one: after the first accident, people got nervous. Someone got hurt, so everyone started acting extra careful. They were paying so much attention to each little detail of their performance, it became less fluid. When you rehearse a routine enough times, it becomes ingrained in your mind and body until it's a natural extension of you. It gets to a point where you don't need to think because muscle memory takes over. But that first accident made a lot of the performers start overthinking the routines. Which made them more self-conscious. And when you get self-conscious, you're not gonna be in the flow, and you'll be more prone to making mistakes. I think that's why there was a second accident, then a third, then a fourth. It set off this unfortunate chain reaction."

I'm curious to learn what this second reason is, and Violet can tell she has me on the hook, but something in the quirk of her mouth dares me to be less predictable. So instead of waiting for her to provide this second reason, I take the dare and go back to the topic of *Higher Dimensions*. I ask what she meant about not getting the full story.

This seems to instantly revitalize her. She moves the drink pitchers aside so she can lean in closer and lowers her voice, as if we might be overheard.

"I think there are things science either can't or won't explain. There are ancient tribal mythologies involving shadow people, and some claim to see them to this day. Who's to say they aren't some sort of interdimensional beings? I haven't seen them myself, but I've seen other strange shit. Orbs, weird distortions. Before you ask, no, I wasn't on drugs—I don't take them, remember?—and yes, my carbon monoxide detector was working properly.

"It's more than reality glitching out. I think we're catching hints or residue of these other places. This book proposes that some enlightened beings—your Buddhist monks, Indian gurus, South American shamans—are able to raise their consciousness to levitate, teleport, all kinds of wacky stuff. Then you have theorists who believe multiple worlds exist on different vibrational wavelengths, but we're tuned into a single one. I don't know, it seems like those more enlightened individuals have already found a way to tune into other wavelengths. I just wish that this book would tell me how to do it, specifically, step-by-step, instead of vaguely chalking it up to deep meditation."

Once again, I'm rendered speechless. Violet seems disappointed that I have nothing to add, so she returns to the topic of her Vegas show.

"Anyway, the other reason I think all the accidents were happening—and I expect to get shit for this, but I'll say it anyway—was because the show was cursed. Not in a witchy way, per se . . . I hate the term 'witchcraft,' it's so reductive and stigmatized. But I do believe people can influence the world around them with their energy.

"When my sister and I were little, we were once playing on the beach in Brigantine and this creepy old lady walking by told my parents what a pretty little girl Sasha was. As soon as she walked away, Sasha cut open her foot on a broken bottle in the sand. You might call that a coincidence. My mom called it the evil eye. From that day on, she made us wear red strings tied around our wrists to ward us from it.

"Intentions can manifest themselves in the real world, in a negative or positive way. After feeling like I was the target of so much negative energy, I used that as fuel, determined to transform it into something beautiful. That's how *You Are Magic* came about. My hope is that the book and the seminars will empower people to channel their intentions toward the positive."

Once again, she reads my mind by saying, "I bet you're wondering how people can do that. I'll show you." She points to the two pitchers. "Let's say you don't want lemonade or water. What are your two favorite beverages?"

"Alcoholic or nonalcoholic?"

"Doesn't matter."

I think for a moment and tell her milky iced coffee and whiskey.

She nods. "Okay. Now look at these two pitchers and imagine one of them is filled with iced coffee and the other is filled with whiskey. Picture it. Really convince yourself of it. Do you have that picture in your mind?"

I tell her I do, and she grabs my mug, tossing the rest of the water onto the grass. "Which one do you want first?"

"The iced coffee."

She takes one of the pitchers, tips it, and a creamy brown liquid pours out. Pointing to my blazer pocket, she adds, "There's sugar in there if you want it."

Two packets of raw sugar, but the coffee is already sweetened perfectly. It's the best iced coffee I've ever had.

"Now my turn." She moves the manuscript so it's between us, its white corners peeking from beneath the black sweatshirt. "I love turning paper into confetti but that's been done to death. Same with the glitter bombs. Now that I've finished reading this beautiful book, I don't want to dump it into a recycling bin, I want to turn it into something different, but also beautiful. I want to see this stack of papers fly, like feathers on the wind. I want the paper to *be* feathers."

A quiet moment passes and then a gust of wind picks up. In that instant, Violet whips the sweatshirt away and the manuscript is gone, now replaced by a mound of feathers, which immediately scatter in the wind.

I'm so dumbstruck, my mouth hangs open, and one of the feathers flies into it.

"Wow," I say.

"You look like you could use a real drink." Out of god-knows-where, she produces a rocks glass and picks up the other pitcher.

Before she even pours, I know what comes out won't be lemonade or water. This liquid is a golden amber. I take a sip. It's the finest whiskey I've ever tasted.

Date: March 6, 2018, at 2:42 PM
To: checkmate@protonmail.com
From: cfrank@sidecarstudios.com
Subject: Next Steps

I am in receipt of a package with a rook on it. What happens next?

Date: March 6, 2018, at 5:19 PM
To: cfrank@sidecarstudios.com
From: checkmate@protonmail.com
Subject: Re: Next Steps

Dear Mr. Frank,

What happens next is that we converse.

Instruction to follow.

Sincerely yours,

‡

Date: March 7, 2018, at 8:55 AM
To: cfrank@sidecarstudios.com
From: twoods@sidecarstudios.com
Subject: getting off track

Your vigil coverage was decent (though more Sasha would've been better), but the interview with Antoinette was a bit much, just as I suspected it would be when I heard the rough cut. Let's keep the weirdos to a minimum, yes?

I'm getting tired of pestering you for updates on the Sasha interview, so I'll make this simple. Make it happen by the end of the month or we're going to find a new host for *Strange Exits*.

—TW
Tobin Woods
Editorial Director & Cofounder
Sidecar Studios

Date: March 7, 2018, at 9:24 AM
To: twoods@sidecarstudios.com
From: cfrank@sidecarstudios.com
Subject: Re: getting off track

You'll get your Sasha interview, but with all due respect, considering the title of the podcast, I'm going to need some leeway on the so-called weirdos. Especially considering downloads of SE have been increasing week over week, including the Antoinette episode. The lead I'm currently following is offbeat, to be sure, but it may end up being the most fascinating episode to date.

—CF

Date: March 7, 2018, at 9:34 AM
To: cfrank@sidecarstudios.com
From: twoods@sidecarstudios.com
Subject: Re: Re: getting off track

Hopefully it won't be one of your last episodes.

—TW

Sasha

March 8, 2018

"Be careful!"

"Don't get too close!"

It's cold, there's a tangle of loud whispers talking over each other, and I'm lying on the ground in the fetal position. Brightness floods my eyes and I sit up with a shriek.

"Hey, don't shine that thing right in her eyes," a male voice admonishes, and the light shifts down a few inches.

"What the fuck?" I try to scramble backward but hit a wall. Terror liquifies my insides as I try to get a handle on where I am, what this is. I can make out a handful of silhouettes, mostly male if I had to guess. One is holding a long stick pointed a foot above my head and another balances something boxy on his shoulder, which is marked with a glowing red dot.

Down the hall, another light appears as a dark figure wearing a headlamp approaches. "Hang on, I think I know her."

Using the wall for support, I finally stand, craning my neck at the man coming toward me. I'm more familiar with the smarmy voice than the face, but I'm pretty sure of who this is. "Cameron?"

"Sasha? How did you get here?"

As my eyes adjust, I get a better sense of my surroundings. The boxy object with the red dot is a video camera. The stick dangling above me is a boom mic. Some of my fear dissipates as I register the film crew around me.

"Are we . . ." But I'm still too disoriented to speculate. "Where the hell are we?" Wherever it is, it's freezing. There's a tingling in my toes and grit digs into my heels. Oh god. A quick feel of my arms and legs—yep, flannel. I'm barefoot in my pajamas again. And this time, I have an audience. With recording equipment. Fantastic.

Cameron stops a few feet away from me and his expression mirrors my own confusion and dread. "We're in the lower level of the Witkin Theater. What are you doing down here?"

They're all looking at me. Waiting for me to answer this very legitimate question. What *am* I doing down here?

I don't have a good answer.

Cameron cocks his head, frowns down at me. "Are you okay?"

I don't have a good answer for that, either.

"What's happening over here? Why did we stop filming?" A stocky woman in a puffy green vest pushes past the men, using her clipboard to swat them aside. She stops short when she sees me, her hand flying up to her throat. "Jesus Christmas, I thought you were a ghost." Before I can assure her that I am indeed corporeal, she fires off a series of questions, asking my name, what happened to me, whether I need medical attention.

At this point, my entire body is trembling. Hard to say whether it's nerves, the frigid temperature, or a bit from column A and column B. "I'm not hurt or anything," I say, using the stone wall behind me to help me get to my feet. "Just a little cold."

The woman raises exasperated hands at the film crew. "Have you all just been standing around watching her freeze to death? For the love of Pete, get her a blanket, socks, *something*." Turning back to me, she unzips her vest, slips out of it, and drapes it over my shoulders, ignoring my halfhearted protests.

"Do you need us to call the police?" she asks me.

"Oh, no. Definitely not." Someone hands me a thick pair of socks and I nod my gratitude.

"Then how did you get in here? This place is locked up and we've had cameras monitoring this hall for hours. You appeared out of nowhere."

"Oh. Um . . ." I balance on one foot and struggle to pull on a sock with fingers stiff from the cold. "That's strange." Everyone around me has gone silent and still, waiting for more of an explanation. There's a dropping sensation in my stomach, like the moment you trip over an uneven sidewalk and aren't sure if you'll catch yourself before you fall. I brace my back against the wall, and a few small stones come loose with a clatter. I lurch forward as a few more give way, first from the wall, then the ceiling.

"All right, grab the equipment and let's get out," says the woman. "Right now." The percussion of more loose stones tumbling down makes everyone move quickly. Everyone but me.

Abject fright immobilizes me, triggers my worst childhood memory. Trapped underground, alone, my surroundings crumbling all around me. No way out. I will be buried alive. I will die here.

"We need to go," Cameron says, pulling me away. "No telling how unstable the rest of the structure is down here."

I snap back to the present, taking short jagged breaths. I'm not in a mining tunnel. Not alone, not trapped. There is a way out, right through here, up these steps. I steady my breathing and follow the others.

As we head upstairs, the woman continues interrogating me. "What just happened? Were you pushed? Did you see or hear anything?"

"Not that I know of," I say. "Why were you filming me?"

"We've been monitoring some unusual activity at the theater these last few nights," she says. "Where did you even come from?"

I have zero good answers tonight, so I stay quiet.

"Hey, let's get you cleaned up," Cameron says when we're one flight up. To my left, twenty feet away, is the exit.

"I can find my way out from here," I say.

"Let's have a little chat first. Maybe find you some shoes." He gestures down the hall in the opposite direction of the exit.

Part of me is tempted to make a break for it, but there are various ways the situation could get more embarrassing. This time the exit door could be locked or set with an alarm. There could be a second film crew or additional cameras ready to capture my hasty escape. Or local police on their way to check out the disturbance I caused. And even if I get away, there's no telling what Cameron might say about the incident on his podcast. Not that I care what the majority of his listeners think, but I know Quinn is one of them. Better to smooth things over with Cameron now than deal with my daughter's inquisition later. "Sure, a chat sounds great." I can't quite keep the sarcasm out of my voice.

"They haven't set up any cameras on this floor yet." It takes a few tries until he finds an unlocked door. "We should be okay in here." He ushers me into a narrow dressing room crammed with empty wardrobe racks, its walls plastered with old playbills. It smells of stale cigarette smoke and some kind of varnish.

I cross my arms and perch on a sunken plaid sofa as Cameron pulls up a stool. "I didn't get attacked by some kind of ghost or demon," I say. "I just leaned against an old wall and part of it crumbled. Nothing otherworldly. It's an old building."

"And the subbasement hasn't seen any major renovations in over fifty years. I wouldn't attribute the loose stones to anything paranormal." His reasonable tone should put me at ease, but we both know there's more to this. "What I'm puzzled by is your sudden appearance."

"Yeah, me too." I chew my lip and regard the floor's tattered carpeting, which is a color so dreary it doesn't know whether it wants to be brown or gray or beige. "Did I just . . . I mean, did anybody see where I wandered in from?"

"We all saw, on the monitors upstairs. Which is why we all came rushing down. But I still don't understand how you could've gotten to the theater's lower level without anyone seeing you. Hang on, I'll show you." He takes out his phone, taps on the screen a few times, and turns it toward me.

It's a photo of a monitor with a grid of video feeds. "This is how they did the setup. The crew placed night vision cameras in various areas of interest, most of them in the auditorium—the stage area, the wings, backstage, the catwalk. There's also one in the trap room—that's the room beneath the stage, which was the site of the wine cellar when this place was the Worthington Estate. And a couple a floor below that, in the subbasement, which should look familiar." The next photo is a closer shot of the monitor, zeroed in on the upper-right-hand corner, which shows a stone-paved corridor with an arched ceiling. And there I am, a partially blurred gray figure curled up on the floor, face hidden in the crook of my arm.

A tremor zips up my spine.

"At first, we weren't sure what we were looking at." Cameron swipes to the next image, a grainy close-up of my upper body. It's like looking at a photographic negative of myself as interpreted by the night vision; my black hair registers as white strands splayed across the dark sleeve of my shirt, which is actually beige. "I mean, we knew it was a person, but didn't know . . ."

"Whether I was a human or a ghost? For future reference, when in doubt, go with the former," I say.

"Hey, if you saw some of the footage this team has collected over the years, you might not be so sure. But in this case, what made your appearance unusual—there are a few things. First of all, this camera is motion activated. Presuming this is some kind of sleepwalking situation, if you came from the end of the hall, you should've been captured entering into the frame before taking your little nap on the floor. But the motion sensors weren't triggered until you were already lying down. Also, there's only a single entrance at the end of that hall, and it's locked. The other entrance is from the stairs, and there's another camera there that didn't pick up anything." He brings the phone in for a closer look, a preoccupied frown clouding his face.

First Violet appears in a photo where she doesn't belong, now I do. What an unexpected thing for us to have in common.

I have a sudden urge to flee. Would he try to stop me? My breathing quickens at the thought. "I-I don't know what to tell you," I stammer. The fear and uncertainty in my voice repels me, so I sit up straighter and try again. "Your cameras must've malfunctioned and whatever locked doors I made it past must not be all that secure. Like you guessed, I've been having some sleepwalking issues. No idea how I ended up here, but the last time I checked, I wasn't one of the X-Men, so it's not like I can walk through walls. I mean, you just saw me almost crash through a wall—I'm closer to being the goddamned Kool-Aid man than a superhero." This infusion of sass clears my head and propels me to my feet. "Now, I hope we can avoid making a big deal out of all this, and save me some embarrassment. I'll leave you to your ghost hunting or whatever this is. Right now, I'd like to get home and finish sleeping in my own bed." I take slow, shuffling steps backward, flashing Cameron a phony smile as I retreat.

"I wish you didn't act like you think I'm out to take advantage of you. I don't blame you for it—I'm sure you've had shitty experiences being fame-adjacent, but . . ."

"But what?" I stop my slo-mo moonwalk. "You're not like those other guys? You're just trying to help?"

"Actually, yeah. I *am* trying to help you." His voice is two parts faux-wounded, one part self-righteous.

It would be more sensible to keep my mouth shut and resume my exit, but this disorientation is too much and the majority of my energy is dedicated to keeping my shit together. Which leaves very little in the way of impulse control. "Are you trying to help like the people who went through my trash for a month and then blogged about it? Or the so-called private detective who claimed to have irrefutable proof of my sister's whereabouts and conned me out of five grand before fleeing the country? I'm at the point where I don't think I can handle getting any more help." My voice cracks.

"Sasha, hold on. I really do want to help you." Now he almost sounds sincere.

"What I think you really want is to get on my good side, so I finally grant you that podcast interview. Or to sweet-talk me into signing a release so you can use that basement footage of me for whatever spooky series you people are making here. Neither of those things is gonna happen." I turn to go but Cameron's next words freeze me in place.

"Just to be clear, *Off the Beaten Path*—that's the 'spooky series' being filmed here—doesn't need you to sign a release to use your likeness. There are signs posted outside and all over the building stating that the theater is being used as a filming location the next few days and anybody who sets foot on the property automatically gives consent if they end up on camera. In all fairness, I also don't need your permission to discuss the incident on my podcast."

My jaw goes so stiff, it's a wonder I don't crack a tooth. I throw a disgusted glare over my shoulder but don't leave the room.

"Sasha, listen. We're in a position to help each other here. I'll talk to the producers and get you edited out of the show. In exchange, I'd like an interview with you for *Strange Exits*."

"Yeah, I don't think so." It takes an astronomical amount of will-power not to add, *Go fuck yourself.*

"You have two choices. Be presented on TV however the producers decide, or present yourself, in your own words, on the podcast."

This time I can't hold back. "Go fuck yourself." But I also can't leave. I stomp over to him, waving a finger in his face. "Those are shitty choices and you know it."

"Agreed." He flashes his palms and ducks his head in concession. "Any chance I can get you to sit for a minute?"

Now he's being all nice again. What a jerk-off. The worst thing about it? I have to hear him out in case he can help me avoid some deeply awkward publicity. I return to my spot on the plaid sofa.

"Just keep an open mind," he insists.

That's my cue to start cringing. Whenever someone tells me to keep an open mind, they may as well be promising to inundate me with bullshit they expect me to believe as fact.

"There's someone you need to meet," he says. "She might be able to offer you some guidance, and she's been dying to talk to you."

"And I've been dying to be left alone. Yet you still keep badgering me to talk and talk and talk."

"This part doesn't have to be for *Strange Exits*. The whole thing can be off the record. I don't even need to be there. I just want to set up a meeting with you two."

"A meeting with a certain person named Antoinette?"

"How'd you know?"

"I listen to your stupid podcast, okay?" A flush creeps up from my collarbone.

"Really? You listen to *Strange Exits*?" The boyish pride in his voice says he's choosing to ignore my derisive modifier.

"This isn't the fangirl moment you've been waiting for."

"No, of course not." He shakes the smug grin off his face. "So you must've heard the last episode."

And all the others. How could I not? "Yeah, I heard that one and somehow my eyeballs didn't become detached despite my violent eye-rolling." I can't resist a quick demonstration. "I've tried to be pretty tolerant about the crazy theories surrounding Violet's disappearance—aliens, the Illuminati, dimensional rifts. People can believe what they want to believe. What bugs me is when they try to foist their beliefs on others without any solid evidence. Like your girl Antoinette."

There's a sudden flutter in my peripheral vision. I turn as a sheet of paper becomes unglued from the wall, drifts down, and lands in my lap.

It's a playbill for a ballet performed at the Witkin Theater some years back. *Swan Lake*. The poster's two central figures are kneeling, clad in tutus made of feathers. Two swans framed by a swan-shaped silhouette. Three swans.

The playbill quivers in my unsteady hands. A shiver tickles the back of my neck.

The swans mean something.

This was supposed to be over once Violet was a no-show at the vigil.

It's not over until you follow the arrows.

Why is my brain trying to lure me into a labyrinth of synchronicity? This ballet has nothing to do with me or my sister. Neither do swans. So why do I experience the same magnetic pull to this poster and the swan figures in Renatta's office? It's like there's a clue I'm meant to pick up on, a code I'm expected to decipher.

My teeth begin to chatter.

"What's wrong, Sasha?"

Typically, my automatic response is "nothing," but my life is veering down atypical paths and unvarnished honesty feels more appropriate here. "I'm afraid . . ." The words a breathy whisper but their truth provide unexpected armor. "This show, your podcast, the unending Violet mania, my nosy daughter, everybody digging and digging. For any trace of her or who she was."

"Why is that scary for you?" Cameron asks.

"You sound like my therapist." Which is who I should be saying all this to. Unfortunately, you can't always control when your emotional volcano will erupt. I clasp my elbows, as if buckling myself into an invisible straitjacket. "I'm so tired of pretending to keep it together. I'm not even that good at it. My husband knows something's wrong but acts like he's afraid to ask. My daughter isn't afraid to ask me anything but gets annoyed at how little I tell her."

"About Violet?"

"About Violet, about how fucked-up I am, about how fucked-up things were with me and Violet." A hard swallow and I raise my head to look at Cameron head-on. If this is when the postoutburst wave of cathartic euphoria is supposed to hit, it's taking its sweet time. "I don't know what happened to my sister, and I don't know how to live with not knowing. All I do know is, weirder and weirder shit is happening, and therapy isn't helping, and I don't think some podcast host or random curly-haired lunatic is gonna help, either."

"Okay, fair enough." He rubs his knees and looks at me sideways. "It's not like those are your only options, though."

"No offense, but the only options I'm interested in right now are the ones that involve me going home." I uncross my arms and stand up. "It might be too much to ask for this to be off the record, but—ouch!" Something angular embeds itself into the arch of my socked foot. I sit back down and bring my heel across my knee, expecting to retrieve a pebble or tack of some sort. "Are you fucking kidding me," I mutter, pinching a small hair clip between my thumb and forefinger. It's black and plastic and shaped like a butterfly. Violet owned hundreds like it back in the day.

"What is it?" Cameron leans in but I close my fingers around the clip before he spots it.

"It's nothing. Or maybe it's something. I don't know . . ."

Something thaws within me. This little plastic butterfly, along with the twos and the swans, the series of synchronicities littering my path . . . it's all so maddening. Even though part of me wants to dismiss it as nonsense, deep down, I can't help but find something lovely about it, too.

"I'll think about being on your podcast. For real. In the meantime . . ." I fight an onslaught of reluctance and quickly lose. "You think you can set up a meeting for me and Antoinette?"

FAX COVER SHEET

April 28, 2003

Violet,

Thanks for offering to look after Quinn these next two weeks. I'm sure she'll have a blast with you. And it'll be good for Sasha to have this time to get back on her feet.

Here's the release form you requested. I still don't love the idea of our daughter appearing on TV, but if you say it'll be a fun surprise for Sasha, I'll take you at your word. Remember: nothing crazy!

—Gabriel

Roses Are Red, Violet Is Red-Hot

By Noriko Tomlin

MAY 7, 2003

My Violet Volk obsession/girl crush was born when I saw her Vegas show a few years ago. After that, I'd TiVo every one of her TV specials and random appearances (I still cry every time I see that clip of her surprising the boy with the brain tumor at his elementary school graduation). My friends joked about restraining orders when they saw my bedroom covered with magazine pics of Violet, but I'm not the stalking type. I just thought she was a badass chick taking over a male-centric industry and giving it a much-needed makeover. I mean, how could you not love her style? She was like the Gen-X love child of Morticia Addams and Liberace. The woman wore a dress made out of playing cards to the Oscars! (Confession: when I got married last year, I wore red glitter lipstick and rhinestone butterfly hair clips in tribute to VV.)

It drove me nuts that Violet didn't give interviews, though I also kinda loved it. I didn't love when she announced a hiatus from magic, though. Did that mean I'd have to go back to watching cheesy guys in leather pants making scantily clad girls disappear? Ugh, no thank you. A year passed with no word from Violet and the whole world began to feel so blah. And then BAM! A VV book announcement! BAM! A VV tour announcement! BAM! A VV cover story in *PopArk*! BAM! A VV appearance on *LateFridayLive*!

I haven't read the book yet (spoiler alert: I'm gonna love it) but I've maxed out two credit cards getting tickets to see her in multiple cities (whatever "an evening of magical inspiration" means, I'm in!). I've also framed the *PopArk* cover (whoever came up with the idea of putting her in a neon electric chair is a friggin' genius) and I've watched her *LateFridayLive* segment like ten times since it aired yesterday.

First of all, let's talk about the costume. I don't know what I'm more enamored with: the silver catsuit or that black cage skirt she wore over it. Second of all, how adorable is her niece? I died when she came out in a matching outfit, down to the sparkly red lips. Too cute!

Then there was the illusion itself, which was pretty much the most breathtaking thing I've ever seen. I was in tears just from the pep talk Violet gave her niece, about how she can be anything she wants to be, and not to put any limits on herself. And then you have this precious little girl say she wants to be an angel and a mermaid, but her mother tells her those are both impossible. And while everyone watching is reaching for the tissues, Violet tells Quinn that her mother is wrong, that nothing is impossible.

I'm getting goose bumps remembering it, and I didn't even get to the magic yet!

Here it comes, though. After Violet says nothing is impossible, both she and the little girl start floating up. First, they're just hovering a few inches above the stage, then a foot. The girl says she's scared, and Violet tells her she shouldn't be, because she's an angel. A second later, the girl sprouts wings (where did they come from??) and flies like fifteen feet into the air. She gasps, laughing in pure delight. Now this is motherfucking magic.

My jaw's already on the floor at this point, but Violet is still hovering a foot off the ground, chill as can be, while her niece is way above her. At this point, Quinn starts looking pretty freaked-out, but Violet reassures her, as a humongous tank of water is wheeled onto the stage, that if she gets tired of flying, she can stop anytime she wants to because the girl is not only an angel but also a mermaid. All of a sudden, there's a huge explosion and all you can see is a cloud of feathers and glitter and all you can hear is this little girl screaming before she splashes into the water, which is now bubbling like a massive Jacuzzi. There are flashes of the girl's dark hair and silver leotard, and it seems like she's struggling in this tank and—holy shit, is she going to drown?

Violet runs to the tank, ready to climb in and rescue her niece, but then this little hand comes out of the water, then part of an arm. A trapeze is lowered over the tank, the hand grabs hold of it, and the girl is slowly pulled up, soaking wet, stunned like all the rest of us. And as her bottom half emerges—if you're guessing mermaid tail, ding-ding-ding! It's iridescent and gorgeous and I kinda want one.

If that's not a mic drop moment, I don't know what is.

Now pardon me, I need to go watch it again.

Strange Exits

Episode 8: "Use Her Illusion"

CAMERON FRANK [STUDIO]: If I looked at your book collection, I'd bet there's a fifty percent chance I'd find a copy of *You Are Magic* or *Life's Great Illusion*—maybe both. To date, the books have sold a combined total of over fifty million copies. They've been translated into dozens of languages and make periodic reappearances on bestseller lists, particularly around the holidays. The two titles also spawned a successful line of journals, workbooks, and page-a-day calendars. It would not be an understatement to call Violet Volk's brand of self-help a global phenomenon.

Violet was instrumental in building this phenomenon, touring the world as a motivational speaker in support of her books. In fact, she spent much of the five years leading up to her disappearance on the road.

And by her side during that time was Rudy Serrano, who I'll be speaking with today.

Rudy was born into theater royalty. Both Tony Award winners, his father, Javier Serrano, has been one of Broadway's most lauded directors and producers since the 1970s, and his mother, actress/singer/dancer Linda Driscoll, still graces the Great White Way, currently starring in the musical adaptation of *Requiem for a Dream*. Having followed in his parents' footsteps, today Rudy is a Tony Award–nominated

Broadway theater producer and talent manager. Earlier in his career, he was Violet Volk's tour manager. And there are few people who can provide a better glimpse into her life during those final years before she vanished.

CAMERON FRANK: Rudy, it's good to have you on the show. To begin, talk a little about how you and Violet first met.

RUDY SERRANO: My parents were good friends with Joyce Belote, Violet's manager. In the mid-nineties, I was just out of high school and still living at home, working various theater jobs. Joyce would come around to dinner once in a while, and I tried to be around for those meals. The woman was a character: in her sixties, foul-mouthed, chain-smoking, with a red bouffant wig and bright green eye shadow. She was funny, bawdy, and sarcastic, like all four Golden Girls rolled into one. And she'd tell the best showbiz stories.

CAMERON FRANK: Did she talk much about Violet?

RUDY SERRANO: Oh yeah, like a proud grandmother, bragging about the bookings she got for her, that sort of thing. But I didn't actually get to meet Violet for a few years, not until after the Vegas show closed and she came to New York for a couple of weeks. Joyce threw a small dinner party for her. This must've been sometime in early 2002.

CAMERON FRANK: What was your impression of her? Were you already a fan of her work?

RUDY SERRANO: So, about that. Um . . . not really. I was more of a snob back then, and I didn't consider stage magic high art. So even if I saw Violet in passing on TV, I might've watched for a minute, then changed the channel. If anything, I was just happy for Joyce, that one of her clients got so popular. Even if I did think of that client as a cheesy attention whore.

CAMERON FRANK: And what did you think seeing her in person?

RUDY SERRANO: Not as cheesy as I considered magicians at large, but still very much an attention whore. Joyce sat me beside her, so I had to endure an entire evening of Violet turning forks into spoons, making bread rolls levitate, changing the white wine into red, you get the idea. The other guests found it downright delightful. I pretended I did, too, but I just wanted to eat my dinner in peace, without her making my broccoli burst into flames. Then there was Joyce, who sat on my other side and gave me these encouraging smiles throughout the night, talking me up to Violet, how smart and ambitious I was, how I was moving up in the world. Then I remembered she'd mentioned Violet being divorced, and how she was always on me about meeting someone special . . . I couldn't believe it. The whole thing was a setup.

When Joyce went to check on dessert, I followed her into the kitchen. I mustered up something about how lovely and talented Violet was, but firmly stated she wasn't my type.

Joyce burst out laughing and said, "What kind of fucking idiot do you think I am that I'd set up Violet with a gay man?"

At that point, I still hadn't come out to my parents, but Joyce said she could tell as soon as she met me.

CAMERON FRANK: So if it wasn't a romantic setup, why was she talking you up so much to Violet at dinner?

RUDY SERRANO: To lay the groundwork for Violet to see me as a professional figure she could trust. I'd been working with some touring theater companies for the last couple of years, and Joyce had been hearing great things about me. She felt I was ready for the next step and offered me the opportunity to be Violet's tour manager. I said yes without knowing anything about the type of show it would be, the pay, nothing. I know, so much for my highbrow ways.

CAMERON FRANK: Why were you so quick to accept the position? Didn't you have misgivings, considering you weren't a fan of magic?

RUDY SERRANO: Some, but I trusted Joyce. She'd never steered me wrong before when I'd asked her for professional advice—hell, her life was dedicated to shaping other people's careers. If she believed this was the right move for me, I'd listen to her.

We got to work the next day, Violet, Joyce, and I, figuring out what sort of tour to do in support of *You Are Magic*. The book wasn't even done yet, but the venues she wanted to play get booked six months to a year in advance, so we needed to plan early.

Without a dinner party of guests to entertain, Violet was a different person. She wasn't trying to be coy and charming and mysterious. Once she dropped that shtick, I could talk to her. I preferred her more direct, bitchier.

Violet was already butting heads with her publisher about what kind of promo to do for *You Are Magic*. Empirical wanted a traditional book tour with bookstore visits, Q&As, signings, the usual. That didn't appeal to Violet. She wanted to do something unconventional.

CAMERON FRANK: Like what?

RUDY SERRANO: She was still figuring that out. She wanted to incorporate magic in a way that tied into the book but wasn't as grandiose as her Vegas show.

CAMERON FRANK: Wasn't "grandiose" pretty much out of the question given the previous accidents and rising insurance premiums?

RUDY SERRANO: It might've been out of the question in Vegas, but she had other options. A couple of touring magic shows offered her a headline spot, but she saw that as a step back. She also turned down not only my father, but other theater producers who approached her about doing a Broadway show. Joyce said she could've even done a solo tour, playing arenas if she wanted.

CAMERON FRANK: That's surprising, considering the media at the time painted Violet as too much of a liability, with nobody wanting to take a risk on her.

RUDY SERRANO: That was Violet creating a narrative.

CAMERON FRANK: I don't understand.

RUDY SERRANO: Her reputation did take a hit after Dominic Puglisi's death, but once the divorce followed, and then getting dropped by the Kintana, she knew she needed to ride that negative wave for a while. She saw her celebrity as a form of storytelling. It wouldn't make a good story if she made a comeback too quickly, professionally or romantically. The public needed to see her suffer, to put those accidents behind her, and to get to a place where they'd root for her again. So when she moved back to LA from Vegas, even though things were great with Mayuree, she played out that relationship like a trainwreck in public, picking fights with her when paparazzi were around to document them. Eventually, Mayuree had enough of the charade, and she took off. The tabloids painted Violet as emotionally unhinged and speculated about addiction issues, after which it was easy to plant stories about her career being in trouble. It was a tricky gamble, and Violet did lose out on film and TV opportunities at that time.

CAMERON FRANK: Was Joyce advising her to do all this?

RUDY SERRANO: Oh, hell no. Joyce wanted Violet to step out of the spotlight entirely for a year and let all the shit cool off instead of stirring up more of it. Joyce used to say managing Violet was an oxymoron. "Stubborn as a fucking mule, that one."

But she was always there to support Violet no matter what. After the Mayuree breakup, when Violet said she wanted to write a book instead of putting together a new stage show, Joyce was encouraging. After three years of nonstop performing, it could be the break Violet needed.

Of course, it wasn't long before she talked about returning to the stage anyway. Though the show she initially conceptualized was very different from the act we took on the road.

CAMERON FRANK: How so?

RUDY SERRANO: Initially, Violet wanted to forgo working with assistants and rely entirely on audience participation. And we're not talking about picking a card, any card, but extreme illusions involving pyrotechnics, barbed wire, sealed glass boxes. Violet's reasoning was, having everyday people create these illusions alongside her, they'd be harnessing their own magic, which would reinforce the ideas in the book.

Of course, there were two huge challenges to creating a show like that.

CAMERON FRANK: The first thing that comes to mind is safety.

RUDY SERRANO: Exactly. And Violet didn't know how all of these effects would work, looking dangerous and dramatic but being safe enough for a novice to participate in, so we hired the best magician consultants out there to help design the show.

The second challenge was trust. After the onstage injuries in Vegas, after Dominic, how were you going to convince members of the audience to get up there at all, then stay up there when they saw the crazy shit she had planned for them?

CAMERON FRANK: Is this where Quinn Dwyer comes in?

RUDY SERRANO: Almost.

We're in spring of 2003 at this point. The *You Are Magic* tour was already sold out, with all this secrecy surrounding what kind of show it would be, apart from a press release that promised inspiration with a dash of magic or something to that effect. Violet's *LateFridayLive* appearance would be the first preview of the tour to come.

It was always Violet's intention to perform that illusion with a little girl. What better way to regain the trust of her audience? It just so happened that her niece was visiting at the time and willing to be part of the act.

It went great, too. The audience loved it, the press raved about it. We were two weeks from kicking off the tour and already being inundated with requests to add dates.

I don't know the details of what happened next, but less than twenty-four hours later, Violet demanded we tone down the act, and said she wouldn't be performing any effects with audience participation, which was about fifty percent of the show. Everything had to be reconfigured at the last minute. It was a creative and logistical nightmare.

CAMERON FRANK: Did Violet tell you why she decided on these major last-minute changes?

RUDY SERRANO: When I asked her, she said she wasn't confident enough to do the bigger illusions, especially the ones with volunteers, without something getting fucked up. She refused to take a risk like that again and face more accusations of caring more about her career than about people. She was so adamant, she said if I tried to change her mind, she'd fire me on the spot and cancel the tour altogether.

I thought maybe Joyce could reason with her, but she said Violet made the same threats to her.

So we cut the bigger illusions, repurposed the set pieces as best we could, focused on interesting ways we could use light and sound, and . . . it's a testament to Violet's charisma that she pulled it off. The first couple of weeks were rough, but she kept getting new ideas on how to create this special experience for her fans. It obviously worked out because we spent a good four and a half years touring.

CAMERON FRANK: What was that like? What was *she* like during those years?

RUDY SERRANO: After getting a taste of her high-strung diva side, I braced myself when we got on the road. And I did see that side of her again, but not as often as I expected. I was actually really surprised by how . . . nice she was.

CAMERON FRANK: That's probably the first time I've ever heard someone refer to Violet Volk as nice.

RUDY SERRANO: And she'd probably hate me for saying it. I don't mean nice in a bland way. It caught me off guard how caring she was.

The woman was like a rock star at that point. She could demand anything she wanted and have it handed to her on a platter. A state-of-the-art tour bus with a custom-made isolation tank? Done. Fresh local produce and a vegan chef preparing all meals? Done. Every step was taken to make sure Violet was comfortable on the road.

But she made sure it went both ways and prioritized the well-being of her entire crew, all fourteen of us. Sometimes she could be annoying about it—not all of us enjoyed the meditation and smoothies she foisted on us daily—but she took care of us as much as we took care of her. She made sure we were eating right, getting enough sleep. Scheduled more days off than any other tours I've done. Depending on the place and season, she'd take us on bike rides or hikes. If we were having a tough week, she'd try to do something to raise our spirits, like hire a masseuse or throw us a pool party. Sometimes it would be something offbeat, like laser tag or country line dancing. Most of the crew was busy setting up the show during the day and breaking it down at night after she performed, so they didn't see much of Violet. But she still tried to spend one-on-one time with each of us, inviting us to watch movies or play video games on her tour bus.

CAMERON FRANK: Violet played video games?

RUDY SERRANO: Oh yeah. She especially loved the survivor horror ones like *Silent Hill* and *Resident Evil*. Her favorite was *GTA*, though. I wasn't allowed to schedule any shows for the forty-eight-hour period following a new *Grand Theft Auto* release and made sure she was not disturbed for that duration.

CAMERON FRANK: I wouldn't have expected Violet to be so carefree at this point.

RUDY SERRANO: She wasn't. I think she was very lonely and stayed on the road so long because it kept her distracted. That's why she had me schedule so many private after-hours shows for her, too. If she could be up late enough performing, she could sleep through the day and not have as much time to kill before she had to go back onstage.

She was happier when Mayuree joined the tour—those two were on-again/off-again for years—but she didn't come around often and sooner or later they'd start fighting, and Mayuree would leave. That's when Violet would be at her lowest. Nothing we could do would help except waiting for her to come out of it. We all knew she was estranged from her family, so we never mentioned them. But we felt bad that she didn't really have anyone, so we made sure she could rely on us. The crew was very protective of her.

CAMERON FRANK: It sounds like you formed your own makeshift family.

RUDY SERRANO: That's what happens on the road.

I'm not saying Violet and I became besties—we didn't—and I never grew to care for her act—the only thing I hate more than magic is the world of self-help. But I cared for Violet.

I can't imagine where she might be now. I like to think she's playing *GTA* somewhere, sipping on a smoothie, not giving a shit about what the rest of us are saying about her.

July 22, 2003

Dear Violet,

I didn't expect you to come through the way you did, but you *saved* me making all of Mom's funeral arrangements. Thank you for that. I knew she didn't have long, but even when you see it coming, you never know how it'll hit you, and it hit me like a freight train. I can barely even remember the week you were here, just how comforting it was to have you around. It felt like having the sister/best friend I always wished for.

You came through yet again when you offered to take care of Quinn while I got my shit together and spent some quiet time with Gabriel. It was hard to see you two leave, but she was elated to go to Cali with you.

I never imagined things could improve this much between us after . . . well, after everything. But with Mom gone, all that seemed inconsequential.

And then I saw you on *LateFridayLive*. And then I saw my daughter on *LateFridayLive*. I racked my brain for when you asked my permission to use Quinn in a magic trick or bring her on national TV with you or put her fucking life at risk to clean up your public image. Let's see, that would be never and never and never. Instead, you found a way of manipulating my husband into giving permission. Sounds about right.

I can't believe you'd use Quinn to demonstrate how "safe" your magic is when we both know how much can go wrong when you're dealing with harnesses and heights and water tanks. This was a delicate seven-year-old girl, not a professionally trained assistant (which you don't have the best track record with as is).

On top of that, I told you more than once I never want Quinn mixed up in showbiz. 'Cause, you know, I've seen what it does to a person.

Thanks for going against my wishes.

Did you see how scared Quinn was when she was "flying"? Though not as utterly terrified as when she nearly drowned. You were probably too up your own ass to see it, but I saw. Of course, she won't admit she was afraid, but she's not the same girl she was before. She's skittish, flinching at any sudden noise or movements, she has night terrors, and as much as she used to love swimming, now she's so scared of water, she won't go near it when we're at the beach—I can hardly even get her to take a shower (forget baths—she's convinced she'll drown in the tub).

Nothing and nobody is more precious to me than that child, and I'll never forgive you for what you did to her.

You really don't give a shit about anyone on this planet except yourself, do you?

That's it, we're done. Don't call, don't visit, don't write. Forget you have a sister.

S.

Date: April 14, 2004, at 4:33 AM
From: violet@violetvolk.com
To: theresa.epstein@empiricalbooks.com
Subject: possible idea

Dear Saint Theresa,

How very patient you've been with me. Coming up with something new
has been a bitch, but here's what I've been tinkering with. More of an outline of an outline. Is this something?

xxoo

VV

LIFE'S GREAT ILLUSION
By Violet Volk

Table of Contents

Part 1: Fake It
-Stop Hiding Behind the Curtain
-Risk Manage Your Escape Act

Part 2: Break It
-Cut and Restore Your Life

Part 3: Remake It
-The Art of Artifice: There Is No "You" to Discover, Only a "You"
  to Invent
-Meet Your New Best Friends: Smoke and Mirrors
-Become a Student of Yourself: Practice Your Sleights and Learn
  Your Angles
-Navigate Your Metamorphosis: Craft Your Character, Costumes,
  and Props
-Live and Let Lie: Exceptional Is Better Than Genuine

Part 4: Take It

-Master Misdirection: Show Them Where to Look and What to
See

-Don't Wait to Be Invited: Build Your Own Stage

Date: April 14, 2004, at 9:31 AM
From: theresa.epstein@empiricalbooks.com
To: violet@violetvolk.com
Subject: Re: possible idea

We can work with this. Keep going and let's talk next week.

How annoying is it that Guns N' Roses already took *Use Your Illusion*?

T.

Date: April 14, 2004, at 9:55 AM
From: violet@violetvolk.com
To: theresa.epstein@empiricalbooks.com
Subject: Re: Re: possible idea

Supremely annoying. It would've been the perfect title. Oh well . . .

Date: April 19, 2004, at 1:08 PM
From: theresa.epstein@empiricalbooks.com
To: violet@violetvolk.com
Subject: Re: Re: Re: possible idea

Lovely chatting with you today, as ever.

Are you okay? Something about you seemed off on the phone, more sub-dued. Do I need to stage a touring intervention? The seminars are great for book sales, but you've been on the road for a while now—I don't want you to burn out.

Date: April 19, 2004, at 1:55 PM
From: violet@violetvolk.com
To: theresa.epstein@empiricalbooks.com
Subject: Re: Re: Re: Re: possible idea

Are you kidding? I want to do twice as many dates when the second book comes out. I'm fine. I like being on the move, staying busy.

That said, I've been going at it hard and it's time for a break. Not sure where I'll go yet (leaning toward Nepal and Tibet) but I'll be off the radar all of next month. So you can hold off on that intervention.

If you'll excuse me, I have to go write a great book now.

                                                    xxoo
                                                    VV

Sasha

March 12, 2018

I've been waking up early for my morning runs, to get in an extra couple of miles. Too early today, as indicated by the milky half-moon and sky still smudged with navy peeking through the bedroom curtains. I lace up anyway. Down the stairs, out the door, and a damp chill greets me.

There's something furtive and appealing about being one of the first people up and about, like we're all conspiring to get a head start on the day.

The path I usually take circles Willow Glen in just over five miles. Quinn never joins me on these runs and Gabriel sometimes does, but not this early, so I can lose myself in my thoughts . . . or lose myself outside them. I'd take a bullet for those two, but ever since I came home from the Witkin in the middle of the night (this time they were both up), their earnest efforts to coax me into talking about my sleep-walking have been crazy-making. I don't have much to say about it—dissecting it with my therapist is bad enough. I can't go through the draining process again with Gabriel or Quinn, especially since I still don't know what to make of it all.

As I reach the entrance to Cordova Park, a rhythmic thump behind me snaps me out of my thoughts, sneakers on pavement accompanied by panting.

"Were you ever going to tell me about this meeting with Antoinette?" Quinn calls out to me, her voice breathy.

Instead of taking the hilly nature trails as originally planned, I direct us to the flat jogging track, past a series of pavilions shaped like giant steel mushrooms. "You stalking me or something?" I slow my pace so she can keep up.

"You gave me your account password when you were trying to recover that photo. But isn't it fucked-up how I need to stalk my own mother to find this stuff out?"

Fair point, but I still bristle at her acidic tone. "Your mother had this wacky notion that she was entitled to some privacy. Is that why you're accosting me? To get the dirt on Cameron and Antoinette? Since you won't be hearing any of it on the podcast—it's all gonna be off the record."

"I pretty much figured. Nah, I just happened to be up early and thought I'd try to get hooked on endorphins like you. So far, it's not working."

"You're lifting your knees too high and you're overstriding. You'll last a lot longer with a shorter stride. And loosen up those clenched fists, you're running like you're angry."

She rewards me with a snort, this one borderline irked. One of the things that helped me survive Quinn's teenage years is understanding her lexicon of grunts and other monosyllabic expressions.

"It's okay if running isn't your thing," I say, bringing down the pace another notch. "Gardening isn't my thing."

"Yeah, but you've tried to get into it with me a bunch of times, you just happen to be a disaster around plants. I was always opposed to the basic concept of jogging. If no zombies are chasing me, I don't see the point. But I thought I'd give it another shot."

"How come?" What an effort to keep my voice light and free of suspicion.

"I don't know, maybe you'd actually talk to me, like for real, if we had our thing." Whoa, where is this hostility coming from? "Dad and I have our thing—" She cuts herself off and comes to an abrupt halt. "Oh my god, Mom. I wish you watched *Beyond Bizarre* with us last night. There was an episode about Agatha Christie that was amazing."

I run in place, still processing the undercurrent of hostility coming from her, and muster some polite curiosity. "Oh yeah?" It baffles me, this affinity for true crime, especially unsolved disappearances. No matter how often she explains the odd comfort she gets from immersing herself in these stories, I can't grasp the logic in it. If I had my arm torn off by an alligator, the last thing I'd want to do is watch nature shows about alligators.

"Did you know she mysteriously disappeared in the 1920s?"

We resume a slow jog, beginning our second lap of the track.

"I think I vaguely heard about it at some point, but I don't know the details. They did find her, right?"

"That's the insane thing. They found her, but nobody really knows what happened."

"What do you mean, nobody knows what happened?" I have to keep my gait from quickening, my legs eager to break into a sprint. This isn't enough motion for my body, not enough exertion.

"Hey, we're right near Better Beans, let's grab some coffee."

Rounding the corner, we end up on Audubon Street, the main drag of Willow Glen. Other than Better Beans, only a bakery and an Italian deli are open this early, the scents of baking bread and freshly brewed coffee commingling. With the other businesses still shuttered, the town's full charm won't go into effect for another hour or two, when the outdoor retail displays kick the quaintness up a notch: baskets of flowers, artisanal soaps and jams, knickknacks, secondhand books, racks of colorful vintage clothing, handmade jewelry, petite paintings and sculptures . . . and soon enough, my salon A-frame chalkboard bearing a pithy quote (today's is I REGRET TAKING GOOD CARE OF MY HAIR— SAID NO ONE EVER).

I get us coffees from the Better Beans window counter while Quinn wipes her damp forehead with the bottom of her T-shirt, which is five sizes too big, as per usual.

"Thanks," she says, taking her cup, and we continue strolling. "So the story goes, Agatha was married to some dude who was cheating on her with his secretary. Apparently, the day he told her he was gonna leave her and went off to be with his side piece is the day she vanished. Her car was found abandoned somewhere in Yorkshire, which set off this national panic about where she could be. All these people got involved in the search, including the Sherlock Holmes guy."

"Sir Arthur Conan Doyle?"

"That's the one. I mean, this was Agatha Christie, who was super popular. It's like if Stephen King went missing today."

"I *am* familiar with Agatha Christie's contribution to literature." There's something equally endearing and infuriating when your kid is needlessly condescending toward you.

"Anyway, a week or two goes by, and they finally find her in some hotel like fifty miles from her abandoned car. How did she get there, right? Shrugs all around." Quinn offers her own exaggerated shrug. "But there she is at the Old Swan Hotel and get this: she was checked in under a fake name, pretending to be some rando South African lady."

The coffee cup almost slips out of my hand. "Did you say swan?"

"The Old Swan." Her response is cautious. "It's the hotel where Agatha Christie was found. What it's called today, anyway. Um . . . why the big reaction?"

"I don't know. Something about swans." A warm gust of air passes over us, perfumed with honeysuckle.

I can't worry my daughter about my mental well-being, or worse, send her scurrying down a labyrinth of coincidences that could all hit dead ends. "So why was she pretending to be someone else at the hotel?" Hopefully, Quinn won't press the swan issue.

The corners of her mouth turn down. "Nobody knows. And when they asked her about it, she said she couldn't remember a thing. She was in some sort of fugue state. At the time, people thought it might've been her way of getting revenge on her husband for leaving her— public sympathy and all that. Or maybe finding out about the affair was so traumatic, it sent her over the edge. But there's no official record, just a bunch of speculation."

"What do you think happened to her?" My use of a pronoun over a proper name is deliberate. As much as I'd like to discuss anything other than Violet, that might be what my daughter needs right now.

"What do *you* think happened to her?" The question lobbed right back at me.

The question. Always asked. Never answered adequately.

"I don't know enough of the circumstances," I hedge.

"If you had to guess."

As many times as the question has been posed to me, as many times as I've given variations on the same noncommittal response, it only hurts when Quinn asks it.

"I think, even though it looked like she had a good life on the surface, she was unhappy and needed to escape," I say. "Nobody will ever know why. None of us were in her head, you know?"

"I guess." Her gaze shifts over to me. "I think she stayed quiet because she was afraid that if she told the truth, nobody would understand."

"Maybe." My calves twitch and I flex my feet, then point them. God, I just want to run and run and run. Even if it's a loop, even though I always come back and would never dream of doing otherwise, it's the only escape I have. "Do you want to walk around some more?"

"In a minute." Before I can stand, Quinn's hand on my arm anchors me back down. "You love to complain about how we never have quality mother/daughter time—whatever *that* is—so how about we hang out here a bit?"

"Of course." Why do I feel like I'm being chastised? Another joy of motherhood: doing your best to understand your child and feeling like you're getting it wrong over and over again. "So how have you been doing? *What* have you been doing?"

"I've been spending a lot of time in the library."

"Just what the mother of a college student loves to hear."

"Not at SJU. I've mostly been there." She tilts her head in the direction of the Willow Glen Library two doors down. "Researching local history and stuff."

"Oh yeah?" Every part of me resists asking whether it's a project for school. Instead, I go with, "Find anything interesting?"

"Tons." The word is so loaded and her nod so slow.

"Anything you want to share?"

"It's funny, when I told you what happened with Agatha Christie, I thought some of it might be familiar to you?"

"I get it, you want to talk about Violet. But there's nothing—"

"This isn't about Aunt Violet. This is about you."

Come on now, it's never about me. "I'm sorry, Quinn, but your riddles are going over my head. I told you, I never heard that story before. I'm not hung up on unresolved disappearances like you are."

"Yeah, that's kind of the problem."

"Any chance you can just tell me what you're getting at?"

But she won't spit it out. The way she tilts her chin this way and that, like she's the cat and I'm the cornered mouse, tells me she's going to do this at her own pace, and if what comes next is unpleasant, that's on me.

"Since I've been at the library a lot, I've been talking to Mrs. Toback more." An expectant pause, but I don't take the bait. "I think you give her a bad rap. Sure, she's nosy, but how could she not be, considering? And she's not mean and gossipy about it—she's more of an Aunt Violet fangirl than anything. Says she still gives *You Are Magic* and *Life's Great Illusion* as gifts, and she makes sure the library is well stocked with both. Mrs. T's also been helpful with my research. Willow Glen's library isn't super high-tech, so a lot of local newspaper archives are still on microfilm. You ever use a microfilm reader? It looks like one of those computers in an eighties movie."

My stomach flips as Quinn reaches down and retrieves a folded-up piece of paper from her sock. Shaking it open, she smooths it out on the bench between us and turns it so I can read.

It's a 1987 article from the *Finchley Free Press*. About a cave-in at the mines. About me.

"I don't know what I'm supposed to say here, but I'm guessing it's going to be the wrong thing." She glowers at me. "Quinn, what do you want from me? I'm still a total blank on all this."

"You never even told me about it. Even if you don't remember much, it's a pretty major thing for a kid to go through."

The hurt in her voice pierces me, but I can't resist matching it with my own. "Are you sure this is really about me? Or are you upset I didn't tell you because it involves Violet?"

"It's something I would've liked to know. You could tell me now."

"There's not much to tell. You read the story." Not only am I lying to my daughter again, I'm doing it badly.

"It's so fucked-up, how I have to play the investigator because you keep things from me. You think I want to spy on your phone or spend hours in the library researching our family?" The jut of her jaw brings even more angles to her face. "I'm so sick of asking questions and getting the same nonanswers. Like, why did you keep me from seeing Aunt Violet for half my childhood? Go ahead, give me the usual line about how she was too busy touring."

"She *was* busy touring. I didn't see her for almost five years before the night of her last show." Sweat breaks out on my upper lip.

"And why is that? Could it be because of anything in that takedown you definitely didn't write that you swear is utter bullshit?"

Why have I gone this long propping up the mythology of such a flawed person at my own expense? Am I such a martyr that I'll sacrifice my daughter's respect for me to keep her ideals about Violet intact?

"Listen. Honey. I want to tell you everything, but I can't explain things I don't fully understand myself. I'm . . . working through it, I'm just not there yet." The problem isn't that she's too young. The problem is that I'm too cowardly. No wonder she doesn't share more with me.

"You forgot to add the part about knowing what's best for me. I used to believe it, too, but this sounds like it's more about what's best for you."

Ouch. I have no response to that.

"Can I at least come with you when you talk to Antoinette?" she asks.

"Let me think about it."

"Whatever." Quinn takes a final sip of coffee and stands. "Just to give you a heads-up, I'm headed to LA this weekend. I'll be gone a couple of days. Hopefully, that'll be enough time for you to think about it."

"Los Angeles?" Damn, she is all about surprises today. "But your birthday is this weekend. I thought we were going to do a *Saw* movie marathon and get sushi from the fancy place."

"We can do that when I get back. Or something."

It's hard not to feel like she's punishing me. "A-Are you visiting someone out there?" I stammer, not that she owes me any explanation or needs my permission. She's an adult, after all.

"Yes, I'm visiting someone. Maybe I'll tell you about it when I get back. I don't know why you're looking at me like that. I'm about to graduate college. Unlike you, I don't intend to spend the rest of my life in Willow Glen. You might as well start getting used to me not being around. Thanks for the coffee." She turns to go, but not without throwing a final jab. "You can hold on to that clipping. Maybe it'll jog your memory."

I want to call out to her, but after that verbal pummeling, I'm unable to speak. Even if I could, I don't know what I could say to smooth things over between us right now.

When I return to the house, Gabriel is out running errands and Quinn is stomping around her room, tossing clothes into an open suitcase on her bed. She doesn't acknowledge me when I peek into her doorway, so I let her be and make my way to the linen closet at the end of the hall. On the floor is a large storage bin filled with some of my mother's old hair tools and accessories: hot rollers, Velcro rollers, flexi rods, teaser combs, crimping irons, a myriad of clips and brushes, and various hair gadgets Mom couldn't resist ordering from TV ads. Tucked inside a box for something called the Air Kurl*Mi, which resembles a plastic medieval mace, is a stack of notes and letters held together with a scrunchie. All of them from Gabriel and me. All addressed to my sister.

Someone in Violet's entourage—a lawyer or a manager—sent them to me a year after she disappeared, before her California property was about to go into foreclosure, along with her passport and other legal documents. As I read each piece of correspondence, bit by bit, my personal history gained all these new layers, dark ones and light ones. When I showed Gabriel the letters, he thought I'd be upset with him for meddling so actively behind my back. Initially, the reality of his orchestrations and omissions was painful, but gradually, I recognized his kindness for what it was. How absurd and perfect. By the time I had begun shielding Quinn from Violet's transgressions, Gabriel had spent years doing the same with me. Believing the beautiful lie may be worse than accepting the ugly truth, but I was grateful for those beautiful lies. I just didn't realize they were also an invisible boulder on my back (Violet's moments of selflessness never did ring fully true). The ugly truth hurts more but weighs less.

Quinn is ready for this. It's time to take the boulder of beautiful lies off her back.

Rereading might make me lose my nerve, so I keep the bundle intact and wait for my daughter to finish packing.

When I hear her in the shower, I tiptoe to her room and sneak the letters into her suitcase.

Restless, I go downstairs in search of a momentary diversion. I circle the living room, unable to get Antoinette's instructions out of my mind. Follow the twos. What the hell does that even mean? How are you supposed to follow a number? Is it as simple as—

I snatch up the remote and turn on the TV. *You want me to follow the twos, Antoinette? I'll show you how pointless it is.*

I punch in three twos, not knowing what channel will come up, vowing not to make any tenuous connections between my sister and whatever appears onscreen.

A sepia-toned image of an ivy-covered brick building fills the TV as a male British narrator intones, "It wasn't until eleven days after her disappearance that Agatha Christie turned up as a guest at the Swan Hydropathic Hotel, known these days as the Old Swan . . ."

My arms break out in goose bumps. Mesmerized, I sit and watch the rest of the show.

Missing Girl Recovered After Tunnel Collapse

By Sam Raible

JULY 18, 1987

Many happy tears were shed when a twelve-year-old girl was discovered safe and sound in a collapsed section of the Finchley Mining System. Sasha Volkov went missing two days ago during an impromptu exploration of the tunnels with her older sister. The Finchley Mines have been closed to the public for years, due to unstable infrastructure, which led to frequent tunnel collapses. Unfortunately, this has not prevented exploration of the dangerous tunnels, which have led to accidents and deaths in recent years.

Howard Martindale, the head of the Willow Glen Fire Department, spearheaded search efforts for Sasha. "I don't know what the girls were thinking going down there," he said. "It's a miracle we found Sasha in one piece after two days."

It's also curious that the Volkov girl was discovered in a section of the tunnels that had been searched multiple times. Rescuers found her dehydrated, covered in scrapes and bruises, and unable to recall anything from the previous forty-eight hours.

"It's a head-scratcher, for sure," commented Chief Martindale. "We had three different groups go over every inch of that tunnel. There was no sign of the Volkov girl until this morning. It's like she magically reappeared. When we asked her if she'd been wandering around, she said she couldn't remember."

After being retrieved from the tunnel, Sasha was brought to the hospital, where she was treated for minor injuries and kept overnight for observation. While a subsequent medical examination found no head injuries, it is not unheard of for traumatic experiences to trigger a temporary episode of memory loss, also known as transient global amnesia.

"She may regain her memory at a later date, though there are no guarantees," said Dr. Raymond Patel, a neurologist at Finchley General Hospital. "What's more important is that her other memories are intact, and no other neurological abnormalities are present. At this point, the priority should be for Ms. Volkov to recuperate comfortably at home."

Which is exactly what Sasha is presently doing. Her parents, Anatoly and Regina Volkov, were thrilled to be reunited with their missing daughter, though they did not wish to speak on the record.

Date: March 12, 2018, at 9:04 AM
From: quinndwyer@sju.edu
To: SmokinAce@acemorgan.com
Subject: I guess let's do this

Hey,

No, I haven't changed my mind. Was just looking for a way to tell Mom without stirring up drama. Then I remembered that I'm a grown-ass woman and what I do is my business. Long story short: I'll be on that flight on Friday. But I did tell a friend I'm going to see you, in case you try to pull anything sketchy.

I hope you're not full of shit . . .

Quinn

Date: March 12, 2018, at 11:01 AM
From: quinndwyer@sju.edu
To: SmokinAce@acemorgan.com
Subject: Re: I guess let's do this

Quinn,

I'm full of shit about a lot of things, but this isn't one of them. I promise the trip will be worth your while.

Safe travels,
Ace

Strange Exits

꩜

Episode 9: "Checkmate"

CAMERON FRANK: This episode is going to be a little different.

As a podcaster, I have a certain code I try to adhere to. Coming from a journalistic background, I am diligent about fact-checking and verifying sources, but I also like to explore a story from every possible angle. That means having an open mind to theories that are not so easy to quantify.

When you cover a spectrum of topics that veer into high strangeness, it's bound to attract a . . . colorful array of individuals and claims. And when I can't verify the authenticity of such claims, the best I can do is trust my gut. There are a lot of hoaxers out there, and I believe my gut has steered me away from a fair number of them.

Then there's Checkmate.

My gut doesn't know what to make of Checkmate. I don't even know whether this individual is male or female, or even a single person—perhaps it's a collective of tricksters looking for a little airtime, masquerading as a singular shadowy figure. In any case, I'll refer to Checkmate as they/them.

A few months ago, I began an unusual correspondence with an enigmatic figure who purportedly had mind-blowing intel on Violet Volk. Maybe I should have known better than to play along, but there was something about Checkmate's utter indifference to me that caught me off guard. If anything, it seemed like Checkmate was trying to dissuade me more than persuade me.

Even the process of getting to talk to them was unconventional. After an exchange of formal emails, I was sent a package and instructed to go to a local park early in the morning on a specific day, and only open it then.

In hindsight, I'll admit it was foolish risking my safety like that. But the whole time, Checkmate made it seem like they were the one putting themself on the line.

I went to the park. On my way there, I kept looking around to see if anyone was following me, but Finchley was pretty dead at that hour, and since it was a rainy morning, there were no cars in the lot at Cedar Creek Park. I made my way to a covered picnic area and opened the package.

Inside was a burner phone, a spare phone battery, and a slip of paper with a phone number written on it. I called the number. Someone picked up on the second ring. The voice was electronically disguised. It was Checkmate.

I thought long and hard about whether to air this . . . encounter, and I still don't know what to make of it. You be the judge.

CHECKMATE: I appreciate you following the OPSEC I asked you to employ in protecting my identity and location.

CAMERON FRANK: OPSEC?

CHECKMATE: Operations security.

CAMERON FRANK: Is that an indication that you're involved with the military or CIA or some other clandestine organization?

CHECKMATE: I was with a group instrumental in maintaining national security, though I cannot offer my title or the specifics of my responsibilities. Any tangible proof I could provide would inevitably be traced back to me and would put us both in danger.

CAMERON FRANK: Doesn't having this conversation put you in danger?

CHECKMATE: It does, but lack of evidence offers plausible deniability for anything I am about to tell you. One can dismiss me as a geriatic loon spouting conspiracy theories. Information like this is easier to reveal when it's less likely to be believed.

CAMERON FRANK: And now that we're finally speaking, what would you like to reveal about Violet Volk?

CHECKMATE: We'll get to Ms. Volk, but first I need to provide some contextual information.

How aware are you of collaborations between intelligence agencies and people in the entertainment arts?

CAMERON FRANK: Well, I know government agencies consult with Hollywood and even sponsor projects, like war movies made to ensure the military is perceived in a positive light. I wouldn't be surprised if the CIA, FBI, or NSA get in on the act, too. Movies, TV, music . . . they're all useful tools to spread propaganda.

CHECKMATE: Indeed, they are, and the CIA and Pentagon are involved in shaping and approving scripts to ensure favorable portrayals—they have offices dedicated to such purposes. Aside from that, are you familiar with any specific field missions involving the entertainment arts?

CAMERON FRANK: . . . I can't think of any, other than the movie *Argo*. Didn't that involve the CIA working with Hollywood to create a phony film production as a cover to rescue Americans out of the Middle East? I think it was Iran during the hostage crisis?

CHECKMATE: That's correct. Though the adaptation of those events took liberties with the facts. The actual 1979 operation owed its conception and smooth implementation to the Canadian embassy's involvement. This was downplayed in the 2012 film, which ironically—or perhaps predictably—also involved the CIA consulting on the project.

There are numerous other examples, particularly during the cultural cold war. US intelligence went to great lengths to incorporate the arts in its subversion of communism, from mounting art exhibits and large-scale concerts to using Louis Armstrong and Dizzy Gillespie as "goodwill jazz ambassadors." Some celebrities discovered their role in propaganda operations but grudgingly went along with them, like the aforementioned jazz virtuosos. Others remained entirely unaware, like Nina Simone, whose 1961 tour of Nigeria was covertly sponsored by the CIA.

CAMERON FRANK: Wait, weren't the Beatles and Rolling Stones part of some MK-Ultra experiments with LSD? Or is that an urban legend?

CAMERON FRANK [STUDIO]: For those unfamiar with Project MK-Ultra, it was a top-secret and illegal program of mind-control experiments developed and run by the CIA from 1953 to 1973.

CHECKMATE: There were programs MK-Ultra used to manipulate mass populations with drug use, which did involve the Beatles and the Rolling Stones. Secret agents pushed LSD on members of both bands, for the purpose of popularizing and glamorizing psychedelic drugs. If memory serves, Mick Jagger was the surprising holdout on that one, and the last member of the Rolling Stones to try LSD.

But let's move on to stage magic. After all, this is what you're here for.

Have you heard of John Mulholland?

CAMERON FRANK: I have not.

CHECKMATE: He was a renowned stage magician, and at the height of the cold war, he created a manual for the CIA on misdirection, concealment, and stagecraft.

CAMERON FRANK [STUDIO]: True story. The text was supposed to be destroyed, but it was recovered, declassified, and published as *The Official CIA Manual of Trickery and Deception* in 1973. A sampling of what it covers: creating hidden signals via hand gestures and patterns in shoelaces, concealment of individuals in secret compartments, and techniques on how to spike someone's drink.

CHECKMATE: Mulholland's sleight-of-hand expertise was useful to agents in the field, though he was not the only magician employed in surreptitious government projects. Most have maintained their anonymity, though a few eventually get named. There have been claims of Harry Houdini working with Scotland Yard to spy on Germany and Russia, which have not been fully substantiated. But Uri Geller is another story.

CAMERON FRANK [STUDIO]: Uri Geller is an illusionist and self-proclaimed psychic. He gained fame for television performances involving telepathy and telekinesis—bending spoons with his mind, making watches stop or run faster, describing hidden drawings, that sort of thing. While many magicians have used their influence to debunk fraud in the paranormal community, particularly mediums and pseudopsychics, Geller was an anomaly in his steadfast assertions that his abilities were genuine and not stage trickery. This drew scrutiny and criticism from magicians, scientists, and skeptics, who proposed methods Geller could have employed in tricking his audience. Oh, and did I mention Geller also claimed to be a psychic spy for the CIA? There's that, too.

CHECKMATE: Earlier this year, newly declassified files revealed Uri Geller participated in CIA experiments to determine whether his paranormal abilities were genuine. These included remote viewing tests in which he was placed in a sealed and monitored room and asked to replicate drawings made in a neighboring room. The published results showed a surprising level of accuracy in many instances.

While this does not fully corroborate all of Geller's claims, particularly the more outlandish ones, it does offer some compelling data.

CAMERON FRANK: So how does Violet Volk fit into all this? Was she also part of secret experiments? She never made claims of having paranormal abilities, but many believed she was the real deal when it came to telekinesis.

CHECKMATE: She was the real deal. And she was enlisted in multiple operations.

CAMERON FRANK: But it had to be behind the scenes because she was so recognizable . . . Right?

CHECKMATE: [*long pause*]

CAMERON FRANK: Hello?

CHECKMATE: I'm still here . . . While I'm unable to share any details of the clandestine work she did, I will say one thing. Twenty-five years ago, we had disguises so advanced they could make anybody—*anybody*—utterly unrecognizable. Imagine the technology we've been able to apply since then.

CAMERON FRANK: The implication here that Violet Volk was a spy, psychic or otherwise, is—no offense, but it's ludicrous. She was putting on nightly shows in Vegas, flying all over . . .

CAMERON FRANK [STUDIO]: And that's when I thought of what Benjamin said about Violet's mysterious business trips. How they left her changed, haunted somehow. Basic logic dictates they could've actually been international corporate gigs or private hiking retreats, like the ones referenced by John Arno. Basic logic goes nowhere near the vicinity of espionage.

The thing is, Violet Volk has a way of defying basic logic.

CHECKMATE: Yes, Violet traveled a lot, even during her residency in Las Vegas. She was a tremendous asset to us, though we made a mistake in overscheduling her. It should have been easier once her obligations with the Kintana were concluded. We needed to ensure the contract wouldn't be renewed, so unfortunately, some extreme measures were taken to increase the theater insurance premiums so drastically, it wouldn't be financially feasible for the Kintana to continue working with Volk. And to damage her reputation just enough that she'd want to step away from the limelight. All of which would give her more bandwidth to participate in our operations.

CAMERON FRANK: Wait, so you're saying your people were responsible for those accidents? The accidents that left one assistant, Dominic Puglisi, dead?

CHECKMATE: Collateral damage, I'm afraid.

CAMERON FRANK [STUDIO]: My stomach turned at this response. It's a hideous thought, that people's lives meant so little in the greater scheme of sabotaging Violet's career. It makes me want to doubt Checkmate's claims that much more.

CAMERON FRANK: Huh. Okay, so you got Violet out of Vegas and away from stage magic. How did that work out for you?

CHECKMATE: At first, we were able to find a compromise in which she could reinvent herself as a motivational speaker, still incorporating some magic but not so much that it would be as draining as the grandiose Las Vegas production.

It worked well for a couple of years, but by the time Ms. Volk published her second book, she was becoming more stubborn and difficult to handle. She was adamant about returning to the stage for full-scale magic shows, and she expressed increasing hostility toward us. We became concerned that she would jeopardize field missions or leak confidential information.

CAMERON FRANK: It sounds like more extreme measures were called for. Who took them this time, you or Violet?

CHECKMATE: The way she disappeared had the hallmarks of one of our operations. I wasn't privy to its conception but did learn the details of its execution. Unfortunately, there was an incident that caused my immediate termination, so I never learned the outcome.

CAMERON [STUDIO]: His word choices here make me cringe. *Execution. Termination.* I've been quick to dismiss the idea, but is it possible Violet Volk truly could've met with foul play? And at the hands of the CIA? This goes beyond tinfoil hat territory, into . . . I don't know, tinfoil body armor.

CAMERON FRANK: Here's something I don't understand. If Violet's disappearance was the result of one of your secret missions, why have it take place in the middle of such a highly publicized and well-attended event?

CHECKMATE: Because it's so incongruous. Who would believe a world-famous entertainer would be taken in the middle of her own performance to be silenced by the government? And to "get disappeared" while doing a disappearing act? How ludicrous! Who could ever make such an accusation and be taken seriously?

CAMERON FRANK: Let's say this incongruous scenario is what happened. Even though you can't offer any proof. Why come forward with all of this now?

CHECKMATE: I'm proud of the years I've devoted to keeping our country safe, even though some of the things I've done for the greater good keep me up at night. Violet Volk also did things for the greater good, more than anyone will ever know. I've come forward now because I'm old and unafraid of repercussions. I'm not proud of how we tarnished Ms. Volk's name and sabotaged her career. Any apology I offer will be hollow and spineless. The best thing I can offer is a bit of truth. And hope.

CAMERON FRANK: Hope?

CHECKMATE: Yes, hope that she got my warning in time.

CAMERON FRANK [STUDIO]: And with that, the line went dead.

So? What do you think?

Did I fall for a hoax?

Or is Checkmate's account so preposterous it could actually be true?

One of the guiding principles of journalism is the two-source rule. Some reporters insist on three independent corroborating sources for every fact. I freely admit that my journalism has been shoddy with regards to Checkmate. I don't have three corroborating sources or two . . . or even one, for that matter. There is zero documentation to back up the things Checkmate said. All the background info on the government programs mentioned has been made publicly available. Any connections to Violet's mysterious business trips and her involvement with intelligence operations are tenuous as best. There's nothing to verify it. Any of it.

And yet . . .

As much as my journalistic roots urge me to be rational, there's something about this conversation I can't discard. I can't explain it any better other than to say *it feels true.*

Is it just me?

Sasha

~

March 19, 2018

Quinn returns from LA today. In the morning, she texts to say she won't need a ride from the airport. She also requests a family meeting for tonight. I offer to bring a pizza, eggplant and olives, from her favorite place. Her reply consists of a single letter: *K.*

Did she read the letters? She must've read the letters.

As I busy myself with the day's clients (three cuts, one balayage, two blowouts, and a double process), I try to keep the worry at bay, but it gnaws away at me. Quinn has never called a family meeting before.

After work, Gabriel greets me at the house, taking the pizza from me. He kisses my cheek and whispers, "Let her say everything she needs to say."

Quinn is at the kitchen table, chin resting on her interlocking fingers, her face solemn and vaguely imperious, like she's in a boardroom waiting for her underlings to file in. I'm half-expecting her to break out the PowerPoint. Tonight, she's the boss.

I get a courteous greeting but no hug. Once I've doled out pizza slices, Gabriel and I eat quietly (okay, I don't eat so much as pick at the crust), waiting for Quinn to begin.

"Thanks for getting dinner," she says to me. "Before we get into things, about that meeting with Antoinette—"

"I'd like you to come," I interject. "Both of you." Gabriel squeezes my knee under the table.

"I appreciate that." Her frosty tone warms a few degrees. "And I appreciate you letting me do what I needed to do in LA. It was . . . full of surprises. Beginning with the letters I found hidden in my suitcase."

"I've been going back and forth on whether that was a mistake," I say. "I couldn't find the right way or right time to tell you—"

"That my aunt was an asshole? I mean, it wasn't a total shock at this point, though the stuff with propositioning Dad . . ." She shudders.

I twist a piece of crust in my hands, crumbs raining down on my plate. "I was worried you'd resent me for keeping you away from her. Not letting you have more of a relationship with your aunt."

"In all honesty, Mom, I did resent you. But I get why you cut her off. It couldn't have been easy for you, either."

"It wasn't." For once, I let her see the pain in my eyes.

Quinn's face softens with sympathy and understanding. "We can get more into all that stuff later. Let me tell you about my trip to LA. I went out there to see Ace Morgan."

Apart from my raised eyebrows, I don't move.

Ace came to the first candlelight vigil for Sasha. When the camera crews were out of sight, I pulled him aside and scolded him like he was a little boy, how dare he betray my sister after being her trusted mentor, that sort of thing. I asked him to leave and never bother our family again.

He respected my wishes, until now.

"Mom, you don't have to be all stoic and creepy about it."

"Your mom's not being stoic or creepy, she's listening." Gabriel matches my stiff posture. "That's why we're here, to listen and support you."

"Great, but you guys don't have to act like robo-parents." Exasperation as she gives her head a little shake. "Anyway. He reached out to me. Apologized for not getting in touch these last—well, ever. Said there was some tension between him and the family, but he needed to explain some things. In person. And it had to be in California because—well, I'd see for myself when I got there. He even offered to fly me out." An appraising glance to see how I'm doing, and she goes on. "I knew you'd be against it if I mentioned it, and I didn't need your suspicions on top of my suspicions. I asked Ace why it had to be in person, and he said he needed to give me something. From Violet. And it was imperative he give it to me two days after my twenty-second birthday. Because 222 was her lucky number. Mom? Are you crying? Aw, Mom, it's okay. Really."

She scoots her chair over to me and Gabriel rubs my back while I blow my nose.

"I remembered what Antoinette said about following the twos, and even though the message wasn't for me, it still felt like—Mom, please don't kill me—it felt like a *sign*. But I didn't want to say anything to you guys until I made sure Ace was legit. He gave off a dickish vibe on *Strange Exits*, but there's no law against being a cranky old man." Quinn checks to see how I'm holding up, and I motion for her to continue. "When I met him, he did have a little of that old-school smarm and sexism—he called the waitress 'cupcake' and asked me why I was dressed like a boy—but other than that, he was . . . pretty great actually. He wouldn't stop raving about Violet, what a spitfire she was and how she was the best thing that happened to magic since Adelaide Herrmann."

"Who's Adelaide Herrmann?" Gabriel and I say in unison.

"I wondered the same thing, and he told me all about her. She performed around the same time as Houdini and was called the Queen of Magic. Her shows were epic, and she did tricks nobody else could do—like she did the Bullet Catch with an entire firing squad of six people. As if catching one bullet in your mouth isn't already a big deal, she caught six! You'd think that alone would make her more of a magic legend, up there with Houdini, but she was forgotten by pretty much everyone except hard-core magicians." Quinn takes a bite out of her pizza. "Ace said Aunt Violet used to tell him she was scared of being forgotten like Adelaide, and he'd reassure her that would never happen. Which is sweet and all, but at this point, I had to know what the deal was with *Magic Secrets Uncovered*. You ready for this one?" She's too hyped-up to add suspense at this point. "Aunt Violet was in on it! She knew about the whole thing and even helped him plan which tricks to reveal."

I open my mouth to ask exactly what Quinn goes on to answer. "I know, why would she do that, right? So apparently, she wanted to update her show, to keep up with the newer competing acts, but also because who wouldn't get tired of doing the same thing over and over again? It's the stuff Benjamin talked about on *Strange Exits*. But while Aunt Violet was suspected in rigging the stage accidents, *actually* she was in on having some of her biggest illusions revealed so the Kintana would have no choice but to let her update the show! Baller move, right?"

"Baller move," Gabriel and I echo in a painfully uncool way.

"Anyway, Ace and Aunt Violet only pretended to have a falling-out in public, but privately, they were always besties. He kept encouraging her to return to doing proper stage shows, even though the bigger money was in the motivational stuff she was doing. And if he knows anything about how or why she vanished, he wouldn't tell me no matter how much I badgered him. That's not why he needed to see me. His 'sole objective,' as he called it, was to give me this."

With a flourish, Quinn presents a small gold key. "Aunt Violet had him get the safe deposit box in his name, so it would never be traced back to her. It wasn't at a bank, either, but a private vault. He swore he never saw what was inside—I was skeptical about that, but Aunt Violet kept him on her payroll until she disappeared, and he lives in a ridiculous mansion, so benefit of the doubt and whatnot." Turning to Gabriel, she gives him a mischievous smile. "Dad, it's time to quote your favorite movie."

"My favorite movie?" He looks startled, like a kid not expecting to be called on by the teacher. "*Se7en?*"

"Gimme your best Brad Pitt."

He laughs, clears his throat, and makes his face a mask of anguish. "'*What's in the box?*'"

It takes a long beat for Quinn to answer, her jaw falling open, as if reliving the moment. "Cash. I mean . . . So. Much. Cash. It was amazing but it also kinda freaked me out. Ace started talking about getting a tax attorney and some other things, but all I could do was stare at all that cash." A hard blink, head shake, and she's back with us. "You know what I did next? I puked."

"Please tell me you threw up on the money," Gabriel says.

"Right on the money. It was so embarrassing, but then I couldn't stop laughing."

I wait for the two of them to stop laughing now before I ask, "Was there a note or anything else?"

"Three, actually." She fans out a trio of tiny envelopes, as if they're playing cards. They're like the kind you'd get with a bouquet of flowers and each one bears a single capital letter: *Q, S, G*. "I only read the one for me. It said, 'You'll probably do better things with this than I ever did. Just remember: your mom and dad already gave you everything that matters. Love, Aunt V.'"

Gabriel and I take the envelopes bearing our respective initials. "You first." I nod to him.

"'She's crafty, she gets around / She's sorry for letting you down. Love, V.'" His chest shakes as he swats away an errant tear.

"Isn't that a Beastie Boys lyric?" Quinn asks.

"The first part," I say, tearing into my envelope. The piece of card stock inside bears one sentence and our "222" sign-off. "'Everything's too serious to be so serious.'"

Great. Quinn gets stacks of cash, Gabriel gets an apology, and I get a pithy reminder to lighten up.

Quinn types something into her phone and holds it up. "It's a quote from *The Way We Were*."

While I preferred Streisand's musicals, I did watch that movie whenever Violet would put it on. For the longest time, I could never understand why it was her favorite. Then we watched it together after Mom died. When the credits rolled, we pawed at the tissue box between us, and I said, "I don't know how you can watch this over and over. It's too tragic. You have two people who love each other fiercely but are so different, they can't find a way to live together peacefully."

Sniffling, Violet dabbed at the mascara streaks beneath her eyes. "Yeah, it kind of reminds me of us. That's why it's my favorite."

That made me cry more than the movie, and remembering it now makes me cry even harder.

March 20, 2018

It's 4:00 PM. Gabriel, Quinn, and I meet Cameron outside a teahouse on a tree-lined side street that straddles the border of Willow Glen and Finchley. There's an old-timey SORRY WE'RE CLOSED signboard hanging from a suction cup on the front door, but when Cameron knocks, a woman's voice from inside trills, "Come on in!"

The small room has low ceilings dotted with hanging spider plants, which we duck around, in search of the voice.

Antoinette is tucked away at a corner table but stands to greet us. Between the ornate tea set, the gaudy flowered wallpaper and table-cloths, and her ensemble of stacked petticoats and mismatched velvets, I feel like I've been thrown into a British period film about a quirky headmistress.

After making the introductions, we jam our bodies into cramped wicker chairs, except for Cameron, who remains standing, shifting his weight from one foot to the other.

"I guess I'll catch up with you later," he says to nobody in particular, making a slow exit in case one of us calls him back. None of us do.

"I imagine coming here was not easy for you." Antoinette pours tea for us all as she speaks. "I'm so grateful you did. And how lovely for your family to join you." She motions to the tiered trays of finger sandwiches and miniature pastries before us. "Please. Help your-selves."

But I can't add any food or liquid to my jittery stomach.

"You have a lot to tell us today," Antoinette says to me. "Go at your own pace." Her glasses are tinted yellow and I can't tell what color her eyes are behind them. Still, her overall demeanor is less deranged than I expected.

"I don't know how you know that," I say. "And you probably wouldn't give me a satisfying answer, but . . . Fuck it. I'm just gonna start, before I lose my nerve. I . . ." Only it's become too dizzying, this merry-go-round of the peculiar and nostalgic spinning faster and faster, to center on one thing.

"Why don't you begin with the twos," Antoinette coaxes.

And so I do, recounting the synchronistic parade of triple twos, on clocks, receipts, lottery numbers, TV channels, and misdelivered mail.

"I can't help but think all these surreal and inexplicable things are adding up to something bigger. And that it connects to an incident from my childhood, something I've tried to put out of my head ever since it happened."

I keep my eyes trained on the tea in my cup, my hands warming on the porcelain.

"Violet and I grew up with the lore of the Finchley Mining tunnels. Every year, there'd be at least one kid who went down there and got lost or hurt, or worse. When we were little, our parents would try to scare us into staying away, telling us a nasty man lived down there who liked to shave the heads of little girls and chop off their feet to make soup. I understand wanting to keep your kids obedient, but little girl foot soup? Gotta love how twisted our parents were.

"We heard other rumors of sketchy activity that went on down there. Teenagers sneaking off to smoke weed, have sex, fight, graffiti parts of the tunnels . . . There were even rumors of weird religious rituals taking place down there—the Satanic panic was still a thing back then. Even if there wasn't an actual boogeyman waiting to shave our heads and eat our feet, there was still plenty to keep us afraid of that place.

"The summer before sixth grade, we read a story in the *Willow Glen Gazette* about buried treasure in the Finchley mines. This was a couple years after *The Goonies* came out, which made every child who saw it desperate to search for buried treasure.

"Violet and I took it a step further. You know those doorknobs that look like giant crystals? We used to unscrew the one on our bathroom door and pretend it was a big diamond, then take turns hiding it and make up all kinds of scavenger hunts for each other to find it. Dad got so annoyed having to screw the doorknob back in all the time, he went to the hardware store and got us one just to play with.

"When we read that story about how there might be actual treasure in those tunnels, there was no question that we had to be the ones to find it.

"One Saturday after lunch, we told our parents we were going to play with some friends at Cordova Park, packed some supplies into our book bags, and set off.

"As soon as we entered the tunnels, I was sure it was a horrible mistake. Our flashlights only penetrated a little bit of the darkness, our jackets were too thin against the cold, it was eerie and musty, and some sections smelled like pee.

"Violet had to have been creeped out, too, but every time I suggested we turn around and go home, her resolve only strengthened, and her annoyance with me grew, until she snapped and said I didn't deserve to find the treasure if I was going to be such a baby about it. That was it. I wouldn't let her bully me into what I believed was a dangerous situation, so I huffed and said I was leaving. Only I got turned around on my way out. Once I realized I was lost, I didn't know if it was better to keep looking for an exit or stay and call out for help.

"Then I heard a rumble overhead.

"I started running and screaming Violet's name. There was another rumble, a louder one, and the tunnel shook, and I was knocked off balance.

"When I stood up, this wall of boulders came crashing maybe ten feet ahead of me. It was the loudest thing I'd ever heard, like magnified thunder. I scrambled backward on my hands and feet like a crab, screaming my head off, but there were huge rocks raining down behind me, too. I had nowhere to go. I kept yelling for Violet, but I was drowned out by all the noise and blinded by all the dust being kicked up.

"There's no way I can convey how petrified I was.

"When the dust settled, I checked to see if there were any spaces I could squeeze through, but the tunnel was completely blocked. In front of me and behind me. And Violet wasn't answering my screams. Nobody was.

"I felt another wave of shaking come on, but this time it wasn't the tunnel, it was my body convulsing. There was more noise but this time it sounded like jet propellers roaring inside my head.

"I must've passed out. When I opened my eyes, I was no longer in the tunnel but in my bed, at home. It had been a dream, right? Except I never remembered any of my dreams. And I was wearing the same thing I had on when Violet and I went exploring. And I was covered in scrapes and bruises. When I tried to get out of bed, I collapsed on the floor beside it.

"Mom and Dad were still at work, but Violet must've heard me, because she rushed upstairs. She shrieked when she saw me. How did I get home? How did I escape from the tunnel? I had no idea.

"It hadn't been a dream.

"There was a search going on for me. I'd been missing for two days. Violet had been downstairs watching TV, there was no way I could've just reappeared like that. But I did.

"Violet said I had to go back to the tunnels and be found by rescuers. Otherwise, everyone would think we were lying, and we'd get in trouble—even as a twelve-year-old, she understood the importance of optics.

"I don't know how I let her talk me into going back there, but I did, and it was a nightmarish wait, expecting the tunnel would collapse on me any second. I was finally 'found' an hour later.

"When they asked where I'd been for the last two days, I said I didn't know. I still don't know."

My lips and throat are parched from all the talking. I gulp down my tea. It's lukewarm and too sweet and just what I need right now.

Gabriel and Quinn wear matching stunned expressions, but Antoinette's is more fascinated and a bit bemused.

"Incredible," she says, removing her glasses and massaging the bridge of her nose. "I haven't come across many examples of this happening at such a young age."

"But you've heard of this happening before?" I ask. "I'm still not convinced it wasn't a hell of a vivid hallucination."

"Come off it, Sasha." Her bluntness startles me. "It wasn't a one-time incident, was it? Cameron showed me the video footage. You might as well share the rest."

So I do. I tell them about my sleepy-time visits to the Witkin: waking up outside of it, then onstage inside, then appearing impossibly in the subbasement.

And since this geyser of confessions is running full blast, I explain it's more than the twos, I'm also coming across swans everywhere, but even that's not all of it, and I tell them about the photo of Sally at the salon that kind of . . . maybe . . . no, *certainly and unquestionably* captured my sister in the background.

"I've tried to tell myself it was one of those dumb #violetisback photos," I say. "But I didn't mix up Instagram with my photo app, and Sally saw it first—it was clearly Sally with her rainbow hair . . . and Violet reflected in the mirror behind her. Let's say, for a second, I saw who I think I saw. What did I actually see? I don't believe in ghosts, but was it a ghost? Are you sure you're not trying to get me to communicate with the dead here?" My breath catches in my throat at the thought of Violet being . . . I can't bear to think of it. But the question is already out there.

Antoinette picks up a biscuit as she considers the question, nibbling the edge of it like a rabbit. "I don't think you saw a ghost. Like I said in my interview with Cameron, my contact with Violet, while brief, did not feel like communicating with someone deceased. I think you got a glimpse into . . ."

I scoff. "You're going to say another dimension, aren't you?"

"I was trying to think of a way to put it that you wouldn't be so derisive of, but that ship has sailed." She brushes some crumbs off her velvet jacket. "For what it's worth, I realize how preposterous this all sounds, and how challenging it is for the mind to accept such ideas. It's easy to dismiss as sheer lunacy."

"Fortunately, I've been seeing a nice therapist named Renatta, who assures me I haven't crossed the line into lunacy just yet."

"How is that going?" Gabriel asks. "Is she helping?"

One of my shoulders rises in a half-shrug. "I didn't think so at first, but she says it's a process, so I'm going with it. Talking about things doesn't always make them better. But my strategy of not talking about them at all wasn't working, so it was time to try something new." I turn to Antoinette. "So. What does it all mean?"

"Well . . . Goodness—I don't expect to be able to decipher all of this at once . . . but it's a truly incredible gift you have. Do you know anything about OBEs? Out-of-body experiences."

"Like your soul/astral body traveling around outside your physical body? Yeah, Violet tried to get me to read up on that stuff—she was always into wacky shit—but I disregarded it until I got older," I say. "I don't put much stock into the claims of people wandering around the astral plane. It's more plausible for OBEs to result from the brain making up hallucinations, like what happens during a near-death experience. All trauma induced."

"That is one way of looking at it," Antoinette says. "But I'll give you some literature that may give you a fresh perspective. The collective I'm part of studies unusual phenomena like this, but we like to blend science in with the metaphysical. We're developing a hypothesis that connects to the branches of theoretical physics that propose different dimensions vibrate on separate frequencies. In a nutshell, we believe if a person can change their vibrational frequency, their mind/soul/astral body can travel to those different dimensions. These are not hallucinations, they're explorations of different planes of reality. And while your case is more unique in that it's your physical body doing the exploring, it could be a natural extension of astral travel or a more advanced form of dimensional jumping. When our group met with your sister, she was utterly riveted by the material we shared with her."

"Of course she was. And according to you, she must've gotten proficient at it, seeing as she's not here." My snark snags on an unexpected prick of desolation. I continue in a more subdued voice. "If that's what happened to her, I don't want to do the same thing to my family. I very much want to remain in this dimension. Bearing in mind this is the one percent of me keeping an open mind about all this."

"That one percent is enough for us to work with," says Antoinette. "If it offers you some reassurance, any astral travel you may embark on is connected to intentionality. If you end up somewhere you don't want to be, you can will yourself to return to home base. You've already shown your capability in that regard, both as a child and recently."

Between my outpouring of the strange and Antoinette's confounding rationalization of it, my head feels both helium-light and leaden.

"I don't want to overwhelm you any further, so how about this?" Antoinette retrieves a tote bag from beneath the table and hands it to me. "I've prepared some things for you to read. There's also a link to online audio files containing . . . let's call them guided meditations. If nothing else, you may find the exercises a useful tool in stress management and harnessing your intuition. It's up to you. If you'd like to get in touch to discuss any of this material, you'll find my card in there, and I welcome the opportunity to connect again."

"Thank you." I take the tote and push my seat back. "Let me ask you something. I understand why my brain is seeing triple twos everywhere—my sister and I have a connection to that specific number. But the swans are baffling me. If it were butterflies, it would make more sense, because butterflies were Violet's thing. But I can't think of how swans are relevant to either of us."

Antoinette hands me a scrap of paper and a pen. "Draw a swan."

"Drawing isn't my forte," I say, picking up the pen, "But if this is going to—oh." I've only drawn a hook and a horizontal line connecting to it but it's so obvious now: in its most abstract form, a swan resembles the number two. "Okay. Wow."

As we leave the teahouse, I catch sight of Cameron in his car.

I knock on his window until he rolls it down. "Hey, stalker. I just wanted to say thanks." He tilts his head, expecting more. "Fine. You win. I'll do your stupid podcast."

A quick nod, but he's still not done with me. "Any chance you and Quinn could do the show together?" he asks.

As my daughter lets out an excited squeal behind me, I tell him, "You really are an asshole, you know that?" I scrunch my mouth into something he'll undoubtedly interpret as a smile.

Violet Volk Is a Fraud

By Anonymous

JANUARY 10, 2008

Can someone please explain how Violet Volk became a feminist and pop culture icon? Her entire empire has been built on deception, whether by fooling her audience with her stage tricks or creating a false persona her fans have fervently embraced. Since when do we reward people for being con artists? Since we've bought into Violet's lies and made her a superstar, I guess.

Which isn't to say this media darling hasn't weathered her share of public criticism (accident or no, she *did* kill a guy). But her ability to shake off bad press and reinvent herself, while admirable to some, is maddening when you consider the person in question.

Violet Volk is not a feminist. Or a role model. Or an icon. Or a good person.

Violet Volk is a fraud.

Violet Volk does not deserve your admiration.

I'll tell you why.

Who am I? I'm what the gossip rags would call "a close source."

Why am I coming forward with this? I'm sick of the deception, tired of watching adoration heaped on a woman who isn't worthy of it. It's time you know the truth.

Let's begin, shall we?

First of all, credit where credit is due: Volk is a skilled magician. There, that's out of the way.

Did Volk excel in a field dominated by men? Sure. But for all her complaining about the misogyny she encountered, what did she do to change anything? Did she take any major steps, like naming the magician who sexually assaulted her to prevent him from harming others? Nope. (To be fair, that's something deeply personal, and not every survivor is comfortable confronting their abuser. But still.) Did she take any minor steps to combat misogyny, like petition the Global Magician Brotherhood to change their name to something more inclusive? Nope, not even after the GMB named her Magician of the Decade in late 1999.

Of course, there are other ways Volk could've helped make the magic industry more hospitable for women, such as encouraging female up-and-comers by inviting them to perform with her, either as assistants or opening acts. Except she didn't do either. In fact, all her assistants were male, because she "wanted to flip the script on traditional stage magic gender roles." While she was busy doing that, she forgot something important: a number of magicians start out as assistants, particularly females. As a result, she denied women the opportunity to learn the craft by working alongside her. Oops!

To this day, for all the so-called trailblazing she did, you won't find a single woman in the magic community who would consider her a mentor or even a friend.

I'm not saying role models can't be flawed people. It just helps if they're not utter hypocrites. Volk often touted that women shouldn't use their bodies to get ahead in life, yet she spent her early years working as a stripper—correction, *burlesque dancer*. However you try to class it up, if you're taking off your clothes for money, even if they're vintage duds, let's call it what it is: stripping. Which isn't to say burlesque and other forms of exotic dancing can't be art forms or serve to empower women. It's possible. But typically and traditionally, nudity for pay is about women serving the male gaze. When Volk was discovered by Jackson Cleo at a burlesque club, he was there as a bachelor party guest. He wasn't there to appreciate female empowerment via vintage performance art; he was there to watch women shake their tits and asses.

If you think about it, Violet might not have had her big break if it wasn't for the male gaze of Jackson Cleo.

Of course, Jackson Cleo might not have had his big divorce if it wasn't for Violet exchanging female gazes (and more) with his wife, but that's a sordid tale for another day.

Let's talk about Volk's pivot from magician to self-help guru. Remember how she boasted about living her best life in *You Are Magic*? More lies. The whole reason she wrote that book is because her life was in pieces and she needed a big payday.

We're going back to 2001, just after Violet's life has turned into a dumpster fire. While she claimed she ended her Vegas show to "focus on new projects," she also had no choice, since the Kintana refused to renew her contract. She approached other Vegas venues, but between her reputation for being difficult to work with and the high cost of insuring her productions, due to multiple injuries and a tragic fatality, her credibility took a big hit and nobody wanted to take a chance on her. Romantically, things were even worse: 2001 marked the end of Volk's marriage to Benjamin Martinez and the implosion of her longtime on-again-off-again affair with Mayuree Sakda. Womp womp.

At least she had her family, right? You know, the one that she'd frequently ignored and/or mistreated during her rise to fame. Some examples. She ran off to pursue her stardom dreams in NYC right after her mother was diagnosed with MS and left her sister to foot the medical bills. She got her uncle maimed at a backroom poker game. (Who's got two thumbs and likes to gamble? Not Uncle Slava after that night!) She missed the chance to say goodbye to her father before he died because she didn't want to fly on Friday the thirteenth. She even had to be coaxed into attending her own sister's wedding by Sasha's husband, Gabriel, who spent years playing the peacekeeper between the two (speaking of Gabriel, does anybody else find it creepy how Violet modeled her own husband to resemble her sister's? No way that's a coincidence).

And then, of course, there's what Violet did to her niece.

Remember how Violet never performed with any female assistants? There was one exception to that: her seven-year-old niece, Quinn Dwyer. Let's set aside whether this was nepotism or mere hypocrisy and get right into the illusion. Quinn was a little girl who loved angels and mermaids, who dreamed of being both. Volk was the fairy godmother who'd turn her into one and then the other, making both her dreams come true right there on that stage.

You know what little kids generally don't love? Being suspended from a great height before they're dropped into a tank of water and nearly drowned. That's a good recipe for traumatizing a kid right there. Take another look at that *LateFridayLive* performance. When Violet rushes to the tank in a panic, that isn't her acting—that's a deep-down dread that yet another person has fallen victim to one of her dangerous illusions—this time, a family member.

Is it any wonder that the sisters have been estranged ever since?

Maybe it's just me, but I find it ironic that someone who's been hailed as a feminist icon treated the females closest to her with such disregard.

But what about how brave she was being openly bisexual? There's no denying that took guts during a time when the LGBT community wasn't as readily accepted and fought for certain basic civil rights (a fight that continues to this day). You'd think Volk would've made a bigger contribution as a member of this community. Yet she barely showed up. She didn't speak up for legal rights, social acceptance—hell, she couldn't even be bothered to attend a single pride parade. She was far from resembling anything close to an activist.

And if you're about to argue that Violet being openly polyamorous was also gutsy, I'd counter that only helped build her allure further. An allure she took great pains to cultivate.

It's one thing to stand up for who you are—it's another to openly brag about your promiscuity and treat your romantic partners like props. Volk was eager to be seen anywhere and everywhere dating anyone and everyone, but she never said much about what these partners meant to her. Whether or not the emotions were sincere, it's hard not to view her "throuple" with Mayuree Sakda and Benjamin Martinez, as well as other romantic entanglements, as nothing more than a series of publicity stunts. Frankly, it's hard not to view much of Volk's life through the same lens, her entire showbiz existence based on chasing and basking in the limelight.

Does this not make a mockery of the very thing Violet arguably sought to normalize and celebrate? Doesn't it blatantly reveal her as disingenuous, willing to exploit both men and women in the interest of expanding her fame? Doesn't this make Violet a deeply problematic symbol of women's equality?

Maybe I'm being too harsh. After all, she helped so many people with her books, right? Ah, yes, let's talk about the inane drivel that passed for self-help penned by Violet Volk—if she even wrote her own books (for all we know there's a ghostwriter under an NDA floating around somewhere). If you consider platitudes you could find embroidered on a pillow dressed up in f-bombs to make them "edgy" in any way helpful. None of the ideas she presents in her books are particularly groundbreaking. They're mostly cribbed from the New Thought spiritual movement, which went on to influence *The Law of Attraction*, *The Secret*, and countless other philosophies that claim you can manifest any reality. All Volk did was add a dash of *Rocky Horror*'s subversive vibe and "don't dream it, be it" motto to be more on-brand for her.

The books and onslaught of motivational seminars (insert cash register noises here) basically had Volk doing a handful of magic tricks while proclaiming the key to getting the life you want is to visualize and dream really, really hard. Yeah, because it's that simple.

Dreams are all well and good, but once in a while you need to wake up and stop visualizing an idealized reality. Same goes for people. Sometimes you need to see an individual not for who you want them to be, but for who they really are.

Open your eyes and take a good look at Violet Volk. This is not a quality person worthy of so much adulation. This is an overvalued person who has based her existence on lies and manipulation.

Violet Volk has cemented her place as a cultural icon of the 1990s and 2000s, but let's finally see her for what she really is: a trickster, a phony. A fraud.

Strange Exits

c⸩

Episode 10: "Sasha and Quinn Dwyer"

CAMERON FRANK: When I started this podcast about Violet Volk, there were a lot of people I hoped to interview, but none more than her sister, Sasha Dwyer.

I've long felt an inexplicable connection to Sasha. Here was this woman living through a turbulent time in her life and having to do so in a media spotlight. Sasha showed a level of poise few of us would be able to muster under such duress, and she was criticized for it. Not only that, the few times she's spoken about Violet honestly and was . . . let's say, less than effusive, not only did she receive additional public criticism but she was also the target of threats and acts of vandalism to her home and business. And while both law enforcement and armchair sleuths have dismissed Sasha as a person of interest in her sister's disappearance, her reputation among the Wolf Pack is still tainted, as they remain convinced she wrote the "Violet Is a Fraud" takedown. What evidence do they have to back that up? Nothing solid I could find. Baseless hunches more than anything else.

If you ask me, Sasha's been getting a bad rap. It's been said many times, but it bears repeating: there is no right way to grieve. Just because she doesn't break down in front of news crews doesn't mean she isn't feeling the pain of losing her sister. And if she prefers to avoid the media altogether, that's her prerogative. After all, it's not like Sasha has been shown in the most sympathetic light. Who could blame her for being press-shy?

I certainly can't, and that's why I wasn't surprised when Sasha turned down my numerous interview requests. What *did* surprise me was when she finally said yes and when her daughter, Quinn, also said yes. It's my great pleasure to welcome Sasha and Quinn Dwyer to *Strange Exits*.

SASHA DWYER: Thanks. I know the right thing is to say I'm happy to be here, but I'm still in immediately-regretting-this-decision territory. No offense.

CAMERON FRANK: None taken. Quinn, how are you holding up?

QUINN DWYER: Better than I was at the vigil. Though I'm still keeping an eye on the door. That was a nice intro you did for Mom. So nice, I didn't even mind being mentioned as an afterthought.

CAMERON FRANK: I didn't intend that—I just know how protective Sasha has been about keeping you out of the media—

QUINN DWYER: Relax, I'm just messing with you. Consider it payback for how much you hounded us to come on this podcast.

CAMERON FRANK: Fair enough. I'm sorry if my enthusiasm was too much and I went a little overboard trying to get you to participate.

SASHA DWYER: And I'm sorry if my desire to live a normal life with some semblance of privacy was getting in the way of your career objectives.

CAMERON FRANK: Right . . . [*clears throat nervously*]

QUINN DWYER: Hey, Mom, I didn't fully get it before, but you're right. Apologies that begin with "I'm sorry *if*" do sound totally insincere.

CAMERON FRANK: [*nervous laughter*] I see neither of you are going to make this easy for me. Okay, how about this. I'm sorry, truly sorry, for any discomfort or disruption I caused either of you in pursuit of this story.

SASHA DWYER: That's a much better apology. You can hear the difference, right, Quinn?

QUINN DWYER: Oh yeah. Not just in what he's saying, but how he's saying it. Definitely more sincere this time.

SASHA DWYER: Night and day. Hey, Quinn, how long do you think it's gonna take before he asks if I wrote the takedown?

QUINN DWYER: I think he'll get you comfortable with some easier questions first, like fun childhood stuff about growing up with Aunt Violet. Right, Cameron?

CAMERON FRANK [STUDIO]: When both Sasha and Quinn agreed to appear on the podcast, I was thrilled. But at this point, I was thinking it might've been a better idea to interview them separately. I couldn't help but wonder if they'd concocted a strategy ahead of time to disarm me and take control of the conversation.

At the same time, historically, some of the most successful interviews I've conducted have occurred when I let the subject set the tone and pace, letting the discussion progress organically. I figured my best bet here was to go with it, even if that meant asking a thorny question sooner than I'd anticipated.

CAMERON FRANK: Actually, Quinn, I'd like to ask you about being in Violet's act. What do you remember about performing with your aunt on *LateFridayLive*?

QUINN DWYER: Not much. I was only seven.

CAMERON FRANK: There must be something you could recall about it.

QUINN DWYER: It's funny, because I've seen that clip of me and Aunt Violet so many times, but I don't know how much of it is me remembering it versus creating memories based on watching it. I can picture myself doing the act with her, but I can't bring up anything that was going through my head at the time. I don't even remember rehearsing it. All I remember is how afterward everyone told me I did such a great job, how convincing I was when I was pretending to drown. But I must've not been convincing enough, because things got shitty not long after, and I stopped hearing from Aunt Violet. I thought I must've messed up badly to drive her away like that. Years later, I started getting panic attacks, and I've had issues with anxiety ever since. This irrational part of me became scared that if I did the wrong thing, I'd drive other people away.

SASHA DWYER: Honey, you didn't drive Violet away, I did. And your panic attacks didn't start years after you performed with her, they began as soon as you got back from LA. Along with the night terrors, and your aquaphobia. I could barely get you to bathe because you were petrified of the water. You weren't convincing in Violet's act because you were good at pretending to drown—you almost *did* drown. But I was worried bringing up the trauma would make it worse somehow, so I denied it. Not the best move on my part.

QUINN DWYER: I knew something went wrong, I could just never pinpoint it. So I blamed myself. Like, if I performed better, maybe Aunt Violet would call once in a while, or at least send a postcard.

SASHA DWYER: Quinn, you have absolutely zero fault in all this. I hate that you ever blamed yourself for any of it. Maybe I went too far cutting her off completely, but the more time passes, the more you don't know how to fix things.

QUINN DWYER: I get that now. You kinda had to shield all of us from her toxic side. Though it never fully made sense how weirdly protective you were of her reputation around me. Especially when that takedown came out. Even while you were being accused of writing it.

CAMERON FRANK: Actually, since you brought it up, why not get into it now. Sasha, were you responsible for creating or writing the content for violetisafraud.com?

SASHA DWYER: I was not, but there's no way to prove a negative, so I don't expect people to believe me.

QUINN DWYER: I didn't always believe you. But I believe you now.

Aunt Violet was a phenomenal magician. But she was . . . careless in a lot of ways. That's why Dad protected you from her worst and you protected me from her worst—and kinda the rest of the world, if you think about it. Someone who makes that much of an effort to save her sister's legacy would've never written that takedown.

SASHA DWYER: That means so much to me.

QUINN DWYER: Are you being sarcastic?

SASHA DWYER: Fifty percent. Force of habit.

CAMERON FRANK: So hang on, just to confirm some of the specifics in that essay—

SASHA DWYER: We've gone into enough specifics. Airing out our dirty laundry is bad enough, I'd appreciate it if we weren't forced to describe each tawdry item in detail.

CAMERON FRANK: Understood. Just one last question about the take-down: Do either of you have any ideas about who might've written it?

[LONG PAUSE]

CAMERON FRANK [STUDIO]: As the two women go quiet, Quinn shrugs and sits back, a stunned look on her face, like she said way more than she expected to. Sasha gnaws at her lip and bears a more intense expression, as if waiting for the right words to surface then debating whether or not to speak them.

SASHA DWYER: I have no way of proving this, just like I have no way of proving I didn't write the takedown . . . I think Violet wrote it herself.

QUINN DWYER: Seriously?

CAMERON FRANK: What makes you say that? This was not only damaging to Violet's reputation, but also something your sister fought hard to suppress and remove from the internet.

SASHA DWYER: That's what makes me believe she was behind it. Violet was an expert at publicity—getting it as much as avoiding it. If she wanted that takedown to go away, she would've done what she did every other time something nasty was written about her: she would've ignored it. Violet survived the bad PR of accidentally killing a person. She would not allow herself to be brought down by one little website. The fact that she went to so much trouble trying to get it taken down— she went to court over it when she didn't even sue other magicians for stealing her material!—tells me she wanted more eyeballs on it. Not to mention, she got to live out her own personal Streisand effect. I could see it being a perverse way of paying homage to Barbra.

CAMERON FRANK [STUDIO]: Ironically, several years prior, Volk's favorite performer, Barbra Streisand, went through something similar when she sued a photographer for displaying a photo of her Malibu home online, claiming it violated her privacy. The suit was dismissed, but the publicity surrounding it resulted in more unwanted attention for the photo than it would've gotten otherwise. The resulting social phenomenon has been known ever since as "the Streisand effect."

CAMERON FRANK: But why would Violet want so much attention on something so negative?

SASHA DWYER: I don't know. Maybe it was the closest she could get to actually apologizing for any of it. Or maybe she wasn't sorry but just wanted us to see her as she really was, before we never saw her again.

QUINN DWYER: [*murmurs*] Like a deathbed confession.

CAMERON FRANK: Sasha, do you think you ever saw Violet as she really was?

SASHA DWYER: I think the better question to ask is whether Violet ever saw herself, if she knew who she really was. She was always looking to escape from something or into something. When we were kids, she couldn't wait to get out of Willow Glen and then she couldn't wait to get out of New York and go on tour, and then she couldn't wait to stop touring, and so on. Wherever she was, it was like she wanted to be somewhere else. And someone else. She decided early on she didn't want to be Varushka, so she became Violet. When we were kids, she also wanted us to be Goonies, searching for buried treasure. In high school, when I started dating a boy she liked—one I happen to be married to today—she became a goth, dyeing all her clothes black, blasting Siouxsie and the Banshees nonstop, wearing *all* the eyeliner. Then there was her *Rocky Horror* phase—she already had Magenta's look down, all she really needed was a maid costume. Oh, here's a fun fact: she briefly considered using Magenta as her stage name, but my husband convinced her the double *V* of Violet Volk was more powerful—he was a marketing whiz even back then.

CAMERON FRANK [STUDIO]: As she continues to reminisce out loud, Quinn and I look on with cautious surprise. It's nice to see Sasha this relaxed and open.

SASHA DWYER: Anyway, I think Violet was always playing with identity. I don't remember if she said it in one of her books or someone on this podcast said it, but she didn't believe in finding herself so much as creating herself.

CAMERON FRANK: But you must've seen beyond the person she wanted to portray.

SASHA DWYER: Sometimes.

CAMERON FRANK: Quinn, what do you want people to know about your aunt?

QUINN DWYER: How much she loved nature. It's strange she hid that part of herself from the public. I don't have a lot of memories with my aunt, but my favorite was camping at Joshua Tree with her.

SASHA DWYER: Camping? When did you go camping with Violet?

QUINN DWYER: When I stayed with her in LA. I'll tell you about it sometime. It was something special. But she could even make a walk in Cordova Park special. Aunt Violet said she couldn't live without the energy of a city for too long, and she didn't have the patience for gardening or any of that stuff, but she felt the most at home being in nature.

CAMERON FRANK: Sasha, what about you? What do you want people to know about your sister?

SASHA DWYER: How painfully *human* she was. There's this contingent of people who want to see her as a heroine or some kind of . . . I don't know, ultraterrestrial, or something. I understand the appeal in seeing the extraordinary in the ordinary—Violet had a gift for giving people that vision. It was the beauty of her artistry. But when you mistake a trick for the real thing, you're not being taken with an artist, you're being taken in by a con artist.

CAMERON FRANK: That's a little harsh.

SASHA DWYER: Harsh truths are our love language.
    Yes, Violet was talented, and yes, she had phenomenal charisma. But she could also be self-serving, conniving, even downright spiteful. Violet had flaws. It's fine if people appreciate her work, but it's time to demystify her.

CAMERON FRANK: It sounds like your sister had a special ability to get under your skin. Are you still angry with her all these years later?

SASHA DWYER: Of course. We were estranged for years before her disappearance, but I always thought we'd hash things out eventually. I actually thought it would happen on the night of her last performance. But it didn't. I got nothing. No reconciliation, no resolution, just silence. It hurts. There's a reason our family hasn't moved in the last ten years. There's a reason we've kept the same phone numbers. Yeah, I'm still angry, but there's a part of me that'll always be waiting for her to come home.

CAMERON FRANK: What about you, Quinn? Are you angry at Violet?

QUINN DWYER: For me, it's less anger, more frustration. I wish I could've spent more time with her as a kid and gotten to know her as a grown-up. I'm still uncovering these different sides of her, some of them less than stellar, some of them surprisingly generous. It's frustrating that I don't get to reconcile the legend with the real person, and that I might never know what happened to her. I tell myself—and my parents tell me, all the time—that it's nothing any of us did, that we can't blame ourselves for Violet being gone. Sometimes I don't buy it and think our family wasn't enough—*we* weren't enough—for her to stay. Usually, though, I tell myself if we weren't enough, that's her problem. From everything I'm learning about my aunt, it seems like nothing and no one could ever be enough for her.

CAMERON FRANK: You wouldn't be the first to say that.
    Sasha, you know I need to ask about Cyndi Yanoff's birthday party.

SASHA DWYER: Didn't Eleanor give you all the dirt on that already? She's got a freakishly good memory, so I don't know what I could add.

CAMERON: I'm curious about your impression of the show with Ace. Was that the first big illusion you ever saw your sister perform?

SASHA DWYER: It was. Most of what Violet did around the house was the usual: coin and card magic, cups and balls, brass rings, silk scarves, you get the idea.
    One thing I want to clear up: Ace lied about never meeting Violet before that birthday party. We saw him perform in Brigantine one summer when we visited our uncle Slava and got to meet him afterward. Violet showed him some tricks, and Ace took an immediate interest in her. He wanted her to join a junior magic league, help her develop a routine, and get her performing in front of an audience.
    Our parents were divided on the idea. Mom was worried it wasn't

a "normal" thing for a girl to do and would be too expensive. Dad was also skeptical but open to the idea if Violet would dedicate herself to being the best at it. They needed some kind of proof that it would be worth allowing Violet to pursue magic.

CAMERON FRANK: Was Cyndi Yanoff's birthday party that proof?

SASHA DWYER: Look, it's not fun for me to ruin the mythology surrounding my sister. But it's also not fun to see naive people believe a story as truth without knowing all the facts. The truth is, she did meet Ace prior to that party, and she *could* have rehearsed a routine with him.

In any case, after that, every other weekend, Dad and Uncle Slava would take Violet around to the magic group meetings in Philly, North Jersey, and New York. If Slava had a good week at the poker tables, he'd take her to a magic shop and get her books, tricks, props. If he had a bad week, he'd still bring her a few decks of cards—it seemed like she went through a new deck every day.

Ace started her on more advanced card and coin magic, but when he found out she was double-jointed, he taught her some escapology, too. When Dad wasn't on chauffeur duty, he was making costumes for Violet. Imagine a burly Russian man sewing a straitjacket for a child.

QUINN DWYER: I wish we still had that stuff.

SASHA DWYER: It might be in the basement.

CAMERON FRANK: Did either of you ever have an interest in performing magic?

QUINN DWYER: I never wanted to learn magic because I didn't want to ruin the joy of watching it. Also, I have terrible coordination, so I'd probably suck at it.

SASHA DWYER: For me, it was less about the magic and more about inclusion, being part of a club with an oath of secrecy. Violet did let me join her in a couple of the meetings, but I found them alienating. No offense to any magicians, but it was boring as hell. How many possible ways can you guess my card or make a coin vanish and reappear? And they spend ages on this stuff. You know what it's like? It's like listening to someone play the bagpipes. If they're bad at it, it's torture. If they're good, after the first song, it all sounds the same, and you're still listening to the bagpipes.

CAMERON FRANK: It doesn't sound like something you enjoyed even on a spectator level.

SASHA DWYER: I think I let all my sister issues get tangled up in it for a long time. But I have to admit, I do have a newfound admiration for Violet's work now.

CAMERON FRANK: Where did that change of heart come from?

SASHA DWYER: My daughter. My husband. My therapist. My friend Sally . . . Maybe even this podcast.

CAMERON FRANK: It means so much to hear you say that.

SASHA DWYER: You're welcome.

CAMERON FRANK: Sasha, before we wrap up, could you share one more story about Violet that nobody's ever heard before?

QUINN DWYER: I made him ask that one. It's gotta be one I never heard before, either.

SASHA DWYER: [*faux-exasperated sigh*] Okay. There was one time in high school, we cut class to go to the diner for burgers. We had a booth in the back, and when no one was around, Violet put her hands flat on the table and told me to watch my plate. A second later, one of my french fries wiggled then rose up about a foot and floated over to her. She leaned over and ate it.

QUINN DWYER: No way.

CAMERON FRANK: How did you react to that?

SASHA DWYER: I said "fuck you" and nearly pissed myself.

Violet laughed at me, said something like "I finally got you."

It couldn't be real, though. I racked my brain for a logical explanation, I searched every inch of that table, but there were no strings or any other devices that would've made it possible.

"Do it again," I said, "keep your hands where they are, and this time, I pick which fry." She agreed, and I picked the longest french fry on my plate, even dotting it with ketchup—I had to be absolutely sure there'd be no fry swapping.

CAMERON FRANK: Did she make it levitate again?

QUINN DWYER: Of course she did . . . right?

SASHA DWYER: She did, but this time the fry only made it halfway across, when Violet glanced out the window and saw some guy in the parking lot staring at us. The french fry fell to the table and Violet swept it under a napkin.

"Show's over, let's get the check," she said.

It would've been pointless for me to badger her about how she did it, so I let it go.

QUINN DWYER: How come you never told me this story before?

SASHA DWYER: Because I'm a lousy, withholding mother?

I don't know. It was one more thing I thought would be easier to keep quiet about, since I couldn't make sense of it. I told myself there was a rational explanation I just hadn't figured out yet. What were my choices? To believe the logical or the impossible.

CAMERON FRANK: What do you believe now?

SASHA DWYER: I mean, I still lean logical, but I've made more room for the impossible. Let's say . . . the impossible hasn't moved in but I've cleared out a drawer for it.

Date: March 29, 2018, at 8:15 AM
To: cfrank@sidecarstudios.com
From: twoods@sidecarstudios.com
Subject: The Future of Strange Exits

Cam—

I know I had some reservations about you and worked you hard, but you've really pulled it off. Your work on *Strange Exits* has been outstanding.

Good thing you pushed back on that Checkmate episode. It's getting a ton of social media and blog coverage and is the most downloaded episode of any show we've ever aired, though the Sasha/Quinn episode looks like it's going to break that record. The big picture is even more impressive: *Strange Exits* is nearing a million monthly downloads, well above any numbers Sidecar has seen before. This is exactly the kind of show we need to position ourselves as a premium audio journalism and entertainment provider.

Keep going with the Violet season. Even though we initially planned on twelve episodes, I think we can easily do five to ten more. There's no reason to stop this rocket from reaching the next stratosphere.

Start putting together an outline and proposed budget. I'll need that ASAP so I can squeeze you into our Q2 allocations.

While I still can't draw a direct line between #violetisback and *Strange Exits* downloads, there's no question the viral social media campaign contributed to the overall fervor surrounding Volk, so I'll reimburse your out-of-pocket costs and provide a more substantial marketing budget for next season.

Speaking of which, I want to think ahead and start planning out the next few seasons of *SE*. Violet has been a gold mine, but if we don't have a good subject for another deep dive, branching off into multiple stories could be a better way to go. While you keep churning out the VV episodes, I can hire associate producers to lay the groundwork for the next season, so you can hit the ground running when you're done with this one.

Let's meet next week to brainstorm and get some ideas in motion.

I also want to look into additional crossover opportunities with *Off the Beaten Path*—how about you set up a meeting for us with the Curiosity Network?

Keep up the great work.

—TW

Date: March 29, 2018, at 4:57 PM
To: twoods@sidecarstudios.com
Cc: rfleischer@fleischermediagroup.com
From: cfrank@sidecarstudios.com
Subject: Re: The Future of Strange Exits

Tobin,

I appreciate your positive feedback. It's nice to see you set aside your doubts and finally trust in what I'm doing.

Before we get into any further discussions about this or subsequent seasons of *Strange Exists*, I'd like to introduce you to my agent, Ruth Fleischer, copied here. I signed with Ruth a couple of weeks ago, right around the time you were threatening to fire me. It was reassuring to discover I had a number of career prospects I could explore outside of Sidecar Studios, and Ruth has already lined up a few conversations for me. She was also kind enough to have Fleischer Media Group's legal team review my contract with your company.

It turns out, our original agreement was for only twelve episodes of a "podcast centering around the life, career, and disappearance of Violet Volk," so we'll need to negotiate a new agreement for any additional work I might do with Sidecar.

Our contract also specifies that the content I create—these first dozen episodes—belongs to Sidecar, but I trademarked the name *Strange Exits*—as a podcast and other media—prior to signing that contract. Therefore, I own the rights to the *Strange Exits* brand; something to bear in mind moving forward.

A couple of months ago, you told me my future with Sidecar was not guaranteed. I agree with you. I think we need to sit down and have a bigger conversation about what—if any—kind of future I might have with your company, before I put together any outlines or budgets, before we have any brainstorming chats, before any of that. I do have other opportunities I'm considering, but I'm certainly open to discussing what Sidecar may be able to offer me going forward.

Reimbursing me for my marketing expenses is a good start, though I do have some concerns about how much pushback I've received working on *Strange Exits*. For example, it seems you are still unconvinced that #violetisback brought in downloads, whereas countless stories reporting on the trending hashtag followed up by listing various projects about Volk, with *Exits* named nine times out of ten. If I do stay on with Sidecar, it's important for me to feel that my ideas are being respected and nurtured.

I'm booked up the rest of this week, but I have some availability next week if you'd like to chat. Please be sure to include my agent on the call.

—CF

Sasha

"I know I shouldn't be reading any of the garbage online, but I've been sneaking a peek here and there since Quinn and I did the podcast . . . and some of the things people are writing about me aren't awful. The assholes are still out there, they'll never go away, but I've even had members of the Wolf Pack reach out to me directly to apologize. I don't know what to do with this sudden wave of empathy." I grin at Renatta, who gives me one of her thoughtful smiles in return.

"How is everything going with the sleepwalking?" She crosses her legs, and a beige high-heeled shoe comes into my line of sight.

"I've never seen you in heels before." It's not a practical chunky heel or wedge, either, but something you could use to break up a block of ice. "You usually wear such sensible shoes." *Like me.* I don't add that her pragmatic footwear was something that initially bonded me to her, because that would be trivial.

"I thought it was time to try something new." Renatta points her toe.

All I can muster is a noncommittal grunt as I glance at my own feet clad in black Mary Janes. Have I really been wearing the same type of shoes since elementary school?

"Are you uncomfortable discussing the sleepwalking or are you . . . You seem . . . troubled by my shoes."

I square my shoulders. "You know what? They're not my taste, but they look great on you. And I haven't had any more sleepwalking incidents in over a month. It could've been all the Violet stress getting to me, but I seem to have a handle on it now. I've been doing this . . . program Antoinette recommended called the Portal Approach. It's a set of recordings, each one about a half hour. I guess you'd call it guided meditation, though it's more bizarre than that."

"Bizarre how?"

"You have to listen to the recordings in a specific way, in a dark, quiet room, wearing headphones. There's the usual spiel about clearing your mind and slowing your breathing, but then you also do these vocalizations, like you're tuning your body to a certain frequency. The rest is . . . not white noise exactly, but these electronic tones that supposedly enhance your brain waves in various capacities. If you do the program every day, you're supposed to experience all these positive effects—less stress, better focus, more energy and creativity, overall improved mood." I leave out the part about how the Portal Approach also claims to groom you for astral travel, "an exhilarating journey in which you can explore other planes of existence." Thanks, but no thanks. Not that I'm fully convinced out-of-body experiences are a thing, or that I'm capable of anything resembling teleportation (cue involuntary eyeroll at the very thought). "I don't buy into all of it, but I do think it's helping. I feel more at ease after each session, and it's nice to go to sleep and wake up in the same place."

"Good for you." Renatta smiles wider, and I bask in her approval.

"Not that everything is perfect at home. With all the recent Violet hysteria, it hasn't fully sunk in that Quinn is graduating college next month and will probably leave Willow Glen in the near future. Ever since she received her inheritance, she's been talking more about traveling and going god-knows-where to save the planet—no way is she gonna stick around here."

"How are you handling her newfound wealth?" Her usual pad is on her lap, but there's less scribbling today.

"Quinn is so grounded and earnest and smart, I'm sure she'll be fine with it. Whether she uses it to fund the testing of backlogged rape kits or a sustainable homeless shelter or a Violet Volk museum—all ideas she's considering—I know she'll put the money to good use."

"That wasn't quite what I asked. I'm glad to hear Quinn is managing her windfall well, but how are *you* doing with it? You struggled for many years without your sister's financial help, and now all of a sudden . . ."

"Help arrives when I need it least? And isn't even for me but for my daughter?" I let out a wry snicker. "I'd be lying if I didn't say I was peeved about it, at first. Gabriel and I never asked Violet for money, and she rarely gave it to us. Not that she wasn't generous in her own way. But it drove me nuts how she'd buy me shit like expensive silk scarves that I never wore when having a little more cash would've helped us breathe easier. There was one time, something came up where we urgently needed money—I think it was a roofing issue—and I brought one of the scarves to a vintage clothing store. They offered me a hundred dollars! I was so irritated with Violet, and even more irritated with myself, because I couldn't sell that scarf, or any other gifts she got me that I rarely used. I mean, there's a handbag in my closet that's worth more than the car I'm driving. It was infuriating. But after Violet disappeared, I was glad I'd held on to everything. So yeah, I was a little pissed off about the cash, but only because it brought up some difficult memories. What Violet left for Quinn—it doesn't negate my sister's shortcomings, but it's reassuring to see a nicer side of her."

"What about those letters you gave Quinn? How did she react to them?"

"You know, I think we both helped to fill in some missing pieces of Violet for each other," I say. "It was important for Quinn to know the more unpleasant sides of her aunt—I just didn't want my daughter to become disillusioned. And she's not. At the same time, she's helped me see how quick I was to cast my sister as the villain of my life. And how wrong it was to reduce Violet to one thing." Sighing, I reach for my favorite throw pillow and hug it. "I do wish I'd made more of an effort with Violet. I wish I knew her better. But how do you get to know someone who's always trying to trick you?"

Renatta looks at me like I've said something unexpectedly deep and nods. "I think that's a good place to stop."

April 18, 2018

"So, it's been a month since I got back from LA," Quinn announces over breakfast—she's prepared us a spread of tofu scramble, yogurt, and fruit. "I already had a lot to think about with graduation coming up, and this . . . gift from Aunt Violet weirdly added more pressure to the situation."

Gabriel nods, stirring blueberries into his yogurt. "Your mom and I aren't gonna tell you how to spend your money—"

"*Our* money. That's the first thing I want to make clear. It doesn't belong to me alone, it belongs to the family." The set of her jaw warns against any protest. "I want you to cash in some of your good parent karma here. We can pay off the house and any other debt, and you can hire that assistant for the salon . . . or we can buy a new house and you can retire early or do something else. Anything. Whatever you want."

Gabriel and I are too stunned to respond.

"Did you really think I wasn't gonna take care of you? Come on. In other news, I have a couple updates you might be less thrilled with." Quinn breathes deeply, measuring her words. "I was thinking instead of jumping right into a job, I might want to get my master's in environmental science. But before that, I'm gonna spend the summer in Costa Rica doing a conservation internship. Also, some of the grad schools I'm interested in are kinda far away. Like one I'm considering is in Oregon and another is in Ireland. I still don't know where I'll end up, but . . ."

It's what I've been expecting but still feels like a sucker punch. There's no good way to prepare for this, but my separation anxiety doesn't matter here. All I can do is make sure I don't hold her back.

Hiding my devastation takes work, but thankfully, Gabriel speaks up for both of us. "Costa Rica sounds amazing. You know we'll miss the hell out of you, but wherever you go, we've got your back."

"About that . . ." Quinn spears a piece of pineapple and stares at it. "I know you've been worrying about me—maybe not worrying, but Sally and I talk, and I know you're . . . *wondering* about me . . ."

"And I should've brought all that up to you, not Sally." It doesn't count as taking initiative, since Quinn began the conversation, but late is better than never. "I just didn't know the right way to talk about it, and I didn't want to ask you something you might be uncomfortable with or not ready to answer. It's not my place to put a label on you. And I didn't want you to think I was making any assumptions . . ." I give Gabriel a nudge to chime in.

"We always hoped you knew you could be straight with us—Jesus, bad choice of words—What I really mean—" he stammers.

Before we can make things any more cringey, Quinn shakes her head and bursts out laughing. "Oh my god, please stop, this isn't a big coming-out moment. I just think societal pressure to be a girly-girl is bullshit. In terms of . . . orientation, I'm not sure what label I'd give myself, but I'm actually leaning more asexual. I'm not a virgin, and I haven't had any bad experiences with sex, I've just always been more into the platonic thing. I don't know if that'll change, but that's where I'm at right now." She puts her palms flat on the table and lets out a breath. "Questions? Comments?"

It's such a relief, not what Quinn said, but the very act of her saying it, of knowing she isn't hiding from us.

"One comment," I say.

"Is it about how you love me no matter what?" Quinn asks.

"Pretty much."

"That was gonna be my comment, too," Gabriel adds. "And also, thank you for trusting us enough to share something so personal."

"Well, I was in a quid pro quo mood after Mom pretty much spilled her guts." An irreverent shrug. "Anyway, I have one more announcement. I don't leave for Costa Rica until July, so between graduation and then, I'm taking us on vacation. I don't care where we go, I just think we need to get away for a while."

"Love the idea, and I don't care where we go, either," says Gabriel. "Sasha?"

They both turn to me.

"I've never been anywhere, and you want me to choose our vacation?" Despite my internal protests, I can't help but think this could be a good opportunity to follow the twos. And if the swans also represent twos . . . "Actually, I have an idea of where we could go."

Quinn's face lights up. "Great. Hold that thought." She rushes out of the room and comes back a moment later with her laptop and wallet. Grinning, she swaps my plate for the computer. "Let's book it right now."

"Don't you want to—"

"Nope," she cuts in. "It's more exciting if you tell us after. Dad and I trust you." She busies herself with clearing the table.

Across the way, Gabriel offers me an encouraging wink and pushes his chair back. "We expect a full itinerary by the time I'm done with the dishes."

I pull up a browser, type in a few search terms, and sift through the results to a backdrop of a domestic symphony: running water, clattering silverware, the refrigerator being open and shut. By the time the final crumbs are wiped from the table and my husband and daughter resume their seats, I've just finished entering the credit card info.

My finger hovers over the button that will confirm the trip.

"Do it," Quinn insists.

I hit enter and let out a breath like I just detonated a bomb. "It's done. We're going on a tour of Agatha Christie's England, beginning with a stay at the Old Swan Hotel in Harrogate, North Yorkshire."

"Nice!" they exclaim in unison.

"Hang on, though, I still need to get us flights." As I enter the relevant dates and airports, I feel more and more certain this is where we need to go. There's something thrilling about acting on impulse and intuition; no wonder my sister—

My mouth falls open. There are several options that'll get us to Leeds, but only one real choice.

Flight 222.

Oh synchronicity, you rascal, you.

May 17, 2018

It's an evening flight, and people around us are already yawning as we file into our row. Quinn has claimed the aisle seat and Gabriel offers me the window, but I decline; I'd rather sit in between my husband and daughter. I've flown before, but never outside the country, and the thought of crossing an ocean makes me uneasy.

As we settle into our seats, Gabriel cocks his head. "Is that new?"

I fiddle with the loosely knotted scarf he's pointing to, not used to the feel of silk against my bare skin, unsure of whether I'm wearing it correctly. "Kind of. It's part of the unworn Violet gift collection."

"I like it."

"Me, too." It's one of the more subdued scarves she gave me, with a black-and-gray houndstooth pattern, and it goes well with my standard white button-down and jeans (hey, I can't try *all* the new things *all* at once).

During takeoff, my stomach lurches, and it feels like we're moving in slow motion. If only. Ever since Quinn informed us of her postgraduation plans, life has seemingly gone from a normal pace to warp speed, each day faster than the next. All of a sudden, it's like I'm in a movie montage and every time I blink it's a new scene. Family breakfast. Blink. Quinn's graduation. Blink. England vacation. Before I know it, Quinn will be off to Costa Rica, then briefly home before she's off again to parts unknown. Despite making peace with some of my Violet troubles and having no further sleep disturbances, it looks like I'll still have plenty to discuss with Renatta for the foreseeable future.

Gabriel and Sally have promised to keep me so busy and amused, I won't have time to miss Quinn. We've been talking about joining forces and developing our own line of hair care products, but haven't gotten past arguing over whether they should be branded with the Volk name.

Not all of Quinn's plans have involved being hundreds or thousands of miles away from us. She's also been scouting local commercial properties that would be suitable for a museum, though she's decided it won't be dedicated solely to Violet.

"I think I'm gonna call it the Women of Magic Museum," she informed us the other day. "After Ace told me about Adelaide Herrmann, I couldn't stop thinking about her. So I did more research and came across all these other stories of women who've been overlooked by the magic community. I want to celebrate them along with Aunt Violet."

Being the supportive parents that we are, Gabriel and I have expressed our deep enthusiasm for the museum, particularly if it'll be located in the Willow Glen area and require Quinn to spend a lot of time on-site (naturally, she sees right through us).

As for Violet Mania, thankfully, it's died down. #violetisback activity has dwindled, and while *Strange Exits* remains a popular podcast, fans are grumbling about the decline in episode quality and surplus of advertisements since the episode with Quinn and me aired.

An hour into the flight, half the plane is asleep as I get up to use the restroom. It's tiny, and being in such a tight enclosed space is unexpectedly nerve-racking. I use one of the Portal Approach breathing techniques I learned to steady myself.

A minute later, the plane dips and shakes. Before I can find something to hold on to, I'm catapulted against the door, headfirst. The FASTEN SEAT BELT light dings on, and I try to pull the door open, but it won't budge. The turbulence worsens and there's a roaring in my ears as I slide to the floor. My entire body vibrates, and the edges of my vision are going dark, dark, and darker, until I'm out.

"Now do you believe it?" The question comes from behind me, the husk she inflected in her voice still present, an aural tattoo from a time when she wanted to mask her girlishness and be taken seriously.

Slowly, I turn my head, prolonging the disambiguation. It could be somebody else. It could be a hologram, a mist, or nothing at all. The peripheral glimpse is promising enough that my feet follow through and face the source of the voice.

It's her. My sister stands six feet away. Her lean body in skinny black jeans and a turtleneck, head-to-toe black, as usual. A decade older since the last time I saw her, and all she has to show for it are deeper grooves on either side of her mouth, bolder parentheses framing her crooked smile, which is still painted a sparkling red. A stranger taking their wildest guess would put her well below forty-two. But I am not a stranger, and a closer examination of her face immediately and intangibly adds extra years. It's something about her eyes, the way they're clouded over, a look that says she's seen plenty but you're better off not knowing.

Violet holds out a hand, palm up, and I stretch my arm until the tips of my fingers graze hers.

This should be a moment of gratitude and reprieve. I should be propelling toward her, bear hug at the ready, forgiveness imminent. Bygones and all that crap.

Instead, I remain rooted in place and slowly pull back my arm, searching her face for . . . I don't know what I'm searching for.

"Now do I believe what?" I ask. Even though I felt her tangible form, my eyes travel around her silhouette, checking for flickers, transparencies, any indication that she's not a corporal being. "I don't know where we are or what this is. What am I supposed to believe in here? God? Life after death? Astral projection? Parallel worlds? My unstable grip on reality?"

The angles in Violet's face blur as she gives me a tender smile. "Nobody has a stable grip on reality."

"That doesn't answer my questions."

"Those aren't questions I can answer for you. Perhaps you should be asking different ones."

"Can you even hear how pretentious you sound right now?"

"Can you even hear how judgmental you sound right now?"

"How is it that I haven't seen you in ten years and you've managed to get on my nerves in under a minute?"

"Special sisterly skills. Come on, let's do this." She motions me in for a hug, but I hold her off.

"No, fuck you. I'm still mad at you."

"You're always mad at me about something." Her scorn is unexpected. I was expecting contrition.

"Don't make it sound like I'm overreacting."

"Because you've never done it before? How about the time you blamed me for putting gum in your hair at Wei Zhang's sleepover?" She folds her arms across her chest.

"Are we seriously doing this?" I match her combative stance. "Wei Zhang wore braces."

"Wei Zhang was also in love with Gabriel. Don't you remember she was out like half the week after that sleepover?"

"She had the flu."

"That's what Wei said, but Mom was giving me a trim at the salon when Mrs. Zhang dropped in to reschedule her perm because she had to take her daughter to all these extra orthodontist appointments." Violet gives me a pointed, now-do-you-believe-me look.

I do believe her.

"I'm not saying I didn't do some awful shit, I'll own up to that," she adds. "But I won't have you hating me for shit I didn't do."

"I don't hate you."

"You hate me a little bit. Sometimes." There's that familiar taunting lilt.

"Fine, sometimes I hate you. But only a little bit." Our glares melt away into lopsided grins. "We can do that hug thing now if you want."

Violet kisses my cheek as I put my arms around her, tightly, so tightly, but her small frame is strong, and I know she can take it.

It's nighttime and we're standing on a shoreline, the air salty, water lapping at the sand, a full moon casting a bluish glow over us.

"Seriously, where are we?" I ask. "We could be anywhere."

"Exactly right. We're anywhere. Leave it at that."

"I mean it about still being mad at you."

"I know."

"I put my life on hold waiting for you to come home. I was always putting life on hold."

Violet lets out a here-we-go-again groan. "This is the issue I had with you. You did the martyr thing, but you complained about it. I never denied being egotistical. I even made a website and told the world about it."

"I knew it was you!" I mime strangling her. "You know how many people blame me for writing that thing?"

"I thought, since we were estranged, maybe coming clean would help somehow?"

"After almost five years? Why wait so long?"

"I wrote that thing a month after our last blowup. It took me years to have the guts to publish it. The point is, I finally did have the guts. I owned my selfishness."

"Should I applaud you for that? Selfishness is easy."

"In the moment it is, but not in the long term." Her mouth forms a grim line. "It gets lonely when you end up in an empty house—or on an empty tour bus—with the only person you ever truly put first."

"Why did you invite me to your show if you were going to leave like that?"

"So your final impression of me could be doing something beautiful. Doing what I do best. Maybe that was selfish, too."

"You think?"

"It was something I had to do." Violet paces in a small circle.

I'm already at an angry simmer, but she has an uncanny knack for turning up the heat until I boil over. "That's not an explanation. You *had* to disappear without a trace? Why the fuck . . . *Why?*" I spit out the word, imagining it trailed by a hundred question marks.

"Remember how obsessed Mom was with curses, how she made us wear red strings to ward off the evil eye and all that stuff?" Round and round she goes, staring at her feet as she speaks.

"Of course. Oh my god, you're giving me motion sickness."

She stops pacing. "I think, in some weird way, I was the curse. You were the helper, you made everyone's life better. I made everyone's life worse."

There aren't enough eye-rolls in the world. "Nope. Not happening. This is one pity party I will not be attending."

"I'm not trying to make you feel sorry for me. And I wasn't trying to blow up your life, even before I left. I just wanted you to be a little less serious."

"Right, because 'everything's too serious to be so serious,' like you said in your little note."

"It was such a grind to get you to have fun."

"We can't all live in a fantasy world like you. It's hard to have fun when you're taking care of everybody." This is not the warm and fuzzy reunion I was hoping for. Who am I kidding, Violet and I don't do warm and fuzzy.

"Sasha, it was your choice to take care of everybody."

"Yeah, but why did you always have to make me feel bad about my life choices?"

"I didn't want you to feel bad, I wanted you to dream bigger."

"Not all of us need big dreams. Some of us are fine with small-to-medium ones. You wanted to dazzle the world and get the stardom and big money, and you got all of that. I didn't want that. And anyway, you never seemed genuinely happy. It was like none of the fame and success was ever enough."

"I wasn't happy. It wasn't enough."

"Oh, are you gonna say you wanted my quaint little life, even though you went out of your way to take digs at me in your books? *You Are Magic, Except You, Sasha Dwyer, Are a Loser.*"

"More like *You, Sasha Dwyer, Are Magic. Wake Up and Smell the Glitter.*"

I strain to catch a note of sarcasm in her voice, but she's being sincere. Huh. "I always felt like you wanted to shove your superiority in everyone's face, but especially mine. Like you were forcing me into a series of contests. And you always won."

"I never won. Nothing that mattered, anyway. You were smarter and more beautiful and *nicer*. People cared about you because of who you were, not who they wanted you to be. What you have matters more than anything I ever had."

"Tell me this wasn't all about Gabriel. All those ways you tried to stick it to me, the microaggressions. Tell me it wasn't because of a boy who didn't fall in love with you."

She lowers her head and kicks at the sand. "I thought something more would happen . . . eventually . . . and then you swooped in."

"There was no swooping. You said you didn't like him like that."

"You still should've backed off. Gabriel and I had more in common. He was my friend first."

"So what?"

"So I had dibs!"

"Violet, we're talking about a person, not the last slice of pizza. You can't call dibs on someone's heart." I shake her arm until she looks at me. "And what about when you *Indecent Proposal*-ed Gabriel? Don't give me that crap about it being a joke."

Violet hisses through her teeth. "Yeah, not my best moment. I just had two relationships implode and was starting to change my mind about having kids, because it seemed like a kid would stick around, you know? That night at the bar, I got super drunk. In the moment, all I could think was how impossible it was that I'd find someone like Gabriel, but how amazing it would be to have his baby. Even if he'd said yes, there's no way I would've gone through with it, but there wasn't a second he wasn't anything but mortified. I thought passing it off as a joke might lighten the mood, but . . . not so much." Violet opens her hands and stares down at them. "I could never find a good way to apologize. For what I put you through. And Gabriel. And Quinn. Saying I'm sorry isn't enough. But for what it's worth, I am sorry." When she looks up at me, she's crying. "I wanted a family like yours, but I didn't know how to get it."

"A good way to start is by being decent to the family you do have." My voice is soft, less chastising, more regretful. "And are you sure that's what you really wanted? I think you would've still found a way to be dissatisfied with your life."

"Probably. But you put your whole heart into family, I put mine into work, and I feel like I ended up with nothing. Trust me, you won."

The rising lump in my throat makes it tough to speak. "Come on, Violet. You made people fucking believe in magic."

"Not all people. Not you."

Tears gush out of me.

"That's the real reason I wanted Quinn to be part of my act," she says. "To make her believe things you never could. It wasn't right for me to do it that way, and I hate myself for hurting her. I wish I could undo it . . . but I can't undo anything now."

A few minutes ago, I was this close to launching into a rant, spewing everything I'd pent up over the last decade . . . but what's the point? She knows she was shitty. Better to tell her something she doesn't know. So I do. "For so much of my life, people acted like I must be dying of envy having a famous sister. I denied it, because it was mostly untrue, but it *was* a little bit true. Just not in the way you'd think. I envied how instantly you found your purpose in life, how early it came to you. And how much you loved it."

"You could've become a doctor if you really wanted to." She dabs at my tears with her sleeve.

"That's the thing, though. I only said I wanted to be a doctor because every immigrant parent wants their kid to become a doctor. It would've made Mom and Dad proud. But it's not what I really wanted. I didn't know what that was. My unplanned pregnancy wasn't an excuse not to pursue my dream. I was kinda relieved I could stay in the suburbs and live a more low-key life."

"Which is the last thing I wanted." Hands on hips, she narrows her eyes. "Okay. You wanna know the real reason I left? You want the truth?"

"Why even ask that? Is anybody really gonna say, 'Actually, no. Jack Nicholson was right: I can't handle the truth. More lies, please!' Yes, of course I want the truth."

"Okay, but you can't get mad . . ."

"I totally can, you're not the boss of me, but tell me anyway."

"I wanted to beat Houdini."

"At what?"

"At being a magic legend." She looks out at the night sky behind me. "Maybe he'll still be considered the greatest escape artist, but nobody will ever top my vanishing act. That's gotta put me up there, right? Keep people talking, make sure they don't forget me? Then again, maybe that's what Adelaide Herrmann thought, and people forgot her."

"I think Adelaide Herrmann cared more about the magic itself or she wouldn't have started a new act in her seventies after that warehouse fire destroyed all her props."

"You know about Adelaide?" Her mouth opens wide, surprised and impressed, which makes me stand taller.

"A little birdie named Quinn told me about her. And nobody is gonna forget you or Adelaide if she has anything to do with it."

We sigh in unison.

"I wish you cared more about magic," she says.

"Me, too."

Violet gives me a bittersweet smile. "I think we both got it wrong. I was too frivolous with my magic, too showy and obsessed. You were too oblivious of your magic because you were busy taking care of others. My magic made me greedy, and it made others greedy, until I was drained and lost. Ignoring your magic put limitations on your life. Like, you never wanted to talk about what happened in the tunnels."

"I still don't love talking about it. Because I still can't explain it."

"Something impossible and wonderful happened. Why can't that be enough? Why be tormented by it when you can enjoy how fucking cool it is? Maybe you can logic away all the weird shit that's ever happened to you or maybe you are actually extraordinary in ways you can't begin to comprehend."

"The thought of that freaks me out. It's always been easier to dismiss it."

"But when you dismissed it, you were dismissing me. You pushed me away."

"You pushed me away first!" With that petulant you-started-it response out of the way, I remind myself that I'm an adult. "You shut me out when you stopped telling me how your magic tricks were done. And all because I told Mom and Dad about what that teacher did to you. No good deed—"

"Hang on, just stop." Palm in the air, she jerks her head like she's trying to remove something rattling around inside it. "You think I was punishing you for telling Mom and Dad about that monster who beat on me?"

"Yeah . . ." I stretch out the syllable like I'm explaining something obvious. "That's why you wouldn't share any more of your magic secrets, which, for the record, was the part of your magic I enjoyed the most."

"Sasha, you dummy. I wasn't punishing you. You were sweet and innocent, and you shouldn't have had to see what that asshole did to me. I was grateful you got me away from him." Her tears run freely, and she doesn't wipe them away. I let mine flow unimpeded, too. "I stopped telling you my 'magic secrets' as a way to thank you. I thought, maybe if I could convince you any of it was real, it would . . . I don't know, undo some of that darker shit somehow."

It dawns on me that our entwined lives have been like one of those optical illusions where you can see two completely different images in the same picture. "Yeah, it didn't undo anything," I say. "It just added to my resentment and kept me firmly in my pragmatic bubble. If it couldn't be explained and I couldn't figure it out, I didn't want any part of it."

"At the same time, closing yourself off to things you couldn't explain created these invisible borders you refused to cross. But you finally did cross, and now you're here."

And now that I'm here, an inner tug tells me it's time to go.

"I don't suppose I'll see you at any future Thanksgivings." It's meant to come out jokey but sounds a little heartbroken.

"I need to stay where I am."

"That's so inconvenience stores."

Violet's eyes glisten. "Come see me again," she says. "Bring the kid next time."

"I'll try. I will."

Even if this isn't real, it's nice to believe for a little while.

I close my eyes. It's dark except for a tiny pinpoint of light. There's an upward tugging on my body, like gravity working in reverse, and a static hum in my ears. The hum grows louder and louder. It becomes a roar that reverberates throughout me. When I open my eyes, I'm back on the plane, on the restroom floor, wedged between the toilet and the sink. The plane is flying smoothly. The FASTEN SEAT BELT sign is off.

My eyes and nose are seeping, and I do the best clean-up job I can with the low-grade single-ply tissues within arm's reach. I get to my feet and open the restroom door on the first try. After all that, you'd think

I'd be walking on jelly legs, but they remain sturdy and my steps down the narrow aisle don't falter.

Gabriel is sleeping slumped against the window, and Quinn is also out, her head tilted back. They emit faint synchronized snores that make my heart hurt.

I wish I didn't have to wake Quinn, but there's no other way to return to my seat.

Gradually, after some gentle shoulder-nudges, she opens her eyes, squinting as she takes in her surroundings, then me. She gets up to let me through and when she takes a closer look at me, she's instantly awake.

"Oh my god. You saw her, didn't you?" Her eyes bore into me, spooked, wistful. "How?"

We speak in low voices so as not to disturb the sleeping passengers around us.

"You have to tell me. Everything," she insists.

"I will," I say. "But how did you know I saw her?"

Quinn rummages through her messenger bag and holds out a hand mirror. I use a knuckle to wipe beneath my eyes and brave a look at my reflection to see how well I wear emotional meltdown.

Pretty well, surprisingly. Pale but not too blotchy. Eyes a little bloodshot but electric blue. What was it Mrs. Toback compared them to? Cobalt glass. For some reason, I find this funny. Everything makes me want to laugh.

Quinn puts a hand over mine and guides the mirror to the right side of my face. Even in the low light, I catch the glimmer, and turn my head until I see the source: a sparkling red lipstick imprint stamped just above my jaw.

I gasp, laughing in pure delight.

Acknowledgments

Caroline Bleeke: You were attuned to the story I wanted to tell, as it was taking shape, and you nurtured it every step of the way. Thank you for your insights and encouragement, your warmth and wisdom, and those killer brainstorming sessions.

Philippa Sitters: I'm ever so grateful for your ongoing support—and not just career-wise (handling delicate writer egos is an essential yet underrated agent superpower). I also appreciate your valuable input on this book and your inside stories of the fame-adjacent.

Michelle Hazen: Your gorgeous persistence and positivity helped wrangle me out of a creative conundrum. Thank you for reading early pages with generosity and enthusiasm, and for your continued friendship.

I'm tremendously grateful to the dream team at Flatiron Books and Macmillan, including Sydney Jeon, Claire McLaughlin, Katherine Turro, Megan Lynch, Malati Chavali, Bob Miller, Marlena Bittner, Nancy Trypuc, Keith Hayes, Kelly Gatesman, Jaya Miceli, Jeremy Pink, Donna Noetzel, Eva Diaz, Shelly Perron, Rima Weinberg, Katy Robitzski, Drew Kilman, and Emily Dyer.

Thank you to all the talented folks at PFD, including Rebecca Wearmouth, Lucy Barry, Antonia Kasoulidou, and Lisette Verhagen in foreign rights, and Jonathan Sissons and Rosie Gurtovoy in dramatic rights. Thank you also to Amandine Riche at DGA.

Kayla Drescher: It means so much that you took the time to share your experiences as a professional magician and answer my bazillion questions. I'm also grateful to you and Carissa Hendrix for creating the *Shezam* podcast—its unvarnished and fascinating perspective on being a woman in magic was a vital resource in researching this book.

Bridget McGraw-Bordeaux: thank you for reading quickly, for offering the exact constructive feedback I needed, and for your endless curiosity and enduring sisterhood.

Natalie, Stephanie, Asha, and Jeanine: thank you for your kindness, openness, empathy, advice, and for making our CPSG a safe space.

Librarians, booksellers, book clubs, fellow authors, any and all members of the reading community: I cannot thank you enough. Your passion and tireless endorsements of books and authors are invaluable, and your ongoing support for *Oona Out of Order* has been life-changing. Special shoutouts to Pamela Klinger-Horn, Mary Webber O'Malley, Luisa Smith, Darla Dykstra, Zibby Owens, Robin Kall, Adriana Trigiani, and Jordan Moblo, though my gratitude extends to countless others. I'm also thankful to the staff members at POWER-HOUSE Arena, Porter Square Books, and Peoples' Books & Culture, who hosted me in person during my launch week, just before the lockdown.

There were several books that were instrumental for research and inspiration: *Fooling Houdini* by Alex Stone, *Hiding the Elephant* by Jim Steinmeyer, *Magic Is Dead* by Ian Frisch, *Playing Dead* by Elizabeth Greenwood, and *Big Magic* by Elizabeth Gilbert (while not about stage magic, it massively helped reignite my writing spark).

I also want to take a moment to recognize some of the numerous women who have had an impact on the world of magic, including but not limited to: Adelaide Herrmann, Fay Presto, Dorothy Dietrich, Misty Lee, Minerva, Jade, Ariann Black, Celeste Evans, Lisa Menna, Kristen Johnson, Magic Babe Ning, Judy Carter, and Melinda.

Mom, thank you for all the love, and for telling anyone and everyone about my books. I hope I keep making you proud.

Cooper, thank you for being an eternally adorable diva and for getting me outside more. (Sorry for referring to you as "and dog" in my author bio.)

Terry, you are everything. You are home. Thank you for the pencils. And the sandwiches. And the laughs. And for keeping the rest of the world turning when I'm in a bubble, writing and otherwise. You're so cool.

About the Author

Margarita Montimore is the author of *Asleep from Day* and *Oona Out of Order*, which was a *USA Today* bestseller and *Good Morning America* Book Club pick. After receiving a BFA in creative writing from Emerson College, she worked for more than a decade in publishing and social media before deciding to focus on the writing dream full-time. Born in Soviet Ukraine and raised in Brooklyn, she currently lives in New Jersey with her husband and dog.